NEW MEXICO
Sunset

D0973087

GENERATIONS ARE SUSTAINED
BY FAITH AND LOVE IN
FOUR COMPLETE NOVELS

Tracie Peterson

BARBOUR
PUBLISHING, INC.
Uhrichsville, Ohio

The Heart's Calling © 1996 by Tracie Peterson.
Forever Yours © 1996 by Tracie Peterson.
Angel's Cause © 1997 by Tracie Peterson.
Come Away, My Love © 1999 by Tracie Peterson.

ISBN 1-58660-139-3

Cover design by Robyn Martins.

All Scripture quotations, unless otherwise noted, are taken from the King James Version of the Bible.

Published by Barbour Publishing, Inc., P.O. Box 719, Uhrichsville, Ohio 44683 http://www.barbourbooks.com

Member of the
Evangelical Christian
Publishers Association

Printed in the United States of America.

TRACIE PETERSON

Tracie Peterson, best-selling author of over forty fiction titles and one nonfiction title, lives and works in Montana. As a Christian, wife, mother, and writer (in that order), Tracie finds her slate quite full.

She has over twenty-three titles with **Heartsong Presents'** book club and stories in six separate anthologies from Barbour, including the best-selling *Alaska*. From Bethany House Publishing, Tracie has several historical series, as well as a variety of women's fiction titles.

Voted favorite author for 1995, 1996, and 1997 by the **Heartsong Presents** readership, Tracie enjoys the pleasure of spinning stories for readers and thanks God for the imagination He's given. "I find myself blessed to be able to work at a job I love. I get to travel, study history, spin yarns, spend time with my family, and hopefully glorify God. I can't imagine a more perfect arrangement."

Tracie also does acquisitions work for Barbour Publishing and is a board member of American Christian Romance Writers. She teaches workshops at a variety of conferences, speaking on inspirational romance, historical research, and anything else that offers assistance to fellow writers.

See Tracie on the Internet at http://members.aol.com/tjpbooks/

Welcome Reader!

New Mexico Sunset picks up the saga of the Lucas, Monroe, and Dawson families which first came to life in *New Mexico Sunrise*. I hope you will continue to enjoy the romance and adventure of the next generation. God Bless You!

Tracie Peterson

The Heart's Calling

*Dedicated to my Grandmother Williams,
who shared many stories with me
of her childhood and the good ol' days.
I love you, Grandma!*

Chapter 1

D o you have everything you need, my dear?"

Her grandmother's heavy French accent only increased Pamela Charbonneau's misery. "I have nothing at all," she pouted.

Claudia Charbonneau shrugged her shoulders. "Life is what one makes it, *n'est-ce pas?*"

"No, it isn't so," Pamela insisted, tossing her stylish blond curls from side to side. Only an hour earlier, Claudia's own maid had painstakingly pinned and curled Pamela's waist-length hair, and now she threatened to bring it all back down with her childish tantrum. "I'm eighteen years old, and so far my life is only what others force upon me. I am not allowed to make my life my own!"

"Ma petite fille, you bring most of the trouble upon yourself."

"But *Grand-mère,*" Pamela interrupted, "I'm in love, and my parents don't understand. Bradley Rayburn means the world to me. My parents were cruel and vicious to make me leave him and Kansas City. It's my home, and he's the man I intend to marry."

"Marry him?" Claudia Charbonneau replied with her first show of disgust. "I cannot see why a young woman such as yourself would want to settle down to marriage and the unpleasantness of childbearing before you have a chance to see the world and all that it has to offer. Perhaps then your Bradley Rayburn would hold less fascination for you."

"Impossible," Pamela protested, bringing herself up to her full five-foot, two-inch height. Claudia was no taller than her granddaughter, but because of her elegance and refinement Pamela felt as though the woman towered over her by a foot.

"I love him!" Pamela cried. "I will always love him, and as soon as I can figure a way to leave this south Missouri hick town, I will!"

Claudia was not impressed by her granddaughter's show of temper. It was all to be expected. Pamela's parents had never spent enough time at home to rear the child when she was young, so she had learned her values and principles from nannies and house staff. When her father and mother finally reappeared, it was just in time to find a local ne'er-do-well dandy keeping company with their daughter—and with the audacious intention of marrying her!

"It would be well if you learned to appreciate this town for its quiet reserve and charm," Claudia was saying, but Pamela had angrily turned away.

"I hate it here, already," Pamela muttered and whirled on her heel. "Nobody loves me! Nobody but Bradley!" With that Pamela threw herself across the feather mattress of her bed and cried.

Claudia Charbonneau shook her head and left her granddaughter to have her cry. It was the fourth that day. Sooner or later, Pamela would have to understand that what was done was done, and no amount of tears would change that fact.

～

At noon, Pamela finally emerged from her bedroom to join her grandmother for lunch. She sat at the opposite end of the elegant table, watching her grandmother instruct her servants in a low voice, her words inaudible to Pamela.

When Claudia finished, she gave Pamela a polite nod and lifted a sterling fork. "Shall we begin?"

Pamela ate in miserable silence. Her grandmother had instructed her only that morning that too much conversation at the dinner table would lead to upsetting the delicate balance of one's stomach. Pamela was full to the rim of her reddened eyes with rules that her grandmother intended her to follow.

She was not to leave the house unescorted.

She was not to drink anything cooler than room temperature.

She was not, under any circumstance, to appear outside of the house before ten o'clock in the morning, and she was never to speak to anyone before Claudia's introduction.

Rules, rules, rules! Pamela thought she'd burst from frustration. At least in Kansas City there hadn't been a list of rules to follow. Her parents traveled abroad so often that Pamela had had a free rein. The servants adored her, and she in turn bestowed on them the love she would have given her parents, had they been around to receive it.

Now she was here—and she wasn't even sure where *here* really was. She'd been forced to take the train south from Kansas City, then travel by stage to this small Missouri community where her grandmother had spent the last few years. All this traveling was in order to separate her from Bradley.

Oh, Bradley! Pamela sighed, remembering his boyish smile and curly blond hair. Friends had teased her, saying she would have nothing but blond-headed babies and that, because she and Bradley were such a handsome couple, their children would no doubt be beautiful.

Lifting a forkful of curried chicken to her mouth, Pamela ate while barely tasting the food. Although the scene her parents had caused on the night of her engagement party was almost more than Pamela could bear to remember, she could not help thinking about it.

They were supposed to be in New York for at least another week, and Pamela had planned an elaborate party at which to announce her engagement. She reasoned that her parents couldn't possibly tell her "no" after all Kansas City's social elite turned out to wish her and Bradley well. But something had happened to bring them home early. Perhaps they'd caught wind of the party, or maybe someone had deliberately sent for them. Either way, Pamela would never forgive her father for the way he had barged into the formal dining room, where forty people were celebrating her engagement, and announced that there would be no wedding. If that weren't bad enough, he had ordered Bradley thrown out of the house and Pamela to her room.

"He treated me like a child," Pamela muttered.

"Did you say something?" Claudia asked with a look of annoyance.

Pamela stiffened. "No," she lied. "I was just thinking aloud."

So her life went on that January of 1883. Pamela was a prisoner in her grandmother's home while Bradley was somewhere in Kansas City, no doubt nursing a broken heart.

~

Alexandra Dawson—Zandy to her friends and family—finished buttoning her burgundy wool coat before seeking out her husband.

"I'm ready to go," she said, entering the manly confines of Riley Dawson's office.

"Not without a kiss," he said and patted his lap. Zandy smiled and quickly crossed the room to comply.

"I wouldn't dream of it," she whispered against his ear.

Hugging her close, Riley couldn't help but feel as though he were the most blessed man in the world. Not that long ago, he had confronted Zandy with the experience of seeing him for the first time in over a year. To make matters worse, the encounter took place after she had thought him dead and buried.

"What are you thinking?" she asked, pulling back just far enough to meet his brown-black eyes.

"Just how very good God has been to me," Riley answered.

Zandy appreciated his words of praise for God, especially remembering how adamantly Riley had rejected Him when they had first met.

"It seems hard to believe that I'm the same man who gambled his way into ownership of a Colorado mining town and tried to force his attentions on one young, beautiful, and very naïve girl."

"I was not naïve!" Zandy protested. "You didn't get what you wanted, did you?"

Riley laughed. "As a matter of fact, I did. I just didn't get it the way I intended."

Zandy joined his laughter. "No, God had other plans for you, Riley Dawson, and making me your mistress wasn't one of them. You may own enough silver mines to pave the streets of Denver, but when you deal with me, you deal with my God."

"Our God," Riley said in a contented way that warmed Zandy's heart.

"Yes," she murmured. "Our God."

Riley pulled her face down to meet his and kissed her long and lovingly. Zandy snuggled up against him like a child being cradled.

"I thought you were going into town," Riley mused.

"I am."

"It doesn't appear that way to me," he teased.

"Shows what you know," Zandy countered with a twinkle in her green eyes. "I'm already halfway down the street."

Riley laughed and put her from his lap. "You'd best get on your way before I decide you shouldn't go out on a cold day like this."

"As if that would stop me," Zandy called over her shoulder. "By the way," she added, as she paused at the door, "do you need anything?"

"Only you," Riley replied and pushed back the black hair that had fallen over one eye.

"I believe you could use a haircut. Maybe you should come with me," Zandy offered.

Riley shook his head. "No, I've got to see to these accounts. Your father is doing a fine job of managing the city of Dawson for us, but he always feels better when I give him my report on the matter. You run along, and when you get back I'll play you a game of chess." Zandy nodded and happily took herself off to do her shopping.

～

Zandy entered Mrs. Mallory's dress shop at exactly eleven o'clock. She had promised to come for a dress fitting, and Mrs. Mallory hated it when anyone was as much as a minute late.

"Good morning, Mrs. Mallory," Zandy said, pulling off her black leather gloves.

"Good morning, Mrs. Dawson. I have your dress nearly finished," the heavyset woman said, coming to help Zandy off with her coat. "You know where to change your clothes. I'll bring the dress to you shortly."

Zandy nodded and took herself into the small adjoining fitting room. She quickly changed out of her blouse and skirt and accepted the new creation of cream-colored velvet.

"I'll do up the buttons for you," Mrs. Mallory said, taking Zandy in hand as though she were a small child. "You have such a fine figure to work with. Pity I can't take more after you and less after my husband."

Zandy giggled slightly at the reference to Mrs. Mallory's portly husband. "You have a grace that poor Mister Mallory could never hope to achieve."

Mrs. Mallory smiled and stepped back to survey her work. "Yes, this looks perfect."

Zandy couldn't see the mirror from where she stood, but she liked the feel of the gown and knew that Mrs. Mallory wasn't one to offer idle praise.

The older woman worked diligently at the task of tacking black jets to the bodice and finished by taking a final tuck in the waist.

"I'll have it ready on Saturday," Mrs. Mallory said abruptly. She unbuttoned the gown and moved away. "You may change now."

Zandy was used to these curt dismissals from her dressmaker. Mrs. Mallory was one of the few people in town who didn't love to spend hours chatting about nothing in particular.

Zandy quickly replaced the elegant gown with her more durable blue wool skirt and white blouse. She had just reentered the front room when the bell on the door sounded and two women entered.

"Mrs. Charbonneau," Zandy said, extending her hand to the older woman. "I was going to stop by today and thank you for the invitation to dinner and, of course, to accept."

"Madame Dawson," Claudia remarked with a smile, "it is always a pleasure to speak with you. Might I introduce my granddaughter? This is Pamela Charbonneau, formerly of Kansas City."

Zandy's eyes left the older woman and traveled to the obviously miserable younger one. "Miss Charbonneau, it's wonderful to make your acquaintance."

"Mrs. Dawson," Pamela said with a questioning interest.

"Please, call me Zandy. May I call you Pamela?"

"Please do," Pamela replied.

"I must be on my way," Zandy announced, pulling on her coat, "but, I wonder, would you like to stop by for tea this afternoon?"

"Oh my," Claudia said, holding a lace-edged handkerchief to her throat. "I know I won't have the energy for such an outing, but perhaps Pamela would enjoy it. I would so like for her to spend time getting to know you."

Pamela appeared to perk up. "I'd love to. Thank you, Mrs. Dawson. I mean, Zandy."

"Good. I'll expect you at three," Zandy bade the women good-bye and went to finish her rounds in town.

At three o'clock, Pamela arrived in a hansom carriage of lacquered black and gold. She felt as though a yoke had been lifted from her neck as she approached the cobblestone walkway that led to the Dawson mansion. It was an impressive two-storied house of natural stone with a black wrought-iron fence surrounding the yard.

Bradley and I could have had something like this, she thought. *What am I saying? We'll still have something like this. I'll find a way to get back to Kansas City. Maybe Mrs. Dawson can even help me.* The thoughts ran in whirlwinds in Pamela's mind as she reached out and sounded the brass door knocker.

Expecting an old butler, Pamela opened her mouth in surprise at the dashing figure in his navy blue afternoon suit. She didn't know who this dark-headed man was, but he was certainly handsome.

"Miss Charbonneau, I presume," Riley said, extending his hand. "I'm Riley Dawson, Zandy's husband."

Pamela eased her gloved hand into Riley's. "I'm pleased to meet you, Mister Dawson."

Riley smiled, revealing perfect white teeth. The glint in his eyes made it clear he was a man who enjoyed life. "Call me Riley, and come inside, please. It's much too cold to stand gabbing on the steps."

Pamela allowed Riley to usher her to the sitting room where Zandy was already fussing over the tea. "Pamela!" she exclaimed and quickly crossed the room. "I'm so glad you could come."

"Me too. I was beginning to fret that there would be no one my own age in this town," Pamela confessed.

Zandy laughed. "I know full well what you mean. This seems to be a community of stately, refined characters, who have nothing better to do than garden and take naps. But it is a wonderful town. So peaceful and simple. Riley and I have grown to love it dearly."

Pamela tried to catch Zandy's enthusiasm but could only nod.

"Riley, take Pamela's coat and we'll have tea," Zandy instructed.

Pamela stayed for over an hour and thoroughly enjoyed herself. She found that once the formalities dropped away, Riley and Zandy were entertaining companions and more than accepting of her. She even relayed a bit of her plight and why she'd come to stay with her grandmother.

"I'm afraid my parents don't understand that the heart's calling can't be controlled. And just because my parents don't approve," Pamela said as Riley helped her into her coat, "doesn't change those feelings."

"Maybe you will change their minds," Zandy replied. "Until then, you're welcome to come and visit as often as you like."

"Thank you, Zandy, Riley. I will call again."

~

And she did. Pamela found one excuse or another to make her way to the Dawson house nearly every day. Pamela and Zandy laughed about girlhood experiences until they felt that they'd known one another all their lives. Pamela was only a few years junior to Zandy, who found that the company of a young woman was something that had been missing in her life lately.

"I really like her, Riley," Zandy said one evening as they prepared to retire. She sat brushing her long brown hair, while Riley watched from the bed. It was a habit he'd fallen into, and he now realized it was as much a part of his bedtime routine as putting on his night clothes.

"I worry that you're spending too much time together," Riley finally said.

His words surprised Zandy so much she stopped in mid-stroke. "Why do you say that?"

"Well, she's here almost every day. And I can't help but think that you do too much to encourage her when it comes to this Bradley guy."

"Riley Dawson!" Zandy exclaimed. "You, more than anyone, should understand about falling in love with someone. Especially, I might add, someone that you can't have." The coy smile on her lips told him she wasn't really annoyed.

The look on Riley's face told her that he, too, remembered a time when he had actively pursued her, in spite of Zandy's own protests.

Riley patted the mattress beside him, and Zandy put the brush away and joined her husband. "I just don't want you getting involved in something that's better left to others. This is a problem between Pamela and her folks. You have to remember, you aren't her school chum. You're a respectable married woman, and you shouldn't offer too much advice to a young, innocent woman like Pamela."

Zandy stared in surprise at Riley's mild reproof. "I may be married, but I'm not so old that I can't appreciate the company of a young, single woman. I enjoy hearing about her life. She's known so much and lived in a way that I can't begin to understand. Do you know that every stitch of clothing she owns was made in either Paris or New York?"

Riley pulled Zandy into his arms and nuzzled his lips against her ear. "Would you like me to take you to Paris so you can have your gowns made there too?"

Zandy melted against him with a sigh. "No, Mrs. Mallory would never speak to me again. I just find Pamela stimulating, and I believe her parents are wrong to keep her from the man she loves."

"Be careful, Zandy," Riley warned softly. "You can cause grievous damage by interfering." He gently turned her face to his. "I know how tenderhearted you are, and I don't want to see you hurt. Be her friend, but don't try to be her heart in this matter. Pamela must choose for herself how she'll deal with this situation."

"You're right, of course," Zandy sighed.

"I always am," Riley teased, and he reached over to turn down the lamp.

Chapter 2

W ait until you hear this one!" Pamela exclaimed.
Pamela's enthusiasm for her most recent epistle from home caused Riley to roll his eyes. Zandy caught sight of the exasperation in her husband's expression but said nothing.

Pamela made a regular habit of sharing her mail from Kansas City with Zandy, and because of the frequency of her visits Riley had found himself trapped into being a part of their afternoon gatherings on more than one occasion. Today was no exception.

Zandy took the cup of tea that Riley offered her and delicately balanced it against her emerald green day dress. The color matched her eyes, and Riley often told her that he fancied the shade on her. Today, however, it seemed to do little to appease his frustration with Pamela.

"Glady, she was my maid," Pamela said, glancing up from the letter, "says that Mama and Papa were home for a short time last week. They were positively in a rage because they had been forced to endure the company of Horace Tabor, the notorious Silver King of Leadville, Colorado."

"I know of Tabor," Riley commented. "He's managed to make a fortune in silver. Nothing overly notorious about that."

"Oh, but it isn't his wealth that put Mama into the vapors," Pamela laughed. "It seems that Mister Tabor has not only a wife and child but a mistress." Pamela continued reading and didn't notice the way Riley blanched at the word "mistress."

"Mama told Glady that Tabor seems most open about his affair and doesn't care one thing for propriety. She was absolutely mortified. Seems she told Glady that his mistress is quite willing to be the other woman. Mama couldn't abide even the sight of Mister Tabor and told Papa that all such men should be lined up and shot."

At this Riley nearly spewed his tea across the room and brought even more attention to himself by breaking into a fit of coughing. Zandy glanced up, concern flooding her face for only a moment. Catching Riley's eye, amusement seemed to overtake her, and she grinned broadly.

"Yes, I quite agree with your mother," Zandy mused. "Such lack of character is appalling. Do go on, Pamela."

"Well, there isn't much more. They say absolutely nothing about Bradley.

Oh, Zandy," she sighed and let the letter drop to her lap, "do you suppose I shall ever hear from him?"

"I doubt that your grandmother would allow it," Zandy replied honestly. "Even if you managed to get a letter to him, you know she'd never allow you to receive a reply."

"Yes, I know you're right."

"Why don't we just put it behind us and enjoy our tea," Zandy suggested.

Pamela refolded the letter and put it inside her purse. Just then, a knock at the front door drew Riley's attention, and he found a perfect reason to excuse himself.

"Riley certainly isn't himself today," Pamela said, absentmindedly playing with her teaspoon.

"Oh, he's just a bit on edge," Zandy remarked with a glance at the door. "I'm afraid we ought to cut this session short today. I've been neglecting him sorely."

"Oh," Pamela replied.

Seeing her friend's disappointment, Zandy pushed on to offer some consolation. "Why don't we get together tomorrow and go shopping? I have several things I need to pick up."

"Why don't you have the servants see to it?" Pamela asked in a rather haughty tone.

Zandy frowned, realizing that the girl was every bit as spoiled as Riley had mentioned that morning at breakfast. "I enjoy doing for myself," Zandy answered gently. "Sometimes, it is more gratifying to work with your own hands and accomplish something important than to have others do it for you. Now, shopping isn't all that important, but I enjoy it. If you don't wish to go along, that's entirely up to you."

Pamela put her teacup aside and shook her head vehemently. "No, no. I would very much like to accompany you. I certainly didn't mean to offend you."

"You didn't," Zandy smiled. Hearing Riley in the hallway, she quickly stood. "Shall we continue our talk tomorrow, then?"

Pamela reluctantly nodded. "I'll see myself out. You attend to that neglected husband." Her attempt at a smile was forced, but Zandy pretended not to notice.

At the sound of the front door closing, Riley crossed the sitting room to where Zandy waited and pulled back the edge of the lacy priscilla curtain. "How did you manage this?" he asked, watching to make certain Pamela was really on her way down the street.

"I told her I'd been neglecting you," Zandy smiled.

"And so you have," Riley answered, letting the curtain fall back into place. "I was beginning to despair of ever having a moment alone with you again."

"Now, Riley," Zandy said, coming to place her hand upon his arm, "there isn't any need for you to sulk. I got rid of her, didn't I? By the way, who was at the door?"

"Just the delivery boy from Nelson's shoe shop," Riley replied. "I ordered a pair of boots some weeks back, and they arrived today."

"Are you expecting any more deliveries?" Zandy asked with a flirtatious smile.

Riley immediately caught her mood. "Why no, Mrs. Dawson. I believe that's the last of them."

"Good. Then we have the house to ourselves," Zandy said sweetly. "And the day."

"And just what do you have planned, my dear Alexandra?" he asked with a chuckle.

Zandy laughed. "No plans. Not yet, anyway. But, I'm sure we'll think of something."

～

Pamela Charbonneau was a young woman used to getting her way, and while she knew it was in poor taste to spend so much time at the Dawson house, she couldn't bring herself to do otherwise. She'd even taken to lying to her grandmother in order to avoid a scolding from her on the matter of social politeness.

Throwing herself across her bed and rolling over, Pamela stared up at the floral canopy and sighed.

"Where are you Bradley? You promised you'd come for me. You promised you'd never leave me. Where are you?" The words bounced off the nearly empty walls leaving Pamela more depressed than ever.

～

The next day, Zandy arrived in a stylish one-horse gig. She hadn't even the time to alight before Pamela appeared on the doorstep, fully prepared for their outing.

Zandy smiled and waved, still preparing to dismount and greet Claudia Charbonneau before their trip, but Pamela would have no part of it.

"*Grand-mère* isn't feeling well," she said to Zandy. "I'll give her your best when we return."

"Perhaps we shouldn't leave her alone," Zandy said, reseating herself and pulling wool blankets around her legs.

"No, she'll be fine," Pamela said with a smile. "She's just feeling her age today." It wasn't really a lie, Pamela told herself. After all, her grandmother had complained just that morning of how the cold made her bones ache.

"Well, if you're sure."

"Of course, I'm sure," Pamela replied and dismissed any further thought of the matter.

They spent the day shopping and discussing unimportant matters. Zandy had promised Riley that she'd find a way to talk to Pamela about her frequent visits. She fretted over the idea, however, given Pamela's state of depression over the loss of her Bradley. What if losing her constant contact with Zandy was too much for the girl?

When they finally decided to wrap up the day by having lunch, Zandy found herself praying that God would help her to know what to say.

"I'm positively famished," Zandy said and took the menu offered her by the waiter.

Pamela said nothing but glanced at the list of offered foods and finally settled on petite chicken salad sandwiches. Zandy thought the choice an excellent one and nodded in agreement before the waiter left to bring their tea.

"Might I ask a forward question?" Pamela said suddenly, catching Zandy off guard.

"I suppose so."

"I was curious as to why Riley acted so disturbed yesterday when I mentioned Mister Tabor. Does he know him well?"

Zandy smiled and set her gloves aside. "No, he doesn't know him well at all. Riley Dawson is a most fascinating man," Zandy went on. "When I first met him in Colorado, he was a man of power and control, just coming into his own. He had holdings that gave him control over a small mining town, and he pushed that advantage until he'd built a solid investment."

"I'm afraid that still doesn't explain his reaction," Pamela interrupted.

"Riley wasn't at all interested in doing things properly or in a morally right way. He was a godless man with little concern for the human lives he so completely controlled. If ever there was a notorious man, Riley Dawson was certainly one."

Pamela's eyes widened in surprise.

"He forced his will upon the people of Temperance, Colorado, and did so in such a remarkably smooth manner that the people didn't even know they'd been had. In fact, they renamed the town Dawson, after Riley, then elected him mayor. The one thing that eluded Riley—and the one thing he wouldn't give up pursuit of—was me."

Pamela smiled as though she thought the whole thing was most romantic. Zandy paused long enough to wait until their tea was served before continuing.

"Riley wanted a mistress, Pamela. Not a wife." The shocked expression on Pamela's face told Zandy she'd made her point. "Riley cared nothing about my feelings on the matter, but he did pride himself on the fact that women came willingly to him. I did not, and that moved him to take ugly measures that caused great harm to those I loved."

"How could you possibly have married him?" Pamela asked in disgust.

"I asked myself that about a thousand times. God seemed to have a purpose in mind, and I was very much up against the wall when I finally gave in. I knew it wasn't right to marry an unbeliever, but I reasoned that maybe it was God's way of getting Riley saved."

"Saved?" Pamela questioned ignorantly.

"You know," Zandy said with a smile, "saved from hell. I thought God was using me to guide Riley to salvation in Jesus Christ. Truth be told, He was. Riley became most miserable that he'd forced me into a loveless marriage and, even though we were man and wife, he couldn't bring himself even to sleep in the same house with me."

Pamela's mouth formed a silent *"O."*

"Now, I realize this is a most delicate topic," Zandy continued, "but I use it to share with you just how gracious God was to us and how He worked in Riley's life."

The waiter appeared with their sandwiches, and again, Zandy allowed the conversation to halt until they were alone. Pamela picked at her food, waiting for Zandy to continue her story.

"One day, Riley took me to visit one of his new silver mines," Zandy remembered. "There was a cave-in and Riley was injured seriously. We were buried inside the mine for days, until the people of Dawson dug us out. My folks had me taken to their house, while Riley was taken to the doctor's. I was sick with exhaustion and weakness for a time, and when I came to they told me Riley had died."

"Died?" Pamela exclaimed, dropping the sandwich. "Died?" she questioned in a softer tone, looking around to make sure no one was watching them.

"Yes," Zandy answered. "At least, that was what they told me. In truth, Riley knew he had to come to an understanding with God. He'd accepted Christ while thinking that he was going to die in the mine. Then, as he healed, he was afraid to believe in the reality of it because he feared it was nothing more than a deathbed confession. He couldn't face me again until he knew for certain that his faith was real, so he allowed the townspeople to believe he had died."

"What did he do then?" Pamela asked.

"He went about righting the wrongs of his past life. I didn't see him for over a year, and in all that time I never dreamed he was alive. I tried to make amends for Riley's behavior myself. I gave back to the people of Dawson their money and deeds. Whatever Riley had stolen from them, I sought to return. Then I came here to Missouri, opened the boardinghouse that sits on the west end of town, and tried to start life anew.

"It was a truly bleak time for me for, while I knew God had control of everything, including my widowhood, I was lonely and sad that I'd never really known who Riley Dawson was. One day, he reappeared and begged my forgiveness and told me just what I've told you. It was like being given a second chance at life. That was just last fall, Pamela, and Riley has become the most important person in my life. In fact," Zandy took a sip of tea to settle her nerves, "I had scarcely even spent time with another person before you came to town. It's one of the reasons we haven't any servants, except for the cook. We wanted the privacy." Her teacup rattled slightly as she placed it on the saucer.

Zandy knew that Pamela was still blind to her purpose. "Pamela, I've enjoyed our friendship and hope to continue to do so, but I mustn't put a wedge into the tender union that has been formed between Riley and me. We are still, in many ways, newlyweds, and I need time with him to come to know him better. Do you understand?"

"I'm not sure," Pamela replied, dabbing her lips with her napkin. "What has this to do with me?"

"I'm afraid there is no easy way to say this, but to just come out and say it," Zandy sighed. "It would be best if you were to limit your visits to once a week. I don't want to jeopardize our friendship, but I can't put Riley off, either. I'm blessed in the fact that I have his company on a daily basis, and I know that before long he will no doubt find some new project to absorb his time."

Zandy paused, trying to figure out what Pamela was thinking. "But, until then, I need to spend most of my time with him. It's what we both want and need."

"I see," Pamela said, as a blush crept to her cheeks.

"Please don't be offended," Zandy said, reaching out to squeeze Pamela's hand. "I want very much for us to continue on as friends. In fact, I was hoping that perhaps you would also attend church with us in the near future. We have some wonderful services and so much fun at the socials. The meetings are enlightening, and the pastor is a truly remarkable man."

"Does going to church really make life better?"

Zandy recognized the longing in her question. "It isn't so much attending church, although I can't imagine being without Christians to fellowship with. It's the love of God in your life. It's being forgiven for all the wrongs you've ever committed. It's knowing that you have a friend, a Savior, in Jesus

Christ, and that you never have to be alone again."

"Truly?" Pamela's childish snobbery fell away for the first time.

"Truly."

"And how can you be sure it will work for everyone that way?" Pamela asked sincerely.

"Look at Riley. God completely changed him. Riley was as hopeless as a human being could be, but God found him worth saving and didn't let go until He had him securely in the fold."

"I just don't know," Pamela said, shaking her head. "I've never heard tell of such things. I know from the talks we've had in the past that God is important to you and Riley. I remember your telling me about the peace God gives you but, Zandy, can He honestly take away the pain?" There were tears in Pamela's eyes. "I hurt so much."

Zandy smiled sympathetically. "I know. And, yes, He can take that pain away. Perhaps more important, though, is He will stay with you through the bad times. And, if you let Him, He'll fill the void in your heart with peace and love that is born of Him."

Pamela sobbed softly into her napkin and nodded her head across the table. "Then, do show me how I can be like you."

"Not like me," Zandy replied softly, "like Him."

Chapter 3

The first of March roared in like a lion, and icy snows pelted everything in sight. The next day, the sun came out and melted the frozen wonderland until all that remained was a brown, muddy mess and the fervent hope of spring.

It was during this time that a letter was delivered to Zandy and Riley that caused them much concern. Burley Stewart, Zandy's father and current mayor of Dawson, Colorado, wrote to tell his daughter and son-in-law that things were not as they should be. He cited complications with the miners and an onslaught of lawlessness that put him in fear of even letting the children walk to school.

Riley read over the letter, handing each page to Zandy after he'd finished. She, in turn, devoured the news with fear and apprehension for her family.

"This is awful, Riley," she said, glancing up from the last sheet of paper. "Father says that a gang of outlaws continues to elude capture, and they've even harmed some miners in order to steal their silver."

Riley nodded somberly, knowing full well what the letter said.

Zandy quickly finished reading and handed the pages back to her husband. "What are we going to do about this?"

"I don't know." Riley's tone took on the weight of the world. "I've been unhappy for some time about the reports Burley sent. There has been a continuing downward spiral in the quality of our little community. While all mining towns have their share of disorder and lawbreaking, my heart tells me we shouldn't be a part of it any more than we have to."

Zandy waited for Riley to say more but, when he fell into a thoughtful silence, she eagerly picked up the conversation.

"Perhaps God is directing us to get out of the business of silver mining. Mining always attracts a rowdier group of citizens, what with the saloons, gaming houses, and such. Someone is always looking for an easy way to make money. The proof is in the fact that this outlaw gang seems to hold the town hostage at times."

Riley grimaced and stretched his long legs before him. He rubbed his chin thoughtfully while contemplating Zandy's words. "I think we should go to Dawson," he finally said.

Zandy's eyes lit up. Not because she wanted to see Dawson, Colorado, but because going would mean seeing her father and stepmother, not to mention her young siblings.

"I think that would be wonderful!" she exclaimed. "How soon could we leave?"

Riley smiled at Zandy's enthusiasm for a family visit, but his heart was heavy with the conviction that he was contributing in a big way to the destructive lifestyle of Dawson. God had tested him sorely over the last year and a half and now it was almost as though Riley was being brought full circle. Once again, he had to face how the choices he'd made as a godless young man still affected his life.

"I see no reason why we can't leave right away. Say, maybe in the next day or two. You do realize we may have to stay for some time? This isn't the kind of problem that's going to resolve itself overnight."

"I'll get us packed," Zandy stated, brushing aside his concern, and hurried off to coordinate the effort.

~

The trip was set for the day following the next. They would take the stage, then the train. Zandy figured they'd be in Denver by the end of the week, then another day on the narrow-gauge mountain railroad before they'd finally reach Dawson. It was hard to imagine standing in her Missouri home one day, knowing that within a matter of just a few days, she would be hundreds of miles away in Colorado. Modern progress was a wonder!

Pamela was devastated by the news when Zandy came over to visit her at the Charbonneau house. Claudia kindly agreed to watch over their home while they were away, greatly relieving Zandy.

Pamela sat in silence, toying with a long blond braid.

Waiting until Claudia had left the room for some trivial matter, Pamela asked suddenly, "Zandy, could I accompany you to Colorado?"

Zandy was so shocked at Pamela's forward request that she could say nothing before Pamela continued.

"You know how I detest this town and, since my parents are determined to keep me separated from Bradley, why not add several hundred miles to that separation? I need desperately to get beyond these walls, and perhaps in Colorado I could forget about my heartache and start over."

"Colorado is hardly a solution to your broken heart," Zandy mused. "You would be more lonely than ever."

"I would have your friendship to get me through, and maybe you could introduce me to some of your old friends there."

Zandy had to smile at the remark. She had no friends in Dawson, save her family. In fact, the more she thought about how busy Riley would be with her father and how Ruth had their three-year-old daughter, Molly, to keep up with, the more Zandy thought it might be nice to have Pamela along for the company.

"I promise I won't be any trouble," Pamela said, taking Zandy's hand.

"I never thought you would be," Zandy replied. She wondered silently how she could talk Riley into allowing her to bring Pamela with them. "But how in the world would we convince your grandmother that such a trip would be in your best interest? After all, she'll no doubt miss you terribly."

Pamela smiled confidently. *"Grand-mère* will be happy for me to accompany you, especially if she knows that it will meet your needs."

Zandy scarcely realized the deception Pamela was pulling her into as Claudia rejoined them.

"Grand-mère, Zandy was just telling me that she longs for a traveling companion on their trip to Colorado. I have offered her my services, but we thought perhaps it would be wise to seek your approval on the matter."

Claudia narrowed her eyes slightly before turning to Zandy. "It is true that you wish Pamela to accompany you to Colorado?"

"I would very much enjoy her company," Zandy answered honestly. "I would, however, still need to approach my husband on the subject."

"I see," Claudia remained thoughtful for a moment, then turned to her granddaughter. "I believe it would be a good thing for you to travel. As I said when you first arrived, you've seen nothing of the world and perhaps with a better view of it, you won't pine away for that gold-digging dandy in Kansas City."

Pamela grimaced at her grandmother's reference to Bradley but then offered a sweet smile and nodded. "I know it would ease my suffering considerably."

"Very well," Claudia replied. "Alexandra, I'll have a draft prepared to pay for Pamela's ticket and travel needs."

And so it was settled, at least as far as Pamela was concerned. Zandy, however, knew she had a monumental task ahead in approaching Riley and winning him over to the idea.

~

The next day, Riley, Zandy, and Pamela boarded the stage for Kansas City. Riley hadn't liked the idea of Pamela's joining them but, because his mind was so preoccupied with the problems in Colorado, he gave in easily, only telling Zandy that should any problem result from the matter it would be on her head. Zandy wanted to comment on her husband's words, but she was so relieved to have Riley's permission to bring Pamela that she let the issue drop.

Pamela was elated and in a better mood than Zandy or Riley had seen her since her arrival in town. Zandy could only imagine that the younger girl had contented herself with a change of scenery. Still, it didn't stop Zandy from praying the trip would be a quick and easy one.

It was not to be, however. A washed-out bridge made it necessary for the stage to detour, not once, but twice, and finally the road weary travelers picked up the train in Lawrence, Kansas.

Riley found the ride irritatingly slow and took to pacing from car to car on a daily basis. It was during one of his strolls that he happened upon none other than Horace Tabor, the infamous Leadville Silver King and newly elected legislator from Colorado. He had added to his notoriety, Riley learned in conversation, by divorcing his wife and wedding his mistress, Baby Doe, in a hotel ceremony in Washington, D.C. They were on their way back to Denver, where they would set up housekeeping and start their new life together.

Tabor was a likeable enough man with a drooping mustache and gray at the temples of his receding dark brown hair. His easygoing manner instantly seemed to put Riley at ease and, in talking, the men learned they had a great deal in common. Riley didn't return to the ladies until nearly two hours later, and it seemed that when he did his heart had been lightened considerably. Tabor had a real interest in the town of Dawson. Perhaps, Zandy thought, he would offer them a way out of the dirty game of mining towns and outlaw gangs.

～

Pamela's sullen spirits could do nothing to spoil Zandy's excitement as the train pulled into Dawson, Colorado. She hadn't seen her family in over a year, and suddenly it seemed the most important thing in the world.

"Look, Riley," she exclaimed, leaning across him. "There's Father and Ruth!"

Pamela followed Riley and Zandy from the train to the loading platform and waited grimly while Zandy fussed over each of her family members.

"I can't believe how Molly's grown," Zandy said of her little sister. "She was just a baby when I left Dawson. And just look at you," she said, turning to her thirteen-year-old brother. "Why, Joshua, you're nearly a man." This caused the boy to swell with pride. In spite of his younger brothers' laughter, he felt Zandy had bestowed a high honor upon him.

Eleven-year-old Bart and nine-year-old Samuel took hold of either side of Zandy's wrinkled traveling dress and began tugging on her skirts.

"Guess what, Zandy," Bart began.

"We had a bank robbery," Samuel finished for his brother.

Zandy cast a worried glance at her father, while Riley barely caught the words as he returned with their bags.

"What's this about a bank robbery?" he asked, coming alongside his wife.

"It's true," seven-year-old George exclaimed. "Those bad men rode into town just big as you please."

Zandy had to suppress a smile at the little boy's recitation. Her heart had always held a soft spot for George, as he had been the baby for four years before Molly's arrival.

"George has that right," Burley stated. "But they only managed to get away with several thousand dollars instead of the hundreds of thousands that had been there the day before. We had just decided at the last minute to send the money out on an early train to Denver, and it's a good thing we did."

"God was looking over us once again," Ruth added. Molly began fussing at all the ruckus and attention, so Ruth motioned them to join her. "Let's get out of the cold and head home for something warm to eat. I would imagine you all could use a good rest before we have much more conversation."

Pamela had remained so quietly fixed in the background that Zandy had nearly forgotten her. Noticing her blank stare as she surveyed the town around them, Zandy quickly reached out to pull Pamela into the circle of family.

"This is Pamela Charbonneau," Zandy introduced. "She's a good friend of Riley's and mine, and I invited her to come along with us. I hope you don't mind the fact that we didn't let you know ahead of time that she'd be joining us, but we were so anxious to get here."

"Any friend of yours is welcome," Ruth said, shifting Molly in order to shake Pamela's hand. "We're pleased to have you. Fact is, it's Riley's and Zandy's house anyway. We just take up space there and do our best to keep things running smoothly."

"Don't let her fool you," Riley said with a grin. "This woman is pure organized energy. If you don't believe me, just ask her husband." Everyone, including Ruth, laughed at this, while Pamela forced a weak smile to her lips.

"I'm pleased to meet you," she murmured and followed the entourage to their waiting carriages.

~

Pamela was still miserable even after soaking in a hot bath and eating a hearty meal of the most succulent roast pork she'd ever tasted. She found herself in the company of Zandy and Ruth after the children had been dismissed to play. The housekeeper came and whisked Molly off for a nap, leaving the women to catch up on all the latest news.

"I knew Riley and Burley would be office-bound the minute you got here," Ruth began. She poured tea for Zandy and Pamela before sitting down to her own cup.

"So did I," Zandy remarked. "That was one of the reasons I was glad for Pamela's company. This whole town mess has Riley completely consumed. His spirit is bothering him something fierce, and I know that God is trying to help him put it all in order."

"Riley has certainly changed," Ruth said, then glanced hesitantly at Pamela.

"Oh, Pamela knows all about Riley," Zandy assured her stepmother. "In fact, it was Riley's coming to God that gave Pamela the courage to take the same step."

"Truly?" Ruth questioned, rather surprised.

Pamela ventured into the conversation only half-heartedly. "Yes. I felt moved by the things Zandy told me."

"Pamela is having a most difficult time," Zandy went on. "She had hoped to marry her young man in Kansas City, but her parents are rather overprotective and separated the two. They fear he's just after Pamela's inheritance."

"But it isn't true," Pamela jumped in. "Bradley would never do such a thing. He loves me."

Ruth smiled sympathetically. "I'm sure he does, but you must bear with your parents. We tend to fret and worry over our children, hoping and praying for the very best. I'm sure your mother is no different."

"My mother is a snob, Mrs. Stewart," Pamela promptly answered. "She is only concerned with what the Kansas City newspapers will say the morning after."

Ruth was taken aback by the young girl's bitter words, and Zandy tried to smooth the matter over. "I'm sure I'll be just as protective when my baby comes."

"What?" Ruth questioned. Her eyes widened in surprise. "Are you telling me what I think you are?"

Zandy smiled and nodded enthusiastically. "Yes! I'm going to have a baby in September."

"Oh, Zandy!" Ruth exclaimed and set aside her tea to embrace the younger woman. "How marvelous. What did Riley say?"

"Well, the fact of the matter is, I haven't told him. I was afraid he wouldn't let me take the trip if he knew."

Pamela felt an aching build in her heart. She could be married and having Bradley's children if only her parents hadn't interfered.

"You shouldn't keep things from him Zandy. He is your husband and in accordance with the Bible, you are subject to his authority," Ruth admonished.

"I'll tell him tonight," Zandy promised.

"I have a headache," Pamela said suddenly. "Would you mind terribly if I retired for a nap?"

"Not at all, my dear," Ruth answered. "Do you remember the way to your room?"

Pamela nodded. "I'm sure I do. Thank you for the wonderful meal. And Zandy," she said, turning to her friend, "congratulations."

Zandy beamed in happiness, making Pamela feel even more alienated. The room was smothering her with the joy of the two women, and Pamela hurried for the door, closing it firmly behind her. Leaning there against the heavy oak frame, Pamela felt the first tears flood her eyes. She ran for the stairs and the sanctuary of her room before anyone could stop her and ask what was wrong.

～

That evening in front of her dressing table, Zandy began the long process of pulling out hairpins and letting down her chestnut brown hair. She brushed in long, even strokes while thinking of how she would share her news with Riley. He might be very angry with her for not telling him sooner, or he might be so overjoyed at the news that he'd completely forget the little matter of timing. Either way, she didn't hear him come into the room until he stood directly behind her.

Leaning down, Riley placed a kiss on her cheek. "You're mighty deep in thought, Mrs. Dawson."

Zandy put the brush down and rose to embrace her husband. "That I am," she murmured against his chest.

"I'm sorry I took so long, but I've a feeling you'll see a whole lot less of me before it gets any better. I guess I'm kind of glad you brought Pamela with you."

Zandy pulled away. "You truly are?"

"Yes," Riley smiled down at his wife. "You were smart to bring her, and I was wrong to hesitate. I'm sorry. Do you forgive me?"

Zandy swallowed hard. She felt more than a little guilty for keeping the news of the baby from him. "Only if you forgive me."

"Forgive you? For what?"

"Come sit down," Zandy said, pulling Riley to the edge of the bed.

"If I need to sit down, it must be something big," Riley said, looking deep into Zandy's eyes. "Better come clean quickly, Mrs. Dawson."

Zandy sat down beside Riley and folded her hands in her lap. "I'm going to have a baby."

"What!" Riley jumped to his feet. "Are you sure?"

Zandy couldn't even look him in the eye. "Yes, I'm sure and there's more."

Riley laughed. "A baby! Well, I'll be. I'm going to be a father! When did you find out?"

"That's what I need to talk to you about," Zandy said softly.

Riley immediately noted her sobriety and sat back down beside her. "What is it?"

"I knew about the baby before we left on this trip," Zandy said slowly. "I was afraid if I told you, you might not let me come along. I know it was wrong, and I'm sorry."

"Don't you trust me, Zandy?"

Her head snapped up, and she gazed into his brown-black eyes. "With my life!" she declared.

"But not with the life of our child?" His words hit her hard.

"It was just that I wanted so much to see my father and Ruth and the kids. I was afraid with the way you worry over me that you'd put your foot down and demand that I stay in Missouri and, Riley, I just couldn't bear that."

"So you decided how I would react before you gave me a chance to have any say in the matter?" Riley questioned.

"Well, you can be rather stubborn," Zandy said with a weak smile.

"Me? Take a look in the mirror, Mrs. Dawson, and let's discuss stubborn streaks."

"All right. I've admitted I was wrong."

"Yes, you were," Riley said firmly.

Zandy eased into his arms and snuggled against his neck. "But you forgive me, right?"

Riley laughed and wrapped his arms around her. "I forgive you, but please promise me you'll give me a chance next time. This is some kind of news and, if you'd only told me, I could have made arrangements for you to have an easier trip out here."

"I promise to trust you in the future," Zandy answered, feeling contentment replace her guilt.

"Good," Riley replied. "Now, when is my son due to arrive?"

Chapter 4

The weeks moved slowly, one into the other, without Pamela so much as realizing that the harsh cold of winter was passing into a colorful display of mountain spring. The gardens outside the Dawson mansion had been carefully cultivated by Ruth Stewart and, in spite of the fact that Molly did her best to pick everything in sight, there grew an enchanting array of flowers and vegetation.

Pamela was bored, however. Bored and miserable. The snowcapped mountains surrounding Dawson did little to lift her spirits. She continued to pine for Bradley and spent most of every waking hour concentrating on her memories of their time in Kansas City.

Zandy and Ruth laughed and talked about the baby to come. At one point, they went into town to shop, and Pamela tagged along, wishing that she might find something to interest herself. It was hope ill-spent, as far as Pamela was concerned. She couldn't achieve the same spirit of light-heartedness as Zandy and Ruth. They were content to pick out material and plan baby clothes, while Pamela had nothing but her broken dreams.

Catching sight of a newly placed photography studio, Pamela talked Zandy into allowing her to sit for a photograph. Pamela wanted very much to mail the picture to Bradley, hoping that it would remind him of how much she loved him. Zandy reluctantly agreed to the picture and promised she'd think about whether or not it would be wise to mail the photo to Bradley.

"Pamela, Proverbs 17:22 is just the verse for you," Zandy said one evening while sewing a tiny blanket. "I found it just the other day while I was having my devotions."

Pamela stared curiously but said nothing.

"Anyway," Zandy continued, "It says, 'A merry heart doeth good like a medicine: but a broken spirit drieth the bones.' "

"I have nothing to be merry about, Zandy." The words were given matter-of-factly, and Pamela offered nothing more on the matter.

Zandy put aside her blanket and reached across the small table to where Pamela's hands were folded in idle frustration. "We don't always understand why God allows certain things to happen in our lives. I know I couldn't understand why I had to meet up with the likes of Riley Dawson when he first came to this town. But God sees the bigger picture, and we have to trust Him with it."

"But it is so hard," Pamela said with a heaviness that threatened to break into sobs.

"I know," Zandy said and gave her friend's hand a squeeze. "But just remember this, when Moses' mother put him into the basket and had his sister set him afloat in the Nile, God was already sending Pharaoh's daughter to the river bank."

"I don't think I understand," Pamela admitted.

"God was already planning ahead. He wants us in our living and desires to seek His will and way for our lives. Often, however, we choose another path, and God realizes, as a loving Father, that giving us our own way would be harmful. He gives us the freedom to choose, but He also intervenes to redirect because He knows we are only human. Maybe God realized that Bradley would only bring you heartache and grief. Maybe God has someone better for you. A Christian man who will love and honor you, as he loves and honors the Lord."

"I can't believe that God would be so cruel to me," Pamela said, jerking her hands away from Zandy. She got to her feet and smoothed back the loose pieces of blond hair that had pulled out of her stylish chignon. "I don't want another man, Christian or no. I want Bradley, and if I can't have him I'll have no one!"

With that, Pamela stormed out of the room and from the house. She had a full head of steam and an elongated step by the time she reached the Dawson gardens.

The sky had faded into deep purple twilight, and stars were already visible in the velvety folds. Pamela forced herself to slow down and rethink her words. Zandy hadn't meant any harm, and Pamela knew that full well.

"Oh, Bradley," she whispered against the night skies. Just then someone grabbed her from behind, and Pamela felt steel-like arms pull her tight, while a leather-gloved hand fell across her mouth.

"Don't cry out," the hoarse voice sounded. "I've come to rescue you."

Pamela was nearly beside herself with joy. Bradley had come for her! She tried to turn and speak, but the arms held her tight.

"No, just stay quiet. I'll explain everything later. Just remember, this is for your own good. Now, do what I say."

Pamela nodded mutely, and the hand dropped from her mouth. The man pulled her backwards through the garden to an awaiting horse. Ominous black shadows kept Pamela from getting a good look at the man, but in her heart she was content to believe it was Bradley. After all, he had said he was there to rescue her. An ordinary kidnapper would never say such a thing.

The man hoisted her into the saddle of his horse, coming up behind her at the same time. Pamela settled into the seat and leaned back against the warmth of the man's chest. *Yes*, she thought to herself, *this is my Bradley, and he's come to take me home.*

They rode for hours, sometimes at a steady pace along the well-worn mountain road and other times more slowly, in order to avoid disaster in the pitch black that had become night. Eventually, the rhythmic ride caused Pamela to lose her grip on the saddle horn and fade into a weary sleep. She was safe and warm in the arms of the man she loved. What more could she want?

Pamela dreamed of Bradley's gallant rescue even as she slept. She saw herself laughing at how they'd fooled everyone and escaped the tyrannical rule of her parents. Bradley was gallant and dashing, and Pamela was happier than she'd thought possible. Bradley had saved her from loneliness, and that was all she knew.

The wind picked up and roared down through the tall ponderosa pines, giving a moaning cry that woke Pamela from her happiness. Stretching a bit, Pamela suddenly realized that she was no longer on the back of the horse. Opening her eyes, she was greeted with a warm, crackling fire and the unmistakable aroma of coffee.

Pamela sat up and rubbed the sleep from her face, and that was when she saw it. Two harsh, angry, unyielding eyes, glowing across the fire from her. The man who stared back at her was not Bradley! Nervously, Pamela scooted back a bit before demanding to know the man's identity.

"Who are you? Where's Bradley?" she asked as forcefully as she could.

The man did nothing for a minute. He just kept staring at her with eyes that would yield nothing more than something that closely resembled hatred. His lean, angular jaw was clenched tightly, so tightly in fact that Pamela could see a noticeable ticking in his cheek.

"Well?" she pressed for an answer.

"I might ask you the same," the deep voice sounded from across the flames.

"I presumed you knew. Didn't you help Bradley rescue me?" Pamela asked innocently.

"I don't know what you're talking about, Lady." The man sprung to his feet like a circus cat performing its paces. Pamela shrank away. Her heart was beating wildly. Who was this man?

"I'm talking about this," Pamela finally offered in a weak voice. She waved her arm across the sky. "My rescue."

"I didn't plan to rescue you. I don't know who this Bradley is, and I sure don't know who you are." He came to stand no more than a foot or so away from her before he crouched down. "Who are you?"

Pamela began to tremble so hard that it was instantly noticeable to the man. He grumbled beneath his breath, walked to where his bedroll was, and brought back a blanket. Without any concern for the woman at his feet, he unrolled the blanket with a snap that ended in a cloud of dust.

"Here," he said and threw it down.

Pamela coughed and sputtered in the dust cloud. Anger quickly replaced her fear, and Pamela got to her feet, casting the blanket to one side.

"How dare you!" she exclaimed and rushed at the surprised man. She pounded her fists against his chest while the stranger stood staring down at her in shocked wonder. Finally having had enough, he reached out in a flash and halted her assault.

"Who are you?" he asked in a whisper.

"I'm Pamela Charbonneau," her blue eyes flashed their anger, reminding the man of summer lightning.

A smile broke across his face for only a moment, then faded to a solemn line. "Why were you at the Dawson house?"

"I'm staying there with friends," she said and struggled to pull loose from his grip. "Or I should say, *was* staying there. Now that I've answered your questions, how about answering mine?"

The man shrugged and released her. "Jim," he said casually. "The name's Jim Williams."

"Should that mean anything to me?" Pamela asked, stepping backwards several steps. She felt better putting the distance between them.

"Not unless Zandy told you about me," he replied.

"Zandy? Why would she know a ruthless outlaw like you?"

Jim laughed. "Outlaw, eh? I guess you would think that."

Pamela didn't care that the anger was fading from his face. "I demand that you tell me what's going on. I want to know now!" she screeched and stomped her foot.

Jim stared in wonder. His silence only served to irritate her.

"I mean it!" Pamela's voice was rising to a shout. "I want to know why you took me. I want to know when you are going to release me. I want to know why—"

Pamela stopped as Jim turned to walk away. "Where are you going?"

Jim kept walking and Pamela ran after him, grabbing his arm. "You don't mean to leave me here alone, do you?"

Jim stopped and stared down at her. "I have to think," he declared. "And,

I can't do that with you caterwauling. Sit by the fire and you'll be fine. I'll be back when my head is clear."

With that, he pulled his arm loose and disappeared into the darkness. Pamela whirled on her heel and stalked back to the fire. She was worried, frightened, and just plain mad. The arrogance of the man left her shaking with rage. The memory of his piercing brown eyes left her trembling for other reasons.

Grabbing the blanket he'd thrown down, Pamela pulled it around her and sat down. The trees rustled a haunting melody. Night sounds she'd not heard before became audible in her solitude. Pamela had never really been alone before. All of her life, there had been someone to watch over her or to do for her. Now there was no one, not even the angry man who'd taken her.

Tears came to Pamela's eyes as the distant scream of a mountain lion rang out. She pulled her knees to her chest and hugged the blanket close, pulling it over her head.

"God," she prayed, "please help me."

Chapter 5

All his life, Jim Williams had only one desire. That was to get his own piece of the world and make something of himself. Now, at twenty-six, he was beginning to wonder if that day would ever come.

Even though the night air bore an unmistakable chill from the high-country snows, Jim felt a bead of sweat form on his forehead. He'd taken the wrong woman! To Zandy, he could have explained that it wasn't kidnapping. He'd meant no harm and had only the best of intentions, but how could he tell this to the angry young woman who sat at his fire?

There was no answer in the wind as it blew across his face. There was no reasoning the matter away. When he'd first given thought to the plan of taking Zandy, he'd stopped thinking once he got past the taking part. He'd not even given himself a reasonable plan of action for how they might disentangle themselves from Riley Dawson's wrath once he realized his wife was gone.

Grimacing, Jim kicked at a fallen pine log. "Poor Zandy," he thought aloud. "I sentenced her to a life of misery, and all because I chose to believe what everyone was saying about her."

His memory reminded him that he had seen her leave Riley's house before dawn. That was the morning after Zandy's father had suffered injury in a mining accident.

Jim had presumed that Zandy had spent the night with Riley after fetching the doctor for her father. It wasn't until just recently he'd learned from one of his old buddies that Riley had actually drugged Zandy with the intention of ruining her reputation once and for all. A low growl escaped him as he relived the moment Pat Folkes had informed him of the truth.

He was too late to take back the time Zandy had been forced to spend as Riley's wife, but he'd hoped that he could rectify his angry dismissal and betrayal of their friendship by rescuing her now. But now he had some other woman in his care. A very beautiful woman named Pamela Charbonneau with dark blue eyes that flashed electrically when she was mad.

With a heavy sigh, Jim made his way back to camp. There was nothing to do but apologize and take her back. Hopefully, she'd understand and get over it before they reached Dawson. Jim had no desire to have to answer to the law for his ill-planned scheme.

He reentered the camp silently and came upon Pamela from behind. She heard a muffled sound and turned, as if fearfully expecting to find a wild beast bearing down upon her. Seeing it was Jim, Pamela pulled the blanket down tight around her face.

Jim felt at a loss for words as he took a seat on the ground opposite Pamela. He waited, hoping that she might say something, but when she continued to ignore him, Jim finally spoke.

"Look, I'm sorry for taking you. I hadn't planned it that way. I thought you were Zandy. I just wanted to rescue her." He was trying to offer the most sincere apology he could, but the young woman refused to give him even the slightest consideration.

"Did you hear me?" Jim questioned, irritation edging his voice. He fought for self-control in the face of her silence.

"Look, I don't know what you want me to say that I haven't already said. I'll take you back at first light, but for now we're stuck here."

Pamela kept her face hidden and remained silent, leaving Jim infuriated.

"All right," he said in complete exasperation. "If that's the way you want it, that's the way it'll be." He sauntered over to his saddle and dragged out the rest of his bedroll before plopping down on the ground.

"Remember what I said. We'll leave here at first light, so you'd better get some sleep."

~

In the early morning light, Jim stared down at the child-like woman. Her blond hair had come undone and spilled out from the blanket like a veil. The blanket itself had slipped down far enough to reveal her delicate face in sleep. She had long pale lashes and a pert, almost tiny mouth that Jim remembered, with a shudder, could let go with a most impressive assault of words.

Kneeling down beside her, Jim was struck for a moment by Pamela's seeming frailty. She was so small, he thought. Petite by the standards of most women. How could he have thought she was Zandy? Zandy was at least a head taller and her hair was dark, not golden like ripening grain.

Jim shook his head. What was he doing? Reaching over, he gently shook her shoulder.

"Go away," she muttered and rolled to her other side. The blanket fell away revealing her disheveled state. Her once white blouse was now dirt stained and pulled out from the waist of her tailored burgundy skirt. The skirt itself had ridden up to give Jim a view of silken ankles and dainty satin slippers.

Now he was really disturbed. Seeking to rid himself of his attraction to her, Jim gave Pamela's arm a firm smack and jumped back.

"What are you doing?" Pamela exclaimed, coming up from the ground. She got to her feet and whirled around to face her attacker. "Are you now going to beat me?"

Jim laughed. "At least you're talking to me. Come on. I've got breakfast ready, and we'll be riding out of here in about fifteen minutes."

Pamela put her nose in the air and turned away. "I shan't eat anything you provide." She moved away with a regal step that was almost amusing, given her state of disarray.

"My grub is the only grub here," Jim said with a shrug of his shoulders. "Suit yourself, but it's going to take us most of the day to get back to Dawson."

Pamela seemed to come wide awake at once. "Are we really so far away?" She had thought their ride only a short one.

"We rode for over eight hours. Even if the pace wasn't always very fast," Jim admitted, "it was steady."

Pamela frowned, then noticed her hair. "Oh my," she murmured. "My hair!"

Jim grinned. "Looks fine. I'm just sorry my blanket got you so dirty."

Pamela hadn't noticed the stains on her clothes, nor the way her blouse hung outside her skirt. A gasp escaped her lips as she fought to put everything aright at the same time.

Jim chuckled and walked over to where the coffee steamed aromatically from a worn pot. "Coffee?"

Pamela shook her head vigorously. "I prefer tea, but I suppose you don't have any."

"No, you got that right," Jim replied. "I do have cold biscuits and jerked beef. I know you're used to better, but it's filling." Reluctantly, she gave in and, after combing her fingers through her hair, joined Jim.

Pamela ate silently while Jim watched her for a moment. In spite of her desire for tea, she eventually took a cup of coffee in order to wash down the biscuit.

Jim could stand the silence no more. He pressed forward to ease his curiosity by asking her questions. "Why did you come so willingly with me? Why didn't you fight?"

"I thought," she finally answered, "that you were someone else."

"That's right," Jim remembered. "You kept mentioning some other guy. Bradley, wasn't it?"

Pamela nodded. "Yes. Bradley Rayburn, the man I love."

Jim digested the information for a moment. "Is he your intended?"

"I hope so," Pamela said miserably. "It's been so long since we've been together, he may well have forgotten me by now."

"A man would have a difficult time doing that," Jim mused aloud.

Pamela gave him a quizzical look, then continued. "My parents separated us. I thought perhaps Bradley had come to take me away. When you said you'd come to rescue me, what else was I to think?"

"So you just climbed on the first horse offered, mindless of the danger and stormed off into the night?"

Pamela glared at Jim and narrowed her eyes. Again Jim noticed how blue they were. "I thought you were Bradley! I wanted you to be," she added in a wistful voice.

"Well, I guess I can sympathize with that," Jim answered. Seeing that Pamela had finished her fare and that the sun was even now peeking up over the snowy eastern range, Jim started collecting his things. "We'd best be on our way."

~

Pamela stood uncomfortably and frowned. "I would like a moment of privacy," she murmured.

Jim immediately understood and nodded. "I'll saddle the horse and stow this gear."

Pamela watched him move away, totally unconcerned with her urgent need. She looked first in one direction, then another, somewhat bewildered by her predicament. Jim glanced up and realized she'd probably never had to see to nature's call in the great outdoors.

"Just pick a direction," he called over his shoulder. "One way is just about the same as another."

Pamela reddened and stalked off toward a thicket of brush. She could hear Jim chuckling in the background, and it irritated her more than she could say.

"We'll see how he laughs when we get back to Dawson," she muttered.

The mountain trail was winding and laborious for the horse. He struggled against the weight of two passengers for, while Pamela barely weighed a hundred pounds, Jim was a good-sized portion of baggage. From time to time, he dismounted and led the horse while Pamela rode alone.

For the first time, Pamela began to notice the scenery. The land around her was both beautiful and deadly. At times, the roadway was barely suited to accept the width of a horse, and Pamela felt herself leaning toward the rocky wall as loose gravel and rock shifted and plummeted down the ravine.

A heavy cloud bank moved in and rained on the valleys below them. Pamela watched as it blanketed everything in billowy blackness and lingered on as the morning passed into afternoon.

When they stopped to rest the horse and eat a meager lunch, Jim watched the skies, shaking his head. "It doesn't look good," he said.

"What doesn't look good?" Pamela asked curiously.

"It looks like we're going to get wet," he replied and motioned behind her. "There's another storm moving in."

Pamela glanced at the heavy sky and shrugged. At least she'd be back with Zandy and Riley by nightfall. Thinking of Zandy, Pamela remembered Jim's words from the night before.

"Why did you want to take Zandy?" she suddenly questioned. "I mean, why did you think she needed rescuing?"

Jim pulled his hat down low before shoving his hands into his jeans. "I wronged her a long time ago," he finally said. "I was partially to blame for her ending up in a loveless marriage with that no-good Riley Dawson."

Pamela nearly choked on her food. "Loveless marriage?" She began to laugh gaily. "There were never two people more in love than Riley and Zandy. She worships the ground he walks on. He stares at her with such devotion that I honestly think he'd perish if she were taken from him."

Jim's eyes narrowed and his face grew flushed. "I don't believe you!"

Pamela got to her feet and smoothed her burgundy skirt into place. "Well, it doesn't much matter what you believe. It's true. Zandy and Riley are very happy. In fact, they're going to have a baby in the autumn."

Jim moved away angrily. He threw things back into his saddlebags, muttering all the while. "No one could be happy with Riley Dawson."

"But Zandy is," Pamela said, refusing to give an inch on the argument. "Riley has changed from the man he used to be."

"What would you know of the man he used to be?" Jim raged. "I knew him then. I worked for him and he was a cutthroat, no-good person who. . . ." His words faded into a growl. "He was just ruthless, that's all."

"He got saved," Pamela offered. "Zandy says God made Riley a new man, and she loves him."

"I can't believe this trash," Jim said, throwing the reins over the horse's neck. "Get up there," he said, motioning to the saddle.

"I will not be ordered about. You're just mad because the woman who you thought needed you, doesn't. You should have checked things out a little better."

"Get over here so I can help you into the saddle," Jim muttered between clenched teeth. Pamela's news just couldn't be true. Surely he hadn't been even more stupid than he'd already figured.

"I won't," Pamela said, striking a pose with hands on hips.

"Suit yourself," Jim replied and swung up into the saddle. "You can walk for awhile." He nudged the horse forward and didn't even look back to see if Pamela followed him.

She did, though. She was angry at Jim for refusing to apologize for his temper and even angrier at herself for losing her ride. She grimaced at each step, feeling the sharp rocks as they cut into her thin-soled slippers. Then the rain began to fall.

First it only misted, making everything damp and cold. Then it fell in earnest, with huge drops that saturated everything in its path. Pamela struggled to keep pace with the horse and finally could take no more. Crumbling to the ground, she panted in exhaustion, near to tears for her folly.

Without a word, Jim got down from the horse, lifted Pamela into his arms, and remounted. Neither one said a thing, and a silent truce was born.

Chapter 6

The rain fell in such a deluge that returning the same way they'd departed from Dawson became impossible. Each mountain stream was rising rapidly as the rains continued throughout the day. Finally, they came to a place where they could go no farther.

"We'll have to wait it out. By morning it should go down. This is just a cloudburst," Jim said, his voice laced with uncertainty. "If not, we'll go back a ways and pick up another trail."

Pamela nodded. She was weary and cold and hungry. Nothing could have pleased her more than a warm bed and supper but, next to that dream, getting off the horse was second best.

Jim took a small hatchet and cut branches from the pines to form a shelter. It wasn't much, but it kept a good deal of the water off of them. Eventually, the rain seemed to pass on down the valley and, though the sun didn't come out to warm things, it was a relief.

Pamela succumbed to her exhaustion and fell into a deep sleep. She was mindless of the cold and hunger. When she awoke, it was morning again, and she was stunned to realize she was alone.

"Jim!" she called, crawling out of the lean-to. "Jim!" Her voice held a frantic tone. She hadn't realized until that moment that she'd come to depend on the stranger for her own security.

"I'm here," Jim called, coming from a heavy growth of small pines. "I was catching us some breakfast." He held out a couple of ground squirrels and laughed at Pamela's wrinkled-up nose.

"You'll think they're grand once I get them cooked and you sink your teeth into them."

Pamela rolled her eyes. "I can't imagine feeling that way." But her stomach growled loudly, causing Jim to laugh even more.

Embarrassed, Pamela excused herself to some privacy and didn't return until Jim had the monstrous little things skinned and spitted over a small fire.

"Where did you get dry wood?" she asked, taking her seat beside the fire.

"You just have to know where to look," Jim said with a grin. "The forest is filled with all sorts of wonders, if you know where to find them." With that, he pulled a handful of berries from his vest pocket.

"How marvelous!" Pamela exclaimed and reached out to take some of the berries. She didn't concern herself with whether they were dirty or clean and popped them into her mouth with a smile. "Oh, they're wonderful."

"How old are you?"

"Eighteen," she said in surprise. "Why?"

"I just wondered. You look so young, almost like a child." She frowned indignantly, causing him to add, "No offense."

Pamela relaxed a bit and nodded. "I understand."

"I really am sorry," Jim continued. "I feel bad for all I've put you through, and I guess," he paused, "I just don't want you to be mad at me. I honestly meant you no harm. I'm not the kind of man who goes around taking women on a regular basis."

Pamela laughed, "I'm sure you don't."

It was the only reply she felt comfortable in making. In truth, she was beginning to notice things about Jim that she hadn't before. Like the way he made her feel secure. That had completely surprised her.

She watched him work at cooking the food, turning it until it was golden and brown. She accepted one of the sticks of meat and looked up questioningly.

"I promise, it won't be as bad as you think. Eat it with this," he said and handed her a biscuit. "I brought quite a few of these with me."

Pamela did as he instructed her and found that the taste was bearable. Her hunger appeased, she got up to stretch and walk out the soreness in her back and legs.

Jim was putting things away and dousing the fire when she returned. For a moment, Pamela found herself thinking of his apology and the sincere way his eyes had met hers. He wasn't the ruthless outlaw she'd originally considered him. No, he was just a misguided soul, pining for a love that could not be. Just like she was. The thought shocked Pamela, and her head snapped up to find Jim's warm brown eyes watching her.

"Ready?" he asked.

"Yes, I suppose," she said with a glance at the horse. "Although I'm not thinking overly kind thoughts of the ride ahead."

"Better than walking all the way," Jim mused, and Pamela heartily agreed.

The horse picked his way down the muddy, rock-strewn path. This trail was not as well developed as the one they'd used before, but the rain-swollen creeks prevented them from crossing to the better one so they had to make do with what lay before them.

Pamela found the aching in her back more than she could bear and finally gave in and leaned against Jim. He didn't seem to mind, and she tried to forget the impropriety of the entire matter, reminding herself that the last two days had been filled with improprieties.

"We'll stop and water the horse," Jim said, sliding over the animal's rump. "We're making good time in spite of the rain and flooding. We'll probably be back to Dawson before dark."

"It can't be soon enough," Pamela remarked, letting Jim lift her from the horse's back.

When he set her down, she remained fixed for a moment, looking up into his eyes. Then the screech of a jaybird broke her thoughts, and she moved away to let him work with the horse.

Jim led the animal to the rapidly moving stream and allowed him to drink his fill. With a nervous snort, the gelding lifted his head and flattened his ears. Something was setting the horse on edge.

Jim glanced around, wondering if a bear or mountain lion was nearby. He lifted his eyes to the rocky ledges overhead but, seeing nothing, tried to pull the horse back with him to where Pamela waited.

The gelding whinnied and pulled away, rearing slightly and pounding the damp earth with its powerful hooves.

"What's wrong?" Pamela questioned, then her eyes grew wide, and Jim saw her mouth open as if to say something more.

A sharp blow landed on the back of his head, and Jim instantly lost consciousness, slumping to the dirt. The horse reared, slamming its hooves down inches from Jim's face before charging away from the scene.

Pamela stared at the three men who faced her. They were leering and ugly and frightfully filthy. She backed away a step or two, not wanting to leave Jim to their mercy, yet knowing that if they caught up with her, her own fate could be worse than death.

She turned to run and managed to get several yards away before the youngest of the three caught up with her and threw her roughly over his shoulder.

"See if that fool has anything of value on him," the man yelled. "I'm taking her with us. Ma will know what to do with her."

"I know what to do with her, Joe," one of the others called back. This drew laughter from all three and left Pamela with a sickening feeling in the pit of her stomach.

The stench of the man rose up to assault her nose. Though she was more than a little dirty herself, this man smelled of death and rot. She struggled against his hold, but he only tightened his grip and laughed.

"You might as well cooperate, Missy. You ain't going nowhere." By this time, the other two had joined him and Pamela could see that they were appraising her intently.

"I'd say she's a proper lady," one of the men said, coming alongside her. Pamela could see that a long hideous scar marred his face. It cut a path across his nose and ended just above his lip.

"Now, Knifenose," the other one said, running his tongue over his large lips. "You ain't pretty enough to be courting a proper lady. Iffen she really is a proper lady, then you'd best leave her to me." They snorted laughs, leering and commenting, until finally they reached the place where their horses were tethered.

The man called Joe pulled Pamela from his shoulder and threw her across his horse. The saddle horn pounded like a knife into her ribs, and Pamela let out a cry.

"Keep quiet," the man said, taking a seat in the saddle. He pulled her across his lap, then urged his horse forward.

"Was he dead?" Joe asked Knifenose, and Pamela held her breath waiting for the answer.

"Will be soon enough," Knifenose replied. "He didn't have much of anything on him so I didn't figure he deserved to be eased out of his misery."

Pamela shuddered at their cruelty and felt herself grow faint.

Chapter 7

D on't try to move, Son," a deep voice was saying.

Jim opened his eyes and squinted against the light of day. A white-haired, bearded stranger came into view overhead.

"Who are you?" Jim asked, putting a hand to the painful throbbing on the side of his head.

"The name's Caleb Emerson," the man replied with a warm smile. "Look's like you've been bushwhacked. They robbed ya clean, took all your goods, and left ya for dead."

Jim moaned and tried to roll onto his side. "I have to go after them."

"Whoa there, Fella," Caleb said, putting a strong arm out to restrain Jim's movement. "You took a nasty hit to the head. I stopped the bleeding, and it's not life threatening, but you're gonna have to rest awhile."

"I can't," Jim said. He lifted his eyes to the sky. "They've taken more than my goods."

"Nothing worth your life," the man offered.

"Yes, I'm afraid there was." Jim remembered blue eyes and a face that was only beginning to smile in his presence. "I wasn't traveling alone," Jim finally said. "There was a woman with me."

"Your wife?" Caleb asked in a concerned tone.

"No," Jim said and fell back against the ground. "It's a terribly long story, but I'm afraid I am responsible for the young woman, and now I have to find her."

"Well, you ain't going anywhere just yet," Caleb said sympathetically. "Why don't you just rest for a spell and eat some grub? After that, maybe you'd best tell me the whole story."

Against his will, Jim ate a bit and slept a great deal. He didn't awaken again until midmorning the following day, but his head hurt less and his vision was clearer.

"What time is it?" he asked, struggling to sit.

Caleb gave him a hand before glancing up at the sky. " 'Pears to be about eleven."

"What day is it?"

"Now that's a little more difficult," Caleb replied with a smile. "Best I

45

can figure, it's Thursday."

"If that's true, then I've only lost a day," Jim said, thinking aloud and rubbing his head.

"You gonna tell me what's going on?" Caleb asked.

Jim nodded. "I will if you'll give me some more of that stew you fed me yesterday."

Caleb chuckled and pulled out a tin plate from his saddlebag. "Sure thing." He dished up the stew from where it warmed over a dying fire. "By the way, I've got some good news for you."

"You found her?" Jim asked hopefully.

"Not your lady friend," Caleb said, sorry to see the hope leave the young man's face. "But, I did find your horse."

"That is good news," Jim admitted. He'd need a mount if he was going to find Pamela.

Caleb waited until Jim had eaten his fill of the stew, then curiosity got the better of the old drifter. "Who are you, Son? You and that young lady elopin'?"

Jim shook his head. "Nothing so honorable," he replied. "The name's Williams. Jim Williams." Jim held out his hand to take the stranger's. They shook firmly before Jim continued. "I made a big mistake. In fact, I made several. One mistake I acted out a long time ago, and the most recent came because I was trying to right that wrong."

"I think you just got me more confused than I was to begin with," Caleb said with a laugh.

Jim eased back against a small boulder and rested his head. "I thought a certain young lady, a friend of mine from the past, needed rescuing from a bad situation. I decided to sneak down to where she lived and take off with her. I thought I'd get her to safety and let her decide from there what she wanted to do. But, instead of the woman I planned to take, I ended up taking someone completely different. Someone I didn't even know, until just a few days ago."

"I see," Caleb said without any emotion betraying how he felt on the matter.

Jim grimaced at the dull ache that haunted his thoughts. "She came willingly. Fact was, she thought I was someone else who'd come to rescue her."

"So this young woman needed saving too?"

Jim laughed. "You could say that, I suppose. She thought she did. Fancied herself in love with some city slicker. She thought he'd come to save her in the dead of night and, because it was dark, she didn't know that I wasn't him. We rode through the night, and she fell asleep in my arms. I really thought I was doing a noble thing. When I stopped for a spell to rest the horse, I put her on the ground to sleep, then I built a fire. That was when I realized she wasn't at all who I thought she was."

"What happened then?"

Jim looked down at his booted feet. "I got mad. I got real mad, in fact. I couldn't believe I'd grabbed the wrong woman. When she woke up, she was mad. Scared too, and who could blame her? Here she was, just a little bitty thing, and some big ol' brute of a man had dragged her off in the night. She ranted and raved at me, and those blue eyes of her flashed brighter than any summer lightning storm you've ever seen."

Caleb smiled at the reference. "My wife used to be the same way."

"You're married?" Jim asked, forgetting for a moment to continue with his story.

"Was," Caleb said with a sadness to his voice. "She passed on a few years back. I know I'll see her again someday, but I sure miss her now."

Jim didn't say a word.

"Now, what about your little bitty gal? What happened after her rantin' and ravin'?"

"I'm afraid I stormed off and left her alone by the fire. I knew it was a mean thing to do. She was obviously not used to outdoor life, but I wanted to put her in her place. I had to think too, and I couldn't do that with her yelling and screeching at me like a hoot owl on a wildcat's back."

Caleb laughed out loud at this. "Did your leavin' settle her down?"

"Yeah, and then some," Jim admitted. "She wouldn't even talk to me when I got back. But, the next day things kind of mended themselves. I apologized and explained myself and promised I'd get her back home safely. Now it appears I've caused her harm once again."

"Don't fret about it, Son. You need to get well, then we'll go out after her."

"We?" Jim looked the older man in the eye.

"Sure," Caleb said with a nod. "I can't let you go out there all alone. Now, did you see who took your little bitty gal?"

"Her name's Pamela," Jim said, though he liked the nickname. "All I saw was a vague image of the man who ransacked my pockets. He had a hideous scar that ran over his nose and down to his lip."

"That'd be Knifenose McCoy," Caleb muttered under his breath.

"You know them?" Jim said, sitting up abruptly.

Caleb ran a hand through his rough white beard. "I've been drifting these here parts since my wife died. There's a gang of outlaws that goes down into Dawson on a regular basis and wreaks havoc on everybody. It's the Owens gang, headed up by the mother of two of the men. Old Knifenose McCoy has been riding with 'em for awhile now. If it's them, then I've got a good idea where they've taken your gal."

"Then let's go!" Jim exclaimed and got unsteadily to his feet. His head pounded, but he was undaunted.

"Nah," Caleb said and reached out to pull Jim back down. "That old mama of theirs ain't gonna let anything happen to Little Bitty. She's a real smart one, that woman. She's cultured, and the real brains behind most of their activities. You just rest and get your feet back under you steadylike, and we'll head over to their hideout tomorrow."

"We can't let her spend another night in their company," Jim said in complete exasperation. "Those men might. . .well, they could. . . ." He couldn't even bring himself to say what might happen.

"You gotta trust the good Lord to look over her, Jim. Christianfolk know that He's got all the answers, and He's the one looking out over those who can't look out for themselves. That'd be your little bitty gal. We'll just pray about it and ask Him to mosey on over to where she's at and surround her with His angels. You know the Bible says in Psalm ninety-one, verse eleven that 'He shall give his angels charge over thee, to keep thee in all thy ways.' "

"You believe that, Caleb?" Jim asked wearily. He was giving in to the misery of his body and hated himself for doing so.

"You bet I believe it!" Caleb said enthusiastically. "Ain't you a Christian, Jim?"

Jim put a hand to his head and stretched his legs back out in front of him. "My ma and pa were both God-fearing people. They brought me up to respect the Word of God and to go to church on Sunday. I listened to Ma tell me Bible stories and, one day, when I was just a tike, she asked me if I wanted to go to heaven when I died. I said sure. I mean, I figured it beat all out of going to the other place."

Caleb chuckled, "That's no lie."

"Anyway, I repeated a prayer she told me. When I was done, she explained how all a body had to do to get saved and go to heaven was to accept Jesus as their Savior. She told me that when I accepted Jesus and asked Him to forgive my sins, I became a new person."

"That's for sure too!" Caleb agreed.

"Well, I figured she wasn't lying," Jim continued, "but, in truth, I never felt any different. I mean, I didn't go out of my way to do wrong, but I didn't feel exactly called to preach, either. I guess over the years I figured being a Christian and all just didn't take."

"Sinful critters have a hard way of looking at life," Caleb said softly.

"They see the things they've done, and they know they're no good. God sees the things they've done and knows there's a chance for them to do different. Satan comes along, though, and tells them that there isn't any other way, and that they're the most miserable excuses for human bein's that ever existed. Satan makes sure he stands planted between those struggling folks and God, just to block out the view. But it don't work that way for long."

"It don't?" Jim questioned.

"Nope," Caleb replied and leaned back. "God sends them angels to surround you. They beat back old Satan and tell him to mosey on out, 'cause this property has God's mark on it."

"And does he?" Jim asked. "Does Satan back off?"

"You bet he does. God looks after His own, I told you that, Son."

"But what if I'm not His own? What if Pamela's not?"

"Everything is God's, Jim. The world and all that's in it. The people, the animals, the trees—it all belongs to Him. It's just that some folks don't reckon God is theirs."

Jim felt the need to lie down and stretched out beside the glowing embers. "So you think I belong to God too?"

"I think you need to answer that one for yourself, Son," Caleb replied. "Give God a chance. He's not likely to hold a grudge for your lack of understandin'. Just seek Him out and ask His forgiveness. It's never too late to change the path you're on."

Jim closed his eyes, and a bit of peace began to trickle into his heart. "Sounds like good words to think on," he muttered before dozing off into a deep sleep.

Chapter 8

Pamela stared fearfully into the gray-blue eyes of an older woman. The woman was taller than Pamela by half a foot and had an athletic youth to her that led Pamela to believe she was perfectly able to hold her own in any situation.

"What's your name?" the woman demanded.

"I might ask you the same," Pamela said, lifting her chin defiantly.

The woman studied her for a moment, then gave a brief laugh. "You're a spunky one, just like the boys said." She paused, eyes narrowing. "But you'll learn that cooperating with me will get you a lot less aggravation. My name is Esther Owens. I run this group of ruffians, and I'm no dawdling fool to be taken advantage of. I'm Eastern-educated, and I know well the ways of this world, so it would be best if you got it into your head now that I'm fully capable of running this show."

Pamela stared openly at the woman. Her reddish brown hair had been carefully pulled back and neatly knotted at the nape of her neck. Her dark brown riding skirt and snug matching jacket showed off a still youthful figure. But it was Esther's eyes that held Pamela's attention. They were purposeful and firm, and, just as Esther had stated, they betrayed a look of intelligence that Pamela couldn't deny.

"My boys tell me they killed your man," Esther began again. "Do you have other family?"

Pamela still refused to speak. In truth, she wasn't sure she could after Esther's reference to Jim's death. Pamela felt her hands trembling and clutched them tightly together to avoid giving herself away.

Esther shook her head. "I'll leave you to yourself for a time. Maybe staying in this hole will give you reason to talk to me." Without any other word on the matter, Esther pulled the heavy wood door closed, and Pamela heard the unmistakable sound of her barring it from the outside.

Now Pamela was truly scared. She'd been livid at the way Esther's "boys" had treated her. They seemed inclined to speak suggestively, reminding Pamela that she was under their complete control. But it was Esther's words about Jim that left Pamela void of hope. Jim was taking her home. He alone knew where and why she'd been removed from Dawson in the first place, and now he was gone.

Pamela looked around the dimly lit room. The place was hardly wider than her arm span and only about half again as long. The rough, plank walls had never seen a coat of paint and the floor was dirt. There was nothing but a filthy cot for furniture, and a six-inch slit in the wall overhead offered the only light.

"What do I do?"

~

Esther Owens looked down the table at her gang and shook her head. Two of those present were her own sons, the rest were drifters and renegades who'd learned of her business dealings and sought to join up.

The men argued among themselves over one thing or another while Esther waited for a heavyset woman to serve their lunch. The sound of several riders approaching brought instant quiet to the table. Esther got up quickly and crossed to the window.

"It's just the rest of the boys," she said, coming back to the men.

Several grunts confirmed they'd heard her speak before they launched into a new set of arguments. Esther tapped her fingers on the table, waiting for the new arrivals to join them. They would be bringing her supplies from Denver. Hopefully, they'd bring a newspaper or two, maybe even a book.

Several men burst through the door, two of them carrying wooden crates.

"Take those to my room," Esther instructed and got up to follow the men from the room. "The rest of you men finish your eating and get back to work. We've got a big job to pull tomorrow, and I don't want anything to go wrong," she called over her shoulder.

Silence fell across the table. Although she was just a woman, these men knew her mind to be the keenest they'd encountered. There wasn't a man, young or old, sitting there who didn't know just how much they needed Esther Owens.

Esther directed the men to place the crates on her bed. "Now get yourselves some food. I'll need to talk to you when you're finished." The men nodded and left the room, closing the door behind them.

Esther began sorting through the boxes. She smiled broadly as her hand came to the newspaper that lined the bottom of one of the crates. Pulling it out, she took herself over to her rocking chair and began to read.

The price of silver was climbing, as were railroad stocks. The Atchison, Topeka, & Santa Fe Railroad was advertising tracts of land to entice immigrants to come west and settle along the train routes. There was some speculation that the Santa Fe desired to place a route across the southern U.S. territories, all the way to the coast, but no one was taking that venture very seriously.

Esther read on, drinking in the news and realizing, as she did every time a newspaper came her way, that she missed big-city life and knowing what was happening as it happened. She was about to put the paper aside when a photograph caught her eye. Staring at it hard, Esther began to smile.

The story below the photograph told of a young woman who'd disappeared from Dawson, Colorado. The picture was unmistakably that of the woman who was now captive in her shed out back. Esther wanted to shout when she read that Pamela Charbonneau was a wealthy socialite from Kansas City. There was good money to be made in this, and Esther was already putting together the ransom note in her mind. Tossing the paper onto the bed, Esther made her way back to the shed. She would confront Pamela with her news and decide from there how they would address the issue of a ransom.

～

Pamela had tried every way possible to escape her prison. She'd pulled and pushed at the door, only to realize that it was a hopeless case. She'd checked the walls for any hint of weakness but, finding none, could only pace out her frustrations.

She remembered something Zandy had once told her about God. She'd said that God would never leave her and that, no matter what happened in her life, He would always hear her when she prayed. Glancing up at the sagging ceiling, Pamela wondered if it were true. Would God really hear her if she prayed?

"I guess it's worth trying," Pamela muttered, seeking to convince herself. She tried to remember just how Zandy started her prayers. "Father," she whispered, "Zandy told me I could pray and You would hear me. Well, I'm in quite a fix right now, and I could certainly stand to be heard. Fact is, I need a great deal of help, and I don't know where it might come from. God, nobody but You and these outlaws even know I'm here. Please help me to get away from these people. Help me to escape to safety. I promise I'll never be difficult again, if You will just answer this prayer. Amen.

"There," Pamela stated in complete resolve, "that's done." She waited a few minutes, not moving a muscle, as if to see how God would answer her request. The silence washed over her in waves, but nothing seemed changed or the slightest bit different.

"I wish I knew more about this Christian stuff," Pamela sighed aloud. "Does it happen right away? How do you know if God hears you?" Just then the sound of someone outside the door startled Pamela.

Esther Owens opened the door and with her came a flood of daylight. Pamela squinted her eyes and stepped back a pace.

"Well," Esther began with a strange smile, "I've just come upon a bit of news from Denver. It was rather fascinating, and I thought perhaps you would enjoy hearing about it. Would you?"

Pamela lowered her head and said nothing.

"I asked you a question, Miss Charbonneau."

Pamela's head snapped up at the name. Esther laughed heartily and leaned back against the wall.

"So, you are Pamela Charbonneau of Kansas City and lately of Dawson?"

"Yes," Pamela finally admitted.

"The article in the Denver paper stated that it was unknown as to whether you had been taken or had simply disappeared on your own. Which was it?" Esther questioned curiously.

"It's none of your concern," Pamela retorted in a defiant tone. "What do you plan to do with me?"

"Well, the article also said that you are from a very wealthy family. Don't you imagine your poor folks would pay well to see you returned safely?"

Pamela realized the woman meant business. "I suppose they might. However, we are rather estranged at the moment. I came to Dawson with friends and, in truth, those friends would probably pay a hefty reward to have me returned. After all, I was in their care." Pamela's mind was moving way ahead of her mouth. Returning to her parents would put her in Kansas City, but they'd no doubt just ship her off again. No, perhaps it would be better to go home to Zandy and Riley. Then maybe Zandy could make a plea to her parents for her return to Kansas City and her marriage to Bradley.

Pamela was still lost in selfish thought when Esther spoke again. "Who are these friends in Dawson?"

"Riley and Alexandra Dawson," Pamela stated matter-of-factly.

Esther's eyes widened a bit before she resumed her mask of sober indifference. "*The* Riley Dawson? The one who owns the town?"

"The very same," Pamela admitted and folded her arms across her dirty blouse. "I was staying with them. Mrs. Dawson is my dearest friend."

"Umm," Esther said, letting the information soak in.

"This bears consideration," Esther muttered. "It also means taking a little more care with you. I'm moving you up to the house. I'll keep you there and maybe even let you clean up. You'll cooperate with me, though, or I'll move you right back here. Is that understood?"

Pamela nodded her head. She wasn't about to pass up the chance to move from the shack. Wherever she was going would surely present a better chance at escape than this place.

"Good," Esther said and took hold of Pamela's arm. "Don't think to try anything. We're located in a box canyon so there's basically only one way out.

The walls around us are jagged granite, more than one hundred feet straight up. Beyond those are the harshest mountain wastelands you would ever want to contend with. The nearest civilization is far enough away that we don't consider ourselves civilized." She pulled Pamela with her into the yard.

"This is our hideout. No one but us knows the way in and out, and no one leaves here without an escort because my men are trained to shoot first and ask questions later. Do you understand what I'm saying, Miss Charbonneau?"

"I believe so."

"Well, just in case there's any question left in your mind, I'm warning you good and hard right now. Don't try to leave or you will die."

"But what of your ransom?" Pamela questioned, almost smugly.

"I don't need a warm body to convince people to pay a ransom note. I can forward them a corpse easier than I can worry about running you down every time you get it in your head to try and escape."

Pamela blanched at the easy way Esther spoke of killing her.

"Now," Esther said, coming to a full stop. "Do you understand me?"

"Yes, I believe I do," Pamela replied, giving the woman her full attention. "My life is obviously in a precarious state of balance, and you are the one who will decide my fate."

Esther smiled. "It's such a pleasure to listen to another intelligent soul speak. I shall enjoy having your company while we decide this matter. Now give me your word that you won't try to leave."

Pamela grimaced. "I promise."

"Good enough."

With that, Esther pulled Pamela toward the rough looking log house. Pamela tried to take in everything. She considered where each building lay in relation to the house, without looking obvious, and tried to commit it to memory for later use. The Owens gang would no doubt kill her anyway, so therefore her promise meant nothing. She would seek a means of escape—the sooner the better.

Chapter 9

W hat do you mean she's gone?" Riley questioned his wife.

A teary-eyed Zandy stood, arms akimbo, shaking her head. "I don't know. I just know that Pamela was with Ruth and me earlier in the evening, but then she took her leave. I thought she'd gone to bed, but when I went up to check on her, she was gone. I've covered the entire house, Riley. She's nowhere to be found."

Riley crossed the room and took Zandy in his arms as she broke into sobs. "Hush, we'll find her. You can't get yourself all worked up. It might harm the babe, and you wouldn't want that."

"But I promised to look out after her," Zandy said in between ragged breaths. "I promised Claudia Charbonneau that no ill would befall her granddaughter. I promised you that I could handle the situation. Now just look. For all I know she could be hurt or even dead!"

"Maybe she's just found a way back to Bradley Rayburn," Riley suggested. At this, Ruth stepped forward and agreed.

"That's right, Zandy. You did say she wanted to get back to him awfully bad. So bad in fact, that the girl's grandmother made you promise not to allow her any money, lest she buy a train ticket home."

"I know," Zandy replied, "but all of her things are still here. Pamela is too devoted to her looks and finery to leave it behind. She would have at least taken as much as she could carry. I checked her room, however. Nothing is missing. Her brushes and combs are still there. And all of her clothes are hanging in the wardrobe, except what she was wearing."

"What was she wearing?" Riley asked. "We'll need to get a description to the sheriff."

"The last I saw," Ruth replied before Zandy could, "she was wearing a white blouse and, I believe, a red skirt."

"Burgundy," Zandy corrected. "It was a burgundy color with black braid trim on the bottom."

Riley led his wife to a brocade chair. "Sit here, and I'll send someone down to the sheriff's office. He'll probably want to look around and see if there's any sign of where she might have gotten off to."

Zandy did as she was instructed. She'd no sooner taken a seat when a fluttering in her abdomen caused her eyes to widen.

"Oh!" she gasped in surprise.

Riley turned sharply to inspect his wife. "What is it? Are you in pain?"

Zandy laughed, amidst her tears, "No, I just felt the baby move!"

Ruth smiled, and Riley seemed stunned. "You felt the baby move?" he questioned.

"I'm sure that was what it was," Zandy answered.

"It's a good sign," Ruth said, coming to pat her stepdaughter's shoulder. "Maybe God has given it to you in order to help you concentrate on something other than Pamela. You need to rest and keep a happy heart for your baby's sake, if not your own."

Riley smiled and knelt down beside Zandy. He took her hand in his and kissed it gently. "You aren't to blame for this. I could never hold you responsible for Pamela's well-being. She's much too headstrong, and we both know it. You have to stay calm for the baby. I'll turn this town upside-down and, no matter how difficult the task, I'll find her. You trust me to do that, don't you?"

Zandy looked deep into the loving eyes of her husband. He gave her great confidence that there was nothing too big for him to undertake. "I do," she whispered.

"Good. Now you and my son need to get to bed. It's late, and nothing can be gained by your collapsing on the floor." With that, Riley lifted Zandy into his arms and carried her down the hall.

～

After seeing his wife to bed, Riley went alone to search the immediate grounds for Pamela. Perhaps she'd fallen asleep somewhere. Riley felt angry that she would be so heartless as to leave Zandy wondering and fretting over her safety. But, even if she had run off, Riley reasoned, he wasn't about to let it bring harm to his wife and child.

Seeing nothing unreasonable, and no sign of a sleeping or otherwise entangled Pamela, Riley decided morning would be soon enough to bother the sheriff. Now, he only had to reason with Zandy and see to it that she kept herself from doing something foolish.

Before Riley could make his way from the house the next morning, a note was delivered by a young boy. Riley looked down at the paper addressed to him and asked the child who'd sent the letter.

"Don't know," the boy said with a shrug. "Somebody I ain't never seen afore. Gave me a nickel and said I should bring this note to you in the mornin'."

Riley opened the folded letter and read:

I've taken your wife because you don't deserve her. If I'd known of your ways and how you planned to force her into a love- less marriage, I would never have let you take her. Now she's safe and can make the choice for herself.

Riley reread it quickly, the truth only now starting to stink in. The boy was already halfway down the path, but Riley called him back.

"What did the man look like?" he asked the child and flipped him another nickel.

The boy's face lit up as he caught the coin. "He weren't any taller than you. He had brown hair. Jes sorta regular lookin'."

"Nothing special about him?" Riley asked. "Think hard."

"Nope," the boy answered, shaking his head. "He was just a man." Riley nodded and let the boy go.

"What's your name, Son?" Riley thought to call out.

"Brian," the boy answered. "Brian Masters."

Riley wasted little time. He pushed the note deep into his pocket and went to saddle his horse. It was now all too clear that Pamela had been taken. But, Riley reminded himself with barely controlled rage, it was Alexandra the culprit had been after!

Riley explained the situation to the sheriff and gave all the details of Pamela's disappearance before heading back to the mansion. He left out the news of the note, fearing that if he told anyone, word would get back to Zandy. He had no desire to further worry her with thoughts that someone was after her. Riley wondered what the kidnapper's next step would be, once he realized that Pamela wasn't who he thought she was.

At home, Zandy met him at the door and questioned him about his visit with the sheriff.

"Did you tell him that she might have run away?" she asked.

Riley put his arm around her. "No, I think you were probably right. I think someone has taken her."

Burley and Ruth Stewart stood inside the library's open doors. They exchanged a glance before Burley stepped forward. "What makes you so cer- tain, Riley?"

Riley wouldn't give away the fact that he'd received the note, but he had to offer something that seemed logical. "Zandy made a good point in regards to Pamela. She wouldn't have left her things behind. Not only that, no money or horses are missing, and the things of value that she owned, like her silver comb and brush, are still on the dresser upstairs."

Burley nodded. "You suppose that Rayburn guy came and took her?"

"I kind of doubt it," Riley said with a sigh. Zandy lifted her face to note the weariness in her husband's eyes. She thought she saw fear there too, but dismissed it as Riley continued, "I know Rayburn's type. He's probably already working on another conquest. That's the trouble with young women of means. They often easily fall prey to undesirables who seek only their fortune. Pamela's parents were probably well within their rights to be concerned for their daughter."

"But what if he wasn't like that? What if they really loved each other, Riley?" Zandy couldn't help but ask.

"Then time and distance won't hurt them, Love. Look what happened between us."

Burley interjected, before Zandy could respond, "Besides, that really isn't the issue here. The problem is that Pamela has disappeared, most likely not of her own will. It might be wise if we were to telegraph her parents."

Riley agreed, but added, "I'd like to give it a day or two and see what happens. There's no sense in worrying them if she turns up to have just wandered off in a pout."

"Riley Dawson! Wandered off in a pout?" Zandy exclaimed indignantly. "What kind of woman do you think Pamela is, anyway? She wouldn't leave us to worry like that."

Riley felt the heat of her words, but didn't dare explain that he wanted to see if the man who'd taken Pamela would return her when he realized she wasn't Zandy. Riley shrugged his shoulders and gave a sheepish grin. "Sorry, I guess I put my foot in that one."

～

The days that passed waiting for word about Pamela were sheer torture for Zandy and the rest of the household. Riley seemed genuinely worried that Pamela hadn't returned, or at least puzzled that they hadn't received notice giving a clue to her whereabouts.

On the fifth day of Pamela's absence, a letter arrived with the mail. It was from a kidnapper who demanded over one million dollars for Pamela's safe return. Otherwise, the letter stated, she would be killed.

Zandy was present when the letter was received, and Riley, not knowing what the contents were, had no way to shield her from its impact.

"Dear Lord," she whispered in prayer. Zandy landed on the floor at his feet.

"Alexandra!" Riley quickly lifted her into his arms. He carried her to a nearby sofa and laid her out. "Ruth!" he shouted into the air. He patted Zandy's face and tried to wake her. He quickly read the note.

"What's wrong, Riley?" Ruth questioned, half running into the room.

When she saw Zandy, she emitted a cry of concern and hurried to her side. "What happened?"

"We had a note from Pamela's kidnappers. Zandy read it before I could keep her from it. Next thing I know, she's in a dead faint on the floor," Riley explained.

"Stay here with her," Ruth instructed. "I'll get some smelling salts and a wet cloth." Ruth hurried from the room to retrieve the needed items.

She came back quickly and handed Riley a cloth. "Here," Ruth told Riley, "wipe her face with this." He took it and touched it to his wife's cheek, while Ruth waved the salts under Zandy's nose.

A moan sounded from Zandy as she suddenly came to. She pushed away Ruth's hand and tried to sit up. Riley kept a firm hold on her.

"You just took a nasty fall," he said. "I think you should lie still."

"What happened?" Zandy asked weakly.

"You fainted."

Her stepmother's words seemed to awaken her instantly.

"The letter!" she gasped.

"It's all right," Riley assured her. "You have to relax and let me take care of this."

"But it's all my fault. If I hadn't insisted on bringing her along, she'd be safe back in Missouri with her grandmother. This is all my doing!" She shook her head from side to side, while tears streamed down her cheeks.

Riley took hold of her. "You're always telling me you believe God is in control of our lives. You helped Pamela to God. Don't you realize that she's in His control, and He watches over His own? I know I've heard you declare the same thing on more than one occasion."

Zandy heard the words, but refused to be comforted. "Sometimes we grieve God by interfering," she protested. "You said I was sticking my nose in where it didn't belong when we were back home. Maybe this wouldn't have happened if I'd just listened."

"Maybe," Riley admitted. "Then again, maybe it would have happened back there. We can't second-guess this situation. Either you trust God to keep her in His care or you don't. Is God any less God just because things aren't going your way?"

"No, of course not," Zandy conceded.

"Good," Riley answered with a smile. "Now, I'm going to carry you upstairs, and I want you to stay in bed for the rest of the day. If you don't, I know ways of putting you to sleep and insuring the matter."

Zandy saw a bit of a twinkle in his eyes and couldn't help but smile. "Very well, Mister Dawson. I shall be an obedient wife."

"That'll be a first," Riley said, lifting her in his arms.

∽

Zandy was true to her word and waited out the day in bed. In the days that followed the note's arrival, she even tried her best to leave the entire matter in Riley's hands.

Mostly she busied herself with Ruth and played with Molly and her brothers.

Riley was grateful for the reprieve from Zandy's usual desire to help. He wanted very much for her to remain calm and at peace, but he knew she was worried for her friend.

Daily, he went to retrieve the mail, always looking for another letter from the kidnappers with further instructions. At one point, he was sitting and considering how he would approach the monetary demands when Burley entered and pulled up a chair.

"Any word yet?" he asked his son-in-law.

"No. I'm getting mighty tired waiting on it too."

"Kidnappers are queer creatures," Burley said with a shrug. "Who can know their minds?"

"I didn't expect this, though." Riley hadn't intended to speak the words aloud.

"Why not?" Burley questioned. "You were, after all, the one that believed so adamantly that she'd been taken. You were sure of it, in fact, even when it didn't seem all that sensible to me."

Riley said nothing, hoping that Burley would drop the subject. He didn't want to explain the first letter and cause Zandy's father any undue worry. Still, there was the matter of the ransom note. Riley was completely baffled that a man who'd thought Zandy in trouble and wanted to help her out would turn kidnapper when he realized he'd taken the wrong woman. It just didn't figure.

"You're keeping something to yourself, aren't you?" Burley asked seriously. "I think if it involves any of us here, you'd best come clean and share it with me."

Riley ran a weary hand back through his dark hair. There really was no reason that he shouldn't tell Burley. The man had a right to protect his family.

"A boy named Brian Masters brought me a letter the morning after Pamela's disappearance. It explained why she'd been taken. That's how I knew she hadn't just wandered off or run away."

"Why didn't you say so?" Burley questioned. His voice was edged with irritation. "Did you tell the sheriff?"

Riley shook his head and reached into his desk. From the very back of the drawer, he pulled out the letter and handed it to Burley.

Burley unfolded the note and quickly read the contents, then lifted his eyes to meet Riley's. "He meant to take my Zandy?"

"It would appear that way."

"But who would want to do that? I mean, most folks around here know how happy she is. This feller obviously thinks she's being forced to stay with you."

"I've asked myself the same thing, Burley. Who in the world would believe her miserable? She fairly lights up the day with her smile, and the happiness she knows from anticipating this child is more than anyone could doubt. But, what really confuses me is why this same man would now hold Pamela hostage. Why not just return her and lay low for awhile? I mean, I realize he would be concerned, since he left the note for me, but he'd have little trouble bringing Pamela back, then disappearing."

"Maybe he read that story you gave the paper," Burley offered.

"I suppose that's a possibility. It was just that I figured if Pamela was seen by other folks, and they knew she was missing, they might offer help in returning her to us," Riley remarked. "I knew her parents were slated to go to the springs in New York, and I didn't figure word would reach them from the article before I had a chance to get word to them myself."

"Maybe this feller realized the potential for a big pay-off. If he knew Pamela was worth a fortune, he might just have decided to make his mistake a profitable one."

Riley shook his head, not knowing what to think. Raising his arms in exasperation, he sighed, "Anything is possible."

Burley handed him back the note and noticed an elaborately scrolled envelope postmarked Washington, D.C. "You in some kind of trouble?" he asked, pointing at the letter.

"No," Riley smiled. "In fact, it might be the only truly good thing that's come in the mail in a long while. It seems the honorable Mister Horace Tabor intends to come to Dawson in the near future. It says that he has a matter of great importance to discuss with me."

"Honestly?" Burley seemed dumbfounded. "What could he want?"

"Dawson," Riley replied. "At least I hope that's what he wants."

Chapter 10

Pamela lost track of the time. For well over a week, she was confined to a bedroom that was next to the one Esther used for her own. No noise went unchecked, Pamela soon learned, so her attempts to find a way from the house faded into discouragement. The only time she was allowed out of the room was when Esther escorted her to the privy out in back of the house.

Pamela was just as glad to be locked up, however. Each and every time she ventured from the room with Esther, the men would taunt her with lewd comments and whistles. Pamela's cheeks would flame red at some of the things said. Never had she been exposed to such lasciviousness.

Pamela tried to pass the time by praying and by thinking of the things Zandy had told her about God. From time to time, her mind lingered on Jim Williams, then guilt ate at her fiercely.

"He may have taken me from Dawson," Pamela whispered to no one, "but he didn't deserve to die."

She couldn't help but think of Jim's warm brown eyes. A sadness filled her until she forced the image from her mind. "I can't think of this anymore!"

One day, as evening came, Esther appeared with Pamela's supper. "Venison stew and biscuits," she said and placed the tray on the end of the bed. "Have you still got water in the pitcher?"

"Yes," Pamela said and came forward to peer into the bowl. "I suppose I can't complain that I haven't been well fed. At least, well fed in a rustic kind of fashion."

Esther laughed. "It isn't Delmonico's in New York, that's for sure."

"Delmonico's!" Pamela exclaimed with surprise. "That's one of my parents' favorite places."

"It used to be one of mine too," Esther admitted. "They served an aspic *de crevette* salad that would bring the world to its feet in applause. I went there every time I could talk someone into taking me."

Pamela shook her head. "And now you're here, kidnapping other socialites? It must seem terribly ironic."

Esther shrugged her shoulders. "It's just the way life is." She turned to leave. "For now," she added, and pulled the door closed.

62

Pamela sat down to eat and wasn't surprised to find the stew delicious. The biscuits were as light as any she'd ever had, and Pamela hungrily devoured them, knowing that there would be nothing else until morning.

She'd just finished eating when Esther returned, bringing with her a copy of *Peterson's Ladies' National Magazine*. It was patterned after *Godey's Lady's Book,* and Pamela knew its issues well.

"I thought you might want to take a look," she said and tossed the magazine to the bed.

Pamela picked it up and glanced at her captor. "Thank you."

Esther retrieved the dishes. "You'll probably not find anything terribly useful for your stay with us, but I thought it might break the boredom."

"I wonder if I might make a trip out back before you retire for the evening?" Pamela requested.

"Sure," Esther replied. "I'll take these to the kitchen and be right back." It was a strange, casual sort of relationship between these two women.

Pamela flipped through the magazine while waiting. There was an article on how to arrange cut flowers. Another, equally uninteresting, article gave helpful suggestions for arranging a formal parlor. Of course, there were new dress fashions, and these caught Pamela's eye, but only for a moment. What could she do about them here?

Esther returned and held the door open for Pamela. She obediently walked a pace or two ahead of Esther and wondered if the time would ever come when Esther might drop her guard.

They moved out back through the quarter-moon darkness and passed the place where Esther's sons Joe and Bob were nose to nose in a heated argument.

"Robert Joseph! Joseph Robert! You cut it out here and now. I don't need to break up any childish tantrums tonight. We've got plenty of work that still needs to be done." The men grudgingly parted company with a "Yessum" muttered under their breath.

Esther continued to the privy with Pamela. "You named them nearly the same thing," Pamela commented.

Esther laughed. "It was their father's doing. He said that way he'd only have the two names to worry about. Don't know what we'd have done if there'd been any more."

"Where's their father now?"

"Dead," Esther said without emotion.

Pamela said nothing more but cringed as a hideous sound came from where they'd left Esther's sons. Shouts and curses rose on the silent night air, and Pamela knew the boys had decided to have a go at one another, after all.

"You see to your business and I'll see to them," Esther said in exasperation. "I swear I'm going to have to beat them both. Grown men ought to know better."

Pamela laughed and did as she was instructed. She could hear the fight raging on and Esther yelling at the top of her lungs. When she stepped away from the outhouse, Pamela was still laughing when suddenly a hand clamped down tight on her mouth. Someone pulled her into the darkness behind the privy.

"This is getting to be a habit," Jim said as he let his hand drop from Pamela's mouth.

"Jim!" Pamela exclaimed, forgetting her predicament. Without realizing what she was doing, Pamela threw her arms around him. "You're alive!"

"Shhh," he said and embraced her close to him. "You'll get us both killed."

"I thought you were dead already," Pamela said stiffly and pulled away from him. She grew uncomfortable as she realized how much she cared that he was still living.

"Come on," he pulled her away from the buildings and into the darkness. "We have to go!"

Pamela let Jim lead the way without complaint. She feared they would be caught any moment, and every sound or missed step was absolute torture. Nevertheless, even when she twisted her ankle, Pamela didn't complain or slow the pace. When Jim began their ascent of the canyon wall, however, Pamela felt moved to speak.

"I can't climb these rocks," she protested. "I know I haven't the strength."

"You'll do it or stay here," Jim said over his shoulder. "You'd be surprised what a body can do when pushed to do it or die."

Pamela nodded and realized he was probably right. She had no desire to go back and face the wrath of Esther and her gang. "All right," she said with new determination. "Just let me tuck up this skirt, and I'll do it."

"That's the spirit!" Jim whispered. His pride in her choice to fight was evident.

They climbed the canyon wall without once stopping to rest. Jim had picked a place that was lower than the rest of the canyon. Jim explained in brief that he had been watching the place for only a couple of days, but it was enough time to learn the routine and make a plan.

They could hear shouting in the yards below and Esther calling for Pamela, but they ignored it and pressed upward. Several times, Pamela felt her strength giving out, but just then, it seemed, Jim would know and reach back to take her hand. His warmth gave her strength and hope.

After what seemed hours, they reached the top, and Pamela was surprised to find another man waiting with two horses.

"Come on over here, little bitty gal," Caleb called in a low voice. "We've got a hard ride ahead of us, and we'd best be about it."

"Who's that?" Pamela questioned, cowering against Jim. He put his arm around her protectively and pulled her forward.

"Caleb Emerson. He's a drifter who saved my life after the Owens gang left me for dead," Jim answered. "Come on," and he lifted her up to the saddle. "We'll have to ride double again."

"No matter," Pamela said gratefully. "If it means getting out of there and back to Dawson, I'd ride an elephant."

"No need for that," Caleb chuckled. "These mounts will do us a whole heap better." With that, they pushed out and rode as fast as they dared. Their horses labored against the altitude, while Pamela shivered as cold mountain winds blew down upon them.

They rode for several hours. Finally, when Pamela knew she couldn't stay another minute atop the horse, Caleb called a halt and began unsaddling his mount.

"We'll camp here tonight," he announced.

"Is it safe? I mean, are we far enough away?" Pamela questioned.

"They'll never find us," Jim said, helping Pamela down. "Caleb and I put out a dozen false trails the night before. Even if they are stupid enough to set out in this darkness, they'll never be able to figure out which way to go first. Once they figure out the real trail, we'll be nearly to Dawson."

Pamela heaved a sigh of relief. "How did you find me?"

"Caleb," Jim said with a nod. "He's drifted these parts for a long time and just happens to be familiar with this gang of thieves."

"Thank you, Mister Emerson."

"You're welcome, Little Bitty," Caleb said. The nickname surprised her, but Pamela said nothing. "Always glad to help a lady in need," he added with a chuckle, then pointed to where Jim was tethering his horse. "That young man over there nearly fretted himself into the next world worryin' about how to get you back," he whispered against her ear. "So, I'd be sure and thank him proper too."

Pamela leaned up and gave Caleb's weathered cheek a kiss. The action surprised her almost more than the old man. "I will," she whispered.

Pamela walked back over to where Jim already had a bed fixed for her. "This ought to block out the wind," he said, nodding toward the rocky ledge under which he'd placed her blanket.

"Where will you be?" she asked, straining to see his face. The small amount of moonlight offered little help, and Caleb made no move to put together a fire.

"I'll be right here," Jim assured. "I'm not about to lose you a second time." His words seemed more serious than they needed to be.

Pamela stepped closer. "Thank you for rescuing me, Jim. I know I'm not Zandy, but I appreciate what you've done and risked for me." She leaned up to kiss his cheek as she had with Caleb, but Jim surprised them both by pulling her into his arms. He kissed her full on the lips for just a moment, then released her. The action had taken them both off guard.

Pamela hurried to take her place on the blanket, but before Jim walked away he leaned down to whisper in her ear. "I'm glad you're not Zandy."

Pamela was grateful for the cover of darkness, knowing that she was blushing. Bradley Rayburn's stolen kisses had never left her feeling the way Jim's did. In fact, Bradley was about the farthest thing from her mind at that moment.

She pulled the blanket around her and listened as Jim thanked Caleb for his help.

"It was my pleasure," Caleb told the younger man. "God always gives us a job to do, and often we have to do it alone. But, sometimes He knows we can't stand alone, then He gives us a friend."

"I'm proud to call you friend, Caleb. I don't know when our paths might cross again, but I'll be there any time you call," he reached out and shook the older man's hand.

"I'm proud to call you friend too, Son," Caleb replied. "You keep your feet firmly planted on God's road, and you'll never go wrong. He's a good partner to take on, and you'll never really know what it is to be loved, until you accept His in full."

Pamela felt a strange comforting peace flood her heart. She snuggled down into the blanket and smiled. The contentment she felt was twofold. God had answered her prayers for rescue, and Jim wasn't dead.

Chapter 11

A steady rain was pouring when Pamela awoke the next morning. She was grateful for the small ledge under which Jim had thoughtfully put her bed. Pressing back against the rock wall, Pamela peered out from her blanket and wondered where the men had taken cover.

Suddenly, it seemed too quiet, and Pamela grew fretful. What if the Owens gang had found them and had already done away with Jim and Caleb? Sitting up abruptly, Pamela couldn't help but call out.

"Jim!"

She heard movement to the left and found her fears relieved as Jim scooted under the ledge to sit beside her.

"It looks like it might do this all day," he said with a grin. "I swear, mountain rains are the most unpredictable things."

"Where's Caleb?" Pamela questioned. She could see where Jim's horse was still tethered, but there was no sign of the older man's horse or gear.

"He's gone. Thought it best if we split up, and I figure he's right on that point."

"They'll be coming after us, won't they," Pamela more stated than asked. "A million dollars is nothing to let slip away without a fight. It'll keep them riding the trails, come rain or shine, of that I'm sure."

"A million dollars?" Jim's confusion was evident.

"That's the amount of ransom they asked Riley and Zandy for," Pamela explained. She pulled the blanket around her to ward off the cold and leaned back against the rock. "They were going to send another letter today and give the details of where they would meet."

Jim's face twisted into a look of disgust. "Why in the world would they think anyone would pay that kind of money? That didn't come out sounding the way I intended," he immediately added. "It isn't that I wouldn't consider you worth that much money. It's just I can't figure how they would assume Riley Dawson would care enough to part with that much."

Pamela calmed her singed emotions. The last person in the world she wanted to fight with was Jim. "The leader of the gang is a woman. She's very intelligent and has her people bring her newspapers from Denver. Apparently, when you took me from Dawson, Riley and Zandy must have put out a story with my picture, in hopes that someone would know something about my disappearance. The only thing is, the story told too much of my background and the fact that I'm from a wealthy family in Kansas City."

"Are your folks that rich?" Jim questioned innocently.

"My folks are very well-off," Pamela whispered. "I'm their only child, and I stand to inherit a great deal. That's why they didn't trust Bradley Rayburn."

At the spoken name of the man she loved, Jim's fascination with Pamela's delicate face ended abruptly. He tried to distance himself by moving away just a bit, but Pamela would have no part of it.

"It's so cold. I know it isn't proper, and it would be most unacceptable were the circumstances different, but I wonder if you would mind. . .I mean," she paused as Jim looked back at her. "Would you sit very close and maybe even put your arm around me?"

Jim hesitated for a moment and moved closer. Taking the blanket, he pulled it around both of their shoulders and let Pamela move under his arm to lean against his chest.

Pamela tried to seem oblivious to the physical contact while, in truth, she was shocked with herself for suggesting such a thing. After a few moments of silence, she spoke of a matter on which she'd reflected for most of the night.

"I heard some of what Caleb said to you last night," she began. "His words about God were so comforting, and I truly felt that I was protected under God's care. I was just wondering, are you a Christian too?"

Jim sighed, releasing a bit of the tension he felt.

"I guess so," he said in a noncommittal way. "I asked to be saved when I was just a boy, but I've never really done anything that would prove that it took. Caleb told me to seek God out and ask His forgiveness. He said a lot of times we're inclined to get sidetracked. God knows we aren't strong creatures, and that's why He's so good about forgiving us. I guess right now I'm just trying to work things out so that I can be on good terms with Him again."

Pamela smiled. "I went to church with nannies and maids. Sometimes, once in a very long while, I would go with my parents. But you know, until I met Zandy, I hadn't a clue what God was truly about. How can somebody sit in church, listen to the preacher tell of hellfire and eternal damnation, and still not understand that they needed saving?"

"I don't guess I have the answer to that one either," Jim replied. "I never was one for church after Ma died. For that matter, I've never been one for much of anything."

"What do you want to do with your life, Jim?" Pamela asked softly.

"I can't rightly say," Jim responded. "I've tried my hand at mining, cattle, horses, farming, and I was even a lawman for Riley Dawson when he first came to Colorado."

"Back when he was so very evil?"

"Yeah," Jim replied. "But I suppose he's changed now, eh?"

Pamela lifted up her head and met Jim's dark brown eyes. "He honestly has, Jim. Zandy is very happy with him now."

"I guess I'm glad for that," Jim said and grew thoughtful. "If Riley can change that much, I guess God won't have such a hard time with me."

Pamela laughed out, and the sound echoed off the rock ledge overhead. "That's the same kind of thing I told Zandy when she helped me to find God's direction for my life. I figured if one man could be so changed from the worst possible character to the kind of person I saw in front of me, then I knew God could help me. I guess I'd come to the place where I had nothing and no one else."

"What about your Mister Rayburn?"

Pamela shrugged. It was funny how over the last week or so, she'd given much more thought to Jim than Bradley. "I'm not sure. I suppose my parents could have been right. They could also have been wrong. I think when we go back to Missouri, I'll sit down and write a long letter and apologize for the way I treated them. I suppose we'll just have to work it out from there."

"You've changed," Jim said suddenly.

"I suppose I have," Pamela replied, not taking the slightest bit of offense. "I had so much time to think about things. I realized how demanding I was and how bitter and angry I'd grown. Being in a place where the only thing people thought of was how much money they could make off you, I realized how much I'd harmed the ones I loved."

"How so?" Jim questioned.

"At the Owenses', nobody cared if I wanted things done a certain way. No one gave a thought to how I dressed or what I ate. I was totally and completely at their mercy, and that caused me to see how demanding I've always been. The rest. . .well, I think a lot of my reason for wanting to marry Bradley had to do with making my parents take notice of me." The words surprised Pamela, for she'd never truly allowed the revelation to surface in full. Speaking them seemed to validate the possibility, however, and she felt relieved for having said them.

"I did. . .do. . .love Bradley," she continued. "But I'm not sure that I understand in full what that even means. Zandy told me about God's love and how He loved us enough to send Jesus, His only Son, to die for me and all the other people in the world. And all because if He didn't, we could never get close to

God. God's love for me is such a wonder that I can't begin to imagine."

Jim's eyes locked with Pamela's. "I know what you mean," he said hoarsely. The words would barely make themselves heard. "Caleb made me realize the same thing. I'm glad God cares enough to not have given up on me. I feel in many ways like I've just been saved. Maybe that's the truth of the matter. Either way, I'm just a babe at this walking with God stuff."

Pamela sat up with a smile. "Yes, that's it exactly. I'm so much an infant when it comes to understanding God and the Bible. I've never even given much of a reading to the Word of God, yet Zandy says it holds all the answers for our lives."

Jim smiled. "Zandy would say that. I remember her faith well. I always admired her for it and wondered how a person could give themselves over so completely to something like a book filled with words. Now, though, I think I'm beginning to understand."

Pamela leaned back against Jim and nodded her head in agreement. "It's like God calling the heart to a new way of beating."

"I guess we have that in common, anyway," Jim said, not thinking.

"What do you mean?"

"Being new Christians," he replied. "We're both just starting a new way of living, and both of us have a heap to learn."

~

It was nearly two hours later before the rain let up. Jim knew the flooding in the valley below would most likely be bad. He took Caleb's suggestion of heading down an obscure little path that led into Central City, offering a silent prayer that God would give them safe passage.

Easing into the saddle behind Pamela, Jim was more than a little aware of her close presence. It was becoming increasingly difficult for Jim to ignore the fact that he had, indeed, come to care about this "little bitty gal."

Chapter 12

A great cloud of disorder and lawlessness settled over Dawson. That, along with the heavy rains, left decent folk confined to their homes. Riley watched the situation with growing apprehension. When the town wasn't busy burying those who'd been shot or knifed in the streets, it was building gallows for those who'd committed the crimes.

Riley insisted that Zandy, Ruth, and the children remain inside the mansion. He hired extra men to police the grounds and watched every shadow with a wary eye. The problem continued to grow by leaps and bounds, and there seemed to be nothing Riley could do to change the immediate circumstances.

One idea continued to give him hope of at least taking his loved ones from the conflict. Horace Tabor had made him a very substantial buy-out offer. Riley hated to just walk away from the town. The fact was, he felt largely responsible for what it had become. He was the one who'd brought the town back to life when it was nothing more than a ghost town called Temperance. He was the one who'd taken possession of the mines through gambling and underhanded dealings. Was God now making him face the fruit of his past labors?

Shaking his head, Riley pulled out the Bible. He longed to spend more and more time reading the pages of this book. He forever felt inadequate when it came to being the spiritual leader of his family. Zandy knew much more, in the sense of having years of Bible stories and reading in her memory. The times when he tried to guide or direct them in some choice or decision, Zandy inevitably upstaged him with some Scripture that left him feeling stupidly misguided.

His salvation was real, of that he was certain. His spirit was in close communion with God. That, too, was undeniable. Why, then, couldn't he be the husband Zandy needed? What was it that kept him from being a proper spiritual leader in his home?

A knock on the door brought his attention from the open Bible.

"Come in," he called, pushing back from the desk. The large leather chair creaked in protest as Riley got to his feet.

Zandy entered the room. Her face was radiant, even though a frown lined her lips. Her worry for Pamela was evident, as was her growing condition.

71

Riley watched her cross the room to him. He couldn't help but smile, and he placed a hand against the delicately belted blouse that covered the oversized waist of her skirt.

"And how are my two most favorite people today?" he asked softly.

Zandy's eyes met his, and Riley couldn't keep from moving his hands to cup her face. "We're fine," she answered with the hint of a smile. "Have you had any word?"

Riley shook his head. "I imagine we'll hear soon enough. And when we do, I'll be ready. In the meantime, I think I've made a decision about Mister Tabor's offer."

"Oh?" her eyes widened in anticipation of what her husband would say.

"Yes," Riley replied and rubbed his thumb against her cheek. "I believe I will sell all of my holdings in Dawson to him."

"Truly, Riley?" Zandy reached up to take hold of his hands. "Can we honestly be rid of this awful place?"

"The offer Tabor made is generous, and I can't help but believe there comes a time when a man has to walk away from his mistakes and start anew. Tabor believes he can control this riffraff with his own style of law and order. He has far more power and say than I could ever hope to hold, or even want to, for that matter. When I told him about the difficulties we'd been having with the Owens gang and other like them, Horace Tabor actually laughed."

"Laughed?" Zandy asked.

"Yes," Riley admitted. He kissed his wife's hands and pulled her with him to the sofa. They sat side by side with Riley's arm protectively around Zandy. She hesitated only a moment before leaning her head against Riley's muscular shoulder.

"Is it that Mister Tabor is confident he can control the evil element in this town, or is he so much a part of their world that it no longer bothers him?" Zandy finally questioned.

"I don't honestly know," Riley replied. "Whatever his thoughts on the matter, I'll simply be glad to be rid of this place."

"Me too," Zandy wholeheartedly agreed. Suddenly, she asked, "What about my family?"

"I've already considered their needs. I'll give your father enough money to start over wherever he'd like. I think he'll be relieved to get the children out of Dawson," Riley answered.

"I know Ruth will be," Zandy said. "She told me the boys had picked up bad language at school. I guess the schoolmaster has no control over the larger boys, and the younger ones seem to just naturally fall into bad habits."

"Well," Riley began, the frustration in his voice evident, "I'm grateful for now that the school term is finished. By the time fall rolls around, we'll be long gone, if I have anything to say about it."

"Judging from his kick, I'd say that suits your son as well."

Riley smiled at her reference to a boy. "Coming around to my way of thinking, eh, Mrs. Dawson?"

Zandy smiled, "Occasionally, it seems to agree with me to do so."

Riley returned her smile and placed a kiss on her temple. "First things first, however. We'll do all we can to get Pamela back. Did I tell you that her parents wired me to say that someone will be arriving in Dawson to see to their interest in this matter? Imagine, your only child is taken hostage, and you do nothing more than arrange to send someone on your behalf."

Zandy shook her head. "I told you that Pamela had a bad home life."

"Yes, I know. But, I told you that we can't save her from all the hurts and pains that this world will offer. Only God can do that. Remember?"

Zandy nodded with a sigh. "But it is so hard to do nothing."

"Like you once told me, often we have to live through the rough times in order to learn from the choices we've made in error. Either way, God is still God, and He's the one dealing the hand, so to speak. And, Jesus is right there too, always coming to His father on our behalf. In fact, I was just reading an interesting verse," Riley stated and went to retrieve the Bible from his desk. "It says here in Hebrews seven, verse twenty-five, 'Wherefore he is able also to save them to the uttermost that come unto God by him, seeing he ever liveth to make intercession for them.' That verse is about Christ and the fact that He always lives to intervene for you and me. Imagine that Alexandra," he said, using her given name.

"I've honestly not ever read that Scripture before. It's wonderful, and I'm glad you shared it with me."

Riley felt strengthened in his role of leader by her statement. "If Jesus is interceding for us, and the Holy Spirit is interceding for us, as Romans 8:26 says, how can we possibly doubt that God will hear our petitions?"

Before she could speak, the housekeeper came to announce that Pamela's uncle had arrived. Riley and Zandy went quickly to greet him.

"I'm Riley Dawson, and this is my wife, Zandy," he said, stepping forward to take the stranger's hand.

"Robert Charbonneau," the man replied. He was nearly matched in height to Riley's tall frame and had pale blue eyes that seemed somehow harsh. "Have you had further word on my niece's whereabouts?"

"No, but I expect to hear almost any time," Riley stated.

"I had the carriage driver bring me here first, just in case she'd already been returned," Robert said. "I'll take a room at the hotel."

"Nonsense," Riley interrupted. "We've over twelve unoccupied bedrooms in this house. There is surely no need for you to stay in town. Besides, the kidnapper knows to contact us here. You'll want to stay close in order to keep informed the very minute we get notification."

Robert nodded. "I appreciate that Mister Dawson."

"Please call me Riley. I'll have someone bring in your luggage. Would you care for something to eat or drink, Mister Charbonneau?"

"That would be very much to my liking," Robert admitted, "but you must call me Robert if I am to call you Riley."

"Deal," Riley said with a smile.

"Come along, gentlemen," Zandy said, leading the way. "I'll have Cook provide us with some sandwiches and lemonade."

~

That afternoon, the second ransom letter arrived and with it the instructions for the exchange of money. Robert Charbonneau was unemotional as he read, then reread the letter, while Riley waited in silence.

"Do you have any idea who's holding her?" Robert asked, handing the letter back to Riley.

"I thought at first that I did," Riley replied. "The reason being, and this is in strictest confidence, the kidnapper originally intended to take my wife."

"Your wife?" Robert's surprise seemed to justify further explanation.

"A long time ago, there was a man who was interested in my wife. He left town thinking that she was being forced into a loveless marriage with me," Riley explained. He'd only come to remember Jim Williams' interest in Zandy over the last week or so. "I don't know for sure that it was the same man who took Pamela, but he did leave a note explaining that his intention had been to rescue Zandy from me."

"I see," Robert said rather stiffly. "So Pamela's life has been endangered because some lovesick idiot thought to make some grandiose gesture toward your wife?"

"I suppose you could put it that way. However," Riley stated, meeting the man eye to eye, "I question whether it's still the same man who's sending the ransom notes."

"Why do you say that?"

"I ran a story in the Denver paper. It might have been foolhardy and brought us undesired attention in the matter of Pamela's disappearance. In fact, it is entirely possible that the person responsible for the ransom demands is just someone who learned of Pamela's disappearance and hoped to make a tidy profit."

"I suppose that is a possibility," Robert had to admit. "But why would the man who hoped to rescue your wife still have my niece?"

"That's what I don't understand," Riley replied. "Unless of course, she talked him into helping her get back to Kansas City and that Bradley Rayburn character."

"I'll wire back to the house so they can be on the lookout, but Rayburn isn't even in Kansas City anymore."

"Where is he?" Riley couldn't help but ask.

"On his honeymoon," Robert answered dryly. "It seems in his pining for my niece, he up and married the first wealthy widow who'd have him. They're now in Europe, or so the papers all say."

Riley shook his head. "Let's hope she didn't go back home, then."

After Robert Charbonneau had telegraphed the Charbonneau residence, he stepped into the muddy streets of Dawson. The rain had temporarily stopped.

Robert intended to see to the matter of Pamela's safe return. Having enjoyed life as a man of means, Robert thought he knew that money was often the only way to accomplish anything. Going into the first saloon he passed, he quickly sized up the clientele and began the task of rounding up men-for-hire who would go out in pursuit of his niece and those who held her captive.

"You understand," Robert said to the seedy crowd. "I will pay you each ten dollars now and another twenty when you return with her. But, you must see to it that the kidnapper is brought in alive. I want to watch his neck stretched from the gallows when they declare him guilty."

The men around him nodded their approval and held out their hands for the pay. Robert did as he promised and sent them on their way in search of Pamela. Riley Dawson might take comfort in waiting the abductors out, but he didn't. He was a man used to taking matters into his own hands and this time would be no exception!

Chapter 13

Making her way through the muddy streets of Central City, Colorado, Pamela realized that she'd begun to savor Jim's quick sense of humor and open honesty. Enjoying the companionship of a man such as Jim had never been in Pamela's agenda. He was ill educated, dirt poor, and socially deficient. Beyond that he needed a shave, haircut, and thorough washing. Under normal circumstances, Pamela would have considered him totally worthless. But there was something more to Jim than met the eye. Something that Pamela could no longer ignore.

She couldn't help but smile, watching him lead the horse through the town. He tried hard to avoid the messier places in the road, but all of it seemed to hopelessly ooze muck.

Central City was much the same as Dawson. It was yet another of the infamous mining communities that had seemingly sprung to life overnight. Saloons and gambling houses lined the path while dry goods stores, apothecaries, and other businesses were interlaced between them. Jim finally settled on the nearest store of respectable appearance and tethered the horse to the hitching post.

"I'll see what I can do about getting us some grub. I don't have much left in the way of money, but maybe I can trade for something." Giving a look up and down the street, Jim lifted Pamela from the horse and carried her to the boardwalk. "I think you'd best stay close to me," he whispered in her ear.

Pamela readily agreed, finding the raucous laughter and swaggering patrons of the nearest bar a bit unnerving. She was only too aware of the sheltered life she'd lived. Although she and Bradley had spent many of their evenings on the town, the upper crust of Kansas City had never associated with the likes of what she was exposed to at the present. But her feelings weren't a matter of snobbery here. They were a matter of survival.

Latching onto Jim's arm in a possessive manner, they made their way into the store.

Several miners milled about the narrow room. Some seemed intent on tools at hand, others just drifted around aimlessly. Pamela squeezed closer to Jim, and when she did, she accidentally stepped on his foot.

"Oh!" she exclaimed, startled and in complete embarrassment. "I'm so sorry."

Jim chuckled. "No problem. I only walk on the bottoms." Pamela tried to smile, but, in truth, she was scared to death. When several gunshots sounded outside, she felt herself grow faint. Life in the past few weeks had offered her more excitement than she desired.

"Can I help you?" the shopkeeper asked from behind a filthy counter.

Jim began to talk with the man, while Pamela tried not to notice the noise outside. She was lost in thought until her eye spied a Denver newspaper. Completely forgetting her fear, Pamela stepped away from Jim and took a copy of the paper from the counter. She scanned the front page, wondering if anything else had been written about her disappearance. Seeing nothing there, she continued to flip through the pages until her eye caught a startling announcement. Pamela's hands began to shake as she reread the tiny article.

> *Mrs. Alison Timbre of Kansas City married Mister Bradley Rayburn in an elaborate ceremony on Saturday. Mrs. Timbre, formerly Alison Cavanaugh of the Chicago Cavanaughs, is said to be worth several million dollars and intends to finance her husband's new business, which is yet to be announced. The couple will set up housekeeping after touring Europe for the summer.*

There was a dry ache in her throat and, for some reason, Pamela couldn't seem to put the paper down. How could Bradley have married this woman? *He said he loved me. He promised he'd wait forever to be at my side again,* Pamela thought to herself. Now only months after her father's ugly scene at their engagement party, Bradley was touring Europe with his new wife.

She didn't realize when Jim had come to stand behind her. She glanced up when she felt his hand brush hers at the paper's edge. Their eyes met. The pain was so evident in hers, while the sympathy in his was spoken in a mere look. He took the paper from her, replaced it on the counter, then led her out of the store and back to the horse.

Her vision blurred, and Pamela was grateful that Jim held her arm firmly against his waist. She never thought to ask him how he'd fared in getting provisions. All she could think of was the fact that Bradley had found someone else. A very rich someone else.

"I'm sorry, Pamela," Jim said, lifting her into the saddle. He stuffed their supplies into the saddlebags.

They rode from the town in silence, while all around them was utter chaos. Pamela didn't even notice. She felt the numbing of her shock as it seemed to spread through her veins, leaving her cold and dead.

How could he? I loved him, she thought. *I gave my heart to him and refused to hear any ill of him whatsoever. I stood up for him before my father and mother and argued with all that I could dream up to convince them that he was more than the ne'er-do-well that they saw. Now, they've proven their insight to be correct and I'm the fool.*

In complete defeat, she slumped back against Jim. The tears gave way and poured from her eyes. There was nothing left to go home to. No reason to go on.

~

Jim tightened his hold on the reins and in doing so, tightened his hold on Pamela. She appeared so frail and broken, and his heart ached to make everything better. He struggled for something to say, some encouragement he could whisper into her ear, but nothing came to mind. She was just a little bitty gal, he reasoned, just like Caleb had nicknamed her. How could she possibly be called upon to bear up under such devastating news?

Jim felt like kicking himself for having allowed his feelings for Pamela to deepen. What he'd convinced himself was just admiration and friendship felt like considerably more in the wake of seeing her obvious attachment to a man who'd jilted her so completely.

He could feel the sobs racking her body, and it nearly deprived him of his self-control to seem unmoved. He kept reminding himself that what she didn't need was another man romancing her with sweet words and eloquence. Not that he had either.

He was doing fine at hiding his feelings until Pamela lowered her face into her hands. It was as if she thought she could somehow block out the world and all that hurt her.

"Hush," he whispered against her hair. "Shhh. Crying won't help." The words seemed to settle her a bit, and Jim tried to think of something more to say. Finally it came to him in a startling revelation. "God's with you, Pamela. He won't let you bear this alone."

Pamela lifted her face and turned to meet Jim's eyes.

"I won't let you bear it alone, either."

Pamela managed to put her tears aside and, when Jim felt she was better composed, he began to converse on anything and everything to keep her mind from her misery.

She heard him say something about being in Dawson by morning, but it didn't register as being important. In her mind, Pamela was replaying the events of her life. She thought of first meeting Bradley and how she'd fallen helplessly in love with his gallant nature and zest for life.

Considering these matters, Pamela realized that what hurt the most was the fact that her parents had been absolutely right about Bradley. He was hunting a fortune, and with Pamela he'd found one. She was wealthy and fully capable of seeing to his needs, which, as Pamela couldn't help but remember, included starting a new business venture with several of his close friends. He would never really divulge what type of business he intended to found, but then again, Pamela had never cared. She'd openly promised that whatever it took, she'd make Bradley's dreams come true just as he had made hers a reality.

But now there was nothing left of that dream. She chided herself mentally for being so gullible. She seethed in rage, considering all the things he'd said to her. The promises he'd made. The future he'd planned. All of it was to be theirs together, and now he was living those dreams with another woman. His wife!

By the time the sun started fading behind the mountain peaks, Pamela was no longer hurt. She was mad. Enraged at her stupidity and appalled at the fool Bradley Rayburn had made of her, Pamela became sullen and stiff. She no longer leaned against Jim for support, and the change in her was evident to him.

He wanted to say something, but what could he say that he hadn't already said? He couldn't very well tell her that he was starting to have feelings for her. He couldn't say anything without jeopardizing the thin veneer of friendship that had developed between them. He was still the man who'd taken her from Dawson, Jim reminded himself. He had been solely responsible for her plight from the moment he'd taken her from Zandy's and Riley's care. How could he offer her anything that would matter?

Without warning, Jim reined back on the horse and dismounted. It had suddenly become unbearable to be that near her. Just thinking the thoughts he had contemplated made Jim painfully aware that he'd come to care a great deal more for Pamela Charbonneau than he'd ever thought possible.

If Pamela thought his actions strange, she said nothing. Her face was frozen in a disinterested stare that was fixed straight ahead. Jim doubted she saw anything but the images in her mind.

Leading the horse forward, he could only offer up a prayer for God's intervention. Jim found himself begging God to ease her pain and set things right again. He could only silently wish that things might have been different between them. With a shake of his head, Jim began the descent toward the roadway that would take them back to Dawson. It had once been home, he reminded himself. Now it was just a place of reckoning, and Jim couldn't help but wonder what fate awaited him there.

Chapter 14

Pamela couldn't sleep that night. She restlessly paced the ground just outside the campfire's circle of light. She had no desire for Jim to see the anguish in her face. She was so confused and angry. Why did her heart have to be so willing to jump in where others had bade her to see reason? Why, oh why, did they all have to be so right about Bradley Rayburn?

In complete frustration, Pamela finally plopped down on the ground where Jim had left her a blanket. The summer air was surprisingly cold, and Pamela suddenly realized that she'd taken a chill. Shivering down under the cover, Pamela stared blankly into the fire and was almost startled to find Jim's eyes staring back from across the way. She had thought him asleep.

Without smiling or nodding, she acknowledged his gaze with a look, then closed her eyes, hoping against hope to blot out the events of the day and the raging emotions that surged through her heart.

Pamela awoke with a start to find it was still dark. She sat up and noticing that the fire was getting low, retrieved a few pieces of wood and stirred up the flames. Sitting back down, Pamela hugged her knees to her chest and rested her chin. The fire crackled and popped, while the yellow flames danced in a hypnotic frenzy. She watched the performance for some time, wondering why she couldn't find peace for the situation at hand.

"God," she prayed in a whisper, "I don't know what to do. I feel so hurt, so betrayed. Yet, it isn't really that at all. I feel like a fool." She nodded silently to the fire. Yes, that was what bothered her the most. Pamela Charbonneau was used to having her own way. She'd rarely been challenged, and now she felt ridiculous and stupid in the wake of Bradley's marriage to someone else.

"My parents were right, as were the others who tried to warn me. How stupid I am, Lord," Pamela sighed. It was then she realized that she didn't even love Bradley. "I don't love him," Pamela declared to the fire. "How could I have been so convinced that I did?"

The wind moaned down through the trees and whispered softly against the silent night. The fire died down to a gentle, quiet glow, and with it, Pamela decided to try again to sleep.

"I've been so blind, God," she whispered to the starry sky overhead. "Feelings I thought I had were nothing more than the rebellious imaginations of a spoiled child. I just wanted to get back at my parents for never being there. For never loving me." The realization that this was her heart's most deeply buried secret produced the same effect as if a weight were lifted from her shoulders.

"I still don't know what to do or how to make amends. Oh, God, help me to see clearly what Your will is for my life. Help me to recognize the heart's calling, when the real love of my life comes along." Aching and lonely, Pamela pulled the covers tightly around her shoulders and fell into a troubled sleep.

～

The road into Dawson was barely dry enough for passage, and Jim took special care to lead the horse, while Pamela nervously fidgeted with the saddle horn.

"I'm sorry I was such poor company yesterday," Pamela called down to Jim. "I had a hard time dealing with the shock of what Bradley did, but I'm much better now."

Jim glanced up and smiled. "I'm glad to hear that. I knew God would see you through."

Pamela returned the smile with one of her own. "I intend to tell everyone how you rescued me from the Owens gang. I even hope to encourage my parents to give you a reward."

"No," Jim replied, shaking his head. "That would be totally uncalled for. If it weren't for me, you'd never have been taken from the safety of the Dawson house. I have a lot to own up to, and one of the first things I got to do is face up to Riley Dawson for what I planned to do in the first place."

"He doesn't have to know," Pamela insisted.

"He already does," Jim answered. "I left him a note, and even though I didn't sign it, I'm sure he knows it was me."

Pamela didn't say anything. She didn't know what she could say. Jim had his own problems to resolve, just as she had hers. She knew she still needed to sort through things with her parents and, for that matter, to confess her misdirection and rebellion to Riley and Zandy. After all, she reasoned, she'd put them through plenty of complaining and bitterness. They had a right to see her humbled and sorry.

They were just rounding the final bend, when they were suddenly surrounded by six riders. All the men were heavily armed and pulled their guns to halt Jim's and Pamela's progress.

"Dear Lord," Pamela whispered prayerfully, feeling her heart catch in her throat. Her first thought was that these men were somehow connected to Esther Owens and her gang of thugs.

"What do you want?" Jim questioned the men. "We ain't got much to hand over, so if it's cash or goods you're looking for, you're out of luck."

"We ain't after loot," a particularly seedy character replied. He pushed his horse forward just a bit until it stood nose to nose with the one Pamela rode.

"What's your name?" the man asked Pamela. His cold hard stare caused her to tremble.

"Pa. . .Pa," she stuttered, "Pamela. Pamela Charbonneau."

"That's what we figured. Your uncle hired us to find you and bring you back. This here man is going to be under arrest for kidnappin' you."

"He didn't kidnap me!" Pamela exclaimed. "Well, not intentionally. He did, however, rescue me from outlaws who intended to hold me for ransom."

"I don't see as it's any of my business," the man replied. "The boys and me were hired to bring you back. We get a hefty balance when that's done, and I don't much care how the matter gets solved with this here man after that. You're coming with me, and he's going to jail. You and your uncle can work out the details later."

"Now, wait just a minute," Jim protested.

"No, you wait a minute," the seedy man spoke. He reached down and yanked the reins from Jim's hands. "We got you out-numbered and out-gunned. I don't want to kill you, but if you won't come right quietly, I'll do what I got to do."

"No!" Pamela cried. "He's innocent!"

"I don't much care, Ma'am," the man replied. "I'm getting paid to do a job. It's the first job I've had myself in weeks, so I intend to do what I'm told and collect my money."

Pamela cast a pleading glance at Jim. He seemed surprisingly calm, almost relieved.

"Jim, I promise I'll get my uncle to see reason. He doesn't understand what's happened. I don't even know how or why he's here, but I'll straighten everything out," she said. She watched as Jim was moved away from the horse and surrounded by four of the men.

"We'll be takin' you on back to your kin, now," the man said to Pamela. Leading her horse down the road, Pamela glanced back with a look of help-lessness on her face. "I'll send someone to the jail, Jim. I promise." Jim's dark eyes met hers across the distance and left Pamela with a strange feeling. Why did she suddenly care so much what happened to him?

~

By the time they reached the Dawson mansion, Pamela was nearly hysterical. She had to find a way to make everyone understand that Jim was sorry for his involvement in her disappearance.

When they came to a halt just to the side of the house, Pamela threw herself off the horse and, hiking up her skirt in a most unladylike fashion, she made a dash for the front of the house.

"Uncle Bob!" she yelled, pushing back the huge door. "Uncle Bob!"

The room was instantly filled with people. Zandy came from one direction with Riley right behind her, while Robert Charbonneau appeared from the opposite direction where he'd been working in the library. Burley, then Ruth, with Molly on her hip, came from upstairs, and Zandy's little brothers moved in behind Pamela through the open door.

"Pamela!" Robert said, instantly taking his niece into his arms. "You're alive and safe. Did he hurt you?"

"Uncle Bob, you must help me!" Pamela pleaded, pushing away from his embrace.

"I will, Sugar. I will. Just tell me everything, and I'll see to it that your abductor gets his just rewards," Robert replied. He reached out to push back his niece's disheveled hair, but she would have no part of it.

"You don't understand," she said, nearly in tears. She was exhausted beyond her means, having slept so very little the night before. "I have to talk to you about this. You can't put him in jail."

Robert shook his head in confusion. "Put who in jail?"

"Jim," Pamela replied. "You have to let him go. He saved me from the Owens gang. He risked his life. He didn't mean to take me. Your men have taken him to jail, and he's not responsible."

"Your men?" Riley questioned with a sharp glance at Robert Charbonneau.

"Pammy, you're making no sense," Robert said.

Zandy stepped forward and put her arms around Pamela. "You're exhausted. Come have a bath and some rest. Are you hungry?"

Pamela shook her head. She didn't know whether or not she was hungry. All she knew was that Jim was going to jail for nothing more than a terrible misunderstanding.

"You have to listen to me," Pamela said, sobbing the words. "You have to listen!"

Robert stood back, uncertain what to do. Riley looked on just as helplessly, as did Ruth and Burley. Zandy looked up at Robert and, with a nod, turned Pamela toward the stairs.

"Robert, I'm taking Pamela to have a hot bath. Please see to her concerns about this, ah, Jim?" she said with a questioning look at Pamela.

"That's right. Jim," she said, clinging tightly to Zandy's arm. "Jim Williams. You know him, Zandy. He said you did."

After staring at Pamela with her mouth open in surprise, Zandy lifted her gaze to meet Riley's eyes. Amazingly enough, he didn't seem at all surprised.

"Are you all right, Zandy?" he questioned.

Zandy nodded. "You'd better see to Jim, and I'll take care of Pamela."

"Let me help you," Ruth said, putting Molly down to run her own way. "Burley, you'd best keep an eye on her, or she'll be tearing down the draperies again."

Burley nodded and went in the direction of his youngest child, while Ruth moved to Pamela's side. "I'll have the bath readied," she said and went ahead of Zandy and Pamela on the stairs.

Pamela refused to move until she'd stressed her concerns once again to Robert. "Please, Uncle Bob, don't let them hurt Jim. He's not the one you want."

Robert started to speak, but Zandy wisely shook her head. "I'm sure your uncle will do what is necessary to see to justice. Right now, Pamela, you must rest."

Pamela finally gave in to Zandy's mothering and allowed her to lead her from the room.

~

Riley and Robert faced off in the open vestibule, each wondering what the other would say first.

"You hired men to go after her?" Riley questioned.

Robert shrugged. "I had to do what I could to ensure she came home safely. Your sheriff and his men didn't seem capable of doing the job, so I offered an incentive to men who could."

"You could have jeopardized everything and gotten her killed. Besides that, what if she's telling the truth? What if Williams isn't responsible for the ransom notes?"

"It doesn't matter," Robert replied. "She's back, and at this point I only want to know what Williams has done to her, then I intend to see him hanged from the nearest tree! Right now, however, I have some business to settle." With that, Robert stormed off, leaving Riley to stare after him.

Chapter 15

P amela had to admit she felt better after the bath, but she refused to sleep until Zandy agreed to sit at her side and listen to every word of her ordeal.

"I just have to make someone understand," she said in a way that Zandy couldn't ignore.

With a nod, Zandy moved to the bed and took a seat beside her friend. "Then tell me everything."

"You do remember Jim Williams, don't you?" Pamela asked.

"Of course, I do. Jim and I were once good friends. I thought he cared a great deal about me, but it turned out—"

"He did care. Does still, for that matter. He planned to take you that night, instead of me," Pamela interrupted.

"What?"

"He only knew about the person Riley used to be, and apparently someone told him, long after you had come to love Riley, that you'd been forced into marriage. Jim thought he was responsible because of the way he had treated you. He told me that he hated himself for the way he'd judged you falsely, and that if he'd stayed and helped you, you might not have had to marry Riley Dawson," Pamela explained.

Zandy 's voice betrayed her disbelief. "He came back here for me?"

"Yes," Pamela replied. She leaned back wearily and yawned. "He didn't know about Riley coming to God. He didn't even know you were living in Missouri. He just thought he'd come here and rescue you from your misery. You should have seen his face when I told him you and Riley were madly in love with one another. I even told him about the baby. But that was before—" she stopped suddenly.

"Before?" Zandy pressed.

"That was before so much. It's hard to believe that only a few weeks have passed. It seems like an eternity." Pamela sighed and looked away.

"Why don't you rest now?" Zandy said and started to leave.

"No! I have to tell you the rest. There's so much you don't know."

"All right, but you must sleep once you've finished."

"I will," Pamela promised. She hesitated for a moment, then began to tell the whole story of what happened after Jim realized he'd taken the wrong woman. Pamela stressed that he'd treated her with the utmost care, leaving out the time she had walked to exhaustion in the rain.

"Then the outlaws from the Owens gang took me. They told me that Jim was dead, and that's when Esther Owens, the leader, read about me in the Denver paper. Zandy, she was the one responsible for the ransom notes. She told me herself that she intended to make at least one million dollars out of my disappearance. She wanted to wire Mother and Father, but I told her she'd have better luck with you and Riley, only because I felt more confident that you and Riley could get me back alive."

"That's high praise, indeed," Zandy said with a bit of smile.

"I know that Uncle Bob believes that Jim was responsible for my kidnapping, and it is true that he took me at first, but only because he thought he was doing you a favor. Jim rescued me from the Owens gang. He risked his life with some drifter named Caleb something-or-other, and he was bringing me home when Uncle Bob's men found us. Zandy, you can't let him pay for this. Jim never intended me harm. He never intended anyone harm."

"I can believe that," Zandy replied quietly.

"Zandy, I prayed and prayed about all of this. I've been so stupid and foolish. Can you forgive me?"

"What are you talking about?"

"Bradley has married someone else, a very rich woman in Kansas City. They are even now on their honeymoon in Europe, or so the paper tells."

"I'm sorry, Pamela."

"I was so hurt, Zandy. I thought I loved him, truly I did. But when I realized what had happened, I knew I was only agreeing to marry Bradley because it would hurt my parents as much as they'd hurt me. I knew their social standing was important to them. A great deal more important, I might add, than I was. I wanted to get their attention, and I wanted to make them pay. But now God has shown me that this isn't the way to be. I know nothing would ever have been resolved between us, and maybe it still can't be, but at least I didn't marry a man I didn't love."

"God has a way of interceding," Zandy said. She smiled, remembering Riley's verse about intercession. "It's His way to keep us from hurting ourselves in our lack of knowledge and direction. He loves us very much, and even though it often seems He has rejected us, He never will. The Bible says He will always be with us."

"I believe that. Probably now more than before," Pamela admitted.

"That's because your faith has been tested. You have found it necessary to rely on God, not because I said He was good or because of what you saw Him do for Riley. You went to God with your own need, and from that moment on, He worked through your faith to help you trust Him."

"It was the only comfort I had, but now I fear Uncle Bob will hang Jim before the truth is told. Zandy, will you please help me? Can you go to the jail and talk to Jim? We have to see what the sheriff plans and how soon we can free him."

"I don't know," Zandy said slowly. She knew Riley would never allow her to go into town, and she couldn't very well send Riley to appear on Jim's behalf. Not when Jim had planned to take her in the first place.

"Does Riley know that Jim planned to take me?" Zandy suddenly asked.

Pamela nodded. "He left a note. He didn't sign it, but he figured Riley would know it was him."

"I see," Zandy said. "That complicates matters even more, but I'll do what I can."

Pamela's look of worry lessened with her friend's promise of help. "Then I'll rest. We can talk more later, but there's one thing I have to know."

"What is it?" Zandy questioned.

"You will forgive me for putting you in the middle of all of this, won't you? I mean, I practically forced you to bring me to Colorado, and I was hideously overbearing back there in Missouri. And all of it was because I was such a spoiled child, but, Zandy," Pamela paused and sat up to take Zandy's hand, "I'm not that child anymore."

Zandy smiled and gave Pamela's hand a squeeze. "I know that, and of course I forgive you. Now get some sleep. I've got some planning to do."

Zandy knew that in order to get to Jim, she'd have to leave the house unseen. This would be a difficult task, at best. Someone was always coming to see her about something, if for no other reason than to talk. Finally settling on saying nothing to anyone, Zandy slipped out the back door and made her way into town.

She moved slowly, cautious for the sake of her oversized stomach. She would have relished the comfort of a buggy, but she knew that sending for it would only draw immediate attention to her departure. Besides, she chided herself, the jail wasn't even half a mile away.

Since it was only midday, the town of Dawson was moderately quiet. There was the normal mining traffic with wagons of ore being hauled to processing and the scales. The train whistle blasted, startling Zandy for only a moment. Somehow she figured Riley's voice would closely resemble the same noise when he learned of her absence. Especially when he found out she'd gone to visit Jim Williams.

She pulled her shawl tight around her roomy brown calico dress and kept her head down and eyes to the boardwalk. She passed by several men who made suggestive comments about her condition, and even though her cheeks felt hot from their words, Zandy refused to acknowledge that she'd heard them at all.

Pushing open the door to the jail, Zandy lifted her face and met the eyes of K.C. Russell. Remembering K.C. as one of the deputies Riley had hired when he'd first come to Dawson, Zandy felt a little more confident in her mission.

"I've come to see Jim," she stated firmly.

K.C. eyed her suspiciously. "I can't let you do that, Missus Dawson."

"I'm not leaving until I talk to him face to face," Zandy said with her hands planted firmly on her hips.

Just then, Mike Muldair, another of the men Riley had hired for law and order in Dawson, appeared. "K.C., you'll be havin' to come help me!"

"What's the problem?" K.C. asked, momentarily forgetting about Zandy.

"It's that fool Jake Atkins and his brother Tom," Mike said, his Irish heritage betraying itself in his speech. "Jake's a wee bit in his cups, if you know what I mean."

K.C. nodded. Everybody knew about Jake's drinking habits. "Well, the fool has gone and shot up the Red Lady Saloon, and now Tom is tryin' to keep him from shootin' the barkeep for denyin' him whiskey. We need to give ol' Tom a hand before he puts a bullet in Jake, himself."

K.C. moved to the door, then remembered Zandy. "I can't leave with her here."

Mike moved to help usher Zandy outside, but the sound of more gunshots sent him away from her and out the door. "Ferget the fool woman and come on. We'll be in for it with Tom if we don't help him corral that brother of his."

K.C. finally gave up worrying about Zandy and ran after Mike. Zandy thanked God for the reprieve. She opened the door that separated the cells from the office and called out, "Jim? Are you in here?"

The light was dim, but Zandy could see a man rise from the cot in his cell. "Zandy?"

"Yes," she answered and came to stand directly in front of him. "Pamela begged me to help you, and I've come to do what I can." Jim looked tired, and Zandy couldn't help but feel sorry for him.

"You shouldn't be here," Jim replied. "I never wanted you to get involved in this."

"You involved me, or don't you remember?" Zandy questioned in a gentle tone.

"She told you?"

"Yes," Zandy replied. "I guess in a way I feel honored that you cared so much. I often wondered if you'd forgiven me for the wrongs you'd presumed me capable of."

"Me forgive you?" Jim laughed. "I think we both know it's the other way around. I need your forgiveness, Zandy. I wronged you something terrible, and I've had to live with it all this time. Even before Pat told me the truth of the matter, I knew down deep inside that you weren't capable of doing what I said you'd done."

"I forgive you, Jim."

"Just like that?" Jim questioned. "Even after all of this?"

"Just like that," Zandy replied. "If you had taken me, Jim, then found out I was content—in fact, happy—wouldn't you have brought me back home?"

"Of course."

"You tried to bring Pamela back home too, and, as she tells it, it nearly cost you your life. I think I know that you never intended harm to anyone, and I will see to it that everyone else knows it as well. I'll find some way to get you out of here. Just don't give up."

Jim went back to the cot and slumped down in complete dejection. "There's no way they're gonna let me out of here. I've got no way to prove that anything I say is true. It's my word against theirs."

"And Pamela," Zandy insisted. "She seems really concerned. She was nearly hysterical trying to get someone to see reason. I think she cares a great deal what happens to you."

Jim crossed his arms and sighed. "It won't do any good if that uncle of hers is out for blood, like his men said. He's gonna find a tree and string me up. This whole thing is impossible."

"Nothing is impossible with Christ," Zandy said. "The Bible is clear on this matter. You must put your faith in God, Jim. He's your salvation in this situation, and He won't let you down. I'll be praying for you, and you must do the same. Remember, the Bible says in Matthew 18:20, 'For where two or three are gathered together in my name, there am I in the midst of them.'

Between you, me, and Pamela praying, God will be with us, and He'll answer. He won't let you be falsely punished."

"I'd like to believe that," Jim said, lifting his head.

"Then believe it. God won't let you bear this alone."

"All right, Zandy. I'll be praying."

Chapter 16

Z andy walked from the room with a new determination to free Jim. She noticed that K.C. was still absent from the office and breathed a sigh of relief that she'd not have to explain herself to anyone. Her relief was short-lived, however. She walked out the door of the jail and straight into the waiting arms of her husband.

"Riley!" she gasped. Looking into his angry face, Zandy steeled herself for his rage.

"Alexandra," he said between clenched teeth, "we need to talk." He took a firm grip on her arm and pulled her with him.

"I can explain, Riley."

"Oh, you will definitely do that," he replied, barely controlling his temper. "Starting with why you came into town when I left explicit orders that you were to stay in the house."

"I had to come. Pamela said that Jim is innocent of trying to get ransom for her. He was bringing her home, Riley."

"It still doesn't answer my question. I gave you orders for your own good. I didn't do it just so I could have the upper hand with you. This town isn't safe, and you know that full well. If you couldn't respect my wishes for your own safety, how dare you risk the life of our child!"

Zandy felt herself close to tears at his accusation. She was more angry than she'd ever been. "How could you, Riley? How could you?"

Riley stopped and looked into her angry green eyes. "I don't want to bury you. This town is out of control, and decent folk aren't safe. The sheriff spends his day running from one end of the town to another, just to identify the bodies. You knew the risk, yet you figured that man in there was worth more than your own life or your baby's."

Zandy raised her hand to slap Riley, then halted, suddenly realizing what she was about to do. Taking a deep breath, she pushed away, but Riley wouldn't let her go. Instead, he moved her toward the carriage he'd brought.

"Get in," he said, helping her up.

Zandy did as she was told. She was mortified that she'd been angry enough to hit her husband. What was wrong with her? She'd never in her life felt like this.

Riley quickly joined her and slapped the reins against the horse's backside. With a jerk the buggy moved down the street, and when Riley turned away from the road that would take them home, Zandy turned to question him.

"I thought I was supposed to be at home," she said in a sarcastic voice.

"We're going to talk about this first, and I don't need an audience," Riley replied. Once they were outside of the town proper, Riley directed the horse off the road and into a small clearing. Pulling back on the reins, Riley turned to face his wife. "I love you, Alexandra. I've tried to be a good husband, a proper husband, but you challenge me at every turn. How can I lead if you won't let me? We can't even face life side by side, because you continue to take matters into your own hands.

"You've insisted on interfering in things that aren't of your concern, and this time it could have well cost you your life. Pamela's problems are her own making, just as Jim's are. You have to leave them alone to resolve the messes they've gotten themselves into."

"You don't even care that an innocent man may die," Zandy declared. Her eyes were ablaze with the fire of her anger. "Jim may be hanged because of something he didn't do. He never intended to kidnap Pamela."

"I know," Riley replied, matching her anger. "He intended to take you! Did you know that?"

Zandy sighed. She felt the baby move restlessly in her belly and wondered if she was causing her child harm by arguing with Riley. Finally, she nodded, and when she spoke, her tone was less harsh.

"Yes, I know. Pamela told me first, and Jim and I discussed it. Why didn't you tell me?"

"I couldn't. I thought it might be Jim, but I couldn't be sure. The thought of anyone trying to take you from me, for any reason, left me cold. I didn't want you to worry and wonder, and that was one of the biggest reasons I insisted you stay in the house."

"But Jim didn't want to hurt me. He thought I was living in misery with you," Zandy stated.

"It doesn't matter what he thought!" Riley declared.

"It does!" Zandy exclaimed. "He didn't mean to hurt anyone."

"Well he did. Alexandra, you have to stay out of this." Riley's insistent tone caused Zandy's anger to rekindle.

"I can't!"

"You will or else!" Riley demanded.

"Or else what? Are you going to lock me in my room?"

"If I have to." Riley was nose to nose with her by this time.

Zandy clenched her fists in her lap. "Take me home."

"Not until you understand how things are going to be," Riley replied.

"God expects us to fight for the right," Zandy said. "He doesn't expect us to hide in fear just because something bad might happen. I know Jim is innocent, and you expect me to say and do nothing to try and stop an injustice being done. That's not of God! You simply can't forgive Jim for caring about my happiness. Forgiveness is a part of your responsibility as a child of God as well. Luke 17:3 says, 'Take heed to yourselves: If thy brother trespass against thee, rebuke him; and if he repent, forgive him.' Jim asked my forgiveness, and I gave it. You should learn to do do the same."

Riley shook his head. There was no reasoning with her. She drew on her years of Bible teaching and verse memorization and used it like a mighty weapon against him. Taking the reins in hand, Riley urged the horse forward.

They said nothing on the way back to the house. When Riley stopped the horse just beyond the back entryway, Zandy climbed down awkwardly from the buggy and ran into the house.

Riley wanted to call out to her. He wanted to stop her and ease the anger between them, but he couldn't. He couldn't find a way to get past her consistently placing herself beyond his authority. He couldn't help her to see that he didn't want to dominate or rule her as a king would a subject, he just wanted to protect her and see to her safety and the safety of his child.

Inside the house, Zandy let go the tears she'd been holding back. Why was she so angry when she knew that Riley was right? Maybe it was because he was right that she was mad. All her life, she'd tried to live by the Word of God, and now she almost hated herself for throwing it in Riley's face. She knew full well that wasn't the way God had intended it to be used.

Moving with weighted steps, Zandy felt as though a burden was crushing her down. She had never allowed there to be this kind of anger between her and Riley. How could she resolve it? How could she make him see that Jim's life was just as important and just as worth saving as her own?

She made her way to Pamela's room and knocked lightly.

"Come in," the voice called from within, and Zandy pushed back the door. Tears still streamed down her cheeks, and Pamela immediately took notice. "What is it, Zandy? Is Jim. . .is he. . .?"

"No, Jim is fine," Zandy said, getting control of her emotions. "I just had a horrible fight with Riley. He found out that I'd gone to the jail. He was livid, of course. Oh Pamela, I can't convince him that we need to fight Jim's cause. He just won't listen to reason."

Pamela nodded in complete understanding. "I know exactly how you feel. I tried to talk to my Uncle Bob, but he won't listen to reason, either. I told him everything, including how Jim saved my life, but he just doesn't see that it merits helping him now. He says that Jim made those kind of choices when he decided to take me in the first place. Oh, Zandy. What are we going to do?"

"I don't know," Zandy replied in complete exasperation. There didn't seem to be any answer. Then her conversation with Jim slowly came back to her. "Yes, I do." Her words held more confidence. "We'll do exactly as I told Jim to do. We'll pray. The three of us will pray for Jim's deliverance. There is a thing called intercession. Riley himself told me about it. It's a kind of coming before someone on someone else's behalf. Jesus intercedes for us, as does the Holy Spirit. Now we are going to intercede for Jim," Zandy replied confidently.

Pamela seemed to pick up on her enthusiasm. "Just tell me what I must do."

For a time, they prayed together. Then Zandy left Pamela and went to another of the empty bedrooms and locked the door. She had no desire to see Riley. Her heart was still filled with anger toward him, and it became very clear to her that it hindered her prayers.

"God," she prayed, getting to her knees beside the bed. "I've served You for so long and believed that Your Word was true. I know You have a purpose in this situation, yet I can't see what possible good can come from Jim's imprisonment. I feel so angry with my husband, because. . . ." Zandy fell silent. Why was she mad at Riley?

"I don't know how to live with him," she finally said. A bit of a laugh came out, surprising Zandy. "I've been married to him for some time now, yet I still don't know how to be a good wife. He hasn't the years of spiritual training I've had, and I suppose that makes me feel like I have to lead him. But I don't, do I Lord?" It wasn't really a question, because Zandy already knew the answer.

"I don't need to lead him, because You will. But You can't help him if I'm always interfering. Forgive me, Father. I don't mean to be so foolish and blind. It's hard to follow Riley," she whispered. "It's hard, because I'm afraid he won't know what Your will is on the matter. I suppose I've become a bit of a snob when it comes to my Christian teachings. I can't seem to accept that You can fill Riley with all the wisdom and knowledge he needs in order to be a good husband. Help me, Father. Help me to trust You to guide Riley. Help me to be a wife who is a helper, not a hinderer. I don't want to cause Riley to give up in discouragement."

Zandy immediately felt better. She could suddenly see how she had tried to lead the spiritual matters in their home for some time. It wasn't that Riley didn't want the responsibility, as was the situation for the husbands in some homes, it was that she wouldn't let him have it.

Getting up from the floor, Zandy sat on the bed and began to wonder how she could deal with the situation in a way that would put all the wrongs to right. She loved her husband, of this she had no doubt. But Jim was innocent, and someone had to convince Robert and Riley in order for him to go free.

"God, You are our only hope," Zandy whispered. "Please help Riley and Robert to see the truth, and help Pamela and me to leave it in Your hands. Amen."

Chapter 17

Robert Charbonneau stood amidst the men with a determined look on his face. Four of the original men he'd hired to find Pamela waited in silence for their temporary boss to speak. Robert sized each man up as the type who had no conscience, then proceeded with his plan.

"I find it necessary to call upon your assistance once again," Robert began. "My niece is creating quite a stir with stories of her ordeal. She's completely lost her sense in the matter and truly believes Jim Williams innocent of her abduction. Personally, I think it's just one of those addle-headed female infatuations, but I find it most impossible to persuade her otherwise.

"And, as you know," Robert continued, "our friend is still sitting in his jail cell awaiting some type of justice. I for one am growing weary of the wait. It's been four weeks, and I don't care how much flooding there's been, we're entitled to a speedy trial for this man. Whether a judge can get through the pass or not, I intend to see justice carried out swiftly."

"What are we supposed to do?" the leader of the group asked. He was a stout man with red hair that hadn't seen a washing in more than a month of hard riding. He spat tobacco juice on the ground, and Robert was silently grateful that he'd decided to hold this meeting in the barn instead of the house.

"I'm sure we can think of something," Robert replied.

The man stared blankly for a moment, then seemed to catch Charbonneau's meaning. "We can't very well hang him properly in his cell."

It was as he made this comment that Pamela came upon the men. They didn't see or hear her, so she crept into one of the empty stalls and listened.

"No, that's true," Robert said, thoughtfully rubbing his chin. "However, he could be shot trying to escape. Desperate folks attempt extreme measures when faced with the possibility of their own death. How hard would it be for a man to attempt such an escape?"

The red-headed man leered a grin. "Not hard at all with the proper kind of encouragement."

The stall was hot and dusty, and Pamela felt sweat pouring down her back. Still, she couldn't risk being seen and give away the fact that she knew what her uncle was planning.

"Well, gentlemen," Robert said with a satisfied smile, "I suggest we be about our business right away. This is Saturday, and Saturday nights in Dawson seem to be a most laborious night for our sheriff and his deputies. What say we plan a little diversion just in case the town rowdies don't accommodate us?"

"A fire would bring just about the whole town to help," one of the other men offered.

"A fire would be good," Robert said with a nod. "It must be threatening enough, without doing too much damage. After all, we wouldn't want the entire town destroyed."

"There's some old shacks down at the south end of town, just across Meiers Gulch," the leader remembered. "They're used for storing mining equipment and such. We could set those on fire, and with Corner Creek between it and town, it would bring folks to put out the fire, without risking the Main Street district."

"Good. Then that's what we'll do. Can you get enough help to set the fire and still have enough men to offer the encouragement needed for our friend to escape?" Robert asked, eyeing his watch. It was nearly five. "Say we set the fire around six. Then have things set up at the jail. Just in case you can't get the deputy to leave the place, have another man wait outside to announce some problem. Maybe you could tell him that someone was breaking into the assay office. Just use any old excuse to clear the jail."

"We can handle it, Boss. When the money's right, we can do most anything we need to."

Robert laughed, "A man after my own heart."

Pamela shuddered to think that her uncle could so cold-heartedly plan the death of another. In the weeks since her return, while Jim waited in prison for the circuit judge, she'd only managed to slip notes to Jim by way of one of Zandy's brother's friends. He, of course, couldn't write back, but he usually gave the boy a message for her, and though it often came to her in a most garbled fashion, Pamela knew that Jim was not giving up hope that God would send him a reprieve.

When the men departed for town and Robert hurried back to the mansion, Pamela made a dash for Zandy's room. Mindless of the straw that still clung to her skirt, she rushed up the back servants' stairs and knocked softly on the door.

Zandy opened the door, not at all surprised to find Pamela.

"What is it?" she asked, however, when she saw the look of terror in her friend's eyes.

"Uncle Bob plans to kill Jim!" she exclaimed barely above a whisper.

Zandy motioned Pamela inside. She quickly closed and locked the door before pulling Pamela toward the far end of the room.

"No one will hear us if we talk softly," Zandy said.

Pamela stared for a moment, as if seeing her friend for the first time. Zandy was obviously very expectant, and Pamela knew it would only be a matter of weeks before the baby would be born. How could she even begin to involve her in this mess?

"I'd better just handle this alone," Pamela finally spoke. "You aren't in any condition to be helping me, and there isn't time to get anyone else."

"What are you talking about?" Zandy questioned. She reached out to force Pamela to stay where she was.

"My uncle is planning a jailbreak for Jim. It's going to happen in just an hour or so. I overheard them talking in the barn. And, Zandy," Pamela said, with tears in her eyes, "they plan to kill him."

"No!" Zandy exclaimed louder than she'd intended.

"Uncle Bob is just convinced that I'm too stupid to see Jim for what he is. He thinks I wear my heart on my sleeve and give it to every man that comes along," Pamela explained. "Now, he's convinced that I'm lying to save Jim because I'm in love with him."

Zandy's eyes widened. "Are you, Pamela? Are you in love with Jim?"

"I don't know, Zandy. I care very much for him. He was so kind and gentle. Yet he was firm with me too. He never once allowed that spoiled, little-girl attitude of mine to run the show. He made it clear that he'd not tolerate my selfishness, and I guess I needed that to show me what I'd truly become."

"But that's not the same as loving him. You must know whether or not you care that much," Zandy pressed.

Pamela put her hands to the sides of her head as if to press out the images that were flashing through her mind. She could easily see the plan her uncle made coming true. She could see Jim lying dead in the muddy street of Dawson.

"I've thought constantly of him since our return," Pamela admitted. "I've thought of the way he consoled me when we learned about Bradley. He was so tender, and yet he helped me to see God's hand in it all, and he made me understand that I didn't have to face my pain alone. I've slipped notes of encouragement to him on more than one occasion, but the message I get back is never one that shows anything more than curt acknowledgement of having received them."

"What do you expect, love letters?" Zandy asked with a smile. "You need to listen to that heart's calling you're always talking about. I think if you listen long enough, you'll find that you care more about Jim than you're willing to admit."

Pamela nodded, then paled when she heard the clock chiming half-past the hour. "We've only got a little less than half an hour. They plan to set some shacks on fire to create a diversion on the opposite side of town!" Pamela exclaimed. She pulled away from Zandy and hurried to the door. "Is Riley back yet?"

Zandy shook her head. "His meeting with Mister Tabor must have lasted longer than he planned. He wired to say he'd arrive on this evening's train."

"Then he can't very well help us," Pamela replied and fumbled to unlock the door. "What about your parents?"

"They're out visiting friends, and I don't know when they'll be back," Zandy answered and crossed the room. "Look, whether you like it or not, you're stuck with me. They won't threaten Jim if we're there. I mean, how would it look? A respectable young woman and a mother-to-be standing between them and their man. What are they going to do, shoot us?"

"They very well could, Zandy. That's why I don't want you to come with me."

"Nonsense," Zandy replied. "You run ahead and make certain your uncle isn't going to see us leave. I'll be downstairs directly and meet you at the back door." Pamela nodded reluctantly and hurried to do what Zandy suggested.

After a hurried prayer for guidance, the two women slipped into the dusky shadows of twilight. Zandy directed Pamela to take the garden path, for the extra coverage of the shrubbery and vegetation. The lingering scent of flowers and pine lent the lavender sky an air of romance, but the thoughts in the minds of Zandy and Pamela were far from that pleasure.

Dawson was already enjoying an overzealous celebration for the week's end of work. The last shift at the mine was just finishing, and Zandy knew that six o'clock would be signaled by the explosion that would be set off to blast ore from the rock face of the mines. She knew they would need to be in place at the jail before that, and she hurried, in spite of her cumbersome burden, to keep pace with Pamela's lithe and graceful form. They had to make it time. They just had to!

~

A hot and exhausted Riley Dawson stepped from the five-forty-five train. He glanced at his house up on the hill and sighed in relief to know that very soon it would be Horace Tabor's problem to contend with. The sounds of gunshots and laughter from the brothel and gambling districts hurried his step toward the sanity and safety of his home.

His mind had been greatly preoccupied with thoughts of Zandy. There was so much that needed to be said between them, and he wanted very much to put an end to her worries about Jim. But how? How could he get Zandy to see reason where Jim was concerned? She cared too much, and that bothered Riley more than he could say. Was it possible that Zandy cared more for Jim than she was letting on? It was something that Riley had to find out. He had to know why she was so persistent in defending him.

The walk did him good and helped Riley to clear his head. He was glad to be home, yet completely reluctant to deal with his wife. "God," he breathed the prayer, "give me the guidance I need to do what I must. Let my words be carefully chosen, and please let Zandy speak honestly to me."

The house greeted him in silence, and Riley couldn't shake off the feeling that something was wrong.

"Zandy!" he called out as he took the stairs two at a time. Their bedroom revealed nothing. Perhaps she was spending time with Pamela.

Riley walked quickly to the end of the hall where Pamela's room was. He knocked loudly, and when no one answered, he opened the door. Nothing!

Now Riley was worried. He hurried back downstairs and nearly ran through each room, trying to locate the women. When he reached the library, a single cough let him know the room was occupied.

"Robert?" he questioned, coming into the room.

"I see you made it back," Robert replied from where he sat.

"Have you seen the women?"

Robert shook his head, noting the worried expression on Riley's face. "Not since this afternoon. After lunch, Zandy went to take a nap, and Pamela went to her room. Why?"

"They aren't in the house, and I didn't see them on the grounds when I came home. I'm going to check the gardens, but as dark as it's getting, they both know better than to be out there. Where are Burley and Ruth and the kids?" Riley called out from the doorway.

"I don't know," Robert said. He seemed completely confused as to why Riley was so disturbed. "I wouldn't worry too much, Riley. They're probably just off sewing for the baby or some such thing. I've not seen them leave the house all day, and I've been here the whole time."

Riley ignored the man's assurance. He knew how determined his wife could be if she felt the need to see to some matter. A quick examination of the gardens revealed them to be as empty as the bedrooms had been.

Riley ran a hand through his sweat-soaked hair and returned to the house. Where were they?

Coming back to the library, Riley heard the clock chime six. This was followed by the rocking explosion that signaled the end of the mining shift. Robert glanced up and started to speak, but Riley's look silenced him.

"If they aren't here, there's only one place I can imagine the two of them would have gone," Riley stated. "They must have gone to the jail to see Williams."

Robert paled and got to his feet. "They wouldn't! They couldn't have. I would have seen them leave."

"Be realistic, Charbonneau. Those two are fully capable of giving you the slip if they so choose. They aren't here, so that means they must be somewhere. My guess is the jail."

Robert glanced at the clock and back to Riley. The look on his face changed from calm to anguished. "They can't be at the jail."

"Why not?" Riley said, coming forward. "What is it that you're not telling me, Robert?"

"I. . .well, you see, I—"

"What is it, man? If you know something that can help me find them, you'd best tell me now," Riley said, nearly taking hold of Robert.

"I arranged for Williams to escape from the jail. I set it up so he'd be shot, and we'd be free once and for all without having to wait for a judge to hang him!"

Riley felt the color drain from his own face. He wanted to wring Charbonneau's neck, but that wouldn't change a thing.

"When?" Riley questioned, throwing Robert a murderous look.

"Right now," Robert answered.

Riley didn't say another word. He could only offer up a prayer while running at desperate pace to reach the jail before Robert's plan could be executed.

Chapter 18

When Zandy and Pamela arrived at the jail, it was empty. Fearing that somehow the hired thugs had already coerced Jim from the cell, Zandy rushed through the office as fast as she could.

"Jim!" she called, stumbling through the darkness.

"Zandy? What are you doing here?" Jim questioned from his cell.

"Oh, Jim!" Pamela exclaimed, coming behind Zandy. "They plan to kill you. I heard them talk, and they're going to stage a jailbreak and shoot you while you run."

"Pamela?" Jim's voice revealed his surprise. "You two shouldn't be here, especially if what you say is true."

Pamela came to the cell where Jim stood. She could barely see his face in the fading light. "We had to come. We had to warn you and see if we couldn't stop it. My uncle won't listen to reason. I've tried to explain the matter to him over and over again, but he won't listen. Now there isn't time to go for help. He and his men planned for the jail to be empty except for you."

"Look, you and Zandy have to go back to the safety of the house. I can take care of myself, and we have to trust God to look out for me as well. I'm not running anymore. The last time I did, I ended up causing more hurt and trouble than it was worth."

Zandy stepped forward at this. "Jim, the past has been resolved. I forgive you, now you must forgive yourself. You have a great deal to live for, and I won't see you putting yourself into the hands of those madmen."

"Forgiving is the easy part," Jim said softly. "The forgetting is a whole heap harder."

"We haven't got time to worry about it just now," Zandy said firmly. "They mean to show up here any minute."

Pamela turned to Zandy. "Would you mind giving me a minute alone with Jim? I think I can convince him that we need to help him."

"I'll be just outside," Zandy said with a quick squeeze of Pamela's hand. "I'll keep watch."

Pamela waited until Zandy had closed the door before she spoke again. "Jim, I've got to say something to you, and you've got to listen to me carefully. I can't stand by and watch them kill you. I've come to care too much about you." She paused for a moment, wishing she could better see his face. Stepping closer to the bars, Pamela was surprised when Jim's hands reached out to touch her arms.

"I care about you too," Jim remarked. "That's why I don't want you here."

"But I can't leave!" Pamela exclaimed. "I love you!"

The silence that fell between them caused Pamela to fear Jim would reject her feelings. He knew her foolishness over Bradley. Perhaps he'd give her declaration no consideration at all.

"Did you hear me?" she finally managed to whisper.

"Yes," he replied. "I love you too."

"You do?" Pamela questioned, leaning forward against the bars. Jim slipped his arms around her as best he could.

"I've loved you for awhile now. I guess I was just waiting for you to heed the heart's calling, as you'd put it."

Pamela pressed her face to his.

"Yes, I suppose that's it," she whispered.

Just then, Zandy came back and slammed the door closed. "Something's happening out there!" she exclaimed and surprised both Pamela and Jim by pulling a small revolver from her skirt pocket.

"Zandy!" Pamela cried and moved to her friend. "You can't mean to use that."

"I'll do what I must to keep them from killing Jim. He doesn't deserve to die in a shoot-out." Zandy strained her eyes in the dim light to see if there was anything she could use to keep the ruffians from entering.

"Look," Pamela said and reached up to a small bolt on the door. She quickly slid the lock into place.

"I don't remember that being there," Zandy said, breathing a sigh. "It won't keep them out, but it will slow them down. Now, Pamela, you get back in the corner by Jim."

"Zandy, you've got to stop this," Jim said, to no avail. "You can't risk your life and your child's for me. I'm perfectly willing to put my life in God's hands."

"That's where all of us are at the moment, Jim," Zandy countered. "You can't protect yourself in there, so I'm just doing what I feel I must. You'd do no different if it were me or Pamela in there and you out here."

"But that's different," Jim protested.

Just then shouting from outside the jail could be heard. The ruckus grew until several shots were exchanged. Zandy began to tremble. On the other side of the door, she could hear men's voices. She slowly backed up against the bars of an empty cell and leveled the gun at the door.

The latch was tried, and when the door wouldn't budge, Zandy, Pamela, and Jim could hear someone kicking against it. These outlaws would beat the door down, Zandy realized, then she'd have to face them. Could she do it? Could she actually take a life in order to save one? For the first time, she questioned the sanity of what she was doing. If Riley found out, he'd be furious. Smothered in guilt, Zandy waited for the inevitable.

The door gave in with a resounding crash, and from the doorway rose the shadowy figure of a man. Zandy lifted the revolver higher.

"Stop or I'll shoot," she said in a shaky voice.

"Alexandra!"

It was Riley. She'd nearly shot her own husband! Sickened from the entire episode, Zandy lowered her arm as her knees gave way.

Riley stepped into the room, secured the gun, and lifted Zandy into his arms. She shook so hard that her teeth chattered loudly.

"Are you hurt?" he questioned.

Robert rushed in behind him. "Are they all right? Where's Pamela?"

"I'm here Uncle Bob, and I'm fine. I just couldn't let you put an end to Jim's life. I love him, and I won't let you hurt him. He's not responsible for those ransom notes," Pamela said firmly. She stepped forward putting herself between Robert and Jim.

Robert studied Pamela for a moment, then shook his head. Turning, he saw that Riley was leaving with Zandy. "Is she all right?"

"I don't honestly know," Riley replied. "It's the first time I've found her speechless, and the only time I've ever wished she'd rant and rave at me, if nothing else."

"I'm not hurt," Zandy managed to say, then added, "Just scared half-witless."

"Good," Riley retorted. "You deserve to be."

Just then the sheriff returned, having just found several men tied up and face down in the dirt outside his office. "What's going on in here?" he questioned, lighting a lantern. Turning up the light, he was surprised to find his jail so full of visitors.

Riley exited the cell room and deposited Zandy onto a chair with the order to stay put or else. Pamela quickly followed her uncle into the office, while Jim was forced to wait it out in the cell.

"I'm afraid you had a little problem here tonight," Riley said.

The sheriff snorted in disgust. "I've had a little problem all over town tonight, Mister Dawson. I'm afraid you're going to have to get yourself another sheriff. I quit."

"You can't!" Pamela exclaimed. "There are those who intend to see Jim

Williams hang, and I'm here to tell you that he's not the man responsible for my kidnapping. He didn't send those ransom notes, and I will not be a part of any scheme to see him charged with such nonsense."

"Ma'am, by your own admission, Williams is the man who took you from the Dawson grounds," the sheriff replied.

"That's true, but it was a mistake, and there were no hard feelings between us. He was bringing me back when I was taken by the Owens gang. You have to believe me!" Pamela pleaded. "Please, Uncle Bob, I know what I'm saying. I'm not addlebrained."

"That's for sure!" a voice called out from the open doorway.

"Caleb!" Pamela exclaimed.

"Hello there, Little Bitty Gal," he said with a smile broader than Corner Creek during a spring flood. "Good to see you lookin' so well. What's all this about, Jim?"

"Oh, Caleb," Pamela said and moved across to pull the man by the arm. "They mean to hang Jim because they think he's responsible for my kidnapping. You know the truth. Please tell them!"

The sheriff eyed Caleb suspiciously. "Who's this?"

"He's Caleb Emerson," Pamela said, suddenly remembering his last name. "He was drifting through the area when Jim and I ran into trouble. He helped Jim after the Owens gang nearly killed him. When they took me, Caleb helped Jim rescue me."

"That true?" the sheriff questioned.

"All but the part about me drifting through," Caleb said. He opened his worn out vest to reveal a badge. "I'm a U.S. marshal. Been after the Owens gang for some time now. Just happened that when they took Little Bitty here, I was around to help get her back. Old Jim was in pretty poor shape for several days, and I had to fight him down to keep him from stumblin' after her and bleedin' to death in the process."

Pamela's mouth dropped open at Caleb's declaration. "You're a marshal?"

Caleb laughed. "Yup. I'd been stakin' out the Owens gang for some time. That's how I knew about their hideout."

"Then Williams is truly innocent?" Robert questioned, looking first at his niece, then at Emerson.

"He sure is," Caleb confirmed. "In fact, he risked his life to go down into the box canyon the Owens gang used and pull this gal to safety."

Robert shook his head. "I thought for sure. . ." His words died out. He'd nearly caused the death of an innocent man because of his unwillingness to believe Pamela's story.

"Given the fact that the marshal here is backing up Williams's story, I'll have to let him go," the sheriff told Robert.

"Of course," he replied. "I'll drop everything."

"Well, that's all fine and dandy, but you and me have a bit of business to settle, if I'm not mistaken," the sheriff said.

"You'd better clear out your cells, 'cause you've got more company than you'd figured on," Caleb stated. "I've brought in what's left of the Owens gang. You're gonna have to jail 'em for me until I can make arrangements to take them to Denver."

Pamela looked up at Caleb and swallowed hard. "They're here? Outside?"

"Yup, but don't you worry," Caleb added with a smile. "I've got 'em wrapped up prettier than Christmas presents. They aren't gonna be any problem for you." With that, he went to see to his prisoners.

The sheriff, in turn, went in to release Jim while Riley turned to speak to Robert. "Your hot-headed stupidity nearly got my wife and your niece killed. That same shoot-first attitude is what's wrong with this entire town. I'm going to be mighty glad to be rid of it." He moved to retrieve Zandy, when Robert reached out and touched his sleeve.

"I'm sorry, Riley. I truly am. I know I'm to blame for this, and I intend to take my due. I'd have never seen either of the women placed in danger. You have to believe me."

Riley nodded, but the look of disgust still lined his features. Just then, Jim stepped into the room and, in spite of his bedraggled condition, Pamela thought him the handsomest man in the world. She threw herself into his arms.

"Oh Jim," she cried, burying her face against his chest. "God did it. He sent the miracle we needed."

"I heard, Little Bitty Gal," he said with a laugh. Pamela pulled back at his use of Caleb's nickname and joined his laughter.

Riley lifted Zandy in his arms, in spite of her protest, and started to leave. He turned to face Jim for the first time, and swallowing his pride, he spoke. "Williams, I want to see you at the house. There's a room for you there, and I think it would do us all good to have a long talk."

Jim nodded, knowing in his heart that he still needed to reconcile with Riley. "I'll be there."

Riley turned his face to Zandy and smiled. "Of course, first, I'm going to have a long talk with this young lady about wifely obedience and what I intend to do should she decide to go gunning for outlaws again."

At this, everyone but Zandy laughed. Zandy bit her lip and tried to ignore the look in Riley's eyes. It was the same kind of look that she'd seen some years earlier when he'd told Zandy he intended to be a part of her life forever. It was such a look of determination that it left Zandy in little doubt as to just who would have his way in the future.

Riley passed Caleb just outside the door. He was startled to find that one of the marshal's prisoners was a woman. A rather beautiful woman, at that.

Caleb pushed Esther Owens and her two remaining cohorts through the door to the sheriff's office. The men Riley and Robert had tied and left in the dirt were quickly retrieved by the sheriff himself, making the small jail office rather crowded.

Esther gave Pamela a curt nod of acknowledgement, and Pamela couldn't help but feel sorry for the woman. She'd treated her well during her captivity and, in all truth, Pamela couldn't really bring herself to hate the woman. Perhaps, in another time and situation, they might even have been friends.

When Caleb had secured his prisoners, he returned to greet Jim. "Sure good to see that you're staying out of trouble, Son," he said with a smile.

Jim extended his hand and gave Caleb's a hearty shake. "I can't thank you enough for all you've done. You were my answer to prayer."

"God does work in strange ways," Caleb replied, "but I don't recall any-one, save my wife, ever saying I was an answer to prayer."

"Well, you are," Jim reaffirmed. "I don't know how to repay you."

"Just take care of that little bitty gal and stay close to the Lord. That'll be thanks enough," Caleb said with a laugh.

Jim grinned from ear to ear. "I intend to make that little bitty gal my wife. That is, if she'll have me."

All eyes, including Robert's, turned to Pamela. Pamela squealed in sur-prise and threw herself into Jim's arms. "Of course I'll have you!"

Jim looked over Pamela's head at Caleb. "I kind of thought she would," he said with a laugh.

Chapter 19

A long, hot August gave Jim and Pamela many fine days in which to get to know one another better. It seemed as though their close calls with death had produced changes and maturity in each of them that made all their old problems seem unimportant.

Three days before Jim and Pamela's September wedding, Riley signed the final papers that would give Horace Tabor ownership over all his holdings in Dawson. He felt much as if a weight had been lifted from his shoulders.

Zandy, finding her movements greatly restricted, was growing restless to bring her child into the world. Even so, she gave her best efforts to help with Pamela's wedding plans, fussing over the blond beauty as though she were her own daughter.

Horace Tabor had agreed to wait until the end of the month before the actual transfer of property would take place. Riley had insisted on this due to his concern that Zandy would need time after the baby's birth to rest before she could travel back to Missouri. It also allowed for Pamela to have her wedding in the mansion, something that seemed to give Zandy a great amount of pleasure.

When the wedding day finally appeared and the house had been decorated from top to bottom with orange blossoms, orchids, and ribbons, Zandy stood at Pamela's side and helped her to place the wedding veil on her carefully pinned and curled hair.

"You make a radiant bride, Pamela. I'm sure I've never seen another who could rival you."

"I'm so nervous. I'm afraid I'll pass out on the stairs," Pamela admitted.

"Nonsense," Zandy said with assurance. "I made it through my wedding under considerably more pressure and tension than you'll have. I never fainted once, although I felt like I might. You'll do fine. Now let me look at you and make sure everything is perfect."

Zandy stepped back, her emerald green, high-waisted gown rustling softly as she walked. She appraised Pamela's appearance for any flaw and found none. Her wedding gown was elaborate and completely current with the latest fashion. In a gesture that surprised everyone, Pamela's parents had arranged for the dress to be shipped from Paris, using Pamela's measurements to place the order. Even more surprising was their acceptance of her marriage to Jim, even though they declined to attend the wedding. They were, after all, invited to share company with a visiting Viscount and could not tear themselves away.

Zandy knew that Pamela was hurt at her parents' absence. She had confided in Zandy that the only reason they weren't making a fuss about her marriage was that Robert wholeheartedly approved of Jim as a husband. It seemed that after many hours of conversation, Jim and Robert had put aside their differences. Robert had even agreed to help Jim get established in some type of business, and in a bizarre stroke of fate, they had become the best of friends.

Studying the silk gown trimmed in Brussels lace, Zandy could only smile her approval. "You look beautiful. I can't imagine a more perfect bride."

"You don't think the gown is too much?" Pamela asked, suddenly fearful that she was unreasonably overdressed for such a small wedding.

"Never!" Zandy declared. She reached out and smoothed one of the many satin bows that trimmed the collar of the dress. "A bride can never be wrong in what she chooses to wear. It is her wedding, after all. Now turn around and let me make sure that the train is lying properly over the bustle."

Pamela turned, and Zandy ran a careful hand beneath the veil to straighten the lace cap of the silk overdress. "There! Now it's perfect!" proclaimed Zandy, arranging the veil to fall gracefully behind the bride. "Now, where are your flowers?"

"Over there," Pamela replied, pointing, and she took a deep breath.

Zandy brought the bouquet to Pamela, then turned her to the cheval mirror. "See for yourself."

Pamela moved to the mirror and gasped. "Oh," she whispered in awe.

"My thoughts exactly," Zandy said. She put a supportive hand to her back. Her burden was daily growing more uncomfortable.

Just then a knock sounded, and Pamela's uncle announced that it was time to come down. Zandy opened the door, and Robert, in his resplendent morning suit of dove gray, entered the room to admire his niece.

"Pammy, you look smashing!" he exclaimed.

Pamela beamed under his attention. "I'm so glad I have you to give me away. Mother and Father," she nearly choked on the words, "have never cared for me like you have." She moved to her uncle, lifted her veil, and bestowed a kiss upon his cheek. "I shall always love you for all that you've done."

Robert offered Pamela his arm, and Zandy hurried ahead of them. "You realize," Zandy stated at the top of the stairs, "you will have to give me ample time to descend as gracefully as this child will allow. That could very well take hours," she teased.

Pamela smiled and shook her head. "Jim and I have a lifetime, thanks to all of you. Take your time."

Zandy nodded and, in spite of the pain that tightened her abdomen, she smiled sweetly and gripped the banister for support. She wasn't about to spoil Pamela's day by announcing that she'd just had her first contraction.

In the large, front, morning room, Jim and Riley waited beside a short, balding man whose flowing black robe marked him as the preacher. Pastor Brokamp smiled broadly as Zandy appeared in the archway.

Zandy looked across the room to where Riley stood beside Jim. Both men were handsomely dressed in black claw-hammer tailcoats, with silk waistcoats and gray striped pants. She couldn't help but smile at the natural way Riley wore the clothes, in contrast to the most uncomfortable-looking Jim. She was grateful that Jim and Riley had put aside their differences to such a degree that Jim had asked Riley to stand up with him at the wedding.

Riley had easily forgiven Jim when he pointed out that someone as precious as Zandy deserved to have folks looking out after her happiness. Riley had realized then that Jim's only concern hadn't been for himself but for Alexandra.

Burley, Ruth, and their children were the only other people in attendance. Both Jim and Pamela had hoped Caleb could attend, but he'd made it clear that his marshaling duties wouldn't permit the break. He promised to be there in spirit, however, and expressed happiness that the young folks were tying the knot. Taking her place across from the gentlemen, Zandy joined the others in watching Pamela process forward.

Jim's face bestowed a look of radiant approval as he gazed upon his bride. Zandy was more convinced than ever before that theirs was a love match.

Coming to stand in front of Pastor Brokamp, Robert presented Pamela's small hand to Jim. Jim stared down at Pamela through the veil and winked at her. Pamela smiled.

The ceremony was short and simple, for which Zandy was most grateful. She stood without a word or movement through four very painful contractions. They were coming closer together, and Zandy remembered from the times her stepmother had given birth that the closer the contractions came, the sooner the baby would be born.

"You may kiss your bride," Pastor Brokamp said, and Jim lost little time in lifting Pamela's veil to do just that.

Everyone in the room rushed to congratulate the couple. The boys were laughing and shouting, while Molly squirmed out of Ruth's arms and ran to the various decorative flowers to pick her choices from the arrangements.

The cook and housekeeper appeared, bringing in two large serving carts. One boasted a two-tiered wedding cake, and the other held a silver punch bowl and glasses.

"Oh boy, cake!" George declared and made his move to be one of the first to be served.

Riley was speaking to Robert when he happened to glance up and see Zandy's contorted face. She quickly turned to hide the pain she was feeling and tried to appear as though she were interested in the lace that edged her neckline. With one hand clamped securely against her stomach, Zandy waited for the pain to pass and nearly jumped out of her skin when Riley whispered against her ear.

"Are you all right?" he asked.

"I'm fine," Zandy replied. She nearly gasped from the intensity of the pain.

Riley tried to turn her to face him, but Zandy couldn't move. "Please, wait a minute." Her voice held an unmistakable tone of pain.

Riley took his hand from her shoulder and moved to face his wife. "What is it?"

"The baby," Zandy whispered. Just then, her water broke and hiding the fact that she was in labor became impossible. "I'm sorry!" she gasped and gripped Riley's arm for support.

Riley stared dumbly for a moment. Then a grin spread across his face. "I'm going to be a father," he announced, lifting Zandy in his arms. The children were oblivious to his announcement, while six adults, including the cook and housekeeper, dropped open their mouths in surprise.

Zandy winced against the pain, while Riley laughed, "Leave it to Alexandra to upstage the wedding."

"Oh, Pamela," Zandy moaned from her husband's arms. "I'm so sorry."

"Please, Zandy, don't be. This is a wonderful thing. I'll always remember my wedding as being the birthday of your first baby," Pamela reassured her. "But what can I do to help?"

Riley glanced at Ruth with a helpless look on his face. Zandy's stepmother appeared to recognize the need and instantly organized everyone into their appointed duties.

"Boys, take your little sister to the playroom and keep her occupied. Stay there, and I'll have cake and punch brought to you. Burley, go for the doctor. Riley, come with me. We'll get Zandy to bed."

Pamela, Jim, and Robert stood by helplessly while everyone else seemed to have some task to busy themselves with.

"I think I'd like to change my clothes," Jim announced.

Pamela hated to put aside her wedding finery, but knew she'd be of no help to anyone dressed as she was. She blushed slightly and followed Jim upstairs. Robert trailed after the couple and, finding nothing better to do, took himself to his own room to change.

Some minutes later, when everyone hurriedly reappeared in the hallway, they found Riley nervously pacing outside his own room.

"Ruth told me to wait out here," he said with a sheepish smile. "I told her I thought I ought to stay with Alexandra, but she said I'd done enough already."

Robert and Jim laughed and pulled Riley along with them. "Let's go downstairs and wait this out together." Riley threw a glance back over his shoulder, but Pamela only waved him on.

"She'll be just fine, Riley. I'll let you know the minute the baby comes," Pamela reassured him.

Throughout the day, Pamela moved back and forth from Zandy's bedside to the waiting men below. She gave what little help she could in the way of reports, and she finally convinced Robert and Jim to get Riley into some more comfortable clothes.

"All my clothes are in our room," Riley announced with an upward glance.

"I'll bring you whatever you want," Pamela said. "Just tell me where to find them."

All four of them progressed up the stairs with Riley trying to remember where he'd put the things he wanted. Pamela finally directed Robert to take Riley to his room with the promise that she'd find the needed articles and return to them there.

She had just reached out to open the door when the unmistakable cry of a baby rang out, filling the hall. Riley blanched slightly, while Jim and Robert let out a whoop.

Pamela went into the room only long enough to make certain nothing was amiss.

"It's a boy, Riley!" she announced, coming back out. "You have a son, and Zandy is just fine."

Riley moved to the door, but Pamela put out her hand. "They aren't ready for you yet. So just relax. I'll call you when you can see them."

Riley turned to face his friends. A broad smile parted his lips to show his perfect teeth. "I told you," he laughed. "I told you it would be a boy!"

~

Ruth saw the doctor out, while Pamela stayed with Zandy. She smiled over the downy-headed child at his new mother. "He's a beautiful baby," Pamela declared.

Zandy nodded in complete awe.

"I want to apologize to you," Pamela added, getting to her feet. "Looking at him, I can't believe I could have ever been so thoughtless as to endanger your life, much less his. Please forgive me."

Zandy looked up in surprise. "There's nothing to forgive. I did what I had to do. I'd do it again."

Pamela nodded. "I know what you mean. It's just that you and Riley have come to mean so much to me. I can't believe all of the trouble I've put you through. In so many ways, I could have been responsible for driving a wedge between you."

Zandy shook her head. "No, the only walls that could come between us are the ones we put up ourselves. Riley and I are learning, just like you and Jim will learn, that marriage is a great deal of work and compromise." She snuggled her sleeping baby close and added with a nod, "But, it's very much worth the effort."

Pamela touched the tiny boy's head. "I'll keep that in mind. And you remember that, should you ever need anything, I am your dearest friend, forever."

"I'll remember," Zandy assured her.

Just then the door opened and admitted a proud Riley. He marched into the room as though he were taking charge of a meeting, and Pamela quickly made an excuse to depart. Standing for only a moment at the door, Pamela couldn't help but feel her heart flutter at the loving look on Riley's face as he reached out to take hold of his son. Someday, she'd give Jim a son and maybe even a daughter.

With a light heart, Pamela nearly danced out into the hall and fell headlong into the arms of her husband.

"Umm," she sighed, as he bent his head to hers. "Don't I know you?"

"I should hope so," he replied and kissed her soundly.

Pamela threw her arms around her husband's neck. "I'm glad you kidnapped me," she declared. Jim only laughed.

"I know I'd have never given up my selfish, little-girl ideals if you hadn't come along to offer a little direction and guidance," she stated honestly. "I could never see how immature I truly was. Now that I have, I hope never again to be so self-centered."

"That makes two of us," Jim teased.

Pamela pushed her husband away and turned as if to walk off. "I bare my heart and soul, and you insult me. Maybe you should just go on the honeymoon by yourself." She'd only taken three steps when Jim crossed the distance, seized her abruptly, and threw her over his shoulder. Pamela giggled loudly, pleased with the turn of events.

"This kidnapping thing could get to be a habit," Jim announced, marching down the hall. "I guess a body just has to listen to the heart's calling in order to know what's best to do. Mine tells me I'm in for quite a life with you, Little Bitty Gal."

Forever Yours

*Dedicated to all the would-be writers out there,
with three supportive suggestions that were once offered to me,
and one extra that I would like to add.*

1. Write what you know.
2. Learn what you don't know.
3. Never give up on the dream.
4. Colossians 3:23

Prologue

Riotous changes, for which the young country was already famous, ushered in the turn of the century in America. As the 1900s quickly added years and headed into their teens, a fascination grew for things mechanical and complicated. America was hungry for change and innovation, and her people were only too happy to comply.

Among those changes were some that would drastically alter the course of history. Skeptical crowds viewed automobiles and airplanes, never believing the contraptions would retire the horse and buggy. Meanwhile, the warm wonder of electric lighting spread like a fire out of control and soon engulfed the young nation. New carbonated drinks, rising hemlines, and a variety of contraptions and conveniences that baffled the mind were part of the flood that swept the country into young adulthood.

The world was, of course, not without its problems. Racial hatred ran rampant, especially in larger cities in the East. Leonardo da Vinci's "Mona Lisa" was stolen in August of 1911 and not recovered until two years later. And in 1912, the nation mourned in stunned dismay the sinking of the *Titanic*.

In an almost frantic frenzy, Americans pressed forward at such an alarming rate that old-timers questioned the sanity of those younger. Where would it all lead? And how could it possibly be good?

In the unspoiled innocence of the recently admitted state of New Mexico, things were no different from the rest of the country. A hunger was growing for the wealth and wonder of all that their sister states enjoyed. Perhaps the old-timers weren't panting for change like the younger citizens, and maybe the natives looked with contempt on the destruction that always accompanied progress. But in the growing town of Bandelero, New Mexico, the children of its founders were now coming of age, and with this came bold ideals for the years to come.

Chapter 1

D aughtry!"
The voice sounded loud and clear from outside the adobe stable.
"In here, Daddy!" a young, auburn-haired woman called. She finished cleaning the hoof she held between her slender, jean-clad legs before making any move to greet her father.

Garrett Lucas bounded into the stable with a look of determined frustration on his face. Now in his mid-fifties, Garrett was still lean and muscular from his years of ranch work. His hair was a salt and pepper brown that he fondly told his children was growing whiter by the minute due to their antics.

"Where have you been?" he asked.

Daughtry patted the back of her horse Poco and moved to put away her grooming equipment. "Daddy, you know very well that I ride before breakfast every single morning. Then I come back here and see to Poco, just like you taught me."

Relief crossed Garrett's face before he nodded to his daughter. "I think you ought to have one of the hands ride out with you," he advised. "Or at least you could ask one of your brothers."

"Daddy! I'm twenty-three years old. When are you going to realize that I'm fully capable of taking care of myself?" Daughtry's voice betrayed the frustration she felt with her father's constant overshadowing protection.

"Just because you're grown doesn't mean I stop worrying about you," Garrett offered by way of apology.

Daughtry sighed and brushed the dirt from her pants. "I know and I'm glad you love me, but I have to have some room to breathe. You have one of the largest ranches in New Mexico to run, so why not concentrate on that and let me go my own way?" Daughtry paused and looked at her father seriously. "Sometimes you and the boys are just more than I care to deal with. I don't know how Mother stands it."

Garrett grinned. "I keep your mother too busy to worry about it. Besides, she likes my keepin' an eye on her."

"Well," Daughtry said, coming forward to place a quick kiss on her father's cheek, "I'm not Mother."

She walked past her father and kept moving toward the adobe-styled ranch house. For all her life Piñon Canyon Ranch had been her home, and all her memories, both good and bad, were enclosed by its boundaries. Now, it seemed more like a prison. The world was changing out there, but here, time seemed to stand still. Her family didn't have electricity, telephones, or automobiles, and often Daughtry had the dreadful feeling that life was passing her by.

"I wish you wouldn't wear your brother's clothes," Garrett said from behind her.

Daughtry stopped in her tracks and turned, and her father quickly covered the distance between them. She fixed an expression on her face that she hoped would prove her determination. They'd argued this before, but she was willing to argue it again.

Garrett sighed. "Okay, I give up. Wear jeans when you work around the ranch. But I better never catch you wearing them into town. They're too revealing, and I won't have every guy there drooling and following you around."

Daughtry laughed. "Oh, Daddy. You are impossible. No man is ever going to drool over me, because you're always two steps behind or in front of me. No gentleman can get close enough to ask my name, much less ogle me."

"Good," Garrett said, putting his arm around his daughter. "Let's keep it that way."

~

Inside the ranch house, a flurry of activity was managing to create absolute chaos. This was typical of breakfast at the Lucas table, and Maggie Lucas took it all in stride. Maggie was still a fine-looking woman, with a shapely figure and dark auburn hair, and Daughtry so closely resembled her mother that people often mistook them at a quick glance.

When her husband and daughter came into the dining room, arm in arm, Maggie couldn't help but smile. Then, just as quickly, a frown crossed her face as she caught sight of her daughter's grim expression. Garrett was obviously making himself a pest again.

Maggie knew why, but it didn't help matters any. Her own heartfelt grief at the loss of their daughter Julie, almost four years earlier, caused her to sympathize with her husband. When Julie had ridden out on a cold December morning, no one thought that only hours later she would lie dead at the bottom of an icy ravine. Her horse had lost its footing, and Garrett had never forgiven himself for letting Julie ride out alone. Truth be told, Garrett had never stopped blaming himself for the tragedy and had become incessantly more preoccupied with Daughtry's safety. Indeed, his concern had rapidly approached a level of grief all its own, for he knew his inability to protect Daughtry from all of life's many dangers. His grief and frustration threatened to drive Daughtry

119

away from her father and their home.

Daughtry's brothers swarmed around the room. Dolan and Don were arguing, as was typical for the seventeen-year-old twins. Joseph, sixteen, was trying to snag pieces of food off the plates as Anna Maria and Pepita hurried around the table to avoid his reach, and fifteen-year-old Jordan, Jordy to everyone except when he was in trouble, was reading as he walked. No doubt another western. Jordy loved to read them and point out the inaccuracies. There was only one author he held any esteem for and that was Zane Grey.

Finally, Gavin, the oldest of the boys at twenty-one, entered, gave his mother a peck on the cheek, whirled her in a circle, more to clear her out of his way than anything, and took his seat at the table.

"I'm starved!" Gavin fairly roared, then grinned up at his mother who was shaking her head at him.

"Well, if we can get everyone to take a seat," Maggie said, "we'll have breakfast." Nearly in unison, four boys took their seat, leaving Garrett and Daughtry standing.

"Well, come on Sis, Dad," Gavin said, reaching out to take hold of his mother's hand. "Let's pray and eat."

Garrett took his place at the head of the table, while Daughtry went to sit across from her mother. Everyone joined hands, while Garrett blessed the food. When his brief prayer ended, the chaos which had existed earlier died away to civility and calm. Maggie Lucas would tolerate no rowdiness at her table.

Daughtry picked at her food, while all around her, her brothers ate as though they were starving. She was hungry, or at least had been until that morning's episode with her father. How could she ever get him to stop worrying that she was going to die tragically like her sister?

"Aren't you hungry?" Maggie asked her softly.

Six pairs of eyes followed their mother's gaze to see what Daughtry's response would be. Sometimes, she felt as though she held the entire ranch hostage, awaiting her answers. But most of the time, Daughtry felt like she was the hostage.

"I'm fine," she muttered under her breath and continued to pick at the biscuits and gravy on her plate.

"We've got a heap of work cut out for us today," Garrett was telling his sons, and Daughtry let her mind wander, knowing that this would keep everyone occupied for a spell.

Why can't I just get away from here? Her mind reeled at the unspoken question. What she wouldn't give to leave Piñon Canyon. At least for a little while. *I've never even been out of New Mexico,* she thought. *There's a whole world out there that I only know from magazines and books. Will I ever see it? Will I ever be able to enjoy the things other people do?* She was twenty-three years old. An old maid by some standards, not that her father cared. If he had his way about it, she'd stay unmarried and lonely until her dying day.

The boys all seemed to be talking at once, and Daughtry nearly laughed out loud at the thought of being lonely. *How could anyone claim such a feat in this house?* she wondered. But she was. She was lonely and bored and unhappy with her life. She prayed about it often. She read her Bible. She even sought the advice of their longtime family friend, Pastor David Monroe, but nothing seemed to help.

David had suggested she mingle more with people her own age, but every time she tried to do just that, her father would come looking for her. She'd hoped that after a little time had passed and the pain of Julie's death had dimmed, her father and brothers wouldn't be quite so possessive of her. But, if anything, it was more of a problem than ever.

What made matters even worse was that Daughtry and Julie had never been that close—and now Daughtry felt as though her sister was to blame for all her misery. That only managed to add guilt to the loneliness and frustration that already smothered Daughtry.

I miss her too, Daughtry thought. *Even if we didn't see things eye to eye, she was my sister, and I loved her.* Daughtry looked around her at the family she cared for more than anything or anyone. *I love them all,* she argued with her heart. *But they're killing me!*

"What are you going to do today, Daughtry?"

"Huh?" Daughtry's mind fumbled to recall the question.

Garrett seemed undaunted. "I was just asking what you had planned to do today?"

"Oh," Daughtry said and glanced at Maggie. "I guess Mother and I are going to finish sewing our dresses for the fair."

Garrett nodded. "Sounds like a good idea. The fair's in two days and I wouldn't want my favorite ladies to show up looking shoddy."

Maggie rolled her eyes. "You wouldn't care if we wore potato sacks, as long as you had one of us on either side of you."

The boys snickered, but Daughtry didn't. Her mother spoke the truth. Except maybe dressing in potato sacks was pushing the boundaries a bit.

"I guess you're right," Garrett said with a smile and leaned over to place a kiss on his wife's temple. "I'd go anywhere with you, Mrs. Lucas, and you could indeed be wearing potato sacks and still outshine everybody else." His gaze betrayed his pride and passion for the woman at his side.

"Well, I for one will not be wearing potato sacks," Maggie replied. "Nor will Daughtry. We have some very special dresses planned. You just wait. There won't be an eligible bachelor in town who won't sit up and take notice of our daughter."

"Not that it would do any good," Daughtry said before she could check the thought.

"What's that supposed to mean?" Garrett questioned. All eyes turned once more to her for an answer.

Daughtry pushed back her chair and got to her feet. "It means just what you think it means. No one is going to look at me twice because my daddy might take offense at their forwardness and put them in their place. And if not him, then one of the mighty Lucas brothers. I'm so tired of being treated like I'm five years old. Did it ever once dawn on any of you that I'd like to meet a nice young man, fall in love, and move away from here?"

Everyone stared at Daughtry in surprise. She had never before given such an outburst of criticism for what they perceived as their dutiful love for her.

"Daughtry!" her mother gasped. "You apologize to your father and brothers, this minute."

Daughtry leaned against her chair and considered the situation for a moment.

"Sorry," she muttered and turned to leave. Stalking down the hall, she added in a whisper for her ears alone, "Sorry that I live in this house and will probably die in this house too!"

~

When the boys had finished with breakfast, leaving their parents alone, Maggie couldn't help but try to ease the tension between her husband and daughter.

"Daughtry does have a small point," Maggie began. She tenderly ran her fingers across the back of Garrett's hand. "She is grown up and does deserve to settle down with her own husband and family."

Garrett's eyes flashed anger, as though Maggie's declaration was one of betrayal. "I just want to see her with the kind of man who's going to respect her and love her. He needs to know what's going on with this world and how to make a living that will support her. You've never taken her side over mine before. Why now?"

Maggie sighed. "I'm not taking sides, Garrett. It's just that I see something in Daughtry these last few months that worries me. I'm afraid if you don't find a way to work it out, Daughtry will put a permanent wall between the two of you. You don't want that, Garrett. You've already lost one daughter."

Garrett stormed from the table without another word. Maggie stared after him for a moment, tears brimming in her eyes. "Help him, Father," she prayed. "Help Garrett to heal before it's too late."

Chapter 2

Daughtry remained silent on the ride into town. The growing community of Bandelero was overflowing with people due to the fair, and Daughtry tried to put her feelings behind her and smile. At least she was away from the ranch and she was wearing something pretty.

She glanced down at the lavender dress she'd helped to make. It had a pleated bodice with hand embroidery and lace to edge the scooped neckline. At the waist, a darker lavender ribbon trimmed the gown and tied in the back to show off her very feminine form. Outlandishly gaudy hats were the rage these days, but Maggie and Daughtry had found little use for them on the ranch. Instead, they had ordered less complicated arrangements from Sears and Roebuck. Her mother predicted the simplicity would do more to turn heads, and, when it did, Daughtry could only hope that her father wouldn't be anywhere nearby.

As Garrett brought the carriage to a halt outside of a two-story adobe house, a sudden ruckus caused the horses to rear and prance. Everybody waited for the smelly, noisy automobile to pass by before even trying to dismount.

"Useless things!" Garrett declared, finally settling the horses. "You won't ever see me in one. I'll stick with horses."

"I think they look like fun," Dolan said from the back of his horse. "I hear they actually have races with those things. They go for days and days, and people even get killed."

"How awful!" Maggie exclaimed, taking her husband's hand as she exited the carriage.

Daughtry stared past her brothers to the street where the car was rapidly disappearing. She silently wished that she could be one of the happy passengers.

"Daughtry, you daydreamin' up there?"

Daughtry looked down at her father and smiled. *If he only knew,* she thought. As she stepped from the carriage, however, they were bombarded with friends, and she was distracted from her thoughts.

"Garrett! Maggie! I'm so glad to see you all," Lillie Monroe called from behind a swirl of people.

"Where's Dan?" Garrett asked, while Maggie embraced her lifelong friend.

"Had to set a broken arm," Lillie said with a shrug. "That's all part of being married to the town doctor. You always have to share him. I'll be glad when he takes a partner."

Lillie's sons, John and James, joined them and soon were catching up the Lucas boys on all the news. Sixteen-year-old Angeline Monroe was nowhere to be seen, much to Daughtry's relief. Angeline only reminded Daughtry how old and outdated she'd rapidly become under Garrett's overprotective hand. Angeline was young and just beginning to live, while Daughtry felt her life was over.

"The fair is going to be a great deal of fun," Lillie was saying, while Garrett and Maggie kept stride with her. Daughtry took advantage of the moment to slip out of sight and wander around town alone. Heaving a great sigh, she rounded the corner and ran smack into the broad chest of a stranger.

"Excuse me," she said, looking upward into soft brown eyes.

"I'm afraid the fault is mine," the man returned. "I just came to town for the fair and I don't know my way around."

Daughtry laughed. "It's not all that difficult, believe me."

The man smiled appreciatively. "Maybe you could show me."

"I'm not sure that would be proper," Daughtry said, glancing around for her father or brothers. "I don't even know you."

"Bill," he replied and extended his hand. "Bill Davis."

"Daughtry Lucas," she replied and extended her small gloved hand to take his.

"There," he said confidently, "now we're no longer strangers. Would you do me the honor of introducing me to your fair city?"

Daughtry laughed, glad to be free for once. "Of course."

The rest of the day passed much too quickly for Daughtry. She ran into Jordy once, but he seemed unconcerned that his sister was on the arm of some stranger. Later, Daughtry narrowly avoided a confrontation with Gavin, when she and Bill happened into a knot of people who stood laughing and talking, blocking the street. As the crowd thinned a bit for them to pass by, Daughtry found Angeline Monroe to be the focal point of the group. Laughing and enjoying the attention, Angeline didn't so much as nod when she caught Daughtry's eye.

"Do you know her?" Bill questioned after they'd managed to slip past the gathering.

"Yes," Daughtry replied, hoping Bill wasn't going to ask to be introduced.

"She seems awfully young to be flirting with so many men. You ought to have a talk with her folks," Bill said, surprising Daughtry with his words.

"People have been trying to tell her folks for years," Daughtry laughed.

"But she's very spoiled."

"Unlike you," Bill said, his sincerity clear in his voice. Daughtry blushed furiously but said nothing as she kept walking.

With Angeline just a memory, Daughtry cast sly upward glances at the sandy-haired man who walked beside her. He was as tall as her father, and the width of his shoulders was also nearly the same. He was dressed in jeans and a light brown shirt, but it all seemed rather regal to Daughtry. Perhaps Bill was her Prince Charming, and he would whisk her away from the stifling life she'd known.

"So how come a pretty thing like you hasn't up and married?" Bill asked her while they walked the festive avenue of carnival games.

"Truth? Or would you rather hear some fabulously devised story?" Daughtry asked, completely serious.

Bill studied her for a moment and laughed. "Truth."

"It won't appeal to you," she said, glancing around her for the millionth time.

"You looking for someone?" Bill asked her softly. "I mean, ever since this morning, you've been looking over your shoulder and down the street. What's the problem?"

Daughtry sighed. "The same reason I've never married. I have a very possessive father—and five brothers who feel it's their duty to fill in for him when he can't be there to do the job."

"I see," Bill said, and Daughtry thought he sounded a little nervous. "Are they the killing kind or just the wounding and maiming type?"

Daughtry laughed out loud, catching the attention of several people around them. Stifling her amusement, she waited until they'd walked away from the listening crowd. "I've only known them to be the ranting and raving kind, actually."

Bill grinned. "Ah, that won't bother me then. My ears can tolerate the hollering."

"Don't be so sure." Daughtry glanced at the railroad depot clock and sighed. "I'd better get back. I've been gone way too long."

"I'll walk you," Bill said and tucked her arm around his.

Daughtry wanted to tell him no, but the truth was, she was enjoying herself too much. Maybe God had decided to smile down on her and allow her to meet a respectable young man after all.

"Daughtry, I've been looking for you." Her father blocked their path, and behind him stood three of her brothers.

Garrett was frowning fiercely at Bill, and the scowl was so intimidating that the younger man immediately dropped his hold on Daughtry.

"I've just been seeing the sights and enjoying the fair," Daughtry said, trying to control her temper. Then, hoping she could smooth matters, Daughtry turned to introduce her friend. "This is Bill Davis. Bill, this is my father, Garrett Lucas, and my brothers, Gavin, Dolan, and Joseph."

Garrett was barely controlling his temper as he reached out and yanked Daughtry by the arm. "Evening, Mr. Davis. You'll have to excuse us now."

Daughtry was livid. Garrett continued pulling her down the street, while her brothers firmly discouraged Bill from trying to interfere.

When they were back in the solitude of the Monroe backyard, Daughtry dug her heels in and stopped.

"How dare you!" she exclaimed, and the hurt in her eyes changed quickly into rage. "I can't believe you would embarrass me like that."

Garrett looked at her for a moment. "Daughtry, I was only looking out for your best interest. You don't know that man, and he had no right to be handling you."

Daughtry shook her head. "Enough is enough. I've had all I'm going to take. You may be my father, but I'm of age and old enough to make my own choices. Good night!"

Garrett called after her, but Daughtry ran into the house without so much as a glance over her shoulder. She knew they were spending the night with the Monroes, but she had no idea where she was to sleep. Gratefully, she ran into her mother.

Tears were blinding her eyes, but Daughtry didn't want to talk about it. "Mother, where am I supposed to sleep?"

Maggie noted her daughter's state of mind. "Daughtry, what's wrong?"

"The same old thing. Now, I just want to go to bed. Where am I sleeping?"

Maggie led her daughter to the small room she was to share with Angeline. "I'm sorry, Daughtry. I don't know what has happened, but I hate the fact that it's hurt you so much." She reached out and hugged her daughter close.

Daughtry wrapped her arms around her mother and sobbed. "I can't stand it anymore, Mother. I love you all so much, but I have to be allowed to grow up." She abruptly released her mother and turned away. "I just want to go to sleep now, please."

Daughtry knew that she hurt her mother when she shut her out, but she could see no sense in discussing the matter any further. Silently, she undressed and slipped into bed for a good cry before going to sleep.

～

Morning light dawned, and Daughtry woke with a new determination and outlook on her life. During the night, after hours of praying and pleading with God, she'd decided to run away from home. At least that's what she called it, though she doubted that someone could actually run away at her age.

Angeline still slept peacefully, and because Daughtry knew the girl had come to bed quite late, she tiptoed around the room collecting her things. After dressing and pinning up her hair, Daughtry made her way downstairs.

"Morning, Daughtry," Lillie called to her from the kitchen. "Did you sleep well?"

"Yes, thank you." Daughtry struggled to sound pleasant.

"Are you hungry? I've fixed enough food for a small army. Of course with your brothers and James and John, it very nearly resembles just that."

Daughtry smiled. "Are Pastor David and Jenny coming over this morning?" Daughtry questioned, referring to Dr. Monroe's brother and his wife. "I was hoping to talk to them before we left for home."

"I think they plan to stop by," Lillie responded. "Did you not get a chance to see them last night?"

"No," Daughtry replied. "I didn't."

"Did you need to talk to them about anything in particular?"

"Yes," Daughtry murmured, "but it's rather, well, personal." She thought maybe David or Jenny could offer some help or suggestions on where she could go.

Lillie smiled and nodded. "That's quite all right, I understand."

Within moments, the quiet talk was forgotten as the room filled with the bodies of young men all rivaling the other for the center of discussion.

Daughtry managed to slip outside with her plate of food. She ate with a ravenous appetite, suddenly remembering that she hadn't had any supper the night before.

"I brought you a peace offering," Garrett said, coming up behind her. Daughtry looked up but said nothing. Garrett held out a newspaper. "I knew you'd want to catch up on what was happening around the world. I managed to latch onto this copy of the *Denver Post*."

Daughtry took the newspaper from her father. He was trying so hard to make up for his behavior, and even though she had no intention of changing her mind about leaving, Daughtry couldn't treat him badly.

"Thank you, Daddy," she said softly and glanced briefly at the headlines.

"I really am sorry," Garrett said.

"I know," Daughtry replied. *You always are.*

Seeing that she wasn't in a mood to talk, Garrett left Daughtry to finish her breakfast alone. Daughtry knew that he wanted her to laugh and think nothing more about the events of the previous night, but that wasn't possible for her.

Flipping through the pages of the paper, Daughtry came across an advertisement. It was like no other she'd ever seen. This was an advertisement for a wife. Quickly scanning the lines, Daughtry read:

Wife wanted to share the dream of building a ranching empire. Looking for a hard-working woman who isn't afraid to love and live with a man who will provide a home and remain forever yours in the eyes of God and man.

It was signed N. Dawson, with an address in care of the post office in a small town in eastern New Mexico.

How romantic, Daughtry thought as she reread the ad. The days of mail-order brides were a thing of the past but, from time to time, people did still seek a mate through that unconventional manner.

Daughtry began to get an idea. A very serious idea about answering the advertisement. She folded the paper and stared at it for several minutes. *It could work,* she thought to herself. It could be everything she'd prayed for.

Back at Piñon Canyon, Daughtry penned a response to the man she could only address as Mr. Dawson. She wondered as she wrote what his first name might be. She imagined Nicodemus or Nathaniel—maybe even Navin or Ned, although those names didn't appeal to her sense of romance.

She stared at the blank paper for several minutes, then began to pour out her thoughts.

Dear Mr. Dawson,

I am responding to your advertisement and would very much like to receive more information about the marriage and dream you propose. I have grown up on a ranch and thus have spent my entire life working at the same dream you seem to have. I would be happy to correspond with you regarding the matter. Please address your reply in care of the Bandelero, New Mexico, Post Office.

Daughtry Lucas

Almost as an afterthought, Daughtry picked up her pen again and added a postscript indicating that she had enclosed a picture of herself. Then, scouting through her desk drawer, she managed to find one that had been taken recently at a church picnic. She thought the photo did her justice.

Slipping the letter and picture into an envelope, Daughtry addressed it and made plans for how she would get away the next morning to mail it. This was a great adventure, she thought to herself, and, for once, she looked forward to the next day with less dread.

N. Dawson, she thought with a smile. *Maybe, just maybe, he will be my answer to prayer.*

Chapter 3

Daughtry had nearly given up hearing anything from N. Dawson when, much to her surprise, she found a letter awaiting her at the post office. Giddy with excitement and grateful that she'd ridden in alone for the mail, Daughtry tore open the envelope.

She wasn't prepared for the many pieces of paper that accompanied the letter. Reviewing the items, Daughtry was shocked to find legal documentation for a marriage by proxy, a train ticket, and photograph. The picture was face down and Daughtry decided to leave it that way until after reading the letter. *This way,* she thought, *I won't be influenced by looks alone.*

Carefully opening the letter, Daughtry eagerly read the contents.

Dear Miss Lucas,

I was enchanted by your photograph and letter. I would like to say that I believe you are a Godsend. My faith being firmly rooted in Him, I can say without a doubt that you are the woman I am to marry.

Daughtry reread that line several times before continuing. A strange feeling was coursing through her, and it made her hand shake ever so slightly as she read on.

Enclosed you will find a train ticket to bring you to me and a legal document which will allow you to marry me before you make the journey. It is most imperative that you marry by proxy by the twenty-fifth of September, otherwise the documents will be null and void.

I hope this answers your questions, and I hope the enclosed photograph will put your mind at ease regarding my appearance and age.

Forever yours,
Nicholas Dawson

"Nicholas!" Daughtry breathed. "His name is Nicholas." Gingerly, she refolded the letter and turned the photograph over. Her breath caught in her throat. He was clearly the handsomest man she'd ever seen. She studied the man who casually sat for the photograph. He was dressed in a smart suit, with dark hair and even darker eyes staring back at her. His eyes seemed to twinkle, if that were possible, and his lips were curled upward.

"Oh my," she said breathlessly. "He's wonderful."

She lost track of time, studying the picture as though trying to memorize each and every feature of the man. Finally, when a train whistle blew and broke her concentration, Daughtry realized she would have to be heading back to the ranch.

After another quick examination of the document and train ticket, Daughtry replaced the papers in the envelope and tucked the letter into the deep pocket of her split skirt. Without much thought, she tossed the rest of the mail into her saddle bag and mounted Poco.

"What have I done?" she questioned aloud. All around her the rich cobalt blue sky stretched out to the purple haze of mountains. The noise of Bandelero faded, leaving Daughtry with only one pounding question in her mind. *What do I do now?*

She felt the side of her skirt to reassure herself that the letter hadn't been dreamed. "This man is serious, Poco," she said, as though the horse might offer her some insight. "He's sent me a train ticket and the means by which to marry him before coming to his place." The horse kept a steady trot, mindless of its owner's ramblings.

"Dear God," Daughtry finally prayed, looking upward to the cloudless sky. "I didn't mean to cause trouble, but maybe this is the direction You're leading me. The man says I have to make up my mind before September twenty-fifth." Daughtry paused in her prayers. "Father, that's only ten days from now."

A trembling started anew in Daughtry. Ten days! That's all the time she had to make a lifelong decision. She argued and reasoned with herself all the way back to Piñon Canyon. How could she leave her home and marry a stranger? Even if he were a very nice looking stranger? On the other hand, Daughtry knew she was going to leave this place, one way or another. She had no idea how she would care for herself alone, and marriage to anyone would be better than dying an old maid, she thought.

～

Three days later, Daughtry was still mulling over her proposal. She'd reread the letter until it was well-worn and she knew every word by heart. Always, she came back to the picture and lost her heart a little more. "Forever yours, Nicholas Dawson," she sighed and stared at the dark eyes of the man who wished to marry her. Only seven days were left.

Daughtry had never been a person given over to moments of spontaneous decision. She always thought things out and, inevitably, reasoned away any urge to do something foolish. This was no exception, and as time passed, Daughtry recognized too many good arguments against accepting Nicholas's proposal.

"I can't hurt Mother that way," Daughtry thought aloud. She had taken Poco out for her routine morning ride, grateful to escape the escort her father thought necessary. Pulling back on the reins, Daughtry slipped down from Poco's back and walked alongside the gelding for awhile. "I can't just walk away from my responsibilities," she continued. Poco seemed more interested in the patches of fading green grass than in his mistress's declarations.

"I've always been a good girl," Daughtry said firmly. "I've always been dependable and reasonable. I'll just have to make it clear to Daddy that I need to be allowed to court and marry and eventually leave Piñon Canyon to make my own home. He'll come around in time."

Daughtry studied the landscape for a moment. The rocky western slopes of their property headed upward into the Sangre de Cristo mountain range. Soon snow would cover the magnificent crests and Piñon Canyon would be blanketed in white.

Another winter, Daughtry thought to herself. *And in January, I'll be twenty-four.*

Daughtry walked on in silence. She had to do the right thing, she reasoned. She had to trust God and endure the situation as best she could. When she got back to the house, she would simply write to Nicholas—no, Mr. Dawson—and tell him that she couldn't marry him.

She was about to remount Poco when a cloud of dust in the distance caught her attention. Riding hard and fast across the open plain was her father. Daughtry remained on the ground until a worried-looking Garrett reined up beside her.

"You're on foot," he said, looking Daughtry over from head to toe. "Is something wrong?"

"No, Daddy," Daughtry said, taking a defensive tone. "I'm just enjoying the morning."

Garrett frowned. "Why didn't you bring someone with you?"

"Because I'm a grown woman and I don't need an escort. I like to spend time on my own, and I don't want to have someone following me around all the time. It's bad enough that you won't leave me alone."

Garrett's eyes revealed his hurt but Daughtry was rapidly growing angry, and her father's pain was furthest from her mind.

"Daddy, you and I have to talk about this," Daughtry said firmly. "Why don't you walk with me a spell."

Garrett quickly complied and joined his daughter on the ground. He started to speak, but Daughtry held up her hand. "Please let me say what I need to say," she began. "Then you can tell me what you think and we'll go from there."

"All right."

Daughtry swallowed hard and took a deep breath. She prayed that God would give her the right words to say. "Daddy, I know how much losing Julie hurts you. I hurt too. I miss her, and I wish that she would never have gone out riding that morning. But the truth is, she did, and I can't change that and neither can you. You can't change it by smothering me or watching my every step. You can't do God's job, Daddy."

Daughtry stopped and looked at her father for a moment. He was still a young man, vital and strong, and Daughtry knew he was perfectly capable of providing for his family. He'd helped her with so many things in life. He was the one who had helped her find Christ as her Savior. He was also the one who had taught her to ride and shoot and a hundred other things that pertained to her life on the ranch.

"I love you, Daddy," Daughtry said, looking deep into his eyes. "But I want to get married and have a family. I want a life of my own, and I want you to let me go."

Garrett looked at her blankly for a moment. "Have you found someone?" he asked softly.

Daughtry smiled ever so slightly at the thought of Nicholas. "I thought I had, but now I'm not sure. I do know, however, that it's what I want for my life, and I believe it's what God wants for me too. I don't want to go to school or hold a job or make a great splash in society. I just want to be a wife and mother. I don't want to grow old taking care of you and Mother. You're supposed to care for each other, and we children are supposed to leave the nest."

Garrett nodded, and Daughtry thought he finally understood. Feeling a bit of relief, she offered him a smile.

"Who is it?" Garrett asked without thinking.

"Who is who?"

"Who were you thinking about marrying?" Garrett questioned, and Daughtry could see the determination in his eyes.

"It isn't important," Daughtry said in exasperation.

"Well, why don't you let me be the judge of that."

"Because I'm a grown woman and you aren't the judge of my life," Daughtry stated in anger. "I'm the one who will decide whom I marry and when. This isn't the Middle Ages, Daddy, and I'm not going to be like Momma and let my father decide for me." Daughtry stormed past him and remounted Poco with a fury in her eyes that Garrett had never before seen.

"You're still under my authority, Daughtry," Garrett said, swinging up into his own saddle. "That gives me a say in what you do."

Daughtry gripped the reins tightly. She tried to steady her voice before she spoke. "Daddy, you're making this very difficult. Will you allow me to make some choices for myself? Will you stop shadowing everything I do in the fear that I will end up dead, like my sister?"

Garrett looked at her for a moment before silently shaking his head. "I can't, Daughtry. God made you my responsibility."

Daughtry refused to answer. Instead she dug her heels into Poco's sides, something she rarely did, and flew out across the ground for home. By the time she'd headed into the stable yard, Daughtry had made up her mind. No matter what else happened, she was going to marry Nicholas Dawson! She would have the last word on this and no one, especially not her father, would stand in her way.

Chapter 4

A t a few minutes before three o'clock in the morning, Daughtry led Poco from his stall. She walked him out past the stables and corrals and moved silently toward the open range. She prayed that she was doing the right thing by leaving, and a part of her sincerely thought she was. She remembered her mother saying on more than one occasion that God often expected a person to step out in faith. Mounting Poco in the New Mexican darkness, Daughtry figured this was as big a step of faith as she could possibly make.

The ride into town was uneventful, and when Daughtry arrived, she quickly tied Poco up outside of the church, knowing that Pastor David would recognize the horse and get him back to Piñon Canyon. She wished she could take Poco with her. At least then she'd have something to comfort herself with at the end of her trip. But arranging to take Poco would require her making her presence known to the freight agent, and he would no doubt remember where she had gone when her father came looking.

Knowing the church would be open, Daughtry took her two heavy bags and slipped inside the dark protection of the sanctuary. Quickly, she pulled on clothes she'd borrowed from Pepita in order to board the train and not be recognized. She pulled a heavy shawl over her head and secured it under her chin. Then, taking her bags in hand, Daughtry made her way to the train depot.

Only a handful of people waited for the five-thirty eastbound. Gratefully, Daughtry didn't recognize any of them. She waited in the shadows, however, just in case one of them recognized her. When the train whistle blasted through the early morning silence, though, Bandelero was just coming awake, and no one Daughtry knew was anywhere to be seen.

Daughtry grew fidgety waiting for her turn to board, but as soon as she took her place on the nearly empty train car, she began to relax. Freedom, she thought to herself, came at a high price, but she was sure it would be worth it.

Looking out the soot-smudged window, she nearly ducked down at the sight of Dr. Monroe, or Dr. Dan as she affectionately called him. He was hurrying down the street, however, black bag tucked under his arm and a look of determination on his face, and he never glanced at the train. No doubt another medical emergency, Daughtry thought.

Soon the train began its journey, and Daughtry breathed a sigh of relief. When they reached the town of Springer, the conductor announced an hour wait while they took on several carloads of cattle. Daughtry realized this would be the perfect opportunity to find a minister and have the proxy marriage ceremony performed.

Hurrying through the town, she wondered to herself what minister in his right mind would marry two strangers together. *What if I can't find someone willing to do the job?* Worry flooded her soul. What if she had to turn back, or worse, meet Mr. Dawson without the marriage in place as he'd requested?

Daughtry's worries were for naught, however. The first minister she approached was more than happy to take her offering of five dollars to perform the proxy service. Armed with marriage papers in hand, Daughtry made her way back to the train, ten minutes before it pulled out and headed east to her new home.

Staring out the window, Daughtry felt something akin to excitement and foolish regret, both at the same time. She was a married woman! She was no longer Daughtry Ann Lucas. Now, she was Daughtry Dawson, wife of Nicholas.

Taking out the photograph of her husband, Daughtry tried to imagine what type of man he was. He looked tall, and she could see that he was broad-shouldered. He looked strong and healthy, maybe even older than she. She realized with a start that she had no idea how old her husband was. Nor did she know whether he'd ever been married before or if he had children.

"What have I done?" she questioned softly, then glanced around quickly to make certain no one else had heard her.

When the train finally arrived at Daughtry's destination, she panicked. Nicholas wouldn't know she was coming. She hadn't sent a telegram or tried to telephone or anything else that would let him know of her arrival. She'd brought a small amount of money with her, enough to rent a room for the night, but fear gnawed at her like a hungry animal. Daughtry had never been on her own before.

She stepped from the train and immediately signaled a man to assist her. "Do you know where the Nicholas Dawson ranch is located?" she asked the man.

"No, Ma'am. I can't rightly say I've ever heard of the man."

Daughtry's face fell. Just as she was about to ask the man who might know, another voice sounded from behind her.

"Did I hear you say you were lookin' for the Dawson place?"

Daughtry turned and met the eyes of a dust-laden stranger. The man was older than her father, but his shoulders and chest were massive.

"Yes," she managed to say. "I need to get to Nicholas Dawson's ranch."

"Well, you're in luck," the man said in a noncommittal way. "I'm on my way out there with this load of freight. I just have to finish picking up the rest of it and we can be on our way."

Daughtry sighed aloud. "You, Sir, are an answer to prayer."

The man snorted at her declaration and pointed to his wagon. "You just wait over there and I'll be with you directly. These your bags?" he questioned, glancing at the luggage beside Daughtry.

"Yes."

"That all you brought?"

"Yes," Daughtry replied and ignored his look of curiosity.

Without another word, the man took the bags, threw them up into the freight wagon, and went off in the direction of the train. Daughtry hurriedly planted herself by the wagon and was relieved when the man returned fifteen minutes later to finish stacking the cargo.

The afternoon was late when Daughtry and the freighter finally arrived at the Dawson ranch. The man had offered her no name, and, in return, Daughtry hadn't explained who she was. Now, as the man unloaded his wagon and stacked lumber and supplies inside a rather rundown barn, Daughtry glanced around nervously for her husband. When the freighter finished and Nicholas had still not appeared, Daughtry grew frightened.

"Are you certain this property belongs to Nicholas Dawson?"

"Sure as I am of anything," the man replied. "I've been bringing supplies out here for weeks now. He's gone a lot, which would explain why he isn't out here to greet us now. I notice his horse is gone, so there's no telling where he is or when he'll be back. Did he expect you?"

"No. Well, yes." Daughtry tried to answer reasonably. "He didn't know what day I would get here. Tell me, what else do you know about Mr. Dawson?"

The man eyed her suspiciously for a moment. "Don't know much. He's new to these parts. Took this old place off the hands of Widow Cummings and declared he wanted to turn it into a fine ranch again. Other than that, I don't guess I know anything else."

"You have met him though?"

"Sure," the man said and scratched his head. "I take it you haven't?"

Daughtry shook her head. "No, I haven't met him yet. I have his picture and a letter, but that's all."

"You kin of his?"

"No," Daughtry replied and smiled weakly. "I'm his wife." The man burst out laughing, and Daughtry felt foolish for having mentioned the matter.

"Well, I'll be. I heard he was after gettin' himself hitched. Didn't find any prospects in our little town though, and I heard tell he advertised in the papers for one. Is that how you came to marry him?"

Daughtry felt completely stupid. "Yes," she managed to whisper, "that's how it happened."

"Well, I wish you the best, Mrs. Dawson," the man said, climbing up into the wagon. "Here." He turned to rummage under the seat of his buckboard and handed her something down. "You might want to order something, then I'll have a reason to come back out this way."

Daughtry stared down at the Sears and Roebuck catalog the freighter had just handed her. Daughtry greatly needed his gesture of kindness. "Thank you," she said softly. "You have been so very kind. What do I owe you for the ride out?"

"Not a thing, pretty lady. Not a thing." He retrieved his hat, tipped it to her, and moved his horses back out to the road. Within minutes, the dust of his wagon faded into the distance, leaving Daughtry all alone in the middle of nowhere.

"I've brought this on myself," Daughtry said, squaring her shoulders with a look of determination. "I've just got to make the best of it."

She took her bags in hand and headed toward the rundown house. Staring at it in the soft glow of early evening light, Daughtry realized it was sorely neglected. No wonder Nicholas needed a woman who was willing to work hard. *Well,* Daughtry thought to herself, *this will be a challenge, and I will meet it head on and with a light heart.*

Her resolve lasted as long as it took to get through the back mud porch and into the kitchen. She could see well enough to realize that the place was hopelessly filthy and in need of more than just a little attention.

Setting her mind to the work at hand, Daughtry decided to do as much as she could to put the place in order before her husband returned. She quickly lighted several lamps and explored the rest of the house in order to determine what should be done first.

Through the kitchen, Daughtry found a small but promising dining room. This connected to a small parlor, and this in turn came out onto a short hall that blended into a vestibule of sorts that ended at the front door. Crossing the hall, Daughtry found a larger sitting room filled with an assortment of odd looking crates, furniture, and a wood stove that had been used recently but not cleaned in a long time. Finding more lamps here, Daughtry lit another and left it to radiate a cheery glow in the room, while she continued to explore.

Back in the hall, she turned and opened the door to a small closet. Farther down, she noticed two more doors and opened one into a small room that looked as though it had been a sewing room at one time. Hadn't the freighter said the ranch belonged to a widow before Nicholas bought it?

The other door opened into the bedroom, and Daughtry became suddenly aware of Nicholas's masculine presence. Several articles of clothing lay around the room in disarray. Putting the lamp on the nightstand beside the four poster bed, Daughtry picked up a black suit coat and held it in front of her. The shoulders were broader than she'd even imagined. Nicholas must be quite a large man, Daughtry surmised, by the look of his coat.

She picked up other items and stared at them, as if hoping they would answer her unspoken questions. Picking up a pair of discarded jeans, Daughtry held them against her, trying to get an idea of how Nicholas' size might contrast to her own. She'd worn her brothers' clothes on many occasions, but they'd always been old clothes they had long outgrown. These were the clothes of a man, not a boy, and Daughtry knew there was no comparison.

Realizing that the sky was getting darker and feeling the need to relieve herself, Daughtry went back down the hall and made her way outside. She instantly spotted the outhouse and started across the yard.

For a moment, she paused to take in the beauty of the sunset. The sun looked like a ball of molten scarlet against the fading colors of the sky. Lavender, so dusty and dark that it was nearly purple, blended into streaks of blue and amber. Daughtry hugged her arms against her body and thanked God for the wonder of it.

"Only God can paint the sky like that," she sighed.

Back in the house, Daughtry realized she could do little about the house's untidiness so late in the day. She found a can of peaches and a tin of crackers and made her supper on these. Morning would surely prove to offer her more understanding of her new home.

When she'd finished with the meager provisions, Daughtry extinguished all the lamps but the one she carried with her. She took her bags and made her way to the bedroom. Her only thought was to get a good night's sleep, but when she was actually in the room once again, Daughtry grew uncomfortable. Should she sleep in his bed? What if he came home in the night?

She was about to make a pallet on the floor, when a mouse scurried across the room and out the door. With a shriek of fright, Daughtry's mind was made up. Nicholas or no Nicholas, she was sleeping in the bed!

Chapter 5

Daughtry tried to ignore her concern for the absent husband she'd never met. Three days had passed since she'd arrived at the ranch, and Nicholas had still not come back. Trying to soothe her worry, Daughtry set up Nicholas's picture on the small table in the kitchen and, as she worked, she talked to him as though he were there.

"I'm going to have to start bringing up wood," she said absentmindedly. "It's getting considerably colder and pretty soon it's bound to snow. I used the last of the coal, or at least what I could find, so I guess I'll just have to go down to that grove of trees and see what I can find there."

Daughtry had worked wonders with the place and, in spite of her nervous state of mind, she was pleased with the way things were shaping up. She'd inventoried the supplies and managed to find a pantry just off the kitchen that she'd not seen in her first day of exploring. Nicholas had laid up quite a store of canned goods and smoked meats, as well as plenty of flour, sugar, soda, and salt. Daughtry nearly cried in joy at the sight of so much food.

Her first project had been to clean the kitchen. She reasoned that if she could have this one room in perfect order, she could easily work with the others at her leisure. Going around the room, she noted what was worth keeping and what was plain and simple trash. The curtains were still in good shape but needed to be washed, so Daughtry removed them and began heating water in the biggest pot she could find.

Piece by piece, she emptied the room, until nothing remained but the dirty black stove and the empty ice-box. She found soap in the supplies that the freighter had left in the barn, as well as brushes and a well-made broom. Taking these, she scrubbed the grime from the walls, floors, counters, and cabinets, until everything was spotless. After this, she tackled the stove, washing it thoroughly until she was satisfied that she could cook food without fear of catching something from the filth.

Bit by bit, the room took shape, and Daughtry continued to talk to Nicholas as though he were there, relating her plans as she continued.

She went to work cleaning the small table and chairs that had set in the kitchen, as well as the pie saver and jelly cabinet that she'd taken outside. She was just about to move them indoors, when she remembered something in the barn.

Setting out across the yard, Daughtry opened the barn door and went inside. After several minutes of searching, she returned to the house with a bucket of white paint and a brush. Maybe Nicholas hadn't planned on the house being painted inside, but Daughtry thought a fresh coat of whitewash would help matters a great deal. If he were mad at her, then she'd just have to apologize and try to fix the matter. That was, if he ever showed up.

More nosing around revealed a wealth of useful household goods, and Daughtry began to take courage from the way the house shaped up. The kitchen was actually attractive now with its freshly painted walls and cabinets. The shelves were lined with sparkling dishes from sets that Daughtry had found in crates in the large sitting room, and the pots gleamed from her hours of scrubbing.

Every night, Daughtry went to bed more exhausted than the night before. After the second day, she'd made notable progress with the bedroom, feeling that this was the next place to be put in order. After wrestling the mattress outside and beating it until the entire yard looked like the middle of a dust storm, Daughtry scrubbed down the room and furniture. Finally, she washed every article of clothing and all of the linens before deeming the bedroom acceptable.

She didn't have long to wonder what she'd need to turn her attention to next. When it rained on the second night, Daughtry learned quickly that the roof was leaky. Steady drips fell from the ceiling in more than one place, and Daughtry knew that her job in the morning would consist of trying to repair and reshingle her roof.

She barely had time to worry about her husband. For all she knew, he didn't even exist, except that she had papers that told her otherwise. Every day, she tried to make ready for his return. She wanted very much to prove herself worthy in his eyes. And oh, what eyes, she thought as she drifted into sleep. Dark, dark eyes that seemed to laugh at some private joke. Dark eyes that Daughtry prayed would behold her with love and devotion.

Daughtry rose early, thankful that the storm had passed early in the night. She pulled on the set of boy's clothes she'd brought with her from home, finding them much easier to work in, and planned her day.

She set bread out to rise and made herself some breakfast before considering the roof. The kitchen was chilly, and Daughtry was grateful for the warmth of the stove. She reminded herself that leaky roofs could be lived with as long as she could keep a fire warming the house. With that in mind, she decided to bring more wood up to the house before worrying herself with anything else.

The day was rapidly getting away from her, and the sky was clouding up again. Daughtry knew she should at least try to check the roof out and see if she could do anything about the leaks, just in case it rained again that night.

Making her way to the barn, Daughtry found an old wooden ladder and took it with her to the house. She climbed up on top, noting several very soft spots, and began picking away at the tattered shingles. She was used to adobe houses, but this clapboard house she now called home was very similar to some of the other buildings at Piñon Canyon. Daughtry had helped her father and brothers on more than one occasion with roofing, repairing, and building. She had loved working alongside her family and learning every aspect of how to make the ranch run prosperously.

This was the first time Daughtry had allowed herself to remember her family and tears came to her eyes. Were they worried about her? Of course they were, she chided herself. Her father would be frantic, even though she'd left them a long letter explaining her need to get out on her own. Would they ever forgive her for stealing away in the night? Would she ever be welcomed back?

Exhaustion overwhelmed Daughtry as she climbed into bed that night. How she longed for a bath in a tub of hot water. But for now, she had to settle for washing out of the kitchen sink, where she poured pans of heated water. Perhaps she could talk Nicholas into purchasing a tub—if he ever showed up.

She drifted immediately into sleep, succumbing to the strain of the days that had passed in heavy, never-ending work. Daughtry dreamed of dark eyes and a handsome face, wondering where her husband was and why he'd not returned. The picture of Nicholas faded into that of her father's angry image, and Daughtry tossed restlessly as she sought to escape his rage.

Then the dream took another path, one that Daughtry had never before envisioned. She was being held safe and warm in muscular arms. Snuggling closer, Daughtry felt a hand run through her long hair. Sighing, she relished the dream. This would be what it was like to be held by Nicholas, she decided.

Then, to her surprise, Daughtry felt warm lips against her cheek. They trailed down to capture her lips, and Daughtry returned the kiss.

In the foggy uncertainty of sleep, Daughtry struggled to open her eyes. A part of her wanted to go on sleeping so that she could enjoy the dream, but another part of her was being beckoned. She could almost hear someone calling her name.

Daughtry tried to concentrate on the voice but it faded, and as it did, she became more awake, until she suddenly realized that she wasn't alone. Opening her eyes wide, Daughtry stared into the amused dark eyes of Nicholas Dawson.

For a moment all Daughtry could do was stare. Was she dreaming or was this real? The shocked look on her face caused the man beside her to chuckle.

"I–I—" Daughtry couldn't speak a coherent word to save herself. Shyly, she pulled her arms from the man's neck and tried to ease away from him, as if he wouldn't notice.

Nicholas sat up and Daughtry could see he was fully clothed and sitting atop the covers she so carefully clutched to her neck. With a grin he spoke. "I sure hope you're my wife."

Daughtry saw nothing amusing about the situation. She was trembling from head to toe, and whether it was from the shock of finding Nicholas in her bed or from the passion he'd awoke in her, Daughtry wasn't sure.

In a flash, Daughtry leaped from the bed and ran for the door. She knew her long flannel nightgown wouldn't offer her much coverage, but she wasn't about to stop and retrieve her robe on the way out the door. She reached for the handle and had just turned it, when Nicholas was beside her.

"Don't go. I'm sorry I scared you. It wasn't very nice of me, but I couldn't help myself." His voice was rich and warm, just as Daughtry knew it would be. Daughtry let her hand slip from the handle, but she couldn't bring herself to face her husband.

Slowly, as if dealing with a terrified child, Nicholas turned her to face him. "I'm Nicholas Dawson, although I'm sure you've already figured that out. You look just like your picture."

Daughtry lifted her face to meet his. "You too," she whispered.

Nicholas smiled and his eyes lit up. "I never figured on getting such a beauty for a wife. I wasn't even sure you'd agree, what with me in such a hurry and all. I'm sorry I wasn't here when you arrived. I had to be away on business, and I just got back this morning."

Daughtry nodded and looked away. Her senses were suddenly raging with all that she was seeing, hearing, and feeling. As if realizing she needed the space, Nicholas stepped back and waited for her to speak.

"I'm Daughtry Lucas, I mean, Dawson," she said nervously. She took a deep breath to steady her nerves. "I didn't know when you'd be back. I took some liberty with the house. I'm sorry if I overstepped my rights, I mean, I didn't know what you'd expect of a wife, and I, well. . ." Daughtry stopped as she realized she was rambling and twisting her nightgown.

Nicholas just grinned at her, making the whole situation even more uncomfortable. Daughtry glanced at the bed, and her face flushed crimson.

Noting where her gaze ended, Nicholas reached out and touched Daughtry's cheek. "I really am sorry for startling you. I should have waited until you woke up good and proper, but I haven't always used the sense the good Lord gave me. What say you get dressed and come on out to the kitchen and we'll talk?"

Daughtry was mesmerized by the way his thumb was rubbing her jawline. His fingers were on her neck, and the warmth of their contact against her bare skin sent tremors through Daughtry that she couldn't control.

Surprising them both, Daughtry jumped from the door and moved back to the end of the bed. "I've got my things in here," she said motioning to the wardrobe. "If you'll wait in the other room, I'll get dressed."

Nicholas nodded, the smile never leaving his face. When he had gone from the room, closing the door firmly behind him, Daughtry's knees gave out and she crumpled to the floor.

"Dear God," she prayed in a whisper, "I've really done it this time. Please help me to know what to do and say, and please don't let Nicholas be mad about the paint. Amen."

Getting dressed as quickly as she could, Daughtry laughed to herself. *Paint? I'm worried about paint?*

Chapter 6

Daughtry hurried into the kitchen to find her husband sitting comfortably at the small table. She pulled her apron from a hook near the door and tied it around her trim waist. Nicholas watched all of this in complete silence, surprised at the control Daughtry seemed to have managed to regain in her few minutes alone.

He watched her as she put wood in the stove and got the fire going. He was more than a little impressed at what he'd found upon his return. Truth be told, he nearly walked back out the door, fearing that he'd entered the wrong house. A double take confirmed that he was indeed in the right house but that a transformation of tremendous proportions had taken place. Now looking at the petite and delicate woman he'd married, Nicholas was even more surprised.

Daughtry put a pot of coffee on the stove and turned to question her husband.

"What would you like for breakfast?"

Nicholas smiled to himself. He hadn't had someone to wait on him since leaving home and that seemed a million years ago. "Whatever you're having," he replied and leaned back against the chair.

Daughtry looked thoughtful for a moment. "Well, I have fresh bread and of course there are the canned foods. I wasn't able to locate any eggs or potatoes, so I can't really do you justice with anything grand. I could make tortillas and heat up some of the meat from the pantry." She fell silent and shrugged her shoulders. "I was just going to have toasted bread and jam."

"Sounds fine for me as well."

Daughtry nodded and went back to work, while Nicholas continued his silent study. He figured she was about five feet, four inches tall. Surely no taller, and she couldn't weigh more than one hundred pounds. She had pulled her hair up into a loose bun of rich copper. He liked the shade, never even imagining from her photograph what color her hair might be. She had a sweet face. Almost angelic, he thought. In fact, she looked so childlike that Nicholas suddenly sat up with a start.

"How old are you?"

"A lady should never reveal her age, Mr. Dawson." Her smile was brief and Nicholas caught her teasing tone. "However, because you are my hus-

146

band and entitled to know full well what you've saddled yourself with, I will admit that I'm quite old."

Nicholas laughed at this, and the amusement lingered in his eyes. "How old?"

"I'm twenty-three. I'll be twenty-four in January," Daughtry said with something akin to regret in her voice.

"A mere baby," he chided and was rewarded with a look of sincere appreciation in his wife's eyes. Had someone honestly told this slip of girl that she was old?

Daughtry brought the toast and coffee to the table, then retrieved two mugs, a knife, and the jam before sitting opposite Nicholas.

"Would you ask the blessing?" she asked rather timidly.

"Certainly," he said without a second thought and bowed his head. "Father, thank You for this food and the hard labors of this industrious young woman. I ask that You would bless this house and this union between Daughtry and me and let us live our days devoted to You, Amen."

Daughtry looked up filled with wonder. "That was a beautiful prayer. Especially asking God to bless our marriage." She paused for a moment, then jumped right into the matter. "We do have a rather strange arrangement here, don't we?"

Amused, Nicholas reached out and took several pieces of toast. He liberally slathered jam across each piece and handed two to Daughtry before replying. "Strange doesn't half seem to explain it."

Daughtry poured the coffee and began to feel at ease. "I've always been a very straightforward kind of woman, Mr. Dawson."

"Please don't call me Mr. Dawson. Call me Nicholas or Nick, but not that."

Daughtry smiled. "All right. As I was saying, I like to be honest about things and I don't like to play games, at least not people games. Do you know what I mean?"

"I think so," he said with a gentleness in his expression that further dispelled Daughtry's anxieties.

"I've never been the kind of person to jump into things without real regard to the consequences, but this time seems to be an exception. I'm not sure I did the right thing in marrying you, but it is done and I don't believe in divorce or annulments. I just wanted you to know that I take our marriage very seriously." Nicholas stared at her soberly while she continued. "I intend to make you a good wife. I will work hard, and I know a great deal about ranching. I'm not weak or fragile, and I've spent most all of my life working outdoors alongside. . ." Daughtry stopped abruptly. "Well," she continued hesitantly, "I've spent a lot of time working at the kind of things that will build this place into a respectable and profitable ranch."

A smile played at the corners of Nicholas's lips. "Anything else?"

Daughtry put her coffee down and took a deep breath. "I suppose I should say that I'm a Christian. I believe in walking close with the Lord and reading the Word every day. I like to go to church and fellowship with other believers, and I will never do anything willingly that goes against the laws of God."

"I see."

Daughtry pressed on lest she lose her nerve. "I'm a very devoted person to those I love and care for. I will endeavor to be whatever you need me to be." She was blushing profusely at this point. "And, while I know very little about you, I am very teachable and happy to learn."

Nicholas reached out and put his hand over hers. "What about children?"

Daughtry's eyes flashed up to meet his. "I love children."

Nicholas patted her hand and smiled. "Good, because I do too and hope that we can fill this house with a dozen or more."

Daughtry's eyes widened at his boldness. "Well, I don't know if I love them that much." Her teasing was clearly evident and Nicholas laughed.

"I think I'm going to enjoy being married to you, Daughtry. I, too, have had my misgivings about marrying a person of which I knew nothing more about than the fact that she had beautiful penmanship and took a lovely picture."

Daughtry started to thank him for the compliment, but he continued to speak. "I did, however, pray about this matter and felt that God's answer was found in your letter. I worried that perhaps my desire to rush the marriage would put you off, but again I prayed and asked God to intercede and bring the event about. And, well, here you are, and I must say that I am more than a little bit impressed with the answer God's given. Not only are you the loveliest woman I've had the pleasure of knowing, but you're intelligent, witty, and very charming. Not to mention that you've accomplished in a few short days what I believe would have taken most men weeks to do."

Daughtry remembered the paint and grimaced. "I used your paint," she said, still not sure why it upset her so much. "I saw it with the supplies in the barn and, while I was cleaning the kitchen, I thought it looked like it could use a good coat. I hope you aren't upset with me. I didn't mean to use something without permission."

Nicholas stared at her rather sternly for a moment before replying. "What I have is yours, Daughtry. How could I possibly fault you for benefiting us both? That's just another thing I like about you. You're willing to just get in there and do what needs to be done. That's to your credit. You aren't one of those sad little women who sit around all lost and doe-eyed, waiting for their husband to instruct them in what they should do next. I like what you've done here, so stop fretting." Daughtry relaxed, realizing he was completely sincere.

"I do have some questions, though," Nicholas said, surprising her. Daughtry nodded to show her willingness to answer but was even more surprised with the topic of his question. "Have you ever been in love?"

Daughtry thought back through her life, especially the years before Julie had died. She'd found more than one cowboy fascinating company, but only on friendly terms. She couldn't honestly remember feeling anything akin to what she was feeling for Nicholas, however, and that gave her reason to believe that she'd actually fallen in love with her husband.

"No," she answered softly.

"Me neither," he offered. "I just wondered if there were any ghosts that needed to be laid to rest. You know, broken hearts, lost loves, that kind of thing."

Daughtry shook her head. "I can honestly say there was no one."

"Why were you inclined to answer my advertisement?" he continued.

"I guess," she began, "that your advertisement intrigued me. I thought the whole notion sounded, well, rather," she hesitated and looked away, "romantic."

"I've never been called romantic before."

"I find that hard to believe," Daughtry replied without thinking.

"Why's that?" Nicholas questioned, honestly wanting to know what was going through his young wife's mind.

Daughtry shifted uncomfortably. "Do I have to answer that?"

Nicholas laughed. "I'd sure like it if you did."

"Very well," she murmured and tried to reason out her words before speaking. "You strike me as a very considerate man," she began, "a man who would be most sought after by the ladies of his community. You are very. . ." She swallowed several times, then took a drink of coffee.

"I am very what?" He sensed her discomfort but was completely captivated with what she had to say.

"You are very handsome," she said. "I was very taken with your photograph and the way you signed your letter."

"The way I signed my letter?"

Nicholas leaned back in his chair and waited for her to explain. If she took all day, he wanted to hear exactly what she had to say.

Daughtry blushed and confusion filled her mind. "Forever yours," she whispered. "You signed your letter, 'Forever yours.' "

Nicholas smiled. He'd purposefully chosen that very ending after remembering it from one of his father's letters to his mother. His mother had told Nicholas once that the phrase was more than mere words, it was a pledge of sorts, and she had cherished it greatly. Now his own wife seemed to savor the words for the exact same reason.

"Something I learned from my father," he explained.

Daughtry used that introduction to Nicholas's past to question him further. "Tell me about yourself."

Nicholas shrugged. "Not much to tell. Nobody ever baked me bread as good as this, that's for sure."

"I'm serious," Daughtry said, pouring more coffee into her empty cup. "What about your family?"

"What about yours?"

"I'm alone," Daughtry replied.

"Me too," her husband replied and furthered her frustration.

"How am I to get to know you, if you won't tell me about yourself?" questioned Daughtry softly.

Nicholas leaned forward and smiled, revealing gleaming white teeth and eyes that fairly danced. "We have a lifetime to get to know one another," he answered. "I just don't think we need to do it all at one time. I'm going to enjoy getting to know you, little by little."

Without another word, Daughtry got to her feet, left the room for a moment, and returned with papers in hand.

"These are the marriage documents," she said, handing them to Nicholas.

Nicholas read them over and cast a glance upward to meet Daughtry's eyes. "Our wedding day was the twenty-first of September?"

Daughtry nodded.

"Wish I could have been there. I'll bet you were something to behold." Daughtry laughed at this, and Nicholas smiled broadly at her. "Did I say something wrong?"

"No, it's just that I look a whole sight better now than I did that day. Later, I'll show you what I was wearing."

Nicholas got up and went to the front sitting room where he retrieved a lock box, which he promptly brought back with him to the table. Taking a key from his vest pocket, he unlocked the box and carefully put the papers inside. Daughtry noticed when he did that her picture and letter were also inside the box, along with a large amount of money.

"They should be safe here," he announced and held up the key. "If you need anything, money or such, or you want to put something in here, just holler."

Daughtry nodded. "Just a minute, please," she said and went to the bedroom.

When she walked back into the kitchen, she thrust some money into

Nicholas's hands. "I'd like to add this to your savings," she whispered. "It's all I had left after the trip."

Nicholas took the money and met Daughtry's eyes. He knew what she was doing and felt what she was trying to say without even hearing the words. He nodded, placed the money with his own, and shut the box. "Our savings," he said, locking the box and handing Daughtry the key. It was his way of meeting her trust with his own.

Daughtry reached up, but instead of taking the key, simply closed her hand around Nicholas's and smiled. "I'm content for you to have control."

Chapter 7

D aughtry felt as though she lived a lifetime within a single day. Nicholas asked her to share with him all that she'd done in his absence, and Daughtry happily complied. He seemed especially impressed with the large stack of wood she'd positioned near the back of the house.

"I couldn't find any more coal," she explained, "so I did the next best thing."

"Those must be some arms you have," he teased and reached out to gently caress her upper arm. "Hmm, you don't feel like a lumberjack."

Daughtry giggled and looked at him shyly. "I felt like one and I think I probably got as dirty as one. I went down to that grove of trees by the creek," she said and pointed. "There was quite a bit of dead wood there, and I just made good use of it."

"I have a load of coal coming," Nicholas said, reluctantly removing his hand from her arm. "It ought to get here tomorrow or the next day at the latest. I also arranged for the ice man to deliver here until the creek freezes. I figure I can manage to keep us supplied through the winter."

Daughtry felt her skin tingle long after Nicholas had stopped touching her. She barely heard his words as he continued to speak of his arrangements for the ranch.

"I thought we might go into town tomorrow. We could purchase some of the things we'll need for the winter and also get some staples that I didn't have on hand. Milk and eggs ought to be readily available."

"A milk cow and chickens would suit us better," Daughtry said without thinking.

"I suppose that's true enough," Nicholas said thoughtfully, "but with winter coming on and us not having the ranch really prepared for livestock, I thought maybe we'd just rely on store bought."

"I guess that makes sense," Daughtry replied, walking with slow even strides beside her husband.

They paused at the broken down corral, and Nicholas leaned against a piece of fencing. The wind had picked up a bit and blew wisps of Daughtry's hair across her face.

Daughtry noticed the look of hesitancy in her husband's eyes, and she couldn't help but wonder if he were hiding something from her. How could she know what type of man he'd been before or what type he'd be now? Mother had once said that people always proved their true nature by their actions. Well, so far Nicholas's actions had given Daughtry little to fear.

"What do you suppose we should do first?" he asked her seriously.

Daughtry's introspection was released as she shrugged. "It all depends on your plans."

"What would you suggest?"

Daughtry smiled. "Well, being a woman, I suggest the house be put in order first. When I was trying to repair the roof the other day. . ."

"What? You were up on the roof?" Nicholas interrupted.

Daughtry felt her face flush. "Not exactly ladylike, was it?"

Nicholas laughed. "Ladylike or not, I'm amazed at your abilities. Did you actually get up there to fix the roof?"

Daughtry nodded, feeling rather proud. "I was inspired. The second night here it rained so hard that I had puddles all through the house. I can't say I accomplished much, but it was a healthy start."

"I guess that's what I'll do first then," Nicholas said with a thoughtful glance back at the house. "What else?"

Daughtry smiled. He genuinely wanted her to have a say in the matter. "Well, I'd like to cart everything out of the house and clean it good before winter sets in," Daughtry admitted. "As you could see, I only managed to set the kitchen and bedroom to rights before your return."

"Two very important rooms, if I do say so myself," Nicholas remarked.

"I figured it that way too," Daughtry said and, without thinking of the implications, added, "after all, I figured most of my time would be spent in one place or the other." The words were no sooner out than Daughtry realized how they sounded. She clapped her hand over her mouth.

Nicholas laughed until he doubled over, and Daughtry turned crimson, knowing he must think her terribly forward.

"I didn't mean," she started to justify herself, then realized she would only make matters worse by continuing.

Nicholas straightened up and tried to control his mirth. "That's quite all right, Honey," he said with tears of laughter gleaming in his eyes. "I pretty well figured what you meant."

Daughtry had to turn away to hide her embarrassment at her own statement. *Sometimes,* she thought, *I say the stupidest things.*

Nicholas sobered as if he'd noticed her discomfort. "So we empty the house," he said matter-of-factly, "and we wash it all down. Then what?"

"We put it all back inside," she answered softly. "Of course, if we don't want something back in the house, we can store it in the barn. I don't really know where you want things, so it might be nice if you had a part in the sorting through."

"I'm not sure what's even in there," Nicholas admitted. He stared at Daughtry's back for a moment before continuing. "I bought the place as is from a widow woman who wanted to move back East to live with her daughter. She'd let the place run down to this state and was barely able to feed herself. I heard from the sheriff in town that they were considering trying to force her out for her own good, so I came out here and we made a deal. She left a lot behind, but I have no idea whether it's useful stuff or just junk."

Daughtry nodded and finally turned to meet Nicholas's gaze. "I uncrated the dishes," she said, "but I didn't go through much else. I guess we can do that together, if you like."

"It would be my pleasure. Now, why don't you tell me about our grove of trees. Did you see anything of value there?"

"There were several apple trees, and I think I recognized a plum or two. Would you like to walk down there?"

"Yes," Nicholas replied. "I'd like that."

Daughtry began to walk at a fairly good pace. She was disturbed for some reason by the feelings Nicholas brought about. She thought back to the days she'd spent with nothing more than his picture and realized how much she'd lost her heart to him. *He can't possibly feel the same way,* she scolded herself. *Men are much more level-headed about such matters.* Nicholas obviously needed a hard-working wife, and he probably hadn't wanted to waste his time with romantic notions and courting.

Daughtry was so lost in these thoughts that she didn't pay any attention to the ground she was covering. Before she could tell what was happening, she lost her footing on a large rock and fell forward.

Nicholas's arm shot out in a flash and encircled her waist protectively. He pulled her upright, then, as though he were doing the most natural thing in the world, he pulled her close against him.

Daughtry stared up into his face, knowing he would kiss her. She saw the questioning look in his eyes, as though he were asking permission. Without thought, she reached her hand up to the back of his head and pulled his face down to meet hers.

Nicholas needed no more encouragement. He quickly captured her lips with his own and kissed her so ardently that Daughtry forgot for a moment who and where she was. When he pulled away, Daughtry uttered the first thing that came to mind.

"I love you, Nicholas! I have ever since seeing your picture." Daughtry no longer cared that the declaration sounded like that of an infatuated teenager. She meant the words with all her heart. She really did love this man.

Nicholas held her at arm's length for a moment. The troubled look on his face brought Daughtry back to reality. Somehow, she had offended him.

"I'm sorry," she whispered and walked backwards a step. "That must sound insincere. After all, we've known each other for such a short time." She turned to go back to the house, wanting to run away and hide from her feelings and the man she'd so clearly startled.

Nicholas crossed the distance between them and halted Daughtry from going any farther. "I don't believe you could be insincere if you tried," he whispered.

Daughtry lifted her face, revealing all the emotion and misgivings she felt. "Please don't be angry with me. It's just that I haven't had much practice at things like this. Maybe it's because I've never felt this way before." She shrugged her shoulders before continuing. "My mouth gets a little ahead of itself sometimes, as you've witnessed before."

Nicholas shook his head. "I'm not angry. Surprised, yes, but not angry."

Daughtry nodded and tried to think of something she could say to negate her declaration of love. Short of lying, however, she didn't know what she could say. She meant her words of love. As crazy and untimely as it seemed, Daughtry knew they were truer than anything else she'd said to Nicholas.

As if reading her mind, Nicholas took hold of her hand and squeezed it gently. "Just answer me this. Now that we're not in the middle of a kiss, did you mean it?"

Daughtry knew exactly what he was asking of her. "I meant it," she barely whispered. "I know it sounds impossible, but it's true. I never would have married you otherwise."

They walked back to the house in silence, but Daughtry felt the awkwardness between them. She knew Nicholas was taken aback by her statement, but she sensed that something more than just that was troubling him.

Without a word, they sat down at the table and stared at each other. When Nicholas finally did speak, Daughtry felt her heart skip a beat.

"Tell me about your family, Daughtry."

The soft request shouldn't have caused her such fear, but Daughtry felt confident that Nicholas would never allow her to stay if he knew the truth. And more than ever now, Daughtry didn't want to lose her husband and new life. She didn't want Nicholas to send her back home.

"I grew up on a ranch," she said carefully. "I learned just about everything there is to know. I can ride, shoot, rope, brand, mend fence, whatever.

I've nursed sick calves back to health, assisted with birthings, medicatings, and even helped to drive the herds to market. Ranching isn't just something I learned," she admitted. "It's something that's in my blood."

"But that doesn't answer my question. I want to know about your family. You said that you were alone, but there must have been someone with you at one time or another. What became of your father and mother? Do you have brothers or sisters?"

"I had a sister," Daughtry said, feeling it safe to speak of Julie. "She died several years ago when her horse slipped on an icy trail and went over the side of a ravine."

"I'm sorry. That must have been terribly hard on your folks."

"Yes, it was," Daughtry admitted before realizing that Nicholas had led her where she didn't want to go.

He was looking at her intensely now, expecting her to continue, but Daughtry knew she couldn't. "I don't want to talk about it anymore," she whispered and quickly left the room.

~

Nicholas stared at her chair for several minutes. What was she hiding and why did she look so fearful whenever he mentioned her past? Frustration began to build into anger at her distrust, but then Nicholas caught himself and realized that he had no room to express such thoughts. He was just as guilty of hiding from the past as she. Maybe it was what had brought them together. Maybe it was what God expected them both to deal with.

Chapter 8

The weeks that passed were the happiest Daughtry had ever known. She worked at Nicholas's side, laughing, teasing, and falling into a comfortable routine of being Mrs. Dawson. At night, they snuggled down under handmade quilts to share each other's warmth. Beneath the covers, they talked and dreamed about the future.

Daughtry loved it all. Not a single part of her new life caused her regret, except that she had to avoid her past. She started having nightmares about her father coming to tear her away from Nicholas's strong arms, but she choked back her fears and refused to let them surface. She couldn't risk losing all that had come to mean so much to her.

But, try as she might, Daughtry couldn't forget her family, nor could she dispel the building anxieties that haunted her every waking moment. All she could do was pray and ask God to forgive her and guide her steps, convincing herself that nothing else needed to be done.

Sundays were always a joy to Daughtry. She prepared for church with great enthusiasm, though today the sniffles from a passing bout with a head cold caused her some discomfort.

Nicholas popped his head through the bedroom door with a grin as broad as the barn door opening. "You need help with the buttons, Mrs. Dawson?"

Daughtry looked up and shook her head. "You can't appreciate what we women have to go through in order to look just right for our men."

Nicholas rolled his eyes. "You always look just right to me, even when you're wearing those boys' jeans you seem to favor."

"Sometimes I wish I could wear jeans to church," Daughtry said with a giggle. "Especially when the wind whips up and comes blasting across the open range."

"Well, I'd better never find you wearing those things off the property. It wouldn't be decent to have all the townsmen following you around with their tongues hanging out."

"You sound just like my father," she replied without thinking. The words were no sooner out than she realized her mistake.

Coming to her, Nicholas pulled Daughtry into his arms. "Why are you so afraid to tell me about him? Did he hurt you?"

Daughtry shook her head.

"I promise to understand. Whatever it is—whatever he did to you. . . ." His words trailed into silence.

"He was a wonderful father," Daughtry said, still trembling beneath Nicholas's touch. She would say nothing more, though, and in frustration Nicholas released her.

"I'll get the wagon," he said and stalked out of the room.

Daughtry knew she'd hurt him by refusing to deal honestly with him. She comforted herself by remembering that Nicholas refused to share any real details of his own past with her. They were both hurting and hiding, she decided. They might as well do it together.

Daughtry was glad that Nicholas wasn't a man given to holding a grudge. By the time they headed into town he was laughing and joking about first one thing, then another.

After church they enjoyed a leisurely ride home, and Nicholas shared his plans to buy Daughtry a horse. Good horse flesh was something to get excited about, and Daughtry squealed her delight at the news and threw her arms around Nicholas's neck.

"You really mean it?" she asked, hugging him so tight that he had to stop the horses in order to control her.

"Yes. Yes," he said, laughing at her enthusiasm. "Who would've thought that a little ol' horse would have gotten me so much attention?"

"It's just that I've really missed riding," Daughtry said happily. "Back home, I used to ride every day. I had the most wonderful gelding named Poco. He was about fifteen hands high and had the most beautiful gray coat." She stopped talking because Nicholas was looking at her strangely.

Daughtry jumped back and hung her head. She'd done it again. She couldn't keep from bringing up her family and the home life she'd once loved. "He was a good horse," she finally said, when Nicholas wouldn't speak.

Nicholas remained silent and, when Daughtry said nothing more, he snapped the reins and sent the horse down the path to home.

Daughtry tried not to think about her family that night as she curled into her husband's arms. The day had brought on too many memories, and more than once she'd nearly told Nicholas everything just to be rid of the burden.

"Nicholas?" she whispered against his ear.

"Yeah?"

"I love you." Her voice sounded like a child's trying to get on the good side of an adult.

For a minute, Nicholas said nothing. He tightened his grip on her and sighed. "I don't think you can love me and not trust me," he finally replied.

Daughtry stiffened in his arms. "What would you know about it? You don't love me. At least you've never said that you do."

Nick chuckled at her little girl-like voice. "Never said I didn't, either."

Daughtry tried to ease away, but Nicholas would have no part of it. "Daughtry," he whispered her name and it sounded like a song. "Don't leave me."

Daughtry wanted to cry out that she'd never leave, but in the back of her mind that one thing spread panic through her like no other. She might not ever leave of her own accord, but what if her father forced her to leave?

"Never!" she declared in a whisper and settled down into his arms again.

Daughtry faded into a deep sleep, but soon she found herself in the middle of a most realistic nightmare. Her father had learned of her marriage to Nicholas, and now he had come to face him in some sort of showdown, straight out of the frontier days she'd heard so much about.

Tossing from side to side, Daughtry fought with the images, pleading with her father to leave things as they were. He was furious and unyielding, promising to take Daughtry back home where she belonged and to hurt Nicholas if he dared to interfere.

He quoted the Bible to her, as Daughtry fell to her knees at his feet. "Children are to obey their parents," she heard him say. Turning in her dream to face her husband, Daughtry cried out at the betrayal and pain she saw in his eyes.

"You can't be my wife, Daughtry. You are his daughter," Nicholas told her through the misty fog.

"No," Daughtry moaned softly in her sleep. "No."

"Daughtry!" Nicholas exclaimed and gently shook her shoulders.

"Oh, Nick," she cried and fell limp against him as though all of her strength had been drained away.

Gently, he eased back against the pillows, taking her with him. "Why don't you stop all of this and tell me what's wrong. Tell me what you're keeping from me that causes you to have such fitful nights."

Daughtry looked up at him in surprise. Nicholas just shook his head. "This isn't the first time, you know. You nearly flail me to death night after night. It's only getting worse, so you might as well deal with it here and now."

Daughtry knew he was right, but the fear in her heart caused her to hesitate. "You won't like it," she whispered.

"Why not let me be the judge of that?"

"Because I can already tell," Daughtry replied. "You're so serious about everything, and you handle things in such a mature way that I'm afraid this will make you very angry with me."

"Daughtry," Nicholas said, reaching out to touch her cheek, "I could never be angry with you. Tell me."

Daughtry wiped at her tears with the back of her sleeve, took a deep breath, and got up on her knees. "I ran away from home to marry you."

"What?" Nicholas's eyes widened in surprise. "Don't tell me you're really sixteen or something."

Daughtry laughed. "No, I'm honestly as old as I said. A woman wouldn't joke about a thing like that."

"Then why do you say you ran away?"

Daughtry folded her hands. "My father was devastated after my sister died. It will be four years this November—but he only gets worse with each year that passes. Julie's death caused him to become overprotective of me. Everywhere I went, either he or one of my five brothers was there to shadow my every step. He wouldn't let me meet anyone or court. That's why I never fell in love with anyone else. You have to understand, I love my father and brothers, but they were smothering me to death. Even my mother understood how I felt, but she couldn't seem to reason any sense into my father."

Daughtry could not bring herself to look at Nicholas's face as she continued. "We had a terrible argument the night before I learned of your advertisement. When I saw your ad in the paper, I thought it just might be my way out. I decided to write to you and at least learn more about you, but then you wrote back with the proxy and the train ticket." She paused. "And your picture."

She looked up to see that Nicholas had put his hands behind his head and was studying her intently. Fearing what he might say, she hurried on. "I was going to write to you and refuse the proposal. I thought I could reason with my father, but when I tried to ask him nicely to give me more space—to let me grow up and fall in love—he refused. I was so angry, that I wrote them a long letter and slipped out in the middle of the night to come to you. I didn't let them know I was marrying you, and I didn't say where I was going, only that I would be taken care of and safe."

She sighed. "I'm really sorry, Nicholas. I thought I was doing the right thing, or at least I thought it would work out to be the right thing. I saw it as an opportunity and I took it. Now, I keep having these horrible dreams that my father and brothers come to take me back. They're always so angry and ugly, and I never have a chance to save you."

By now she was crying and Nicholas could no longer remain aloof. "Five brothers?" he asked, his forehead wrinkling up in disbelief.

Daughtry only cried all the more and nodded her head. "I don't want to leave you. I don't want them to take me away." She nearly wailed the words, and Nicholas began to chuckle.

"No one is going to take you away from me, Daughtry. Especially not now, not after all this time has passed between us. You're a grown woman, and you made your choice. You're a married woman, and you belong with me." His words forcefully placed the boundaries for Daughtry to see.

"What's done is done," he added. "You can't let them worry about you, though. And you can't go on having nightmares every night. I have to believe that this father of yours must be someone pretty special. Otherwise, it wouldn't upset you so much. Tomorrow we'll go to town and you can telephone them; or we'll send a telegram. Either way, you have to let them know what you've done and that you're all right."

"You aren't mad at me?" she asked through her tears.

Nicholas opened his arms to her with a smile, and Daughtry nestled down eagerly. "How could I be mad at you?" he whispered and reached over to turn down the lamp. "I love you."

Chapter 9

Daughtry felt November's chill air breathe down her damp back. She was working to pull out the last of the brush that had once surrounded her house. Rising up and stretching, Daughtry relished the sun, mild as it was, and put her face upward to catch every single ray. Winter was soon to be upon them and, by all the signs, Daughtry feared it might be a difficult one.

Nicholas watched his wife from his vantage point in the barn loft. She grew more beautiful every day, and every day he knew he loved her more. How good of God to throw them together. He observed her as she went back to work, thinking back to the day they'd gone to the post office and mailed the letter to her father and mother.

"I don't think I can do this, Nicholas," she had said in a pleading tone that begged him to let her forget the whole thing.

"You have to," he'd insisted firmly. "Nothing bad will come of it, Daughtry. If your folks come here, they'll see how happy you are, and they won't even want you to leave."

At least Nicholas hoped things would work out that way. He continued to watch Daughtry, but he was thinking now of his own parents. They'd be livid if he'd pulled such a stunt, but then they were always critical of the choices he'd made in life. If it weren't for them, however, he might never have met and married Daughtry, and that would have been a pity.

Turning his attention back to the work at hand, Nicholas was surprised when Daughtry called up to him in a frantic voice.

"Nicholas! Someone's coming!"

Like he'd done as a child, Nicholas jumped from the loft to the stacked bales of hay, then to the floor of the barn. He bounded out quickly to note the three horseback riders approaching from the west.

"Oh, Nick," Daughtry whimpered. "I just know it's my father and brothers."

"At least he only brought two," Nicholas said with a smile. "Go on in the house. You wait there for me, and I'll talk to them first. You'll see, Daughtry. It's going to be all right."

~

Daughtry did as she was told, not because she felt overly obedient, but because she was a coward. She had no desire to hear the things her father would no doubt have to say to her husband. "Why, God?" she prayed aloud. "Why couldn't I have just done things the right way?"

In only a matter of minutes, angry voices rang loud and clear. Daughtry tried to cover her ears, not wanting to know what was said. What if her father said something really ugly? What if Nicholas refused to let them see her?

Daughtry started to pace. A part of her was certain that she should go outside and try to smooth over the situation. Maybe once her father saw how happy she had become and how wonderful Nicholas truly was, he'd let things be and go back home.

She reached for the door, just as things quieted considerably. A horse whinnied nervously, and Daughtry pulled back. Nicholas had told her to wait inside. She at least had to show him that she could follow his instructions. She might have misled him regarding her family, but that was all behind her now and she wanted to be a good wife.

Just as she'd convinced herself that everything was going to be all right, shots rang out, and Daughtry felt her knees turn to jelly.

"They've killed each other!" she gasped and ran to the window.

Outside, two men lay on the ground holding their bleeding arms, while one man remained on his horse with his hands raised high in the air. Daughtry didn't recognize any of them. She breathed a sigh of relief and turned her attention to her husband.

Nicholas stood with his feet fixed and a rifle leveled at the third man. The rage in his face was terrifying, and Daughtry saw blind hatred in his eyes. She stared at her husband's face and thought, *Who is this man?* He certainly didn't resemble the gentle one she'd married. Daughtry clutched her apron to her mouth to keep from screaming.

Her mind whirled. Who were these men and why had Nicholas shot them? Furthermore, where had he gotten the rifle to do the deed? She'd never seen a gun of any kind on the grounds, although she wouldn't have been surprised had there been one.

Staring at the scene outside her house, Daughtry couldn't hear a word that was being said. She watched the third man dismount from his horse and stare down the barrel of Nicholas's rifle. She couldn't watch anymore.

Daughtry moved to the far end of the house and cowered in the corner. She was wavering between tears and out-and-out hysteria. The more she thought about the scene, the more frightened she felt. A nervous laugh escaped her as she shook her head. Had Nicholas killed the two men? She sobbed and drew a ragged breath. Suddenly, she felt more terrified than she'd ever been in her life. She would have gladly welcomed the sight of her father and brothers at that moment, but she knew she could hope for no such reprieve.

The kitchen door banged, and Daughtry knew someone had come into the house. Trembling, she backed into the corner even tighter.

"Daughtry!" Nicholas called out to her as he moved from room to room. "Daughtry, where are you?" His voice sounded worried, almost panicked.

When he came into the front room, he sighed when he saw her. "Why didn't you answer me? Are you okay?"

Daughtry couldn't say a word. She stared at him, trying to force herself to calm down. It was an impossible task.

"Daughtry, come here, Honey. It's all right now."

Daughtry shook her head, not really seeing him. She saw instead the man who'd held the rifle in black rage. She saw a killer in her mind and felt her breath quicken.

Nicholas stepped forward with his arms extended. When he came to her, Nicholas reached out his hands to pull her into his arms. Daughtry went wild.

"No!" she screamed and fought his grasp. "Don't touch me!" She doubled up her fists and flailed them in the air at his face and chest.

With stunned realization, Nicholas understood that Daughtry was terrified of him, not the men he'd tied up in the barn.

As gently as he could, Nicholas pinned her arms to her side and physically carried her to the sofa. Daughtry was crying and yelling incoherently, begging him not to hurt her. Nicholas thought he'd die inside.

"It's all right, Daughtry. Honey, don't do this," he whispered. Holding her against him with one arm, he began to stroke her face with his other hand. "Daughtry!" He nearly yelled the name, and she immediately settled.

Raising her blue eyes to meet his dark, almost black ones, Daughtry couldn't hide the fear she felt. All of her foolishness in running away, marrying, and hiding here with a stranger had suddenly come home to her. Gasping for breath, she strained against his touch, while at the same time she heard his gentle words.

"Daughtry, those men are outlaws—a part of my past catching up with me. They meant to hurt us. I only did what I had to do in order to protect us. I was only defending myself."

Daughtry let the words sink in. Reason drove out the fear, and she began to relax in his hold. "Who—who—" she stammered, "are they?"

"It's not important. They're wanted by the law, and later I'll take them into the sheriff. I have them tied up in the barn and they can't hurt you." He softened his expression and loosened his hold ever so slightly. "But then, you aren't really worried about them hurting you, are you?"

Daughtry couldn't answer him. She felt so foolish for her behavior.

"Daughtry, have I ever given you reason to fear me?"

"No," she managed to whisper.

"I'm not a bad man, Daughtry. I know there's things I can't tell you just yet, but trust me. I understood about your secrets, now I'm asking you to understand about mine."

She felt her fears give way to sympathy, then relief. He had only defended himself, she thought. Slumping against him, completely spent, Daughtry clung to his shirt. "I'm sorry," she said softly.

Nicholas brushed back her hair with his hand. "It's all right. I can honestly understand your misgivings."

"Why can't you tell me about your past?" she questioned. "I told you about mine."

Nicholas sighed. "It's a long story, but for now I'm just begging you to trust me and to trust God to work it all out. I love you, Daughtry. Please, don't doubt me on that."

"I don't," she replied and sat up. She studied the worry in his eyes. It went beyond concern and seemed like something that bordered fear. Was he afraid she'd stopped loving him?

"Oh, Nicholas," she said and kissed his face several times, "I was so afraid you'd be killed. Then when I saw you with that gun and you were so angry—well, I just didn't know what to think."

"I know, Honey, and believe me, I would have saved you from having to go through it if I could have."

Daughtry nodded. It was all right, she told herself. Whatever his past consisted of, she no longer cared. She only knew that she loved him and that she would stand by him no matter what.

Leaning down to put her face on his shoulder, Daughtry spoke. "We'll just trust God to get us through this," she pledged.

"That's my girl," Nicholas said and leaned back against the sofa.

Chapter 10

Days later, Daughtry had nearly forgotten the unpleasant incident. "Are we really going to get the horse today?" she asked eagerly. Securing her bonnet, she waited for Nicholas's reply.

"Yes, for the millionth time," he said laughing. "I've never seen you so excited about anything in our two months of marriage."

"Well, there was the time that rat got in the house," Daughtry said with a grimace. "Or wait, what about the bathtub? I got pretty excited about the bathtub."

Nicholas's eyes twinkled. "Yes, yes, you did. I seem to recall having some very fine apple cake that evening. Wonder if I'll get another one for buying the horse?"

"We'll see," Daughtry said with a smug look of satisfaction. "Depends on how good the horse is."

"Now, while we're in town," Nicholas said, bringing the wagon to a halt, "I want you to get whatever you think we might need. We've got to make sure we're stocked up for the winter, just in case we have trouble getting into town."

Daughtry nodded and pulled out a small list. "I wrote down things for the kitchen." She glanced up and down the street which was already teaming with people. Several suffragists stood at one end of the street expounding on the necessity of women having the vote. At the opposite end of town there seemed to be an unusual amount of traffic at the railroad depot. "We seem to have come on a busy day."

"Looks that way." Nicholas helped her from the wagon and put a finger under her chin. "Get yourself some warm clothes while you're at it. I was looking through the things you brought into this marriage and you aren't at all well supplied." His mouth curled into a grin, and Daughtry returned his smile.

"Do you need anything?" she asked. "I can sew, you know, and we still have Mrs. Cummings's old sewing machine. I'm sure I could get it in working shape."

"I could use some heavy shirts for winter," he said, then placed a light kiss on her forehead. "But don't worry about me. I want you to make sure you

166

have everything you need. Everything, understood? Even if you worry that I might think it frivolous. I've never had a wife before, so I wouldn't be knowing what one might need."

Daughtry was touched by his generosity. "I'll try to be thorough. Where will you be?"

"Oh, here and there. I have to get the horse and there's a few other things I need to attend to. I'll pick up the mail, so you don't have to worry about it. Now, here's some money, and if that's not enough, tell them to hold whatever it is you want and I'll pay them before we head home."

Daughtry watched as Nicholas took off down the street. He was so kind and loving. Gone were the images of the hateful man with the rifle. All Daughtry could see was the man who touched her heart.

She was headed across the street to the general store when she happened to glance once more at her husband's retreating form. Surprised, she noticed he'd headed to the sheriff's office. Watching him go into the small building, Daughtry quickly made her way down the street to follow him. She wanted very much to know if her husband were in some kind of trouble.

"But why would he come here if he was an outlaw?" Daughtry wondered aloud. Biting her lip, she looked around quickly and was grateful to find herself alone on the boardwalk.

The town was much too small to have a very grand affair for a jail. Daughtry knew from what folks had told her on the train coming here that this was a one saloon, one cell kind of town. She would have been just as happy had they told her it had no saloon, but then, the world wasn't perfect.

Leaning close to the window, Daughtry could see her husband in deep discussion with a man she could only guess was the sheriff. She couldn't hear anything from this vantage point, however. Quietly, she made her way around the building and up the alley. She came to the window nearest the two men and paused. This one had the shade pulled down on the inside. She could see nothing, but she pressed her ear to the glass after a cautious glance down the alleyway.

"You go far enough back with these men to be related," she heard the sheriff saying. He said something more, but his words were garbled and Daughtry couldn't begin to understand.

Then Nicholas bellowed in voice so loud Daughtry had no trouble distinguishing every word, "I didn't ask them to look me up. They rode in looking for trouble and I gave it to them."

The sheriff, equally enraged, ranted back. "Well, you made your bed this time for sure. You brought it all on yourself!"

Daughtry wondered silently what Nicholas had brought on himself, but she was unable to continue listening at the window because someone was coming down the alley. She made her way down the street, crossing to avoid the suffragists and their battle cries.

She quickly entered the general store and furiously began her shopping. Her mind was filled with ugly images and worrisome thoughts. What if Nicholas had once been an outlaw? Maybe he was once partners with the men who sat in the jail cell. She shuddered at the thought. That just couldn't be possible. Or could it?

She toyed with several bolts of flannel material and finally settled on a dark blue plaid and a solid brown. She ordered the yardage and sought out buttons to match, planning in her mind to make Nicholas two good shirts before winter set in. Remembering his instructions to her, Daughtry went through the material a second time and chose several colors of wool to make herself some simple skirts. She finished by securing some plain white cotton and two calico prints for blouses, before turning her attention to colorful skeins of knitting yarn.

She paid for the goods, certain that she'd overspent what Nicholas had given her, but found to her surprise that she had plenty of cash left over. Seeing that she still had enough money, Daughtry quickly instructed the store owner to throw in several pairs of long underwear for her husband.

"What size?" the man asked her as he went to retrieve the goods.

"Oh, my," she said in surprise. "I don't know."

"Well," the man said looking at the blushing woman, "is he bigger than me?"

Daughtry sized the man up for a moment. "Yes," she determined quickly. "He's at least this much taller than me and about this much wider," she said, holding her hands out to indicate the size. Just then, Nicholas came into the store and Daughtry motioned to the storekeeper. "That's him."

The man behind the counter smiled and nodded. "Morning, Mr. Dawson. I didn't know this little lady was your wife."

"We're newlyweds," Nicholas said, coming up behind Daughtry. "Now what did you mean 'That's him'?"

"I was just buying you some. . ." Daughtry blushed again, unable to talk about underwear in the presence of her husband.

The storekeeper quickly brought the requested product to the counter and added it to the stack of things Daughtry had already paid for. "Will these do?" he asked, looking at Nicholas and not Daughtry.

Nicholas had to hold himself in check to keep from laughing out loud at Daughtry's sudden embarrassment. "She thinks of everything," he said with a wink over Daughtry's shoulder to the storekeeper. "They're fine."

Daughtry handed the storekeeper the remaining amount due, while

Nicholas put his arm around her lovingly. "Did you get everything you needed?"

"Yes, and then some. I certainly can't complain about your generosity, Mr. Dawson."

Nicholas picked up their supplies and led Daughtry to the door. "Would you like to get something to eat while we're in town?"

"That might be fun," Daughtry replied, looping her arm through Nicholas's. "But it's also a bit frivolous. We're going to have a great many expenses come spring and. . ."

"Madam," a deep, but clearly female voice called out, "you are a victim of our society."

Daughtry and Nicholas both stopped directly in front of a sour-faced woman who was dressed in black with a white sash that clearly identified her suffrage cause. The woman continued before either Nicholas or Daughtry could comment.

"This man seeks to enslave you! You needn't be chained to him like a dog. The men of America seek to make women their possessions. They want to control them. He," the woman said, sticking a bony finger in the middle of Nicholas's face, "wants to control you. He wants to dominate your every living moment."

Daughtry stared up at Nicholas as if contemplating the woman's words. Nicholas just shrugged and raised a questioning brow.

"That's right," the woman continued. "This man would just as soon see you bound to him—fit only to serve his pleasures and bear his children!"

Daughtry smiled broadly at the woman. "I know. Isn't it great?"

At this, the woman sputtered and stepped back in horror, while Nicholas threw back his head and roared with laughter.

"You, young woman, are the very reason women are oppressed. You are the reason we can't voice our opinions and vote for our own representation," the woman called to Nicholas and Daughtry as they made their way down the boardwalk.

"You certainly made a spectacle of yourself, Mrs. Dawson. Probably set back women's rights a hundred years," Nicholas said, helping her down from the boardwalk.

"Oh dear," Daughtry said in feigned concern. "I suppose that means I'll be bound to you even longer now."

"Only forever," Nicholas said with a gentleness in his voice that warmed Daughtry's heart.

Daughtry stared up at her husband, all the love she felt for him shining clear in her eyes.

"Well, are you going to just stand there or are you going to tell me what you think of your new horse?" he questioned.

Daughtry's eyes widened and she quickly looked around. Standing there, tied to the back of the wagon, was a beautiful chestnut mare, complete with western saddle. "I thought you might like to ride her home," Nicholas whispered against her ear.

"Oh, she's beautiful! Of course I want to ride her home. Oh, Nicholas, thank you!" She threw her arms around her husband, nearly causing him to drop their packages.

Helping to set things back in place, Daughtry composed herself a bit, but the delight was evident in her eyes.

"You're welcome," he said and happily deposited the packages in the back of the wagon before turning to lend Daughtry some help in mounting.

"Does she have a name?" Daughtry questioned, running her hand along the mare's sleek neck.

"She does. The owner called her Nutmeg."

Daughtry cooed and talked to the mare, whispering the name several times. "I think we'll be good friends, you and I," she said to the horse.

Nicholas helped her up into the saddle, then took his place on the wagon. "You sure you want to ride her home?"

"Of course I'm sure," Daughtry replied indignantly. "I could ride before I could walk, at least that's what my father used to say." She frowned only briefly at the reference before moving Nutmeg forward.

Nicholas pulled up alongside her once they were on the road out of town. "It's going to be all right, Daughtry. You can't be worrying all the time about what might or might not happen."

"I know, but it's been awhile since we sent the letter. I figure it won't be long before. . ." She couldn't finish the sentence, but Nicholas understood and conveyed his sympathy with his eyes. Taking a deep breath, Daughtry reminded herself that she had Nicholas's love and that he would protect her. Then an earlier scene crossed her mind and Daughtry grimaced. *But who's going to protect Nicholas?* she wondered. *Who will protect him when his past catches up with him again?*

With the sheriff's words still reverberating through her head and her own imagination running wild, Daughtry couldn't help but fear the truth. She worked almost mindlessly around the kitchen that evening, putting the finishing touches on supper, waiting for Nicholas to reappear after seeing to the horses. She pulled a peach cobbler from the oven and smiled. At least she could offer him a good home-cooked meal. Cooking was one thing her mother had insisted Daughtry learn.

"Umm, smells mighty fine in here," Nicholas said, coming through the mud porch into the kitchen. "And it's warmer in here too."

Daughtry came to him and helped him off with his coat. "It does feel a lot colder," she replied, feeling the chilled night air as it followed him through the open door.

"No sign of snow just yet," Nicholas added, giving his hat a toss to a hook beside the door. "It might just go around us."

Daughtry nodded. "Supper's ready."

"I can see that," he said, staring appreciatively at the table. "You're going to make me fat," he laughed but eagerly took a seat.

"I baked you a cobbler," Daughtry said proudly. She brought the bubbling concoction to the table in order to show it off. "It ought to taste even better with the fresh cream we brought home."

"I'm going to have to keep buying you presents, I see."

"Maybe you could just share secrets with me instead," she replied soberly.

"What do you mean?" he asked, knowing full well what she wanted.

"I just think it would be nice to know more about you. Like those men the other day. I can't just forget about them. Who were they and why did they want to hurt you?" Daughtry sat down to the table and waited for Nicholas to speak.

"It's nothing," Nicholas snapped and began putting food on his plate. Softening his tone, he looked at her with pleading eyes and added, "Nothing that needs to concern you."

"But I heard the sheriff yell at you," Daughtry said without thinking. She bowed her head, ashamed to admit she'd spied on her husband.

"Don't nose into this, Daughtry," he replied sternly, the first time he'd ever sounded angry with her.

"I have a right to know," she protested, lifting her face to meet his.

Nicholas's eyes narrowed slightly. "Stay out of it. I mean it!" He slammed his fist down on the table, causing all the dishes to rattle. Daughtry stared at him for a heartbeat, then got up and ran from the table.

She was out the back door and running past the barn before she realized he was calling after her. Pride wouldn't let her slow down, however, and Daughtry continued until she came to her favorite place. The little grove of trees by the creek offered her a safe haven, but not much warmth. Shivering uncontrollably under the full moon, Daughtry began to cry. Why had he been so mean?

She knew he'd follow her, but when he wrapped his arms around her and pulled her close, Daughtry jumped back in fear.

"Don't," she said between chattering teeth.

She could see the pain in his face. Pain of rejection and fear of loss. "I'm sorry, Daughtry. I didn't mean to lose my temper."

She said nothing, wondering at the strained apology. Did he think that was enough? Just an "I'm sorry?" *What do you want him to say?* Daughtry asked herself and could think of no answer.

Nicholas reached out to her again, and this time Daughtry didn't push away. "I really am sorry," he whispered against her ear. "It's just that the whole episode with those men unnerved me. I can't help but worry that we aren't safe here anymore. I can't help but worry that I've exposed you to something harmful and ugly. Before, when it was just me, I didn't have to worry about things like that. I prayed and asked God to ride with me, watch over me, and take me home when the time came. But now, there's so much more. There's you and. . ." He fell silent. What was the use? He couldn't explain it.

Daughtry's heart softened toward him. His worry for their safety concerned her more than she wanted to admit but, right now, all she wanted to do was comfort him.

"It's all right, Nicholas. I'm sorry to have pressed the matter, and I'm sorry that I spied on you. I do love you and I trust you, so from now on, I'll leave the matter be."

Chapter 11

Thanksgiving drew near and with it the haunting reminder of Julie's death. Daughtry found herself thinking about her sister, even when she didn't want to. Julie would have been eighteen. Thoughts of her naturally turned Daughtry's mind to her father. She was both worried and relieved that he'd done nothing to interfere in her life. Was he so angry that he no longer cared?

"It's a beautiful day out here, Daughtry!" Nicholas called from just outside the back door.

Daughtry made her way outside, wearing only her dark green wool skirt and long-sleeved calico blouse. "Yes," she murmured, relishing the reminder of summer. "I think I'll do the wash outside today."

Nicholas mounted his horse and gave her an admonishing look. "Don't overdo it and don't stay outside if it turns cold. I don't want you getting sick."

Daughtry grinned at his fatherly words. "I'm surprised you're willing to leave me here alone."

"I'm not very happy about the idea," Nicholas said, "but you're insistent on having fresh turkey for Thanksgiving, and since the Shaunasseys offered to sell me one of their birds, I guess I'll just have to overlook my discomfort."

"Oh, go on with you, now," Daughtry said and reached out to smack the horse on the rump. Instead, Nicholas caught her hand and lowered his lips to her fingers.

"Please stay out of trouble," he whispered. "I've grown very fond of you, Mrs. Dawson."

Daughtry's heart warmed to his words. "And I, you, Mr. Dawson."

With nothing more said, Nicholas took off for his five-mile ride to the Shaunasseys, while Daughtry went back inside to ready her laundry.

With most of the wash done by noon, Daughtry was just putting away her wash tub and scrub board when the unmistakable sound of a wagon caught her attention. Peering around the house, Daughtry was pleased to see the freighter, Tom O'Toole, making his way up the long Dawson drive.

She quickly hurried inside to put on coffee and arrange a plate of cookies, while Tom completed the trip to the barn. He was bringing in the last of their ordered supplies for winter, and Daughtry was hopeful that he might

173

have thought to bring the mail as well.

"Afternoon, Mrs. Dawson," the man said, jumping to the ground.

"Afternoon, Tom," Daughtry replied. "When you finish there, I've got hot coffee and cinnamon cookies for you."

"That ought to make my work pass quicklike," he announced. Pulling down a heavy crate, Tom motioned. "This here is a bunch of them canned goods you asked for last time. It just came in from Denver."

"Oh, good," Daughtry replied. "You can bring that on up to the house, and I'll get to work putting it away."

Tom nodded and followed Daughtry into the house, where he deposited the crate, requested a hammer, and pulled the nailed lid off. Daughtry immediately went to work, while Tom made his way back outside.

Humming to herself, Daughtry felt good about their filled pantry. There was more than enough food to tide them over for a great many months, if necessary. Nicholas, however, seemed to think that even if heavy snows buried them, a good strong prairie wind would most likely clear a path to town. With that in mind, Daughtry didn't worry much about the distance.

She was nearly finished when Tom gave a heavy knock on the door and bounded into the room. "All done out there," he said, and Daughtry poured him a mug of coffee and pointed him to the chair.

"You just rest awhile and help yourself to those cookies. Nicholas has gone over to the Shaunasseys' to get our Thanksgiving turkey."

"Me and the missus are planning on heading up to Raton for Thanksgiving. She's got a sister there and nieces and nephews, and since it wasn't that far by train, we thought it might make a nice trip before the snows set in."

"It does sound like fun," Daughtry said half-heartedly, for, in truth, she loved her little hideaway home and didn't desire to travel away from it, even to visit her family.

"You got kin nearby?" Tom asked, draining his coffee and reaching for a third cookie. Daughtry started to refill his cup but he waved her off. "I still have two more deliveries to make, so I'd best be on my way." He got to his feet, and Daughtry followed him out of the house.

"This weather is sure enough pleasant," Tom said, making his way to the wagon. "I could do without the snow for awhile."

"Me too," Daughtry replied. "Well, take care, Tom." She waited while he climbed up into the worn wooden seat of his freight wagon.

"Oh, I plum forgot," he said, reaching under the seat. "I brought the mail for you."

Daughtry's face lit up, hoping that maybe a newspaper or magazine might be included in his delivery. Nicholas had ordered several magazines for her when they were last in town, and Daughtry was beginning to think they'd never arrive. To her disappointment, though, Tom handed down only a single envelope.

"This one's for you," he said and picked up the reins. "I'll be seeing you, Mrs. Dawson." He snapped the reins and took off on his route while Daughtry stared at the unmistakable handwriting of her father.

With shaking hands, Daughtry forced herself to open the letter. She waited until she made it back to the kitchen table, however, to read it. She was feeling weak in the knees and almost green with anxiety by the time she unfolded the single page.

Daughtry stared down at the words in disbelief. Her father was coming! She read the brief statement of when he planned to arrive and found that the date in his letter matched the one on the calendar. Her father planned to arrive today!

Daughtry dropped the letter on the table. If her father showed up and Nicholas were not there to prevent him from taking her back, what would she do? Feeling sick inside, Daughtry got up from the table and began to pace.

"Dear Lord," she whispered, "I know that sinful nature got me here. I know that I was out and out disobedient, but, Father, I love Nicholas and I don't want my father to take me back to Piñon Canyon. I want to stay here and be Nicholas's wife." She paused and realized her prayer was more the uncontrollable babblings of a rebellious child. She folded her hands together and took a deep breath.

"Show me what I need to do, Father. Show me how to make this right. Please forgive me for going against my father's wishes, and help my father to understand why I did what I did and to forgive me for hurting him. Amen."

Daughtry felt only marginally better. She knew that God was in charge and would take care of everything. She even knew that He'd already forgiven her for her willful disobedience. Daughtry couldn't wash away the feelings of helplessness, however.

A quick glance at the clock on the wall started Daughtry panicking again. *He plans to arrive today,* she thought, *but when?* Finally, Daughtry decided she'd ride over to the Shaunasseys' and get Nicholas. She could face anything with Nicholas at her side.

Despite the nice weather, she put on heavy wool stockings and a wool, split skirt. She pulled on her riding boots and grabbed a warm, fitted jacket to throw in her saddle bag in case the weather turned cool. Then suddenly, without really knowing that she was packing, Daughtry found herself throwing together gloves, a bonnet, her jeans, and one of Nicholas's thick flannel shirts. When she'd gathered these things, Daughtry took two wool blankets and rolled all of it together into a pack that would fit behind her saddle.

Somewhere in the midst of her worry, Daughtry knew she was running away again, but her mind wouldn't let her reason out the truth.

"I can't go to Nicholas," she said aloud, "or I might pass Daddy on the way." The thought of being already en route when her father caught up with her made Daughtry believe he'd have just that much easier of a time forcing her home.

Running with the pack into the kitchen, Daughtry laid out provisions for herself, including matches, a small pot, and a generous amount of food. She stuffed as much as she could into her saddle bags, then leaving the kitchen in complete disarray, she grabbed her things and ran for the barn.

Nicholas was in a good mood as he made his way home that afternoon. He had a nice fat turkey confined in a crate on the back of his rather skeptical horse and two warm loaves of pumpkin bread in the saddle bags behind him. His mood was founded on more than the food, however. He was going home to her. Home to his wife. Daughtry!

He hadn't realized how much he'd come to love her until he spent time away from her. This was the first time since she'd arrived that he'd spent nearly an entire day without her by his side. Even the time he'd had to take the outlaws into the sheriff hadn't amounted to more than a couple of hours.

Anxious to hold her in his arms and see her pleasure at the turkey, Nicholas urged his horse into a gallop and hurried for home.

Nicholas approached the house without giving much thought to the cloud of dust that rose to his right. He was preoccupied with his thoughts and didn't even see the riders until he was bringing his horse to a stop just outside the barn.

Nicholas thought to dismount but sat instead with his eyes fixed on the riders. Without being told, he knew they were Daughtry's father and three of her brothers.

"Well, Lord," he whispered against the silence, "I guess this is it. I'm about to answer for what I've done with this man's daughter. I could sure use some direction in how to come under my father-in-law's good graces."

The riders approached, slowing to a slow walk until they were directly in front of Nicholas. The older of the three pressed his horse forward until he was nearly nose to nose with Nicholas.

"You Nicholas Dawson?" Garrett Lucas asked from between clenched teeth.

"I am," Nicholas replied softly. "You must be. . ." He never got the words out, because Garrett flew across the saddle and knocked Nicholas off of his horse and to the ground.

Chapter 12

After two well-placed blows against Nicholas's face, Garrett's sons managed to pull their father off the stunned man. Nicholas refused to fight back and got to his feet slowly. Knocking the dust from his backside, he moved away a step, while Garrett strained at the resistance of his sons.

"You have to answer for what you've done!" Garrett declared. His face was reddened with anger.

Nicholas rubbed his jaw and a hint of a smile played at his bloodied lip. "I think I just did."

Garrett was livid and refused to be humored. "Where's my daughter? Where's Daughtry?"

"I would imagine in the house. As you can see for yourself, I just got back," Nicholas replied gingerly. He didn't believe his jaw was broken, but it hurt nevertheless.

"Dad, you promised to be levelheaded about this," one of the boys was saying. Nicholas watched as the other two nodded in agreement. Maybe Daughtry's brothers were able to see that their sister had a right to make her own choices.

"Don't tell me what I said, Joseph!"

"He's right, Dad. Daughtry told us in the letter that she's happy. Why don't we let her tell us otherwise."

Garrett seemed to relax a bit, and Nicholas's took the opportunity to speak. "I'm sorry, I truly am. Not for having married your daughter, but for the way we went about it. I know what Daughtry put in her letter, so I know that you realize I was completely unaware of your existence when she married me. It's a poor excuse, I know, but I hope in time you will forgive me."

Garrett stared at Nicholas for several minutes.

"I'm Garrett Lucas," he finally said. "These are my sons, Gavin, Dolan, and Joseph."

"Pleased to meet all of you," Nicholas responded. He didn't offer his hand, feeling if he did he might be forcing the issue a bit. Instead, he motioned to the horses. "What say we tie these fellows up and you let me put my turkey in the barn, and we'll go inside and talk this out with Daughtry."

The other men nodded. Nicholas could see the boys speaking in low

177

whispers to Garrett, while they tied the horses to the corral fence and waited for their host. They seemed like good men, he thought to himself, and he smiled. Of course they were good men; they were Daughtry's family.

Making his way to where they awaited him, Nicholas took the lead. "Come on inside."

Nicholas immediately sensed that all was not right when he entered the kitchen. Things were strewn about in a haphazard way that was not indicative of his wife's normal sense of order. For a minute he stood in the silence, while Garrett and the boys glanced around the room.

"Daughtry!" he called out, but in his heart, Nicholas knew she wouldn't answer.

He rushed from one room to the next, and when he saw the same disarray in the bedroom that had greeted him in the kitchen, Nicholas knew that she was gone. Panic filled his soul. Had friends of the men he'd jailed come for him and taken her instead?

The fear was clear in Nicholas's eyes as he returned to the kitchen. "She's not here. I'm going to check the barn and see if her horse is gone. You wait here," he instructed and ran out the back door.

Nicholas began to pray as he'd never done before. "Dear God, keep her safe. Please don't let any harm come to her. Oh, God, please help me find her."

When Nicholas realized the horse was indeed missing, he made his way back to the house with a heavy heart. Where was she? The light was fading and the wind was picking up, causing a chill to fill the air. Where was Daughtry?

The defeat on his face made it clear to Garrett that Nicholas was more than a little upset at finding Daughtry gone. "Where do you suppose she got off to?" Garrett asked, trying to keep his voice even.

Just then, Nicholas spied the letter on the table. He picked it up, praying that it might be some note of explanation from Daughtry.

"She's run away again," Nicholas muttered and handed the letter to Garrett. "She found out you were due to be here and, what with me gone, she was afraid."

"Afraid? Of me?" Garrett nearly growled in disbelief.

Nicholas nodded his head. "She's been in a real stew since we married. Always looking over her shoulder, wondering when you were going to come and take her by force."

"She was afraid of me," Garrett stated sadly as if all the wind had gone out from him. "I don't know why she thought I would try to make her unhappy."

"It's not important now. What is important is that we find her," Gavin offered, and Nicholas nodded.

"I just wanted her to make good choices," Garrett said, trying to explain himself.

"She's a good woman," Nicholas responded without hesitancy. "She makes good choices."

"Ha," Garrett sounded. "She doesn't seem to have made a very good one this time. She's out there somewhere, only God knows where, and she's alone. It's getting colder and. . ."

"I'm going after her," Nicholas said and turned to leave. "You make yourselves comfortable here, in case she comes back."

"No," Garrett replied, "I'm going after her. She's my daughter, and if I caused this like you said, then I'll find her."

"She's my responsibility now," Nicholas said a bit more forcefully than he'd intended.

"And I say she's still under my authority and protection," Garrett replied, coming to stand only inches from Nicholas. "I was there when she came into this world, and God gave me charge over her."

"But I married her, and that authority now falls to me," Nicholas replied softly. "I love her as much as you do."

"You may love her," Garrett answered, "but she's still my daughter. Flesh of my flesh and blood of my blood."

Nicholas nodded. "I know. But she's my wife, and she's carrying our child."

Garrett's mouth dropped open at this sudden declaration. A part of him wanted to fight Nicholas all over again, while another part of him stood in awed amazement.

"A baby?" he questioned in disbelief.

"Yes," Nicholas replied.

"Why don't we stop this nonsense," Gavin finally spoke up. "We should go together. With all of us looking, we're bound to find her sooner."

"He's right," Nicholas said, seeing the change in Garrett. "Let's all go. I've a feeling she won't be all that far."

"Yeah, but we're talking about my sister," Dolan joked. "She's very stubborn, and who knows where that'll take her."

Nicholas grinned. "She's had good training, though. I know Daughtry can take care of herself." Grabbing his coat, he added, "I'll tell you about her fixing the roof while we ride."

～

Daughtry had found the perfect place to make camp for the night. She had ridden for several hours before coming to a rocky wall barrier. As she paralleled it for a short time, the sky began to grow dark, and Daughtry realized she'd have to stop and take shelter. She also noticed that the air was getting cold.

At the first sound of water, Daughtry felt a bit of contentment wash over her. She'd have a good camp for both Nutmeg and herself. Bringing the horse to a stop by the stream, Daughtry quickly went to work, and before the last few glimmers of late autumn sun had faded behind the mountain peaks, she had a nice fire going.

She thought how beautiful the night was and how the tiny pinpricks of light that were millions of stars in the sky seemed to keep her company through the loneliness of her vigil. "I know I've brought this on myself, Father," she prayed. "But I just didn't know what else to do. I wanted to trust You to work it out. I wanted to have faith that everything would be all right, but I was so frightened."

The wind picked up a bit, and Daughtry hugged a blanket close to her. Foolish or not, she was out here alone and had to make the most of it. Garrett Lucas had raised his children to be capable of caring for themselves outdoors, and Daughtry was certainly no exception to that rule. As the fire began to die down, she tossed several large logs on the coals and settled down for the night.

"Oh, Nicholas," she sighed against the haunting sounds of the canyon winds. "I need you."

Chapter 13

Daughtry tried to sleep but couldn't. Perhaps the hour was just not late enough, she reasoned; after all, the sun had only been down for an hour, maybe two. In frustration, she sat up and leaned back against the rock to contemplate her actions.

In the distant night she could make out little noises, but nothing that offered either comfort or fear. She thought of her life and all that she'd known.

This region of New Mexico was still very rustic. They didn't have electricity to the outlying houses, and while most of the towns sported not only electricity but running water, telephones, and automobiles, Daughtry's world hadn't consisted of any of these things. She felt as though she stood between the past and the future, not really taking hold of either one.

She smiled to herself as she thought of Nicholas building the small addition off the kitchen to house the bathtub. He'd seemed so happy when he realized how much pleasure it gave Daughtry.

They were a strange couple, Daughtry thought. "How could two people who had never before met be so perfect for each other?" she questioned the air. Clearly, the hand of God had been working in spite of human rebellion and disobedience.

Daughtry frowned. Her father was no doubt at her house right this very minute. What a coward she was to leave Nicholas to face him alone. She hugged her knees to her chest. *Oh, God,* she prayed, *please help him. Help Nicholas to deal evenhandedly with my father, and help my father to keep his temper under control.*

She must have dozed, or so she figured, because suddenly the sound of horses clipping at a slow, even pace caused her to jerk upright. Getting to her feet, Daughtry was further stunned to see her husband, father, and three of her brothers ride casually into camp as though they were there for supper.

Standing with her mouth open and her eyes wide, Daughtry was speechless. Nicholas jumped down from his horse, throwing the reins to Joseph, while Garrett dismounted and handed his to Gavin. Before she could utter a single protest, Nicholas had her in his arms and was turning her around as if to inspect every single inch of her.

"She looks to be in one piece," she heard her husband mutter.

Still Daughtry could say nothing, and not until Nicholas completely shocked her by handing her over to her father to continue the examination, did Daughtry finally voice her protest.

"Stop this at once!" she exclaimed and pushed away from her father. "I'm not a helpless child, you know. I'm perfectly fine—or at least I was until you all got here."

She looked from the two men at her side to her brothers. "How dare you interfere in my life this way! I'm old enough to know my own mind. You can't just waltz in here and think to control me!"

Garrett glanced at Nicholas and received one of his lazy, I-told-you-so grins. "I think you should spank her," Garrett said with a slow drawl.

"Sp–sp–spank me?" Daughtry sputtered, completely enraged. "You think he should spank me?"

"That's right," Garrett replied.

"If he doesn't want to do the job, I'll do it," Gavin called down from his mount.

"You're all insufferable." Daughtry put hands on her hips and struck a defiant pose. "I'm a grown woman and. . ."

"You may be a grown woman, but you haven't got a lick of sense," Garrett replied.

"I have plenty of sense."

"Then what are you doing out here when you have a perfectly fine home?" Garrett questioned.

Daughtry looked to her husband for help, but Nicholas looked away as if to keep from laughing.

Daughtry crossed her arms. "I wouldn't be out here at all if it hadn't been for the way you treated me. I may have run off, but you forced me to make that decision."

"I know," he said in a dejected tone that immediately softened Daughtry's heart.

Garrett pushed his black Stetson back and drew a deep breath. "I know I've been unfair to you, Daughtry. It's just that ever since Julie died, I guess I felt like I had to keep a better eye on you. I couldn't get past feeling that if I'd only watched her closer, made her take someone with her when she rode, that maybe she'd be alive today. You'll feel different when you have your child. You'll know just how much a child means to a parent."

Daughtry reached out to touch her father's cheek. "I know. I miss her too. And I also feel guilty."

"Guilty for what?" Garrett asked in complete surprise.

"For being angry with her. Angry that she died. Angry that because of the way she died, I had to bear the consequences." Garrett grimaced at the latter, but Daughtry continued. "We all miss her, but overprotecting me won't change the fact that she's gone to heaven and we're still here."

"You're right, of course," Garrett answered and opened his arms. "Will you forgive me?"

Daughtry melted into her father's embrace. "Of course," she sighed. "I forgave you a long time ago. If it hadn't been for our confrontation, I might never have met Nicholas—and, Daddy, I do love him. I didn't just marry him to get away from home. He's a good man, and he loves God."

Garrett glanced over her shoulder at Nicholas.

"I'm glad you love him, Daughtry."

As if reading her father's feelings, Daughtry pulled back. "I'll always love you too, Daddy. Please forgive me for the way I've done things. I know I was wrong. You and Momma brought me into the world and raised me up to love God and my fellow man—and now it's time for me to go on and live my life with Nicholas."

Garrett nodded. "I know. Just as Julie's death isn't the end, I know that your marriage is just the beginning of many wonderful things. Nicholas helped me to see that. He helped me to realize that life and death are just a part of the circle that makes us who we are. Julie may be gone, but now there's your baby and life starts anew."

Daughtry dropped her hold on Garrett and stepped back a pace. "My *what*?" Her mouth dropped open in stunned silence.

Garrett looked at Nicholas. Nicholas stepped forward with a sheepish grin.

"I think Daughtry's been a bit preoccupied these last few weeks even to realize that she's expecting," he offered by way of explanation. "But I feel very confident that she is."

Daughtry felt her face flush. She calculated the days of their marriage, her monthly cycles, and felt a strange knowledge settle over her. "A baby!" She looked up at Nicholas who seemed quite pleased to have known before even she did.

Without warning, she felt her knees buckle and she fell forward into her father. Garrett managed to take hold of her under the arms, and, looking at Nicholas with a telling smile, he unceremoniously handed the unconscious Daughtry over to him.

"Good luck," Garrett said with a laugh. "You're going to need it."

Quite awhile later, Daughtry and Nicholas made their way to bed. Garrett and the boys had taken up residency in the front sitting room, refusing to let Daughtry and Nicholas even think of giving up their room.

Daughtry brushed her long coppery hair and thought of the news that she was to be a mother. How could she have been so caught up in her guilt and fears that she hadn't realized she was with child? She was almost humiliated that her husband had to be the one to point the news out to her.

Just then Nicholas came in, deposited his boots, and got ready for bed. Daughtry turned and stared at him for a moment. He was so very handsome with his dark hair and broad shoulders. She liked the way he moved with cat-like grace and confidence.

Realizing that she was watching him, Nicholas turned and smiled. Daughtry's hand automatically went to her stomach in wonder. How could it be that they were to become parents? Why had God chosen to bless their union so early on with such a miracle?

"How?" Daughtry questioned, getting up and slipping into bed. "How did you know?"

Nicholas shrugged and eased into the covers. "I'm not stupid. I know all about women. I have a mother after all. Not to mention my sisters."

"Imagine that," Daughtry said rather sarcastically. "You have sisters."

"Yes, I have two sisters and a brother," Nicholas replied. "I am the oldest."

"I see."

"Lance is twenty-eight," Nicholas continued, knowing her unspoken questions. "Natalie is twenty-five and Joelle is nineteen. So, you see, I am more than a little familiar with things that pertain to the female species."

Daughtry blushed and shook her head. "I can't believe that I didn't realize what was happening."

"I thought maybe you did," Nicholas replied. "But when we went to town and I told you to get anything you thought you might need, and you only worried about my underwear—well, then I knew that you didn't know."

Daughtry laughed. "You must think me pathetic."

Nicholas opened his arms to her, and Daughtry slid into them eagerly. "I would never think you pathetic," Nicholas answered softly. "You are most precious to me."

Daughtry leaned her head against his chest. "You aren't angry, are you? About the baby, I mean."

"Why would I be angry?"

"Well, it certainly happened a lot quicker than I anticipated, so I figure it must be just as shocking for you."

"It did surprise me," Nicholas admitted, "but once I realized that it was most likely true, I kind of liked the idea."

"It's just so amazing and wondrous," Daughtry said, her hand going again to her abdomen. "But, I couldn't bear it if you were unhappy." She lifted her face to his, her eyes huge pools of blue.

"I couldn't be more happy about it," Nicholas replied and kissed her forehead. "If you'll recall, I was the one who planned for a dozen or so."

Daughtry laughed. "Well, one down and eleven to go."

Nicholas joined her laughter with his own, then suddenly grew sober. "Daughtry, you have to promise me that you'll be more careful. I nearly died when I came home and found you gone. I know you were scared, but so many things could have happened to you out there. Not to mention that I'm still not all that sure we're safe from my past."

His words both startled and frustrated her. Why wouldn't he tell her what past it was that he was running from?

Daughtry eased up on one elbow to study him for a moment. She was about to protest his silence when she saw something in his eyes that made her want to comfort him. She placed her hand on his chest and smiled. "Whatever you decide is fine by me. If you need to leave this place, you'll do so with me by your side."

"No questions asked?" Nicholas whispered, staring hard at his wife.

"No questions asked."

Morning light brought the blended family together at breakfast. For the first time, Daughtry used her dining room table and chairs and enjoyed preparing a feast fit for an army. Nicholas spoke about the ranch with her father and brothers, while Daughtry made sure that all the cups were filled with steaming coffee and that no one went away hungry.

"I've got a great deal to learn," Nicholas confessed. "But Daughtry's been a tremendous help."

"She ought to be. She's grown up ranching all her life. Piñon Canyon is probably the largest ranch in New Mexico, although I've never concerned myself with such things. We do a good business in beef and horses," Garrett said between forkfuls of food. "There's certainly enough business there, and I always presumed it would pass equally to all of my children." As he spoke, an idea came to Garrett and he put down his fork.

"What say you and Daughtry come live at Piñon Canyon for the winter? I could teach you firsthand all that you'd need to know to get this place running, and, come spring, I would send you off with a starter herd of the best cattle this side of the Mississippi."

Daughtry looked at her father in surprise, then to Nicholas. What would he think of the offer, she wondered? She didn't have long to contemplate as Nicholas raised his eyes to hers. They both thought back to the day of the shootout, and Daughtry nodded as if in answer to Nicholas's unspoken question.

"I think we'd both like that," Nicholas replied, and Daughtry nodded and continued seeing to her brothers' plates.

Garrett couldn't have been more surprised or grateful. "Good," he answered, feeling the first real peace since Daughtry left home. "I don't think you'll be sorry."

"I'm sure we won't be," Nicholas replied. "We won't need to do much here, maybe just board up the windows so that no harm comes to them. We'll take our horses with us, and there's no other livestock or obligation to contend with."

"What about our turkey?" Daughtry asked with a grin. "I can hear him out there even now." Everybody laughed, having heard the turkey's protests through much of the night.

"We'll take him with us," Garrett announced. "We ought to be home in time for Thanksgiving, and he'll make a great main course."

Chapter 14

Nicholas stared down at the mammoth ranch that spread across the endless valley. Nestled between the mountains was Piñon Canyon, the home where Daughtry had grown up. He looked in awe from the empire below, to the man who owned it all, and finally to his wife.

"Like it?" she questioned with a grin. "You should see it in the springtime when all the grass is newly green and the wildflowers are blooming."

Nicholas nodded. "I can only imagine. It's easy to see why you love it." Daughtry smiled. She'd only recently told Nicholas of her fondness for her childhood home.

Her father and brothers moved ahead on the trail, leaving Nicholas and Daughtry to themselves. "When I left," Daughtry said, remembering her escape, "I thought I was leaving a terrible place. A prison. Now I can see that it was more the way I perceived things inside and not at all the way it really was."

"Can you be happy here again?" Nick questioned, reaching out to touch her arm.

Daughtry gave him a radiant smile, and, in spite of the blustery cold winds that came down from the mountain, she was warm and content. "I can be happy anywhere that you are."

Maggie Lucas fussed and pampered her daughter from the moment she got down from her horse. Arm in arm, they walked off toward the house, while the men saw to the horses and gear.

"He's very nice looking, this Nicholas Dawson," Maggie said, bringing Daughtry a steaming cup of hot chocolate.

"Yes, he is. He's also very kind and considerate, and he's a Christian, Momma."

"That's good," Maggie said, and Daughtry heard the unmistakable sound of relief in her voice.

"I'm truly sorry for the way I acted." Daughtry put the cup down and looked up at her mother. "I know I must have just about broke your heart in two, and I can't live with myself any longer. Will you please forgive me for running off and hurting you like I did?"

Maggie put her arms around Daughtry and hugged her close. "I could see how bad things were. I only wanted you to be happy, but I knew how miserable you were. I tried to talk to your father, and he only snapped at me. There's nothing to forgive. I knew in my heart, after learning that you'd left, that God was with you and that He'd guide you safely. It gave me a great deal of peace, even when I didn't know where you were."

"Why did it take Daddy so long to show up?" Daughtry suddenly asked.

"He was mad and real hurt. Mostly because he knew he was responsible for your actions. At first he refused to even deal with it but, as time passed, I could see the anger burning inside him like a spark just waiting for kindling to feed its flame. One day, he marched in here, told Gavin and Dolan to saddle up, and announced he was going to find you and this man who'd stolen you from him."

Daughtry smiled and pulled away from her mother. "I take it Joey went along to keep the peace."

Maggie nodded. "You know Joseph." This time Daughtry nodded, while Maggie continued. "That's what happened here. How about what happened at your end?"

"I got Daddy's letter and it spooked me. I'm sorry to say I ran away again, because Nicholas was at a neighbor's house and wasn't due home for awhile. I had no idea how soon Daddy would arrive, so I packed a horse and left. I figured I'd rather camp out in the cold than face his wrath alone. Besides, I was so scared he'd take me away and I'd never see Nicholas again."

"What happened then?"

Daughtry laughed. "They all came riding into my camp as big as you please. Nick was sporting a bruised face, and Daddy was wearing skinned knuckles. I heard later that Nick wouldn't even defend himself. Just let Daddy have at him, then asked him to forgive him for marrying me."

"He is quite a man," Maggie said in surprised awe.

"You don't know the half of it," Daughtry said with a mischievous twinkle in her eye. "I have a surprise for you."

"What?" Maggie cocked her head to one side as if trying to figure out what her daughter would say next.

"Daddy asked us to live here for the winter, so that he could teach Nicholas all about ranching."

"And your husband agreed?"

"He did," Daughtry said with great happiness. "But we're going home in the spring, and Daddy promised to send us with some prime stock to start our own herd."

"Well, I am impressed," Maggie said, taking a seat beside her daughter.

"And," Daughtry added, reaching out to take hold of her mother's hand, "I have one more surprise. I'm going to have a baby."

"A baby!"

Her mother looked as though she might faint, and Daughtry squeezed her hand. "I was so worried about Daddy coming to take me away that I didn't even know it myself, until Nicholas pointed out the obvious things."

"A baby," Maggie said again, this time more steadily. "I'm going to be a grandmother. Wait until Lillie hears this one."

Daughtry laughed. "You'll no doubt have me knee-deep in sewing projects, and before the winter is over, I'll have enough clothes for triplets."

The women were still laughing when the men came in the room. Maggie got up and received a heartfelt kiss from her husband, while Nicholas went to Daughtry's side and waited to be introduced.

"Momma, this is Nicholas, my husband," Daughtry said proudly.

Maggie surprised Nicholas by brushing aside his extended hand as she threw her arms around him in a motherly hug. "Welcome home, Nicholas," she said with love. "I'm so glad to have acquired another son."

$\sim$

Nicholas spent most of his waking hours with Garrett and Daughtry's brothers. He worked harder than he'd ever worked in his life and knew that he was in many ways facing up to whatever tests Garrett could put him through. At night he collapsed into a tub of hot water, which Daughtry always saw was ready for him, then he would crawl into bed, more asleep than awake.

More than one night, Daughtry would lie beside her husband and watch him. His dark black hair would curl just at the collar and beg her touch, but Daughtry was always careful not to disturb him. She knew her father was working him too hard, but she reasoned that both men had something to prove and, for now, she'd not interfere.

Daughtry settled into the routine with misgivings. She missed the days when Nicholas had belonged just to her. Their ranch hadn't been so demanding, and Nicholas could take plenty of time to stop and talk or hold her. Now, however, she rarely saw him until dinner time, and by then he was so tired he didn't care whether he was married or not.

At dinner one night, the family finally began to feel comfortable enough to ask Nicholas questions and one of the first was about his family.

"My mother and father are both still living. They live near Kansas City, where my father handles investments."

Daughtry hung onto every word but tried to appear as though this was all old news to her. She wasn't about to inform her family that Nicholas hadn't seen fit to confide in her.

"And do you have brothers and sisters, Nick?" Maggie questioned and Daughtry jumped in to reply.

"He has a brother and two sisters," she said confidently before Nicholas could get a word in edgewise. She looked over at her husband, daring him to say more, but Nicholas just grinned and went on eating.

"I guess I still don't understand how you could just up and marry a fellow after you read about him in the paper," Jordy said and turned to Nicholas. "No offense, I think you're as good a man for a brother-in-law as any, but my sister's always been rather picky."

Everyone laughed at this but Daughtry. "I'm not picky, just cautious."

"So cautious you answered a stranger's letter out of the *Denver Post* and sneaked away in the night to marry him? He could have been three times your age and given to fits of rage for all you knew," Gavin said.

"He is given to small fits," Daughtry laughed.

"So what made you do it?" Jordy pressed his luck. "I mean, other than getting away from here?"

Daughtry put her fork down and stared at Nicholas for a moment. "I fell in love with his picture."

Garrett and the boys thought this hysterical and started laughing and slapping the table. Nicholas looked across the table at Daughtry and winked at her blushing face, while Maggie cleared her throat loud enough that the others quieted down.

"That's a silly reason to get married," Jordy replied.

"Sure is," Garrett seconded. "Imagine, marrying someone just because you've fallen in love with their picture. Why, for all you knew, he hadn't even sent you a picture of himself. It could have been anyone's picture."

"I seem to recall," Maggie began slowly, concentrating on moving the food around her plate, "a certain love-sick cowboy who fell in love with a 'spitfire of a girl' as he called her. This man had never met this girl," Maggie continued, "but her father had a portrait of her hanging in his house and that cowboy fell in love with her after staring many hours at it."

Everyone fell into silence as all eyes were drawn to Garrett. Garrett looked across the table at his wife and smiled. Their romance had begun very nearly as she said, and now their daughter had gone and fallen for her mate in much the same way.

"Is it true, Daddy?" Daughtry asked with a hint of laughter in her voice.

"No," Garrett said, surprising Maggie. Her eyes narrowed questioningly, but he quickly continued. "I fell in love with her the first time I saw the portrait, not after hours of studying it." Maggie's smile broadened, and the boys broke into laughter.

"What about you, Nick?" Don suddenly asked.

All heads turned and waited for Nicholas to reply. Even Daughtry couldn't imagine what he might say, and her hand froze in mid-air, her water glass clutched in her fingers, as she waited for his answer.

"I prayed a lot about a wife," Nicholas finally answered. "I was never much the courting type, and even though I had plenty of women giving me the chase, I just wasn't interested in settling down. But I guess I started to see the benefits of having a partner, and so I prayed, then put the advertisement in the .paper." His eyes never left Daughtry as he spoke. "Then your sister answered and sent her picture—and while I thought her a remarkably good-looking woman, I can't say that I fell head-over-heels just then."

"What was it then?" Jordy piped up to ask.

"I guess I was intrigued by her letter," Nicholas responded, seeing the disappointment that flickered across Daughtry's face as she lowered her head to drink. "Of course, once I met her I knew she was exactly what I needed. She's everything a man could want in a wife."

Jordy thought the answer reasonable and continued the conversation by telling of a letter he'd received from some girl in town. The laughter around her did little to revive Daughtry's spirits. Something in Nicholas's response troubled her, and while she couldn't quite figure out what it was, it remained between them nevertheless.

Chapter 15

Daughtry let her frustration boil until morning when she had no other recourse but to vent her emotions at Nicholas. She'd had too much time to think about things and her imagination was running wild.

"Why did you marry me?" she questioned while Nicholas was dressing.

"What?"

"You heard me. Why did you marry me? Why did you push for a quick wedding by proxy? Why didn't you just come here if you wanted a fast wedding?"

Nicholas stopped buttoning his shirt and stared at Daughtry for a moment. He recognized the barely controlled anger in her eyes. "What happened to no questions asked?"

"What happened to sharing your life with me?" Daughtry asked simply.

"What's this all about?"

"It's about us," Daughtry replied rather indignantly. "It's about who you are and why you wanted me to marry you. It's about you being intrigued by my letter, but not in love with me."

"But I love you now," Nicholas offered.

"I want to know the truth, Nicholas. I want to know what you are hiding and why you refuse to trust me."

Nicholas winced at her words. He stared blankly at the wall behind Daughtry for a moment, then in a sad voice said, "Proverbs 19:13 says, 'A foolish son is the calamity of his father; and the contentions of a wife are a continual dropping.' "

"Are you calling me contentious? Just because I ask for the truth?" Daughtry appeared truly hurt, and Nicholas wished to ease her pain.

"No," he shook his head and replied. "I use that verse in reference to myself." Then he grinned and tried to ease the tension between them. "However, if you're feeling guilty. . . ."

Daughtry put her hands on her hips and started to say something but held her tongue. Nicholas saw the softening in her eyes. "Why do you call yourself a foolish son?" she finally asked.

Nicholas ran his hands back through his hair and sighed loudly. "You'd better sit down," he said, coming around to her and pulling out a chair from a nearby desk. Daughtry did as he told her, her eyes never leaving his face.

"I did my share of wild oat sowing when I was young. My folks, good people, saw that I was headed into trouble and began working on me, but I already knew it all, or thought I did, and sought my own way instead. Around the turn of the century, I struck out on my own and hooked up with the wrong crowd. I never really did anything myself, but I was always with one of them when they did something. My name started getting just naturally linked to the kind of bad men that could cause me some major entanglements with the law."

"Are you a criminal?" Daughtry asked hesitantly.

"No," Nicholas said and sat down on the edge of the bed directly in front of her. "No, I always managed to stay just inside the law. I was finally taken aside by an older friend of the family and given a good talking to. As a result I ended up getting myself deputized and began working with the law. Unfortunately, my old friends saw it as a means of advantage for their schemes. They figured their old buddy Nick wasn't about to hand them a prison cell in exchange for the good times they'd showed me."

"Were you a Christian when all of this was going on?"

"I thought I was. Thought I knew about the Gospel and how to live. But I was just as lost as those outlaws when it came to salvation for my soul. Anyway, years like this went on, and my folks were getting more and more worried about me. My brother had married and so had my sister Natalie, and here I was outrunning bullets and breaking up outlaw gangs." He paused for a moment to see how she was taking the news.

"Those three men," Daughtry whispered, "the three you had to turn over to the sheriff, were they. . .?"

"Part of the old Chancellor Gang."

Daughtry gasped, and Nicholas realized that she knew full well who and what that notorious group represented.

"A couple of the gang died in prison, but most of them were paroled just months before you and I married. Everybody was afraid if I stuck around Missouri, they'd locate me and kill me like they promised. Guess nobody gave them much credit for tracking me down out here."

"Kill you?" Daughtry hadn't heard a word past those two.

Nicholas reached out and took her shaking hands into his own. "God helped me to see that I needed more than a casual relationship with Him. When I started thinking about my own mortality and how one of the outlaws I'd helped to put away could just as easily get out and come gunning for me, I knew I wasn't ready to die.

"My father and mother were beside themselves, however, even before the Chancellors got out of prison. My father cornered me when I turned twenty-eight and told me that he was through giving me free rein to do as I wished. He offered to take me into his investment house, but I knew that wasn't for me and I refused. So he told me I had until I was thirty to settle down—or else."

"Or else what?"

Nicholas smiled a little sadly. "He said he'd disinherit me for my own good."

Daughtry looked at him rather puzzled. "Your own father would do that to you?"

"He knew what he was doing," Nicholas replied. "He knew that it would shame me into obedience even at twenty-eight. I didn't want to lose out on the money but, more than that, I didn't want to alienate myself from the family. I knew there would be a full-scale war between him and my mother, not to mention my sisters and brother if they thought Dad were picking on me."

"So what did you have to do to meet his demands?" Daughtry said, suddenly feeling fearful of the response. "What constituted settling down?"

"I had to get a reliable profession, a home in one place, and. . ." He paused, unable to finish the sentence.

"And a wife?" Daughtry asked, her eyes wide.

"Yes."

"And you had to do all of this before you turned thirty?"

"Yes."

"And when did you turn thirty?"

"September twenty-fifth," Nicholas replied softly.

Daughtry stared at him in shock for several minutes. "That was the day the proxy would no longer be any good. That's why you pressed me to hurry and marry you before coming to the ranch."

"Yes," Nicholas said and held her hand tightly. "I had to fulfill my father's requirements. It was important to me. Not just for the inheritance, but because his approval meant a lot to me. I wanted to make him proud of me. I bought the ranch and went about looking into how to be a rancher, then, before I knew it, time had slipped up on me and it was almost too late to get a wife."

"You used me," Daughtry said, suddenly feeling ill. The look in her eyes reflected the betrayal she felt.

"Now, wait just a minute," Nicholas said and took hold of her shoulders firmly. "Isn't that a bit like the pot calling the kettle black? Did you or did you not answer my advertisement in order to escape your overprotective father?"

"That's not why I married you!" Daughtry exclaimed. But even as she said it, she remembered only too well having decided not to marry Nicholas.

Not until her father had refused to listen to reason did she change her mind, and she knew that was one truth she couldn't escape.

"And why did you marry me, Daughtry? Surely not because you were head over heels in love with me from all the courting and flowery words I'd spoken. Maybe it was the hours of evening walks by the river or the cards and flowers." His tone was much too sarcastic for her to bear.

Daughtry jumped to her feet. "I loved you when I married you. I'd fallen in love with your picture and your letter. I thought you'd fallen in love with me as well."

Nicholas stood and spoke calmly. "I did fall in love with you. I told you the truth when I said that. I can't help it that I didn't fall in love with your photograph or letter. I can't help it that I felt desperate to meet a deadline and didn't give the matter as much consideration as I should have. I did pray about it, though. I had a good peace about it too. Daughtry, I know without a doubt that God intended us to be together."

Daughtry tried to grasp all that he said. "Just when did you fall in love with me?"

Nicholas smiled, hoping that her question meant they were making headway. "I'm still falling in love with you," he answered softly, "but I think I first knew it when I came into the bedroom that morning and found an angel asleep in my bed. You know, we've never talked about that."

"Yes, I know," Daughtry said, suddenly feeling a bit uncomfortable at the memory. Everything had happened so quickly. Her marriage, getting to know Nicholas, finding herself with child—it had all come on so fast.

Nicholas pulled her to sit with him on the bed. "I came back to the ranch and all I could think about was that you might or might not be there. I knew I wouldn't have much hope of finding another wife, even though I had two other replies."

"You had other replies?" Daughtry asked, sounding like a little girl.

Nick grinned. "Yes, I did. But yours was the only one I answered."

"Oh."

Nicholas continued, "You can't imagine what I thought when I'd seen all the work you'd done. I figured at first maybe you'd lied about yourself and sent me someone else's picture, because there was no way that I figured a little thing like you could accomplish so much in so little time. Then when I walked into the bedroom. . ." He fell silent, closing his eyes to revisit the memory. "When I walked in and found you asleep in my bed, it was like Christmas morning. I knew then that you'd married me by proxy and that my obligations to my father were fulfilled. But," he said, putting a finger to her lips as she started to protest, "I was completely captivated to know that you belonged to me."

He pulled her close to him and breathed in the sweet scent of roses and lavender. "You were so beautiful, just lying there asleep." His words were warm, and Daughtry felt them relaxing her against her will. "Your hair was spilled out across my pillow, and when I reached out to touch it, I just naturally found myself climbing onto the bed. I couldn't believe how God had blessed me, Daughtry. I still can't. I love you with all my heart, and I am forever yours. I want to be a good husband to you. I've told you everything, and I hope you'll find it in your heart to forgive me."

Daughtry looked at him, his dark eyes revealing a conflict of emotions from within. "I can forgive you," Daughtry finally said, "but I don't know if I can forget." She pulled away from him and got to her feet. A shadow of hurt still lingered in her eyes.

Nicholas came to her, but Daughtry held her hand out. "Please don't touch me. I need to think."

"Daughtry, even God forgets the past when we ask Him to. I'm not only asking, I'm pleading with you. This isn't a matter between just you and me now—we have a child to consider as well."

"I know."

"If you can forgive me, then please forget what I've done to hurt you. Just put it behind you. It's insignificant and unimportant."

Daughtry's eyes flashed anger for just a moment. "It's important to me," she said and stormed from the room to contemplate what her husband had revealed.

"Lord," Nicholas prayed even as Daughtry's footsteps echoed down the hall, "help her to see that I love her. Forgive me for the deception, and help her to forgive me. I love her, Father, and I know that You've brought us together for a purpose. I don't know what the future will hold in store for us, but You do, and I'm asking You to direct me so that I don't mess things up again. Amen."

Chapter 16

D aughtry pulled on her coat and made her way to the barn. She had to get away from the house and Nicholas in order to sort through her feelings. Grabbing a bridle, Daughtry went to the corral, intent on singling out Nutmeg for a ride.

Nutmeg saw Daughtry and whinnied softly, but Poco, after months of neglect and an absent owner, was the one that came to Daughtry. The horse snorted once, then pushed its muzzle against Daughtry's neck, almost pleading.

"So you want to go for a run, do you, Boy?" Daughtry asked softly while stroking the velvety nose. She looked across the corral at Nutmeg, then secured the bridle on Poco and led the horse to the stable to be saddled.

Several of the ranch hands immediately offered to assist her. She started to refuse, but because of her condition and her own uncertainty as to what she should or shouldn't do, she finally relented and accepted their help.

Once on Poco's back, she headed out for a trail she'd ridden most of her life. The air was cold and snow had fallen on the high mountains the night before. The open valley in which the ranch was situated had received only a dusting of snow, though, nothing that Daughtry concerned herself with. Instead, she took the opportunity to pray and think about what Nicholas had said.

"Dear God," she whispered with a glance heavenward, "I think I need to talk about this. You're the only One I can explain it all to, because You're the only One who truly knows what I did and why."

Poco was used to years of such prayers and kept plodding along as though this were perfectly normal.

"I realize," Daughtry continued, "that I did wrong in marrying Nicholas the way I did. I wronged him, I wronged my folks, and I wronged You. I made pledges that I shouldn't have—but now that they're made, there is certainly no turning back."

The words of Ecclesiastes 5:2 came to mind. *Be not rash with thy mouth, and let not thine heart be hasty to utter any thing before God: for God is in heaven, and thou upon earth: therefore let thy words be few.*

Daughtry pondered the Scripture for a moment before resuming her prayer. "I did speak rashly and without any real thought of the consequences," she admitted. "But I'm not trying to take back my pledge in marriage and my vows

197

to You. I just need to understand them. I need to know what my marriage really and truly means."

Not that I can do anything to change the past, Daughtry thought to herself. She noted that Poco had followed their old trail high into the rocks, so she slowed the steed down, still contemplating her life before God.

"I love Nicholas," she told God, "but I'm afraid we both married each other for all the wrong reasons. He needed a wife to please his father and keep his inheritance, and I needed to escape my father's ever-watchful eye." She laughed at her choice of words and glanced heavenward again. "I suppose You know all about children who try to escape Your watchfulness."

~

Back at the ranch, Nicholas began to worry about Daughtry. He searched through the house and when he found her gone, he tore out, barely grabbing his coat, and headed for the barn.

"Daughtry?" he called as he entered the empty stable. There was no answer.

"Daughtry!" Nicholas called again, coming from the stable. Just then Garrett rounded the corner.

"What's wrong?" he questioned, seeing the concern on Nicholas's face.

Nicholas gave a sigh. "Daughtry is upset with me. She stormed out of the house, and I haven't seen her for about an hour. I thought maybe she went for a ride, but Nutmeg is right there in the corral."

Garrett quickly surveyed the horses and shook his head. "But Poco's not."

"Poco?"

"Her horse and favorite traveling companion before she left home. Nobody else would be inclined to ride him." Nicholas saw the apprehension in Garrett's eyes.

"I'd better go find her," Nicholas replied and went to saddle his horse.

"I'm coming too," Garrett stated.

The men were saddled and ready to ride within minutes, and without telling anyone else where they were headed, Garrett and Nicholas rode out side by side.

~

Daughtry felt renewed by her prayers. She could see now that though both she and Nicholas had made mistakes, the focus needed to be taken from the past and placed on the future. They had both been wrong in their actions, but they could easily put those things behind them and start anew. Of this, Daughtry was confident.

Realizing she'd been gone for a considerable amount of time, Daughtry turned Poco around and headed for home. Nicholas had asked her to forget the past and forgive him, and Daughtry intended to do just that. Somehow, together, they would put aside the circumstances under which they married and build a marriage that would be strong and faithful. A marriage that would bind them together, forever.

Daughtry smiled and began to hum to herself. She let Poco pick his way through the narrow canyon path and thought absentmindedly about what she would say to Nicholas. She was so deep in thought that the first few bits of rock falling from the steep canyon wall didn't even attract her attention. They did, however, cause Poco to stop and prance back a step or two.

Poco's actions caused Daughtry to snap to attention just as a huge rock slide covered the path directly in front of them. The loose rock combined with small amounts of snow gained momentum and rushed downward to block the passage through the canyon.

"Easy, Poco," Daughtry whispered and stroked the animal's neck to offer comfort. "We're okay." Daughtry glanced around behind her and knew that she would need to dismount in order to get Poco turned around.

Daughtry slid to the ground and reached out to take Poco's reins just as another slide captured the horse's attention and caused him to rear up and whinny nervously. Daughtry barely managed to avoid the pounding hooves.

While backing away from Poco, she lost control of him and the scared horse seized its freedom and ran.

For a moment, all Daughtry could do was stare after Poco's retreating form. "Great!" she muttered. "Now, I'll have to walk home."

Daughtry picked her way through the rubble and moved past the slide area. She knew she would need at least two hours to make the trek home, but what else could she do except begin walking? No one knew where she was, and only Nicholas knew that she was upset. He might even presume that she needed the extra time to sort through her feelings about him. Walking with determined steps, Daughtry would have laughed at herself had the whole situation not been so infuriating.

~

"Do you have any idea where she might have ridden?" Nicholas asked his father-in-law.

"She has her favorite places. One path in particular," Garrett responded and pointed to the west. "There's a secluded path that winds up into the rocky foothills. She always liked to take that route."

"Let's check there first," Nicholas replied.

"Look!" Garrett pointed to the ground. "Tracks! I'd stake my ranch that those belong to Poco."

The two men followed the tracks that led them in the same direction

Garrett had suggested. With a smile, Garrett turned to Nicholas. "Daughtry can be pretty predictable."

"So far, I haven't been privileged to see that side of her."

Garrett laughed. "I think you have. Isn't this about the third or fourth time you've been involved in her running away?"

Nicholas grinned. "I guess I hadn't thought of it that way. She does seem to favor running rather than dealing with issues head on."

"She can be quite stubborn," Garrett agreed. "So can her mother."

The men had progressed along the path for nearly half an hour when they heard the unmistakable sound of horse hooves pounding through the canyon.

Garrett gave Nicholas a fearful look. "She wouldn't be riding like that unless something were wrong."

Just then Poco cleared the canyon and came into view. Nicholas felt his heart in his throat, and Garrett turned ashen at the sight of the riderless horse.

"Dear God," Garrett whispered, "let her be all right."

Nicholas pressed forward to halt Poco while Garrett watched in stunned silence. The horse whinnied and snorted at Nicholas, rearing back twice before finally settling down to allow the man access to the reins.

"What do you think?" Nicholas questioned, turning to Garrett.

"In truth, I don't know what to think. I don't like to think about it at all. It reminds me of Julie."

Nicholas nodded. "But the horse is unhurt. Maybe he just got spooked and threw Daughtry."

"That girl would have to be unconscious to be thrown from this horse. They're too comfortable with each other. Most likely something happened to cause Daughtry to dismount."

Nicholas looked hard at his father-in-law. "Have there been any strangers around lately?"

"None that I know of. Why?"

Nicholas shook his head. "It's nothing. I just wondered if someone could have made her dismount."

"I doubt there's anyone around these parts that would want to do harm to Daughtry. Years ago we had banditos to worry about, but they moved off to the south as Bandelero grew. Most likely she got off Poco to see to nature's call—or some other perfectly logical explanation." Garrett was trying hard to sound convincing, but in truth, he was desperately frightened for his child.

"You're probably right," Nicholas admitted, but the words did nothing to comfort him.

Nicholas tied Poco to his saddle and urged his own mount forward. Before he could go very far, however, Garrett called out to him, "Nick, would you pray with me?"

Nicholas turned to the man who had once wanted to beat him for stealing his daughter. The minute his eyes met Garrett's, a silent bond was formed. Each man acknowledged, without regret, the position the other held in the life of Daughtry.

With a slow nod, Nicholas waited until Garrett came even, then bowed his head and prayed for his wife.

Chapter 17

Nicholas and Garrett proceeded together, each praying silently and fervently hoping that Daughtry would be found unharmed. In the back of Garrett's mind was the lifeless body of his fourteen-year-old Julie, only four years earlier. Meanwhile, Nicholas was envisioning the remaining members of the Chancellor gang trying to force his hand, using Daughtry as bait.

Neither man was of a mind to talk.

As the canyon narrowed and they could no longer ride side by side, Garrett edged his horse forward. "I'd better lead," he told Nicholas, "since I know the lay of the land." Nicholas nodded and brought up the rear, with Poco trailing behind.

At least in the canyon they were more secluded from the December wind, which was blowing hard and cold across the open valley. High mountain snows capped their surroundings in white, while the red-orange and sandy brown of the rock walls bore only minuscule traces of winter's impending touch.

Nicholas thought of their own ranch to the east. There they had no mountains to contend with—but no barriers against the harsh snows either. He wondered if they'd made the right decision in coming to Piñon Canyon. While he'd learned a great deal more in the few weeks since they'd arrived than he'd hoped to learn all winter, Nicholas was troubled.

Where was she? Where was Daughtry?

Nicholas' mind was so absorbed in thoughts of his wife that he had to glance up to see why his horse had suddenly stopped. Directly in front of Garrett were two men, both with guns leveled at his head.

"What's the meaning of this?" Garrett called out.

"Ain't none of your affair, Mister," a man dressed completely in black called out.

"Well, then, just whose affair is it?" Garrett asked, the irritation evident in his voice.

The other man, a short, squatty character, spit out a stream of tobacco juice and wiped his mouth with the back of his hand. "Well, Nick, it's been awhile, but I guess fate just throwed us together again. You ain't looking too bad for a man about to die."

Nicholas's eyes narrowed, and the scowl on his face was enough to make the man rethink his words. Garrett glanced back at his son-in-law and wondered about the connection between him and the men.

"Jeb, for a man who just spent the last years of his life in prison, I wouldn't think you'd want to throw yourself right back into a cell again," Nicholas replied, never taking his eyes from the man.

The man in black cursed Nicholas's smugness, but Jeb was the one who addressed the issue. "I don't care if I do get throwed back in. It'll be worth it just to say I had the honor of stringin' up your miserable hide."

"So you intend to hang me? I figured that'd be too much work. Why not just put a bullet in me here and now and be done with it?" Nicholas took a gamble with his words, knowing that Jeb answered to his older brother, the ringleader of the gang, Aaron Chancellor. With Aaron nowhere in sight, Nicholas hoped he could buy himself some time.

Jeb spit again before answering. His voice was full of anger and frustration. "I ain't going to do nothin' with you just yet. But when the time comes, I intend to see you suffer good and long."

"Still taking your orders from Aaron, eh?" Both outlaws scowled at the reference, but neither one said a word.

Garrett finally broke the silence and drew the attention of the men. "I demand to know what's going on and why you're even on my land." The men exchanged glances, and Nicholas knew immediately that they were up to no good.

"You own this here land?" Jeb questioned.

"I do," Garrett stated without hesitation.

Nicholas hoped to intercede and take Jeb's mind off of whatever he was plotting. "This man is nothing to you. Your war is with me."

"You've got that right, but I'll just bet there's some money to be made. This here landowner might be our ticket to Mexico."

"You can head on over to Mexico any time you want. It's not that far," Nicholas replied dryly.

"Shut up, Dawson," Jeb demanded. "Gus, what say we take the both of 'em and give Aaron a call. He can make the decision then as to what we do next."

"Doesn't he always?" Nicholas said, hoping to goad either one of them into immediate action.

"Tie 'em up, Gus," Jeb said, keeping his pistol leveled at the middle of Garrett's chest. With a smirk he added, "And gag Dawson if he so much as utters another word."

~

Daughtry had worked up quite a sweat on her hike back to Piñon Canyon. She knew she was still a couple of miles away when she heard the unmistakable sound of voices. Hoping that Nicholas or even her father and brothers had come searching for her, Daughtry climbed up on a rocky ledge to get a better look.

Easing into position, Daughtry gasped and flattened herself against the ground when she saw the men who threatened to shoot her husband and father. Immediately, her mind went back to the day when Nicholas had faced three outlaws alone. Were these men part of the Chancellor gang?

She struggled to make out what was being said but could only hear pieces of words. Try as she might, she was simply too far away to make any sense out of them. She lifted her head just enough to watch the scene below her. A man dressed in black handed his pistol to his partner, dismounted his horse, and took a length of rope from the horn of his saddle.

Helpless, Daughtry watched as the man first tied up Nicholas, then her father. In a matter of minutes the entire matter was completed, and the man remounted, claiming his gun and turning it once again on her husband.

"I have to get help," Daughtry whispered to herself. She watched as the men led Nicholas and her father off in the opposite direction from the ranch. Perhaps she could get back and tell her brothers before the men got too far.

Slipping noiselessly from her perch, Daughtry began to run as fast as she could move. She was panting heavily, unused to the activity, before she'd even crossed half the distance to home. She sucked in lungfuls of cold air, praying for strength to continue, and just when she felt her legs giving out, she caught sight of the corral fences and the orange adobe ranch house.

Dear God, she prayed, *please don't let them hurt Nicholas or Daddy.* The prayer continued, the same words, the same plea, over and over until Daughtry collapsed against the corral in order to catch her breath.

Gavin walked out of the barn in time to see his sister fall against the fence. Without hesitation, he ran as fast as his legs would carry him and scooped Daughtry into his arms.

"Are you all right?" he asked fearfully.

"No," Daughtry gasped, still breathless. "I. . .I have to. . ."

"Just be quiet," Gavin said, carrying her to the house. "You can tell me later."

"No," Daughtry said, putting her hand to Gavin's shoulder. "They have Nicholas and Daddy."

Gavin stopped dead and looked down at his sister. "Who has Nicholas and Dad?"

"I don't know, I think they might be part of the old Chancellor gang." Daughtry clutched her brother's neck tightly, the fear evident in her eyes.

"Why would you imagine such a thing?"

"Nicholas used to be a lawman. He was primarily responsible for putting the gang away." Daughtry drew a deeper breath. "You can put me down, Gavin. I'm okay."

Gavin shook his head. "No, we'd best get on in the house and let everybody hear the rest of this." He started walking again and spied Mack, his father's longtime ranch foreman. "Mack, something's happened, you'd best join us in the house." The dark-headed man nodded and followed Gavin inside.

"Mom!" Gavin yelled loudly. He put Daughtry down on a chair and yelled again, this time even louder.

"What is it?" Maggie questioned, coming into the living room. "I'm not deaf, you know."

"We've got trouble," Gavin explained. Maggie looked at Daughtry for a moment, noticing the redness of her face, as well as the dirt and disarray of her clothes.

"What trouble?" Maggie asked slowly and looked from Daughtry to Gavin and finally to Mack.

Just then, as if sensing that something weren't right, Daughtry's other brothers bounded into the room.

"What's going on?" Joey asked. The question was echoed by each of the others before Daughtry stood up to explain.

"Two men have taken Nicholas and Daddy. I went out riding this morning and a rockslide blocked my route home. I dismounted and Poco got away from me. I guess I took too long getting back, because Nicholas and Daddy came looking for me. I heard voices and came up over a rock just above where the canyon narrows. There were two men with guns, and they tied up Daddy and Nicholas and headed off in the opposite direction from the ranch."

"Who were they?" asked Dolan.

"Daughtry thinks they're part of the Chancellor gang," Gavin piped up. "Seems Nicholas used to be some kind of lawman, and they bear him a grudge."

"Daughtry, are you sure?" Maggie asked, trembling.

"I can't be positive. I couldn't hear what they were saying, but something happened awhile back, when Nicholas and I were on our ranch. Nicholas told me then that there was a good chance more of the Chancellors would come gunning for him."

"We'd better round up as many hands as we can," Gavin said to Mack.

"Make sure everybody is armed and has what they need in the way of ammunition. Jordy, go get the guns from the cabinet in Dad's office. Don, Dolan, go saddle our horses and Joseph, get provisions for all of us. We don't know how long it's going to take or how far we'll have to ride." Without a word of protest, the brothers flew into action with Mack fast on their heels.

"I'm going too!" Daughtry exclaimed.

"Oh no, you're not," Gavin said, and the way he looked at her was so much like his father that Maggie had to laugh.

"But I can't just sit here," Daughtry protested. "I want to go."

Maggie came and put an arm around her daughter. "You're expecting a child, Daughtry. You have to think of more than just what you want."

"I suppose you're right," Daughtry replied sadly. The defeat in her voice caused Gavin to give her shoulder a reassuring squeeze.

"We'll get them back," he said, looking into both Daughtry and Maggie's eyes. "I promise you, we'll bring them back safe."

The women watched as their men mounted up and headed out. Daughtry felt hot tears slide down her cheeks. Would she ever get a chance to tell Nicholas that she was sorry and that she understood why he'd married her the way he had?

～

Jeb Chancellor led the way to the range shack, while Gus brought up the rear with Nicholas and Garrett sandwiched in between. Garrett immediately recognized the place as one they used only on occasion. It was well secluded and far enough away from the rest of civilization that no one would have any idea they were even there.

"This place belong to you too?" Jeb asked Garrett.

"Yeah."

"How much land you own, anyway?"

"Enough." Garrett was quickly realizing their game. "If it's money you're after, why don't you just name your price?"

"Just like that?" Jeb laughed. "What then? You gonna ride back to the house and write out a draft?"

"Is that what you want?"

"I don't know what I want yet," Jeb replied.

"Of course you don't," Nicholas sneered, "you haven't talked to Aaron yet. Big brother has to tell him what to think."

"I'm warning you, Dawson," Jeb said in a menacing tone. "Keep your mouth shut and you just might live to see tomorrow."

"He'd better live to see a whole lot more than tomorrow if you want any of my money," Garrett declared.

"What's he to you?" Jeb asked, halting his horse in front of the shack.

"He's family." Garrett's eyes met Nicholas's for a brief moment.

"Well, family or no, whether he lives or dies is up to Aaron. There ain't no amount of money what can buy back a man's years wasted behind bars." Jeb dismounted and slapped his reins around the hitching post. "Get 'em down, Gus, and bring 'em inside."

In spite of the way their hands were tied, both Garrett and Nicholas swung their legs over the necks of their mounts and jumped down unassisted. Gus poked Nicholas forward with the barrel of his gun pressed firmly in the small of Nicholas's back. In turn, Jeb motioned Garrett inside.

"Tie them to the chairs." Jeb took a defensive position with the gun leveled directly at Garrett, while Gus did as he was told. Once Nicholas and Garrett were securely tied, Jeb motioned Gus outside for a talk.

"Can you work the ropes loose?" Nicholas asked Garrett. Although they sat nearly side by side, Nicholas had to strain to get a look at the way Gus had tied Garrett's ropes.

"I don't know," Garrett whispered back. He strained against the hemp, feeling it chafe and bite at his wrists.

"I think, with any luck at all, I can work through mine," Nicholas replied.

"I think we'd best count on more than luck."

Nicholas grinned. "You do have a point there. I've been praying since we left to look for Daughtry." The smile quickly faded from his face. "Daughtry! I'd nearly forgotten." The agitation he felt was quickly mirrored in Garrett's eyes.

"It's in God's hands," Garrett replied. "I guess it always has been, except for the times I yank it back out." He smiled weakly at his son-in-law.

"I know what you mean. I guess I've pretty much messed up my share of living. I can't say that I've always done things to make my folks proud of me, nor can I stand on the memory of always trusting God to see me through." Nick paused for a minute, wondering if he should continue.

"Who are these men to you?" Garrett finally asked.

"Part of the Chancellor gang. I hung out with some of them before I became a lawman. They figured I'd overlook their shenanigans, for old times sake, I suppose."

"But you didn't?"

"No," Nicholas replied. "I couldn't. Like I told Daughtry, I grew up in a Christian home, and even though I felt the urge to spread my wings and buck up against the wind, I never broke the law. Bad thing was, I constantly kept company with those who did. Finally, a friend took me in hand and I became involved with working for the law instead of against it."

"Were you the one to put them away? Is that why they want to kill you?"

Nicholas took a deep breath and looked his father-in-law in the eye. "Yes. They tried once before back at my ranch. Daughtry unfortunately witnessed the whole thing. I hope you'll forgive me for bringing this on you and your family. I figured when you offered us a home for the winter that they'd lose track of me and give up the search. I guess they won't quit until they're all back in prison or dead."

"Don't be so hard on yourself," Garrett replied with genuine affection. "You've proven yourself to me more than once. I happen to think Daughtry made a good choice for a husband."

Nicholas's smile didn't reach the look of worry in his eyes. "If I only knew that she was safe."

"God's watching over her, Nick. We have to count on that. I guess I'm just now starting to see things more clearly. When Julie died, I figured I'd failed somewhere along the way. Now, I know better and my heart is cleared of the guilt. God's timing isn't always something we mortals can understand."

"I admire your faith, Garrett," Nicholas said honestly. "I hope some of it rubs off."

Garrett grinned. "I have a feeling your faith is greater than you know. Now, how are we going to get out of this mess?"

Chapter 18

After several hours, Daughtry had had her fill of waiting. As soon as she saw that her mother was amply occupied in the kitchen, Daughtry pled a headache and went to her room.

At first she didn't know what she'd do. All she really knew was that somehow, some way, she had to help. Without another thought, Daughtry began to discard her dirty riding outfit. Standing in nothing more than her heavy knit chemise and black wool stockings, she glanced into the mirror and smiled as a plan formed in her mind.

Racing to her clothes chest, Daughtry pulled out the bottom drawer and retrieved her brother's hand-me-down jeans. Disguised in boys' clothes, Daughtry figured she could ride into town and notify the sheriff, as well as the two Monroe families. This would get even more men looking for her father and husband and still wouldn't go against Gavin's instructions that she not join them in the actual search.

Rebraiding her hair, Daughtry coiled it around her head, then pulled on a dark brown hat and surveyed her appearance in the mirror. Noting the curvy appearance of her body in the jeans, Daughtry went to the wardrobe and pulled out one of Nicholas's duster coats.

The coat fell to just above her boot tops, but Daughtry knew it would be better than letting either her father or Nicholas catch her in town wearing boys' pants. With an apprehensive glance down the hall, Daughtry made her way to the front door.

Walking with determined strides across the corral yard, Daughtry took a rope and singled Nutmeg out of the few remaining mounts. Within a short time, she had the mare saddled and ready, grateful that no one had come to interfere with her plan.

Daughtry covered the distance into Bandelero in half the normal time. She knew she'd pushed Nutmeg to the limits, and as soon as the town was in sight, Daughtry slowed the mare to a trot. Nutmeg pranced nervously and whinnied softly at the sights and sounds. Daughtry was amazed at the way the small town was continuing to grow. What had started out as a handful of shops and services was now a bustling town, well on its way to becoming a city.

The sheriff's office was at the far end, and Daughtry knew she'd have to ride right through the heart of Bandelero before reaching her destination. Pulling her hat low, Daughtry urged Nutmeg forward, refusing to make eye contact with anyone on the boardwalks.

To Daughtry's utter frustration, the sheriff's office was closed without a single soul to explain his whereabouts. She heaved a sigh and made her way back to Nutmeg, just as a voice called out behind her.

"Sheriff's gone just now, but can I help you?"

Daughtry turned slowly to find Mr. Tate, owner of the hardware store. "I don't suppose you know where he's gone?"

"Daughtry Lucas! Is that you under that getup?" The man's shocked expression almost made her laugh.

"Yes, it's me, but the name is Dawson now. Do you know where the sheriff is?"

"Sure," Tate replied. "He's gone off looking for your father and some other guy."

"That would be my husband, Nicholas," Daughtry replied. She was relieved to know that the sheriff was already assisting in the search.

"Didn't know you got yourself married," the man said, scratching his chin. "Always figured you'd marry one of the local boys."

Daughtry couldn't be bothered with what Mr. Tate thought. Her real concern was what was happening to her husband and father. "If you'll excuse me," she said remounting Nutmeg, "I have things to do." Mr. Tate said nothing as he watched Daughtry settle into the saddle. "Good day, Mr. Tate." Daughtry urged Nutmeg back through town, wondering what she should do first.

Just as Daughtry had convinced herself that contacting Lillie and Dr. Dan would be the best choice, she pulled Nutmeg up short and gasped. The two men who'd taken her father and Nicholas were riding into town as though they were coming to Sunday meeting.

Without taking her eyes off of the two, Daughtry eased Nutmeg into a slow but steady walk. She had no idea what she was going to do, or how she could manage to capture the men, but Daughtry knew she had to do something.

When the men headed in the direction of the train depot, Daughtry felt herself grow frantic. What if they'd already killed not only Nicholas but her father as well? What if they perceived their job as finished and now they were taking the train back to—wherever?

When the men dismounted and tied their horses to the hitching post in front of the depot, Daughtry began to panic. *What do I do, Lord?* She found her heart racing and, in spite of the cold wind, Daughtry felt sweat on her brow.

The men entered the building, and Daughtry quickly dismounted and tied Nutmeg several spaces away from their mounts. Glancing up at the double glass doors of the depot, she could see that the men were deep in conversation with the ticket agent. Without giving it another thought, Daughtry made her way to their horses.

"If they aren't going to leave by train," she mused in a whisper to herself, "they'll come back for their mounts. Either way, they'll be in for a surprise." She quickly slid her hand along the first horse and reaching under his belly, Daughtry loosened the cinch strap. Repeating this action with the other horse, she felt a bit of confidence in her mission. Somehow, she needed to find out what they were doing inside the depot, then she needed to get help.

Daughtry made her way around the building, peering in through the windows to catch sight of the two men. They seemed to be there to use the telephone, and the agent was somewhat disturbed by their request.

Daughtry watched intently, while one man pushed a handful of money across the counter to the agent and waited for his response. Daughtry knew the phone was on the track side of the building and that the agent's bay window was where she'd have her best chance of spying on the two men.

Slipping across the back, barely managing to avoid a man hoisting a heavy crate to the loading platform, Daughtry eased her way cautiously to the bay window. The window was positioned so that the agent could look up and down the track for some distance and Daughtry knew she'd have to keep to the wall beside it in order to avoid being seen. Thankfully, she noted that the two men kept their backs to her when they entered the room and that the telephone was opposite the side she'd chosen to be.

Daughtry felt herself trembling as she strained to hear what the two men were saying. Just then, the heavy blast from the four o'clock westbound blotted out all hope of hearing what the men were saying.

Glancing down the tracks, Daughtry watched as the train eased into the station, blowing off steam noisily. She felt more frustration than she'd ever known possible as she glanced back into the agent's office and found that the men were still on the phone.

"I have to find out what they're up to," she whispered.

People began to leave the train, while others crowded around her to take their place on board. Daughtry felt herself being pushed back through the comings and goings, until she lost her footing and fell forward.

With a shriek of fright, Daughtry found herself caught by strong hands and set back on her feet.

"Whoa, Son," a deep baritone voice called out.

Daughtry glanced upward and gasped, while the man staring down at her did the same.

"Sorry, Ma'am," the man corrected his mistake, "I guess I mistook you in that garb."

Daughtry still couldn't speak. The man before her was the spitting image of her husband, only his hair was gray and his face betrayed his age. How could it be?

"I–I'm," she stammered. "It was my fault. I apologize."

The man smiled broadly, then reached out to take hold of the stately woman beside him. "No harm done," he said softly.

Daughtry stared in amazement at the couple. She looked at the woman for a moment, then back at the man.

"Is something wrong, Miss?" the man asked her, a look of concern replacing his smile.

Daughtry glanced back at the ticket agent's office and saw that the men were still there. Without hesitation she pushed back her hat and looked into the dark eyes of the stranger. "Do I know you?" she asked boldly.

"I doubt it," the man replied, and the woman at his side smiled.

"We're here to surprise our son," the woman said.

"Your son?" Daughtry barely squeaked out the words.

"That's right, perhaps you know where we could find him. His name is Nicholas Dawson. We received a letter from him saying that he's staying with his wife's family. I believe their name is Lucas," the man replied, then shook his head. "Forgive my rudeness, I'm Riley Dawson, and this is my wife Alexandra."

Daughtry stared up in dumbfounded silence at her father and mother-in-law. "Oh my," she finally managed to whisper.

"Are you all right?" Riley asked, seeing Daughtry pale at the news.

"I'm afraid so," she whispered, feeling faint. "I have a bit of a surprise for you," she said with a slight smile. "I'm Daughtry Dawson, Nicholas's wife."

Riley's mouth dropped open, while Alexandra's eyes widened and twinkled with amusement.

"You are Nicholas's wife?" Riley questioned.

Daughtry shifted her weight nervously and glanced back at the agent's office. "Yes, and the fact of the matter is, Nicholas and my father are in trouble, and I need your help."

Alexandra instantly sobered and reached out to Daughtry. "What is it? What's happened to them?"

Daughtry quickly explained to her in-laws why she was dressed as she was and how the two men inside the depot were responsible for their son's abduction.

"I need your help, Mr. Dawson," Daughtry said in such a way that Riley couldn't help but put his arm around her.

"Call me Riley," he said softly. "Look, I'll take care of this." He looked past Daughtry to his wife. "You take Zandy and go back to the ranch."

"Zandy?" Daughtry questioned.

"That's what most folks call me," Alexandra stated, trying to keep her voice calm.

"Oh," Daughtry replied with a nod. Then turning back to Riley she shook her head. "I'm not going back. I have to help Nicholas."

"Look, I know you want to help him, but we have no idea what we're going to run into," Riley said firmly.

"I know that half the county is out there looking for them. I can't just sit back and do nothing. Look, those two are leaving. Either help me capture them or stay out of my way." Daughtry's determination caused Zandy to laugh out loud, while Riley rolled his eyes.

"I see our son married a woman just like his mother. Stubborn to the bone and just as beautiful." Daughtry blushed at the half-compliment but turned to leave.

"Oh, no you don't," Riley said, taking hold of her arm. "You've got yourself a partner."

Daughtry turned and smiled. "Good. I loosened their cinch straps," she said with a grin. "They ought to just about fall into our arms."

Riley shook his head while, Zandy tried to refrain from laughing.

"They have guns," Daughtry said, while leading Riley and Zandy around the building. "But I figure when they fall off those horses, we might be able to get the upper hand, maybe even get their weapons away from them."

"You leave that to me," Riley said in a voice that made it clear to Daughtry he meant business. She nodded and halted when they reached the front of the depot. The men were still nowhere in sight.

"Alexandra," Riley said, turning to his wife, "you secure our bags and stay out of sight. I'll be hard pressed enough to keep her out of danger's way." He motioned to Daughtry who didn't like one bit that she'd gained yet another guardian.

Knowing the outlaws wouldn't recognize her or Riley, Daughtry motioned her father-in-law to follow her as the two men came bounding out of the depot. Without any time to lose, Daughtry and Riley flew into action as the men attempted to mount their horses. When the saddles twisted to the side and dumped the surprised men on the frozen ground, Riley quickly grabbed the revolver of the one dressed in black, while Daughtry put her booted foot firmly on the arm of the shorter, squatty man.

"Get up real slow," Riley instructed the men after he had Daughtry remove the other man's weapon. "Where's the jail, Daughtry?"

"Other end of town," she answered, feeling hope for the first time.

"Come on, I'll lead the way."

Riley motioned the men forward, while Daughtry apprehensively moved out. The men weren't over their shock as they took hesitant steps forward, but the gun in Riley's hand left them little doubt that he meant business.

A crowd started to gather and follow Daughtry and Riley as they made their way to the sheriff's office. The mumblings and whispers were enough to unnerve Daughtry, but she took a deep breath and forced herself forward. *When this is all done,* she thought, *I may very well faint!*

Mr. Tate was there to greet them, and when Daughtry explained the need to put the two men into a cell, he rapidly produced a set of keys and led Daughtry and Riley into the jail.

Once they had the men behind bars, Daughtry sat down hard on a chair in the outer office, while her father-in-law began to question the men.

"You have my son and his father-in-law," Riley said with a menacing stare at the outlaws. He'd dealt with their kind plenty before, even if it were a lifetime before.

"What if we do?" the short man questioned.

"Well, the way I figure it, you can cooperate and tell me where they are, or I can start shooting parts of your body until you give me the information." Riley prayed his bluff would work.

The man stared at Riley as if trying to decide if he were serious or not. Daughtry held her breath, hoping and praying that Riley wouldn't have to shoot anyone.

"You wouldn't really shoot us," the man in black stated nervously. "Would you?"

Riley fired the revolver into the mattress just to the man's left. He glanced down at the gun as if carefully considering its benefits. "I'll do whatever it takes," Riley answered in a cool, unemotional tone.

Minutes later, Daughtry and Riley emerged from the jail to find the small crowd still lingering to learn what they could. Daughtry refused to listen to Riley's suggestion that he get another man to go with him.

"I know our land better than anyone here in town," she protested with hands on her hips. "And, unless you plan to lock me in a cell with those two, I'm going to find my husband and father."

Riley ran his hand back through his gray hair and stared at Daughtry.

"Remind you of someone?" Zandy questioned, coming up behind her husband.

"Frightfully so," Riley replied with a look at his wife that told her he really didn't mind the comparison. "Poor Nick." Zandy giggled at her husband's mock horror.

"Well?" Daughtry questioned. "Are you coming with me?"

"Of course I am," Riley responded. "Nicholas will have my hide over this and rightfully so, but I'm getting too old to fight the feminine wiles. Could you manage to stop long enough to arrange for Zandy to be taken to your folks' place first?"

"Certainly," Daughtry said with a smile. "My Aunt Lillie—well she's really not my aunt, but she and my mother are like sisters. Anyway, she lives in that house right over there. She's married to the town doctor, so there's always someone there. Just tell her who you are and what you need. She'll see to it that you get there."

Zandy smiled and nodded. Daughtry moved to retrieve Nutmeg's reins and motioned to Riley.

"You'd better saddle up one of their horses, Riley."

Riley gave Zandy a quick kiss, then did just as his daughter-in-law instructed. "Nicholas certainly has his work cut out for him," he muttered under his breath, and Zandy's laughter caused Daughtry to wonder at the murmured words.

Chapter 19

L ess than a half-hour after Gus and Jeb had ridden out for town, Nicholas had managed to free himself from the ropes. Crashing the ancient chair's rickety frame against the wall until it fell into pieces, Nicholas had managed to work his arms and shoulders loose.

"If you back up here," Garrett suggested, "I can probably pull those knots free with my teeth."

Nicholas nodded and pushed his hands, still bound behind his back, up to meet his father-in-law's mouth. Garrett worked at the ropes for only a moment before managing to pull the first knot apart. After that it was only a matter of teamwork and they had themselves free.

Rubbing his wrists and the spot in his shoulder that ached from the only sign of age he'd allowed himself—rheumatism—Garrett smiled at his son-in-law. "I guess we'll be quite a surprise for old Gus and Jeb."

"More than they can imagine," Nicholas said, returning the grin. "The way I see it, we'd be wise to lay a trap. There's no way of knowing if they'll come back alone, and I intend to round up every one of those good-for-nothings so I can get on with my life. I can't go on having to look over my shoulder every time a twig snaps, and I'll certainly not subject my wife and kids to it." Looking intently at Garrett for a moment, Nicholas grew sober.

"I'm really sorry for the danger this has placed you and your family in," he began. "I have to admit that one of the reasons I agreed to winter with you here was because I was worried something like this would happen at our place. I figured, and selfishly so, that they'd come around and find our place deserted, with no forwarding address or knowledge of where we'd gotten off to, and they'd give up and go home. I don't want to be responsible for killing any of them, but I won't let them kill my family."

Garrett reached out and put his hand on Nicholas's shoulder. "You did what you had to do. I would have done the same thing, and there's nothing to be ashamed of in thinking of Daughtry first." He grinned, breaking the tension between them. "I put her mother first, often to my detriment and, sometimes, my distraction."

Nicholas laughed. "Yes, Daughtry can be a real distraction too."

"Don't I know it," Garrett said, joining his laughter.

"What are we going to do about this?" Nicholas said, sobering once again.

"We'll have to take them when they come back. We can watch and see if more than just the two of them come back and judge the situation according-ly. The way I figure it, it's going to be about dark before they can make it back from Bandelero. We can use that to our benefit by leaving the place dark."

"Makes sense," Nicholas replied, sizing up the range shack. It was a sin-gle room, with little more than fireplace, table, and chair. The other chair, now good for little more than kindling, lay in a heap beside a small metal cab-inet. "What's in there?" Nicholas questioned.

"A bit of food, some bandages, that sort of thing. No weapons, except maybe a knife." Garrett strode over to the cabinet and opened it. "Looks like Gus and Jeb cleaned it out. There's bandages and some liniment. Nothing else."

Nicholas nodded and continued to stare out the window. His mind imme-diately drifted where he didn't want to dwell. Daughtry was somewhere out there. Maybe she was alone and hurt or maybe she'd made it back safely to the ranch. Either way, not knowing was killing Nicholas.

"You love her a great deal, don't you, Son?"

Nicholas didn't even smile at the reference. "I do," he whispered. "More than I ever hoped I could love another person."

Garrett came up beside him and put his arm around Nicholas's shoulder. "Let's pray." With a nod, Nicholas felt hope return.

~

"We're about out of light, Daughtry," Riley called from his mount.

"I know, but we're nearly there," she replied in a breathless manner. "We'll just have to push them a little harder."

The horses, already more than a little weary from their continuous jour-neys, were sweat-soaked and starting to lather. Daughtry had never abused a mount in her life, but then, she'd never felt the urgency to save another per-son's life. Nicholas and her father might lie bleeding or half-dead, for all she knew. They just had to get to the ranch shack and see that they were all right. After that, she'd give Nutmeg a well-deserved rest, but not until then.

Daughtry felt a wave of nausea run through her, causing her to slow their pace a bit. She prayed silently that the feeling would pass, and when it didn't, Daughtry surprised Riley by pulling up quickly.

"Here!" she exclaimed, tossing her reins to Riley. She barely took four steps before losing the contents of her stomach.

Considerably more pale and slightly weak, Daughtry returned to her horse, ignoring Riley's shocked expression. She rinsed her mouth out, then took a deep drink from the canteen before remounting.

Meeting Riley's eyes, she nodded. "We're going to have a baby."

Riley's expression changed from shock to extreme concern. "You can't be out here doing this."

Daughtry shrugged. "That's what my brother said and no doubt what my father and husband will say. I can probably expect my father to suggest a spanking again—that seems to be his answer for wayward children."

"And rightfully so," Riley murmured, refusing to give in to Daughtry's dry amusement. "You could harm yourself."

Daughtry laughed. "I'm a little more concerned about what Nicholas will do when he sees me out here." Urging her horse forward, she grinned over her shoulder. "But I guess it's a little late to start worrying now."

Riley sat for a moment, still stunned by the news. Nudging the horse in the ribs, Riley caught up with Daughtry and spoke. "You amaze me," he said to her.

Daughtry was surprised to hear those words instead of a rebuke. She glanced up, still shaky from her bout of nausea. "Sometimes," she replied, "I amaze myself. I figure God has His hand most firmly on my shoulder, though. I don't doubt for a minute that He led me to town in order to find those two at just the right time. I was the only one who knew what they looked like." She paused, looking skyward. "God keeps pretty busy with me, but then I try to return the favor and keep myself pretty busy with Him."

Riley smiled. "Remind me sometime to tell you about how busy He had to keep with me."

Daughtry looked at Riley and nodded. "It's a deal."

~

The mountain peaks greedily sucked out the last bits of light, just as the range shack came into view. Daughtry and Riley did nothing to disguise their approach. They were hopeful that the noise they made would be welcomed by living, breathing souls.

Daughtry refused to listen to Riley's pleas that she let him enter the shack first. She raced across the ground without even securing Nutmeg to the hitching post. Riley did likewise and was on her heels.

Daughtry burst through the door into the darkness. She opened her mouth to call out to Riley, but someone knocked her down onto the hard wooden floor. While the beast managed to sit itself square on her backside, the cracking thud of a fist to a face left Daughtry little doubt that Riley had been properly subdued.

"Light a lamp," Nicholas called to Garrett who was now nursing his sore knuckles. Daughtry was so stunned she couldn't speak. She began to struggle furiously, which only made Nicholas twist around to clamp a hand to the middle of her back.

"Get off of me, you oaf!" she managed to gasp as her father struck a match to the kerosene lamp he held.

Nicholas's and Garrett's jaws dropped open with the stunned revelation that they'd managed to capture their rescue team. Without thinking to move, Nicholas stared at the crumpled body of his father, now stirring in the doorway. Daughtry started kicking her legs, but the duster wrapped around them sufficiently and saved Nicholas from any blows.

"Well, I'll be," Garrett finally said and motioned to where Riley was struggling to sit up. "You know him?"

Nicholas moaned, but still didn't move. "Yeah, he's my father."

"Figures," Garrett said, rolling his eyes upward.

"Nicholas! You're smashing me into the floor!" Daughtry exclaimed.

Finally realizing what he was doing, Nicholas shifted his weight and rolled to the side of his wife. Daughtry just lay there for a moment, trying to take in enough air to fill her lungs.

"I'd say while you have her down there like that—" Garrett began.

"Don't you dare!" Daughtry interrupted indignantly. "Don't you dare suggest he spank me. I'm not a child! If you two had bothered to look at who was coming. . ."

Nicholas interrupted as he took Daughtry into his arms and pulled her across his lap. "We did look. We saw that sorrel mare that Gus had ridden out of here and we saw two scraggly looking characters." Nicholas looked Daughtry over from head to foot, then glanced up at his father. "You gonna live, Dad?"

Riley rubbed his sore jaw. "Your father-in-law packs quite a punch."

"Don't I know it!" Nicholas exclaimed, and Garrett turned sheepishly to shrug. "How'd you get involved in all of this?"

Riley tried to smile, but his swollen lip wouldn't allow for it. "Your mother and I came to town to surprise you for Christmas. We ran into Daughtry at the train station where she'd pinned down your captors."

Nicholas turned to see Daughtry looking at him rather smugly. "You went into town wearing boys' pants? After I told you I didn't want to see you doing that?"

Daughtry groaned in exasperation and tried to free herself from Nicholas's grasp. He tightened his hold on her, leaving little doubt that the matter was far from settled.

"I saw the men take you and Daddy," Daughtry explained. "I ran back home and got Gavin and the boys. They're out there somewhere, even now, looking for you two. I couldn't just sit at home, and Gavin told me I couldn't go with them."

Garrett looked at Riley with a look that only fathers could share. "She's never been one to follow instruction."

"Well, she's going to learn real quicklike," Nicholas interjected. "Daughtry, you could have been killed. I could have busted you in the jaw like Garrett did Dad. Then what?"

Daughtry opened her mouth to speak, looking first at her husband, then her father, and finally Riley. Finding not even a shred of support, Daughtry crossed her hands against her chest and pouted. "I can't believe you aren't even grateful for the rescue."

Nicholas gently held her under one arm and got to his feet, pulling Daughtry up with him as if she weighed nothing. "I am grateful," he said softly, "but I'd be a whole lot more grateful if you were safely tucked away back at the ranch."

He looked at his father, shaking his head. "I don't suppose she told you that she's expecting?"

Riley chuckled. "She did. Right after she lost her lunch and we were nearly here. Reminds me of your mother," he added with such joy that Daughtry couldn't help but smile appreciatively.

"I will take that as a compliment," Daughtry replied. "Your wife is a wonderful woman. I imagine she would have come with us if I'd given her time to change."

At this Nicholas and Riley both laughed, and Garrett shook his head. "Sounds like Maggie. I'm sure if we don't make our way home soon, she'll be leading the searchers for us."

"Those horses are pretty spent," Riley said. "In fact, I think I'd better make sure they didn't wander off too far. In our hurry," he paused with a wink at Daughtry, "we left them to fend for themselves."

"I'll give you a hand," Garrett said, coming forward. "I hope you'll forgive the greeting."

Riley patted him on the back. "Forgiven. From now on, we'll fight on the same side."

"Agreed," Garrett chuckled.

When their fathers had gone outside, Nicholas pulled Daughtry to him so tightly she could scarcely breathe. "I was so afraid you were hurt," Nicholas breathed against her ear. "Thank God you're all right."

"I echo those sentiments myself," Daughtry whispered, lifting her face. "I couldn't just sit at home, Nick. I love you and I had to help. I couldn't have lived with myself if I'd done nothing and lost you."

Nicholas tenderly stroked Daughtry's dirt-smudged cheek. "I love you, Daughtry. My life wouldn't mean much without you in it." He lowered his lips slowly to hers, kissing her long and gently as though gaining reassurance from the action.

Pulling away, Daughtry sighed and leaned her head against her husband's chest. "I like your dad," she finally said. "He's just like you."

Nicholas chuckled softly. "I wouldn't have thought that a compliment a few months back."

"And now?"

"Now, I'm pleased you think it so. He's a good man, and I'm proud to be his son," Nicholas admitted.

"You'll work everything out between you?" Daughtry questioned. "I mean the demands he put on you and such. You won't hold a grudge or be angry with him? After all," Daughtry said looking into Nicholas's dark eyes, "it brought us together."

"No, I'm not angry with him," Nicholas smiled. "Grateful, but not angry."

Daughtry nodded and smiled. "And you aren't angry with me? I mean, I made a pretty big mess of things back at the house. I'm sorry for that too. I was riding back to apologize when I lost Poco. I just want you to know that it doesn't matter that you didn't love me when you married me. All that matters is that you love me now and that you'll always love me."

Nicholas kissed Daughtry lightly on the mouth. "I'll always love you, but I may have to tie you to a chair in order for you to bring our child into the world healthy and safe."

Daughtry laughed. "I promise from now on, I'll be good as can be."

"Uh-huh. Sure," Nicholas mused in disbelief, "until the next time."

Chapter 20

Christmas Eve at Piñon Canyon had been a night of precious celebration as far back as Daughtry Lucas Dawson could remember. The house was decorated festively in pine boughs, red ribbons, wreaths shimmering with gold braided ribbons, and a tree that commanded the center of attention in the living room.

Daughtry lovingly touched the ornaments that hung on the tree. Delicate glass spheres, decorated with miniature paintings of the first Christmas, were among her favorites. They were nearly as old as she, and Daughtry remembered fondly, they were a gift from her father to her mother.

Laughter rang out in the dining room, where most of Bandelero, or so it seemed, had gathered to share in the festivities. When Daughtry's mother had come to New Mexico, soon to be wed to Garrett Lucas, she'd left behind her dear friend Lillie in Topeka, Kansas. But Lillie had soon followed and married Dr. Daniel Monroe, brother to the young pastor, David, who had an even younger wife, Jenny. They were more like a family of closely knit brothers and sisters, and their offspring had grown up in a togetherness that seemed natural and secure.

Daughtry had never known a Christmas Eve when they'd not all joined together to celebrate the birth of their Savior. She could still hear the years of gaiety ringing through her memories. She could still feel the warmth that wrapped around her tightly and made her feel that despite what else might happen, in this home, by these people, she was loved.

This year was even more special, Daughtry thought. Nicholas's family was with them. Added to this was the wondrous blessing that Daughtry was carrying her first child. She thought of Mary and how she must have felt as the birth of the Savior to the world approached. What an incredible feeling to know that she carried a life within her body. How much more must it have been for Mary, who carried the world's King.

The boys, now men really, talked boisterously from the dining room, breaking Daughtry's concentration. Anna Maria and Pepita had worked alongside Maggie and Daughtry to bake hundreds of tiny pastries and cookies for the party. Daughtry couldn't help but smile at the thought of her five brothers, not to mention Dr. Dan and Lillie's sons and Pastor David and

Jenny's son, Samuel, digging into the intricately woven display of confectionery delights. No doubt they'd give little thought to the arrangement, but Daughtry knew there would be hours of praise for the taste.

Compared to the seeming army of men in the house, Daughtry knew there were only a handful of women. Besides their mothers, Angeline Monroe, Dan and Lillie's feisty daughter, and David and Jenny's quiet little Hannah, now eighteen and twin to Samuel, would round out the party of second-generation New Mexicans. The biggest surprise of all and most pleasant for the young gentlemen of the family, was Nicholas's dark-eyed sister, Joelle. She came by train only two days earlier and faced the wrath of both Riley and Nicholas at the announcement that she'd traveled alone.

It was of little matter, however, as all of Daughtry's brothers, as well as Samuel, and Angeline's brothers John and James, were quite taken with the beauty, leaving Angeline, who was normally the belle of the ball, with her nose slightly out of joint. No doubt Angeline would work through the competition and find herself the center of plenty of attention.

Daughtry stood alone in the living room and loved it all. She listened to the laughter, the voices, the happiness, and wrapped her hands around her still slender waist. Her child grew here, she thought and smiled. Two warm masculine hands fell over her own, and Daughtry leaned back into the arms of her husband.

"I wondered where you'd gotten off to," Nicholas murmured against her ear. "How's my baby?"

"He's fine."

"I meant you," Nicholas whispered huskily.

"I was just dreaming," Daughtry said with a smile.

"Are you sure you weren't trying to figure out what I got you for Christmas?"

Daughtry turned in Nicholas's arms and stared up innocently. "You aren't really going to make me wait until tomorrow, are you?" She batted her lashes coyly and put on her most alluring smile.

Nicholas chuckled. "I do love you, Mrs. Dawson. So very much."

"But you still won't give me my present tonight?" Her voice was pleading like a child's.

"Who can resist such charm and womanly wiles?"

Daughtry laughed and wrapped her arms around her husband's neck. "I promise to make you the very best wife, Nicholas. I will work hard beside you and together we'll build a ranch every bit as wonderful as Piñon Canyon."

"I've no doubt of it. You seem to make good things happen wherever you go."

"It isn't me," Daughtry replied with a knowing glance upward. "It's Him. God has made all the most wondrous things happen, in spite of the motives we humans attached to them in the first place. He's very good to look out for us that way."

"Yes, He is," Nicholas agreed.

With a tender kiss to Daughtry's forehead, he set her away from him and reached into his pocket. "I was going to wait until tomorrow, but since you are intent on celebrating early. . ." He fell silent and pulled out a small box. "I'm told this belonged to my mother's mother." He opened the box to reveal an elegantly styled ring. The wide gold band was intricately etched with scrolling and leaves. Set in the very middle was a dark red stone.

"It's a garnet," Nicholas said as Daughtry stared in dumb silence at the ring. He pulled the ring from the box and slipped it on Daughtry's still bare left hand. "I never even thought to send you a ring when I mailed you the proxy." He grinned at her, delighted with Daughtry's complete fascination. "Now you have one and no one will doubt that you belong to me."

"Oh, Nicholas," Daughtry replied, choking back tears, "it's beautiful. It truly is."

Nicholas nodded. "It's only part of the gift, however."

"Oh?"

"Yes," he whispered. "I've already talked with Pastor David."

"About what?" Daughtry asked curiously.

"I want us to marry again," he answered, taking Daughtry's hand to his lips. "Will you marry me in a proper church service, Mrs. Dawson? Marry me in front of all of our family and friends?"

Daughtry began to cry and, not finding the words to answer, she simply nodded her approval.

"Merry Christmas, Daughtry."

Daughtry reached up with both hands and pulled Nicholas's face down to meet hers. She kissed him earnestly on the mouth, her tears falling wet against his face. "Merry Christmas, Nicholas. I love you more with each passing day. I don't see how it is possible to love you more than I already did, but I do. I am yours, now and forever. Forever yours, no matter what the future holds in store."

Nicholas lifted her chin and glanced upward to the ceiling. "Forever His," he whispered in reply, "because He knows exactly what the future holds in store."

Angel's Cause

Dedicated to:

Ramona Kelly—*with a glad and grateful heart that God has blessed me with our continuing friendship. I love you!*

Clara Norris—*God crossed our paths a long time ago and I've been the better for it. I love you!*

Chapter 1

Angeline Monroe peeked out from behind her frilly parasol and giggled. At eighteen, she was clearly one of the most beautiful, if not the most beautiful girl in all of north-central New Mexico. The proof of this was the circle of young men that followed her around like a pack of lost pups, each one trying to outdo the other for her attention. Each one completely captivated with the charming wiles of the shapely young woman.

Her parents struggled to take their daughter's popularity in stride. It wasn't that they didn't want Angeline to court and marry, but the attention that seemed to follow their youngest child was often a worrisome thing.

"You don't suppose we could just put her in a convent?" Daniel Monroe asked his wife in mock seriousness.

Lillie Monroe was an older version of her daughter Angeline. Something in the way her daughter moved among the circle of suitors reminded her of herself. With a laugh she turned to her husband. "You're too old-fashioned, Doctor."

Daniel ran a hand through his hair as had been his habit for over fifty years. "She seems too young."

"She is eighteen."

Daniel winced. Where had the years gone?

Angeline was oblivious to her parent's concern. She loved being courted, even if it was by the entire bachelor population of Bandelero, New Mexico. Even if they did it all at one time.

Church picnics were the best, Angeline decided, while demurely evaluating her companions. Everyone got to wear pretty clothes and look nice, because you'd just come from services. Then you'd spread out blankets down by the river, and everyone would eat and talk and laugh. Yes, church picnics were the very best way to get to know each other.

She put a hand up to brush back a tiny wisp of invisible hair. It made her appear quite innocent and positively feminine, she knew. She knew, of course, because she'd practiced doing this very thing in front of her bedroom mirror.

Angeline glanced coyly around her to make certain her audience was still captive to her cause. Causes were very important to Angeline. She'd joined one after the other and always threw herself into the working needs of each.

She supposed the very first cause she'd ever joined was that of Christianity. To Angeline, going to church and participating in the various activities and committees was a prime cause, indeed. And, in this situation, the cause did her a great deal of good. Her parents often felt that she needed to take the matter of spirituality more seriously, but Angeline noted that she lived by the Good Book and was wholly devoted to the various missionary projects. It was hard to understand why her parents would even once question her devotion to spiritual matters.

Leaving the distastefulness of such thoughts behind, Angeline passed a glance over each young man, receiving in return looks that ran the range from shyly embarrassed to boldly inviting. *Men!* she thought to herself, nearly laughing out loud. How simpleminded they were.

Suddenly, as a mother might be aware of one child's absence from her brood, Angeline realized that she did not command the attention of every bachelor at the picnic. One very stubborn man stood off under a tree and looked to Angeline to be quite bored with the entire day.

Gavin Lucas, oldest son of Maggie and Garrett Lucas, refused to join his four brothers in the pursuit of Angeline Monroe. He watched, however, very discreetly so as not to draw attention to himself. He saw his brothers Joseph, Jordy, and twins Dolan and Don while they seemed to dance on a puppet string that Angeline controlled. No, he wasn't about to play that game.

And, it was because he wouldn't play the game that Angeline even noticed him. She'd always liked the Lucas boys. Maybe it was because her parents and theirs were lifelong friends. Maybe it was because for so many years there had hardly been anyone else around. Then one day the railroad came to Bandelero, and the town began to boom, bringing new people, new businesses, and a whole new lifestyle. Overnight it seemed, the town had grown from twenty or thirty to five hundred, then a thousand. It was a little smaller now because interest seemed to pull people south to Santa Fe and Albuquerque or north to Denver and Colorado Springs. But no matter. Angeline knew how to make the most of what she had, and there was always a cause to be found to entertain herself with.

"Why won't you take a walk with me down by the river?" Jordy Lucas was saying. A full year younger than herself, Angeline never seriously considered Jordy when thinking of husband material. And if she couldn't consider him for that, why waste her time walking by the river?

"I'm having too much fun," she said, beaming a broad smile upon all of them. "I want to stay right here and enjoy the day."

It seemed as though everyone started talking at once then, but Angeline's eyes were once again drawn to Gavin. He hadn't moved in the last half hour and Angeline couldn't help but wonder what he was so seriously considering.

~

Gavin smiled to himself, knowing that Angeline, or Angel as he had called her since she was a child, was disturbed by his aloofness. Up until the last year or so, he'd played her game just like the others. Now, Gavin was through playing. He'd made up his mind about Angel over two years ago and now he was just biding his time. Angeline Monroe was the woman he intended to marry. She just didn't know it yet. Shoving his hands deep into his trouser pockets, Gavin pretended to study the leaves overhead.

"What are you doing here all by yourself?" Daughtry Dawson, Gavin's married sister, asked thrusting a small boy into his arms. "You might as well watch over Kent for me while I help get the food on the table."

Gavin's serious expression changed into surprise, then honest pleasure. "How ya doin', Partner?" Kent, barely a year old, looked up at his uncle and squealed.

"I guess that means good," Daughtry replied, tucking a stray strand of copper hair back into place. "Do you mind keeping an eye on him for me?"

"Not at all," Gavin said, burying his face against the baby's stomach and growling. Kent began to chortle in his baby way. Gavin then held him high into the air, bouncing him up and down.

"Thanks, Gavin," Daughtry said almost apologetically and slipped away while Kent was preoccupied.

Gavin looked past the baby nonchalantly. *Good,* he thought. *Now I really have Angel's attention.* He knew Angeline would come to him on the pretense of playing with Kent, but in truth it would be Gavin she was seeking out. That and the reason for why he was no longer playing her game. Turning his back to Angel and her crowd of suitors, Gavin began to count.

"One!" he said and lifted Kent high into the air. "Two!" he counted and swung the boy low to the ground. Kent giggled and clapped his hands, when he wasn't gripping Gavin's arm.

"Three!" Gavin had just brought Kent up even with his head, when Angeline's voice sounded from behind him.

"Hello, Gavin," she said, seeming to purr the words. "I saw that you were playing with Kent and I just had to come see him."

Gavin stopped swinging Kent and turned to face Angeline. Meeting her eyes, a color somewhere between lavender and blue, he hid the effect she always had on him. "Hi, Angel."

Angeline had his attention now, so she moved on to capture Kent's. No man, no matter the age, was safe from her charms.

Holding her arms up to Kent, he immediately went to her from Gavin.

"You are just the sweetest thing." Angeline's voice rang out like a song. Kent reached for a handful of her long blond curls and laughingly pulled them to his mouth.

"Better not, Partner," Gavin said, using the excuse to touch Angel's hair. He gently removed the spun gold strands from Kent's grubby hands and let the hair curl around his own fingers for just a moment. It was soft and fine like silk, and Gavin silently wished he could bury his hands in it as his nephew had.

Angeline smiled smugly at the exchange, knowing that Gavin was now hers to command. "You're such a little darlin'," Angeline drawled softly, kissing Kent on the forehead. Then without missing a beat, she looked up at Gavin and smiled. "How come you're here by yourself? I missed you."

Gavin let a slow lopsided grin overtake his normally serious expression. "I'm surprised you even noticed me. What happened to your choir?"

"My what?" Angeline questioned, feigning serious confusion.

"Your choir. I figured what with the moaning and groaning of that group, they must be warming up for a good song."

Angeline laughed in spite of the fact that she'd planned not to respond to anything Gavin said. "Jealous?" she finally asked.

"Nope," Gavin stated, quite serious, and took Kent from Angeline's arms. "Never did like to sing." With that he walked off to leave Angeline to stare after him. He wanted to laugh out loud at the stunned expression on her face, but he held it back. She'd come around in time.

~

Two days later, Angeline was still stinging from Gavin's rejection. She'd played the scene over in her mind and saw no reason for his rudeness. She evaluated scenes from weeks, months, and even years gone by and wondered silently when Gavin had lost interest in her. Did it matter? she couldn't help but ask herself. Then, deciding that it shouldn't, Angeline went to work to find a new cause to occupy herself with.

At supper, Angeline had decided what she would request. She waited for just the exact moment when her mother put dessert and a fresh pot of coffee on the table. If her luck held, Angeline thought, no one would call for her father to come play doctor. If her luck held, she just might get her own way.

"Mother, Father," Angeline began, and both of her parents looked up warily. "I have something to ask you."

Daniel looked at Lillie as Lillie was looking to Daniel. They were searching each other for a clue as to what Angeline had planned. When both shrugged, they turned their attention to Angeline and collectively held their breath.

"I want to travel." Angeline was never one to beat around an issue. She was well-known for coming right out with what she wanted. "I know I can't go abroad what with that dreadful war in Europe." She made the affair sound as if it were a party out of control, rather than a life and death battle of political issues.

Angeline smiled sweetly at both of her parents before continuing. "I know too, that you miss John and James since they've gone off to join the army." She waited to see if they would say anything. She almost felt sorry for being the cause of the stunned expression on their faces. "Anyway, I would very much like to travel and see some of our other states. California, for instance, and New York. I've read so much about both places as well as Chicago and Kansas City. I really do want to see these cities."

Daniel was the first to speak. "Angeline, you can't very well go off by yourself and your mother and I can't just pick up and leave. We have obligations and duties here."

"Your father is right," Lillie said, but her memory reminded her that she too had enjoyed traveling as a young lady. "We can't very well take you on any extended trips." Lillie glanced at Daniel, hoping he might soften the blow somehow. Neither one was very good at telling Angeline, "no."

Angeline grew very serious. Her eyes seemed to plead from the softness of her heart-shaped face. "I feel so pressured here," she said softly. "Everyone expects me to choose a man and get married, and I'm just not ready for that yet." It was the very thing to get Lillie's and Daniel's minds in line with Angeline's desires.

"Nobody says you have to get married," Daniel stated firmly. "I certainly haven't been pushing you to find a husband."

"Nor I," Lillie added.

"I know," Angeline said in her manipulative way. "But nevertheless, it is expected. Why just the other day I heard, well, it wasn't very nice and I shan't repeat it in full." Angeline paused as if it pained her greatly to continue.

"What did you hear?" Lillie and Daniel asked in unison.

"Well, there was some talk about how dreadfully old Daughtry Lucas was when she got married. She was nearly twenty-four, you know."

Lillie and Daniel smiled at each other.

"Anyway, people just seem to naturally think I should be looking to marry right away. Of course, there are other obligations to consider since I'm the last one at home. You know how people are these days. Especially in regards to obligations."

Lillie's eyes narrowed just a bit. "What do you mean?"

Angeline smiled. "I suppose people just worry that I'll stay here and take care of you and Father. Sometimes it's just expected of unmarried women."

"What is?" Daniel asked, completely baffled by Angeline's line of discussion.

"That I remain unmarried in order to care for you and Mother, in your aging years."

"What!?" Daniel and Lillie exclaimed at once.

"Not that I would mind all that much, but I would like to see at least a bit of the country before I did that."

Daniel started laughing which in turn made Lillie giggle. Angeline pretended to be confused. But even so, it was hard to know what her parents were thinking and some of her confusion was genuine.

"Did I say something wrong?" she questioned respectfully.

"No, Sweetheart," Daniel replied. "It's just that your mother and I are far from ready to be cared for. I think we can surely find some way to stretch your mind a bit, if not your legs. What do you say you let us consider the matter of travel? Maybe we could find a suitable traveling companion for you or maybe I could spare your mother for a week or so."

"Oh thank you!" Angeline squealed in delight and jumped up to hug her parents. "You're both wonderful, and I love you so!"

Chapter 2

For the next few weeks, travel was all that Angeline could speak of. She enthusiastically bought magazines and books, as well as newspapers, all in the hopes of planning an adventure to equal her dreams.

An unexpected damper came upon things when a German submarine torpedoed and sank the British passenger ship *Lusitania*. The ship was only twelve miles from Irish shores and over eleven hundred people lost their lives. One hundred and twenty-eight of them were Americans. The event caused not only a hush to fall over the country, but from that hush rose up an anguished cry that demanded revenge. Collectively, Americans held their breath waiting to see if their country would break neutrality and join the others already at war.

Angeline saw the worried looks her parents exchanged. They were thinking of her older brothers, John and James, both in the army now. Would they be called to fight in the European War?

Angeline stewed and fretted with everyone else. She teetered on the brink of adulthood, with still very childish theories on how the world really worked. It was beyond her to understand why anyone would kill helpless human beings.

Sunday services were devoted to continued prayer for Europe and the survivors of the *Lusitania,* along with the fervent hope that America could somehow escape the nightmare. Angeline sat stiffly prim and proper, while Pastor David Monroe, her father's only brother, offered words of encouragement.

"God is with us," David reminded them. "He is watching over and tenderly caring for each and every soul, even as shots are fired in Europe, even as the war rages on. He knows our fears and our heartaches."

Angeline glanced sideways at her parents, who gripped each other's hands tightly. They had each other to comfort and Angeline suddenly felt very alone. Her own fears made her feel very vulnerable, and that vulnerability softened her normally controlled expression.

With a look that resembled a frightened child, Angeline noted that her mother had tears in her eyes. Gently, her father reached upward and caught one as it rolled down her cheek. The look he gave his wife caused Angeline to marvel. They were so in love and so right for one another. Could she ever hope to know that same feeling?

After watching her parents for another moment, Angeline raised her face and locked eyes with Gavin Lucas. He seemed to sense her need, and the look he offered gave Angeline a feeling of comfort and peace. Then, just as quickly as it was given, Gavin resumed his study of the Bible in his hands, and Angeline was again alone.

First he ignores me, Angeline thought to herself, *and now he acts as though he'd like nothing better than to put an arm around me. What in the world is Gavin thinking?* She continued to contemplate the situation long after Pastor David had directed them to turn to a popular hymn.

～

Dinner at the Monroe house was quiet and reserved. Angeline hardly felt like eating as she pushed her food around the plate.

"You know what I think," her father began with a cautious glance to Lillie. "I think we need some diversion from all this sorrow." Lillie nodded but said nothing, while Angeline gave her father her undivided attention.

"I learned today that Mrs. Widdle plans a train trip to Denver to see her niece. I took the liberty of speaking with her and suggested that you might accompany her."

Angeline perked up noticeably. "Truly?"

"Yes," Daniel replied. "She seemed quite happy about the idea, in fact. She said that her niece had more than enough room to house you, and there would be ample time for you to see the town and visit the shops and museums."

"It sounds wonderful!" Angeline's mind raced with thoughts of what she'd wear. "When do I go and how long will I be gone?"

"Mrs. Widdle plans to leave next Friday. She intends to stay for two weeks, then return in time to head up the Sunday school class graduation ceremonies." Daniel paused. "I know it's not as extensive as you'd like. It certainly isn't New York or California, but I think you will be pleasantly surprised."

Angeline gave her father a reassuring smile. "I know it will be grand!"

Lillie smiled at her daughter. "It will be, but you must be cautious. Denver is a very big city and the likes of which you've never even known. People can't be trusted the way they are here."

"Your mother is right, Angeline. The larger the city, the less personal and more problematic," her father joined in.

"I will be on my guard," Angeline offered, completely unconcerned with her parents' worries. She was going to Denver in less than a week! *Denver!*

~

"She's going to Denver, at least that's what Dr. Dan said," Dolan relayed to Gavin.

"How soon?" he asked, trying to sound like it was unimportant. Inside he felt as though someone had dealt his midsection a severe blow.

"I guess she's leaving Friday," Dolan answered. "Aunt Lillie thought it'd be fun to have a little party to send Angeline off on her trip. She told me to be sure and have everybody come over Thursday evening for Angeline's last night in Bandelero. So she must be leaving the next day."

Gavin took in the news and frowned when his brother wasn't looking. This wasn't in his plans, and given his serious manner of planning everything out to the last detail, the news was rather upsetting.

"Did you tell Mom?" Gavin finally spoke.

"Not yet, I was just on my way into the house. Hey, you gonna help me unload this feed or just stand there and look like you've lost your last friend?" Gavin gave his younger brother a puzzled look. "Oh, quit trying to play games with me," Dolan smirked. "I know you're in love with Angeline."

"Oh, really?"

Dolan shrugged his shoulders. "It doesn't bother me in the least, although it might be wise to lay your claim to her before she gets all the way to Colorado to look for a husband."

"What makes you think she's going to Colorado to find a husband?" Gavin questioned cautiously. Maybe Angeline had said something to make Dolan believe her interest in matrimonial conquests.

"What else would a woman like Angeline have on her mind?"

Gavin laughed at this. "Knowing Angel, she's got plenty on her mind besides husbands."

Dolan laughed and hoisted a heavy feed sack against Gavin's chest and open arms. "I think you'd better talk to her just the same."

Gavin said nothing, but he was still considering Dolan's words an hour later when he saddled up his horse and headed to Bandelero. Maybe it was time to make his intentions clear to Angel. Maybe she was truly too naïve to know how he felt. She was, after all, just eighteen.

Gavin rode straight to the Monroe house and noted the absence of the buggy Dr. Dan used for housecalls. With any luck maybe he'd have a chance to talk to Angel alone.

Angeline answered the door with her long blond hair dripping wet. "Gavin!" she exclaimed and quickly threw a towel over her head to hide her hair.

Gavin grinned sheepishly and stuffed his hands deep in his jeans pockets. "You're looking good, Angel."

Angeline blushed crimson. "Mother and Father are out delivering a baby on the Stanton ranch. Is something wrong?"

"No. I came to see you."

"Me?" Angeline quickly forgot about her appearance as she lost herself in Gavin's blue-gray eyes.

"May I come in?"

Angeline nodded and stepped back from the door. "I was just washing my hair. If you'll wait in the front room, I need to go comb it out." She wasn't at all the same self-confident girl who usually commanded the attention of everyone around her.

"Why don't you bring your comb and come sit with me?" Gavin's words were soft and alluring.

"I suppose I could," Angeline replied rather nervously. She slipped into her parents' bedroom and retrieved the brush.

When she appeared in the family sitting room, she held up the brush, momentarily not knowing what else to do. Gavin motioned her to sit and reached out for the brush.

"I think this looks like fun," he said, and Angeline was so surprised that she couldn't even protest.

Gavin took the brush in his trembling hands and began to run it down Angeline's long, wet hair. The feeling was like nothing she'd ever known, and it was all Angeline could do to remain seated. No one besides her mother had ever brushed her hair, and now it seemed that Gavin's actions were the most intimate she'd ever shared with anyone.

Gavin felt the same way, although he, like Angel, would never admit it. Forcing himself to speak, Gavin remembered his brother's words.

"I hear you're taking a trip," he began, "to Denver."

"What?" Angeline's voice gave away her inability to concentrate.

"A trip," Gavin repeated.

"A what?"

Gavin would have enjoyed her reaction had he not felt the same uncertainty and nervousness. "I heard that you planned to visit Denver."

"Yes," she managed.

"When are you leaving?"

"Uh. . . Friday. I'm traveling with Mrs. Widdle." Angeline's voice was barely audible.

Gavin continued the long brush strokes. "How long you gonna be gone, Angel?"

"Gone?" she sounded like a child and tried to shake herself out of it. "I'm not sure," she answered.

Gavin, always given to getting right to the point, stopped in mid-stroke and drew a deep breath. "I came here to talk to you about us."

"Us?" Angeline was hesitant. The single word brought Angeline to complete awareness. "What about us?"

"That's what I want to know."

"I don't guess I understand," Angeline said, turning to face Gavin.

"I don't like the idea of you going off, but I guess it's because I'll miss having you around. It might also be because I don't like the idea of those city fellows giving you ideas and causes that will take you away from here."

Angeline's mouth opened slightly. "What are you saying, Gavin?" she finally asked.

Gavin looked at her for a moment. Her lavender eyes were wide with surprise, and even with her hair wet and clinging to her back, Gavin thought she'd never looked more attractive.

"Look, Angel, we've grown up together. There's never been a time when I haven't been a part of your life."

"The same can be said of your brothers and sister too," Angeline protested. She was quickly beginning to see where Gavin was headed.

"That's true enough," he replied. Pausing for a moment, Gavin put the brush aside and reached out to pull Angeline to her feet. "The fact is, Angel, I've loved you since you were a little girl. I made up my mind when I was sixteen and you were just twelve, that you were the one I intended to marry."

"Marry?" Angeline took a step backwards. "Marry?"

Gavin smiled. "I think I've been rather patient while you've courted half the town. Now I'm just laying my claim before you go off and get half of Denver to fall in love with you as well."

～

Angeline was stunned. For all the attention she was used to receiving, no one had ever asked her to marry them. Now here was Gavin Lucas, the one man who seemed least interested in her, and he was proposing marriage. No, he was demanding it, she thought.

Gavin seemed unconcerned with Angeline's shock. "Look, Angel," he said stepping towards her, "it's time to consider the future. I want you to be my wife."

Angeline quickly regained her composure and ducked under Gavin's outreaching arms. Putting a chair between them, Angeline shook her head. "I can't believe you think you can just waltz in here and propose like that. Gavin Lucas, I have no intention of marrying you or anyone else!"

Gavin was the one who looked surprised now. Angeline quickly took the advantage. "You've treated me like I have some awful disease these last months. Hardly ever talking to me at parties or picnics. Never so much as saying a single word when we crossed paths in town. Now you come here and tell me that you've chosen me for your wife, like it's some kind of honor."

Gavin grinned at this. "You might consider it just that, after you get the ring on your finger."

Angeline shook her head. "I'm not ready to marry anyone yet."

"You are a bit immature, I'll give you that."

"Why you. . .you," Angeline stammered for something to say.

"Look, Angel," Gavin said, easily pushing the chair aside in order to get to the woman he loved. "I know I've surprised you, but it's not like we've never had anything between us."

"What have we had between us, except friendship?"

"Friendship is a good start," Gavin said softly. "But we've always had more than that. You're friends with my brothers too, but I'll wager you don't feel the same things for them that you do for me."

Angeline shook her head once again. "I don't know what you're talking about. I like all of you. You're like family to me. But, I intend to travel a great deal. I want to go abroad when those European ninnies quit fighting with each other. I want to fly in one of those aeroplanes. I want to sail on the ocean, and I can't do any of that by getting myself married off to you or anyone else." Angeline noted that Gavin seemed completely unmoved by her declaration. "Besides that, there are things I want to do and be a part of. There are important causes out there, things that I can help with." Angel backed up while Gavin just kept coming toward her. "I mean it, Gavin. I don't have those kinds of feelings for you."

Gavin reached out and pulled Angeline into his arms, then very gently he tilted her chin upward and kissed her deeply. Angel was too shocked to do anything. She felt Gavin's strong arms encircle her waist, while his lips commanded her attention.

She held herself rigid, hoping the kiss would end in just a moment, but it didn't. When Gavin continued to kiss her, Angeline couldn't help but feel her resistance give way. It was after all, her first kiss. Although Angeline would never have admitted it to Gavin.

Gavin stopped kissing her abruptly and set Angeline away from him. He grinned when she gripped the back of a nearby chair to steady herself.

Then, completely to Angeline's surprise, Gavin turned and without even stopping to look back at her, called out, "I think you should reconsider what you think you feel, Angel. I have my own causes and marrying you is right at the top of the list."

Chapter 3

Thursday evening arrived, and Angeline forced thoughts of Gavin from her head and replaced them with ones of the party to come. She dressed carefully in a white gown of cotton eyelet which was trimmed daintily with ribbons of pink. Three flounces fell in graceful swirls to make up the skirt, while the bodice fit snug to accentuate Angeline's small waist. She pulled her hair back from her face and tied part of it with a large pink ribbon that matched those on her dress. Twirling before her mother's cheval mirror, Angeline smiled. She'd never looked better, and she was more than a little pleased.

Angeline went downstairs and found everyone in a surprisingly good mood. Letters had come that day from John and James, and her mother was greatly relieved to learn that they were well. Her father, one of only two doctors in the town, happily announced that he had successfully saved the leg of one of the town's older residents. The man had taken a fall on his horse, crushing his leg and breaking it in several places. Dr. Monroe had worked most diligently to restore the limb and now, after ten days of battling a fierce infection, he declared the leg well on the way to mending. Everyone was happy and the tone of the party was set in that mood.

The first to arrive at the party was David and Jenny Monroe and their twins Samuel and Hannah. At twenty, neither of the twins seemed all that concerned with leaving home. Samuel seemed to favor banking, while Hannah had spent the last year diligently working on the Belgian Relief cause. Angeline herself had joined Hannah's efforts for a time, until boredom set in, as it usually did, and she was off and running to right wrongs somewhere else.

Angeline seldom gave too much consideration to her cousins. They were simple people, uninterested in the things that Angeline found fascinating and completely too quiet to be considered fun.

The Lucas's arrived not far behind David and Jenny, and Angeline was relieved when Gavin seemed content to keep his distance and not bring up their previous conversation. Still, Angeline couldn't help but watch Gavin out of the corner of her eye. She felt herself tremble once when she caught him staring at her, but when he did nothing but grin and give her a slight nod,

Angeline calmed a bit and chided herself for being silly.

Maybe he's thought better of it, Angeline decided silently. *Maybe he's sorry and embarrassed for asking me to marry him.* But just as soon as she considered that thought, Angeline knew that she didn't want him to be. She rather liked the idea of having been proposed to, although she had no intention of accepting. A woman should be flattered when a handsome young man asked for her hand.

"But he didn't ask," Angeline muttered, quickly looking up to see who else might have overheard her.

"What was that, Dear?" her mother questioned, but no one else seemed to have heard.

"Nothing," Angeline said, forcing a smile. "Nothing at all."

$\sim$

The Monroe's beautifully cultivated yard was soon filled with several dozen people. Angeline was pleased with the effort her parents had gone to. Her father had strung paper lanterns around the yard, and her mother had decorated a beautiful buffet of food for all of the guests to enjoy. Angeline had never felt so special in all her life.

It didn't take long for the men to begin their courting. Angeline was soon the center of attention, laughing at their stories and pretending to be shocked at the risks they faced in their jobs. But Gavin wasn't among them, and for the first time, Angeline wasn't nearly as interested in what the other men had to say. What was wrong with her?

From time to time, Angeline sought the crowd for Gavin. Inevitably, she found him after searching for several minutes, only to realize that he knew, when their gazes met, that she'd been looking for him. He'd smile smugly, maybe give her a nod, but otherwise he made no attempt to command her attention or greet her. Angeline felt a sense of ineffable disappointment when Gavin finally turned to engage in conversation with Hannah and Samuel.

$\sim$

"Sometimes I think she's too popular," Lillie Monroe said, coming to stand beside Gavin.

"She deserves to enjoy herself," Gavin replied softly.

"Still, a mother worries about such things. Angeline is very stubborn, like her father," Lillie said with a grin that Gavin shared.

"I heard tell it was the other way around," Gavin offered lightly. "In fact, I've heard a few stories about you and my mom that make Angel seem kind of tame."

Lillie laughed out loud. "Gavin Lucas you've been listening to your father again. Or was it Daniel?"

"Both," Gavin admitted. "I guess they just want to train me up so I'll not be shocked when I take a wife."

"Then your mother and I had best get busy and give you our side," Lillie said with genuine affection for Gavin. She looped her arm through his and with a more motherly tone, spoke of courtship. "Stubbornness can be both a virtue and a curse, depending on how you use it. In my case, stubbornness keeps Dr. Dan and I together. But, we love each other a great deal," she added softly, "and just like the Bible says in Proverbs 10:12, 'Love covereth all sins.' "

"It does tend to make you overlook things, doesn't it?" Gavin reflected, his eyes still on Angeline.

Lillie was rather taken back by his response. She followed his gaze to her daughter. "I worry something fierce about her, Gavin. She's so young, and she's not a bit aware of how ugly the world can really be. Now she's going off to Denver and, after that, who knows where? Her heart is so soft and giving, and she'll expect everyone else to be the same way." Lillie stopped, pulled her arm from Gavin's.

Silence engulfed them for a moment, then Gavin turned to his mother's life-long friend. "Don't worry about Angel," he said softly. "I intend to see to it that she's well cared for. I'll never let anyone hurt her if I'm able to do anything about it."

Lillie smiled at Gavin's chivalrous reply. "You can't be everywhere, Gavin. Angeline's bound to take wings and fly away someday, and there's no way I can stop that. Not that I really want to stop her from growing up, it's just that I worry about the kind of people she'll meet; the type of man she'll finally settle down to marry."

"Then stop worrying about it," Gavin said boldly. "I intend to marry Angel and I told her so. She just needs to get used to the idea."

Lillie's mouth dropped open at Gavin's declaration. "You what?"

Gavin looked a bit embarrassed as if suddenly realizing it was Angel's mother he was talking to. "I hope that didn't seem too out of place. I do intend to speak with Dr. Dan about it before just barging into the family."

Lillie was still dumbstruck as Garrett and Maggie came up to announce they were heading for home.

"I'll help you get the wagon," Gavin said to his father and followed him off into the night.

❧

"I've certainly enjoyed myself," Maggie said, then nodded towards Angeline. "Looks like she has, as well."

"Yes," Lillie replied and looked at where Gavin had stood only minutes before. Should she say something to Maggie? Maybe she should asked her how she felt about them finally being joined as in-laws?

"The children always seem to love these get-togethers. I wish Daughtry lived closer. I miss her so much when she's gone, and it seems like when she and Nicholas come for a visit, all we do is talk about Kent and what new thing he's doing. I never seem to get to talk about what she's doing or thinking."

"I know what you mean, and I have Angeline here all the time. It just seems as if she's drifting away. Did you know that she wants to travel abroad?"

"Not a healthy time to do that," Maggie replied.

"No, but she reminds me so much of myself. Remember when I nagged my mother into taking me to London?"

"Do I ever! I was green with envy."

Lillie nodded. "Now it's our children. Now, instead of things happening to us, it's them. Doesn't that seem strange?"

Maggie laughed. "It does indeed. I remember thinking when Daughtry was expecting Kent that it used to be me bringing the new lives into our family. All of the sudden, I changed places with my child and she was a child no more."

"Yes, that's it," Lillie said as though the thought were a revelation. "I felt that way tonight, almost as if I were an outsider looking in. I used to be that young lady," Lillie said, pointing to her daughter.

"Yes, I remember you telling me all about it," Maggie agreed.

"You'd never come to the parties because you were sworn to never marry." Lillie couldn't help but laugh. "Now, just look at you."

"God had other plans," Maggie replied softly. "I thank Him, too, that He did."

"The same goes for me," Lillie happily seconded. Then completely changing the subject, she reached out and took hold of Maggie's hand. "Gavin is so much like Garrett. He's a good man, as are all of your sons."

Maggie's eyes narrowed at Lillie's sudden praise. "What is it?" she questioned. "What are you trying to say to me?"

Lillie looked across the short distance to Angeline, then back to Maggie. "Gavin told me tonight that he intends to marry Angeline." Maggie's mouth dropped open in surprise. "He told me not to worry about her," Lillie continued, "because he intends to take care of her."

"Well, I'll be." Maggie finally breathed the words. She couldn't help but get a mischievous look to her face. "His brothers will never let him hear the end of it for this. Has he asked Angeline yet?"

"I think so, but he said she needed time to get used to the idea."

Maggie laughed heartily. "Sounds like his father. Poor Angeline."

Lillie smirked a grin as she glanced at her daughter. "Poor Gavin."

Chapter 4

Angeline returned home from Denver a changed woman. Her vocabulary was expanded to include words like suffrage, franchise, and equal rights. Furthermore, she now quoted women who had made their marks in history—Susan B. Anthony, Carrie Chapman Catt, Alice Paul, and Elizabeth Cady Stanton, to name a few. In short, Angeline had a new cause. Women's suffrage! The right to vote!

"Mother, you wouldn't believe what I learned," Angeline rambled in animated excitement. "Colorado agreed in 1893 to allow their women to vote and Wyoming even entered the union fully granting suffrage rights to their women!"

Lillie took it all in stride. Angeline was always at one cause or another. It was really a small wonder she hadn't been bitten by the suffrage bug sooner. It wasn't until Angeline announced her plan to join the suffragist Willa Neal on her lecture tour through New Mexico that Lillie stopped dead in her tracks.

"You what?"

"Oh, Mother," Angeline's voice oozed excitement, "I'm going to fight for the suffrage cause! I'm going to be a suffragist and win us the right to vote!"

Lillie eyed her daughter carefully. "Angeline, we need to discuss this more thoroughly with your father. I doubt he'll be very enthusiastic to the idea of you traipsing off with strangers."

"It won't be the idea of strangers that will bother him. He'll be narrow-minded like most men and not see a need for women to vote."

"Angeline, I don't care for your tone. When has your father ever given you cause to believe that he doesn't esteem a woman's opinion?" Lillie asked her daughter in genuine concern. Who had put such ideas into her little girl's head?

"Mother," Angeline began very patiently, as though she were talking to a simpleton or small child, "women have been made to believe for a very long time that they were incapable of sound judgement. We marry and give birth to men, raise them to adulthood, but somehow when it comes to logic and sense, men believe us totally null and void—completely uneducated and without a hope of making responsible decisions. Yet who do they think trained them up? On who's knee did they learn their first words?"

Lillie stared at her daughter in complete shock. Angeline was unconcerned with her mother's surprise. It was to be expected, she reasoned. Hadn't Willa told her that women were as much to blame, maybe even more so, for their own lack of rights?

"Mother, this is a new age, and the men and women of this world need to wake up to the realization that the world is growing up and moving on." Angeline voiced the practiced words she'd heard at one of the many suffrage lectures she'd attended in Denver. "We have the automobiles being mass produced on an assembly line where workers are paid five dollars a week! There are aeroplanes that fly men in the air and moving pictures that can record things as they happen. And with all this technology and progress toward a better world, woman are still suppressed and treated as though they are second class citizens!"

"Enough!" Lillie cried and put her hands on her hips. "Angeline, I'm happy to know that you spent your time learning about the world, but honestly, you rant this suffrage cause like you had been made to endure some horrendous ordeal. Your father and brothers have only treated us with the utmost of respect. Your father, a college-trained doctor, often seeks my opinion in cases of his female patients, simply because I am a woman. You have only known kindness and respect from the men in this community, and I resent the fact that you act as though it has been otherwise."

Angeline was taken aback by her mother's outrage. "While it is true," Angeline countered, "that our menfolk have offered certain deference to our opinions, they still see us as frail, weak creatures who need to be sheltered from the pains of the world."

"I don't think I understand why you feel this way," Lillie said a bit softer.

Angeline came to her mother and took hold of her hands. "Mother, you wouldn't believe the things that are done to women every day all over the world. Women, who because they have no voice and no chance to make changes, are put upon to be all manner of things for all manner of men. Some are bought and sold for the pleasure of others, and when they dare to raise a hand in their own defense they are maimed and often murdered!"

Lillie sat down at her kitchen table, pulling Angeline with her to take the chair beside hers. "Angeline, I know full well of the ugliness in this world. I have chosen not to make it an issue in your upbringing because I hoped I could shelter you from it for as long as possible. Perhaps it was naïve of me. Perhaps it was unwise, but nevertheless, it had nothing to do with equal rights and whether women should or shouldn't have the right to vote."

Angeline took in her mother's words and weighed them against her newfound knowledge. "I didn't mean to sound harsh," Angeline began, "but Willa Neal told me that often women are a worse enemy to our cause than men."

"You mean she doesn't get the reaction she wants from women and so she calls them an enemy?"

"No, of course not!" Angeline exclaimed. "She simply means that sometimes women are too misinformed and need to be educated."

"Sounds like the same argument you told me that men give for why they won't approve women's rights to vote."

Angeline was temporarily silenced at her mother's logical argument. Finally, she decided she needed to put the conversation on a more positive track and switched to another related, but seemingly neutral topic. "I did so enjoy being around learned women, Mother. I always knew that you and Aunt Jenny and Maggie were women of knowledge, but these women have attended college and they seem to know so much."

"Wisdom is a powerful thing, Angeline. Solomon was wise and he still struggled to make the proper judgments."

"Proverbs 7:4 says, 'Say unto wisdom, Thou art my sister; and call understanding thy kinswoman.' Willa told this to me, Mother. God, Himself, gave a clear picture that wisdom is a feminine virtue."

"Is that all you perceive in that verse? Did you pay any attention to what came before it or went after it? You can't rip pieces out of the Bible to fit your causes, Angeline."

Angeline seemed genuinely deflated, and Lillie felt sorry for her daughter. "Look, I would very much like the right to vote." Angeline perked up at this declaration, but Lillie waved her into silence and continued. "However, I will not fight a cause that degrades the rights of one to boost the rights of another. Nor will I see God's hand in a fight that leads people into civil disobedience and self-declared war against one another."

Daniel chose that inopportune moment to come whistling through the back door entrance. Lillie fell silent as she heard

Daniel cast aside his doctor's bag. Entering the kitchen, Daniel noted the stern expression on his wife's face and an even more troubling look of composed anger on his daughter's.

"What are you two arguing about this time?" Daniel asked seriously.

Lillie got up and went to embrace her husband, while Angeline stood and waited by the table. "It seems," Lillie told Daniel softly, "Angeline wants to accompany a leading suffragist on her lecture circuit."

Daniel grinned. "Suffrage, eh?" He looked at his daughter with genuine affection, but she saw it as a patronizing gesture.

"I know what both of you are thinking and you're wrong!" Angeline declared. "I believe in this cause and I intend to fight it for all I'm worth. I may not be old enough to benefit from it yet, but in a few years I'll be twenty-one, then I'll be able to hold my head up high on the way to the voting place."

"Whoa, Angeline," Daniel said, stepping away from his wife. "There's no reason for you to get so upset."

"You and Mother think I'm a child," Angeline protested, "but I'm not. I'm a grown woman and I have rights, and I intend to fight for those rights. Willa Neal is a wonderful woman. She has a great deal of knowledge, and she's graduated from a very fine college back east." She paused long enough to point a finger at her mother. "And while I might have expected this from Father, I thought you would understand. But I see you're just as misinformed and naïve as Willa said most women are." Turning to leave, Angeline paused at the door. "I believe in this cause, and I believe what she says in regards to what needs to be done. With or without your permission, I intend to join her."

Daniel's face changed instantly from compassionate to fiercely stern. "That's enough, Angeline. You'll do no such thing until we deem it acceptable and in your best interest. Now, apologize to your mother."

Angeline turned up her nose and stormed from the room. There was no way she intended to apologize. Not when she was right!

Feeling very much the martyr, Angeline threw herself across her bed and pounded the mattress in rage. Willa had warned her that this would happen and Angeline hadn't believed it possible. Was the entire world blind to the needs of women?

$\approx$

Lillie's astounded expression exactly matched her husband's. When Daniel opened his arms to her, Lillie eagerly sought the refuge he offered.

"She's so different now," Lillie said near to tears. "I thought maybe we could talk through it, but she just kept getting more upset with each thing I said."

"Shh," Daniel soothed. "It has nothing to do with you."

"She thinks I'm stupid," Lillie said, and a sob escaped her. "Stupid and oppressed and blind to my womanly rights."

Daniel smiled over his wife's head. "Yeah, you seem real oppressed, Lillie. Have I managed to keep you chained to my side unable to achieve your God-given potential?"

Lillie pulled back and looked at the amused twinkle in her husband's eye. "Oh, Daniel," she grinned and wiped at the tears in her eyes, "I'll take oppression if it's with you."

Daniel took Lillie's face in his hands and kissed her soundly on the lips. "I feel the same way about you, my dear."

Lillie melted against her husband, perfectly content that after twenty-some years of marriage, they could still argue together, work together, and joyfully love together. They had weathered many storms and would undoubtably face many more.

"What are we going to do about Angeline?" Lillie whispered the question against Daniel's chest.

"Give her time to cool off and come to her senses. Maybe she'll get interested in one of the local causes and forget about her suffragist friend."

"I suppose you're right," Lillie said, wrapping her arms tightly around Daniel's neck. "I hope you are."

"If not, there's always my idea about a convent."

$\sim$

Angeline's tantrum was spent, and now she felt more determined than ever to leave Bandelero and assist Miss Neal. She pulled out a calendar and noted the day when Willa planned to be in Santa Fe for her first speech. With any luck at all, Angeline would find a way to join her.

"I'll show them that I'm more than a simpleminded female," Angeline whispered to the room. "I'll show them that I'm capable of bettering the cause for women! I'll show them all!"

$\sim$

For the next few days, Angeline was the epitome of cooperation and genteel refinement. She didn't utter a single word about suffrage or equal rights and went about her chores as a dutiful daughter. She was content in the fact that no one was wise to her plans. She reasoned away any feelings of guilt, telling herself that even people in the Bible often had to step out of line in order to accomplish God's will.

On what was to be her last evening at home, Angeline sat quietly sewing while her father discussed one of his cases. Her mother was quite engrossed in the conversation, adding her own thoughts on Daniel's procedures. All in all, Angeline thought it a perfect evening. It was the way she wanted to remember her parents. It was the way she wanted to remember her home.

Getting up and excusing herself for bed, Angeline went to her room and double-checked her suitcase. Everything was ready. She opened her window and cautiously lowered her case to the ground by using a rope she'd managed to hide beneath her bed. Then securing that same rope to the leg of her bed, Angeline prepared to descend in the same manner.

She cast a quick look around the room and smiled. She was leaving a child, but when she returned, if she returned, she'd be a worldly, wise woman. She double-checked to make certain they would see her letter of explanation, then pulled on her jacket and hat, and climbed out her bedroom window.

Reaching the ground, Angeline heard the train whistle blast it's announcement that final boarding was taking place. She picked up the suitcase and ran for all she was worth, managing to pat her pocket and reassure herself that her ticket and money were both still within.

She approached the train depot cautiously, for the first time worried that someone might see her and try to stop her. Thoughts of Gavin came to mind more than once. She'd only been home for four days and no doubt Gavin planned to see her Sunday at church. Poor Gavin would be so surprised, she thought and stepped up onto the train car's platform. They would all be surprised, she smiled as she took her seat.

Chapter 5

A ngeline was filled with anticipation as she rode away from Bandelero. The adventure of what she was doing made her giddy, and she couldn't help but succumb to her own joy.

"I'm really doing it!" she whispered, staring out into the pitch blackness of the night.

In spite of her excitement, the gentle rocking of the train against the rails made Angeline sleepy, and without meaning to, she slipped into a deep, dreamless sleep.

"Miss, this is your stop," a gentle voice was calling to her.

Angeline sat up with a start and immediately winced at the stiffness in her neck. She looked up into the face of the conductor and nodded rigidly. "Thank you," she offered and glanced out the window into the predawn.

"Do you have folks to meet you?" the man asked her.

"No," Angeline responded as if it was unimportant. "I'm catching the southbound train to Santa Fe later this morning."

"Well, you'll have a bit of a wait," the man offered.

Somehow, Angeline hadn't considered this possibility. "I'll be fine," she said with a false sense of courage. Taking her case in hand, Angeline followed the man down the aisle and allowed him to assist her from the train.

"You can wait in the depot," he suggested. "At least the ticket agent will be nearby, if anyone tries to bother you."

"Thank you," Angeline replied and made her way into the dimly lit building.

The room was seemingly deserted, and Angeline swallowed hard to keep her nerve. She made her way slowly to a long empty bench and took a seat with a wary glance into the shadowy corners. She clutched her suitcase close and thought to whisper a prayer.

She stopped, however, before uttering the words. Would God listen to her? She was, after all, disobeying her parents, but wasn't that a verse for children? Didn't God intend that to be a guidance for when you were young and didn't know how to care for yourself? Deciding that she was completely within her rights, Angeline offered a simple prayer and waited impatiently for time to pass.

~

When the Santa Fe train finally pulled alongside the depot, Angeline was exhausted and hungry. She made her way slowly to the train, wondering how in the world she would find Willa, but to her surprise, Willa found her instead.

"Angeline!" the older woman cried from the platform.

"Am I ever glad to see you!" Angeline replied.

Willa Neal was a rather severe looking woman. Nearing her forty-fifth birthday, she was the very image of cartoon depictions of suffragists. Although, as Willa had already shown Angeline, the newspaper cartoons were much kinder to the suffragists these days than they had been twenty or so years earlier.

Dressed in her plain brown skirt and jacket, Willa had pulled her mousy brown hair back into a tight bun, without so much as a single wisp to escape the dourness. In actuality, she might have been a pleasant enough looking woman had she styled her hair differently and worn more flattering clothes. But, looking nice was not a concern of Willa Neal. Suffrage was! Suffrage was all she would give her precious efforts to.

"I'm glad you decided to join us, Angeline," Willa said, leading Angeline down the aisle of the train car. "Did you have any difficulty in winning your parents to our cause?"

"Yes," Angeline replied rather curtly. "I had a great deal of trouble. In fact, they didn't want me to accompany you."

"Typical!" Willa expressed with a nod. "Well, I'm glad you used the brains the good Lord gave you and came along anyway. Look here, there's someone I want you to meet." Angeline lifted her face to meet the gaze of a very handsome man. "Angeline Monroe, this is Douglas Baker. He is a great help to our cause and politically aligned to do us much good. He is very ambitious and very well may one day be president of the United States."

Angeline couldn't hide her surprise as she extended her hand to the gentleman before her. Bending over and lifting Angeline's hand to his lips, Douglas Baker kissed the back very gently, then lifted his head to reveal a broad smile. "I am charmed."

Angeline stared long and hard into the most beautiful green eyes she'd ever seen. Douglas Baker was very nearly perfect, she concluded. She pulled back her hand reluctantly and offered a weak version of her own smile. "How do you do?"

"Quite well," he replied, straightening up again. "In fact, much better now that you are a part of our entourage."

Willa laughed. "Douglas is quite the flatterer. He specializes in making women swoon and babies laugh."

"What about the men?" Angeline questioned without giving it any thought.

"I outsmart the men," Douglas answered with a mischievous smile. "Those I can't outsmart, well," he paused and laughed, "I guess I haven't run across that man yet."

Angeline enjoyed his banter and took the window seat that Willa directed her to. Douglas quickly possessed the seat directly across from Angeline, while Willa sat beside her.

Angeline couldn't help but stare at Douglas. He was the kind of man who demanded attention and drew it to himself when it was otherwise unoffered. He was of average height and not nearly as muscular as Gavin, Angeline decided. But, he was more stately in his appearance, and his neatly manicured hands indicated he spent most of his time behind a desk instead of outdoors.

Willa began speaking before the train even pulled out of the station, and Douglas was happy to engage the older woman in debates regarding the suffrage movement. Angeline simply sat back and took it all in. Mostly, she watched Douglas, fascinated with the way he conducted himself. She was so engrossed in her study of his neatly parted blond hair, that she missed hearing the question that Willa posed.

"I'm sorry," Angeline said, blushing slightly. "What did you say?"

Willa seemed oblivious to the reason Angeline had missed her question, but Douglas wasn't. He gave Angeline a sly wink, nearly causing her to miss Willa's repeated words.

"I was curious as to whether you were acquainted with anyone in the Santa Fe area?"

Angeline nodded. "Yes, I know several families there." She hadn't really considered it before, but she quickly added up at least a dozen or more names who were not only acquainted with her family but actively involved in the government.

"It always helps to get local cooperation," Willa stated.

"I haven't seen some of them for a very long time, but many of the families that come to mind are close friends of my parents or at very least, associates of my father, who is a physician."

"Good, good," Willa said and nodded toward Douglas. "Perhaps you will have the opportunity to introduce Douglas as well. He speaks the language of bureaucrats and often can sway them to listen to our cause."

"Do you outsmart them?" Angeline asked with a shy smile.

"Of course," Douglas replied candidly. "In politics it is required to stay two steps ahead of your opponent."

"But what of your allies?" Angeline questioned.

"Ahh," Douglas grinned, "for allies, it's best to stay five steps ahead and two steps behind."

Angeline giggled, while Willa nodded as though Douglas had spoken a profound truth.

～

Angeline soon found it necessary to excuse herself, and once she was gone from the room Willa Neal leaned forward. "What do you think?" she asked in a whisper.

"I think she's incredibly young," Douglas replied gravely. "She's not even old enough to vote, even if she had that right. Are you sure we won't have her parents chasing after us and putting out warning bells to prevent her from accompanying us?"

"I've thought of that, but from all indications, Angeline seems quite capable of getting her own way. My sources tell me she's the only child at home, and the only girl in the family. I'll encourage her to call home and smooth matters over or at least to telegram."

"You'd better hope she has the connections you're looking for," Douglas said, easing back into his seat. "It won't do much good to have her tagging along if she can't get us the audience we need."

"She will," Willa replied confidently. "She's putty in my hands. I'll have no difficulty in controlling her."

"Has she any clue that you're using her?"

"Why, Mr. Baker, whatever do you mean?"

Douglas chuckled to himself and very nearly sneered at the older woman. "You know perfectly well what I mean, but since I'm using you as much as you're using her, I guess I won't protest too much."

Willa's normally stern expression broke into a smug look of satisfaction. "That's good of you, Douglas. Very good of you, indeed."

～

Angeline returned to find Douglas and Willa pleasantly chatting about the barren New Mexico scenery. "I'm positively famished," she said, taking her seat. "Might I dare to hope that there's a dining car on this train?"

"There is indeed, and one of the best," Douglas said with formal bravado. "Perhaps you would allow me to escort you lovely ladies to breakfast?"

Angeline glanced at Willa who shook her head. "I'm not hungry, but you two go on ahead."

"Are you certain?" Angeline questioned her mentor.

"Absolutely. Besides, why would you want an old woman like me along? This handsome young pup hasn't taken his eyes off you since you've boarded the train. It will do you good to get to know an educated man of Douglas's background." Willa's words caused Angeline to blush.

"Don't mind her," Douglas said, tucking Angeline's arm around his own. "Willa's a very smart woman," he added with a smile over Angeline's head at the older woman. "Very smart."

~

Breakfast was a pleasant affair and Angeline was almost sorry to see it end. She followed Douglas down the narrow train aisle on the way back to their car and found herself righted by his strong arm when the train suddenly lurched.

"You must always be prepared," Douglas said with a smile.

His hand firmly held her at the elbow, and Angeline couldn't help but gaze deep into his green eyes.

"Prepared?" she whispered, completely captivated by the man's charismatic appeal.

"Yes." He was already much too close, but if possible he leaned in even closer. "All battles are won with concentrated effort going into preparation."

"Oh," Angeline managed to say, before Douglas pulled away with a dashing grin and another quick wink.

"I think I shall enjoy teaching you the game," Douglas remarked before once again moving down the aisle.

"No more than I shall playing it," Angeline muttered to herself with a smile.

~

"Here you are," Willa said, waiting for Angeline to take her seat. "I was beginning to wonder if I'd lost you to Douglas's wily ways."

Angeline looked from Douglas to Willa and shook her head. "No, I just like to eat a lot." At this Willa joined Douglas's laugh with her own.

"It doesn't seem to have hurt you any," Willa finally said. She shifted in her seat to face Angeline. "I have something very exciting to talk to you about. Something I've been considering while you were gone."

"What is it?" Angeline questioned cautiously. She was still uncertain of what Willa Neal expected of her as a traveling companion.

"When we are finished in Santa Fe and the other towns on the lecture circuit, I thought you might accompany me to Washington D.C." Angeline's eyes widened but she said nothing. "We have a meeting with President Wilson, and we plan to stage a rally and march to the Capitol."

"How exciting!" Angeline gasped, envisioning the possibility of being a part of the event.

"Then you would consider going with me?"

"Of course," Angeline replied, deeply touched that Willa would ask. "I would be honored." Then realizing it might be difficult to arrange, should her parents decide to interfere, Angeline added, "I will, of course, have to think about it and know more about the preparations." She dared a glance at Douglas knowing she'd find his smile at her choice of words.

Willa nodded completely unconcerned. "Of course. I wouldn't have it any other way."

Chapter 6

I can't believe that she defied us and went anyway!" Daniel bellowed after reading Angeline's letter. "It's the new way people look at things these days. Corruption of values and such." He was storming through the house following Lillie, whose red-rimmed eyes told the rest of the story.

"I'm going after her and that's that," Daniel said, considerably less noisy than before. He reached out and touched Lillie's quaking form and pulled her into his arms. "Ah, Sweetheart," he sighed against her carefully pinned hair, "it'll be all right. I'll find her."

Lillie composed herself for a moment and turned to face her husband. "You're needed here," she whispered. "You know half the town doesn't yet trust young Dr. MacGreggor. You can't just break their confidence and leave them to fend for themselves."

"I can't let Angeline just gallivant around the country like she owns the place either." The irritation in Daniel's voice was clear. "What in the world ever got into her anyway? We raised her to know better than to run off with strangers."

"It's her love of causes," Lillie offered. "Her desperate need to right wrongs. In some ways, I admire her gumption, and in other ways, she terrifies me."

"Well," Daniel said, setting Lillie from him, "I'm going to terrify her when I manage to locate her."

Lillie reached a hand out to stop Daniel from leaving. "There is another way," she said softly.

Daniel turned and eyed her suspiciously. "You're not going to suggest we let her have her way, are you?"

"No, never that," Lillie replied. She thought back to the night of Angeline's going away party and smiled. "I don't suppose Gavin Lucas has had a chance to speak with you, has he?"

"Gavin? No, I haven't talked to him since the party." Daniel looked even more perplexed. "Why would Gavin need to speak with me?"

"Gavin Lucas intends to make Angeline his wife." Lillie stated the words so matter-of-factly that Daniel could only stare back in surprise. "And, I do believe the boy, or should I say young man, is quite determined to do just that.

He did, of course, intend to discuss the matter with you first."

Daniel's face erupted in a broad smile. "Gavin and Angeline?"

Lillie smiled and nodded. "He said she just needed time to get used to the idea."

"So he has asked her?"

"That was rather what I gathered," Lillie said and drew Daniel with her to the sofa. "I say we send for Gavin, and if his father can spare him from the ranch, we send him for Angeline."

Daniel's smile broadened. "That would serve her right."

"Better still, I have no doubt that Gavin could get the job done. He has a vested interest, and I must say, I haven't seen such determination in a young man since," Lillie paused for a moment and reached up to run her hand through her husband's gray-gold hair, "you decided to pursue me."

"Me?" Daniel pretended to be surprised. "I seem to recall it was you who chased after me. With a frying pan, if I remember correctly."

Lillie remembered the scene in her mind. She had gone to New Mexico to visit Garrett and Maggie. It had been her hope to find some quiet place to think through her life, but that was not to be the case. One Dr. Daniel Monroe was already a houseguest at the Lucas ranch, and Lillie had endured a rather ugly meeting with him, before even arriving at the ranch.

Throughout their weakly established acquaintance, Daniel had teased her unmercifully about her eating habits. Habits that had led her to a frightful weight gain and deep depression. On the evening in question, Lillie had simply had enough. She picked up a frying pan and ran after Daniel with the serious intention of putting it to the side of his head.

Of course, matters had been made worse when Garrett and Maggie arrived home and found her chasing after Daniel, who was nearly hysterical from her antics.

Lillie snuggled up close, the memory fading in the intensity of her husband's questioning look. "You deserved that frying pan."

Daniel laughed. "Just like Angeline deserves a good spanking."

"I believe she's a little old for that, but," Lillie said with an impish grin, "she's just the right age for a husband."

"Gavin Lucas, eh?" Daniel settled back as if considering the matter. "I'd like to have Gavin for a son. He's a good man and a hard worker, and I can't imagine anyone I'd rather have for in-laws than Maggie and Garrett."

"Me, either."

"Angeline will be hard to convince," Daniel said as if this would be news to his wife.

"I'm sure Gavin will have his own way of convincing her."

"You still have that frying pan?"

Lillie laughed and edged her elbow into Daniel's ribs. "Of course. I have to keep it handy just in case."

～

Gavin Lucas was a little bit surprised when he received a note urging him to come at once to Daniel and Lillie's. He immediately feared that something was wrong with Angeline. She'd only been home a few short days, and he'd purposefully made himself wait until Sunday to see her.

Leaving word with his brother Jordy, Gavin saddled his horse and rode off for Bandelero. On the way, he reconsidered the situation and a more pleasant thought crossed his mind. Maybe Angeline had realized that she loved him and she wanted to tell him that she would marry him. With that thought in mind, Gavin picked up speed, mindless of the hot summer sun blazing down on him.

～

"Gavin," Lillie said in greeting, "please come in, and thank you for being so quick."

"Is something wrong?" Gavin lost his sense of hopeful expectation and replaced it with a nagging dread.

"Nothing we hope you can't help to right," Lillie said. She untied and laid aside her apron and motioned Gavin to follow her. "Come have some coffee with us, and we'll explain."

Gavin went with Lillie to the family's favorite gathering room and began to feel rather nervous when Lillie told him to wait there. She left the room, leaving Gavin to battle the butterflies in his stomach. What was going on? Where was Angeline?

"Gavin!" Daniel came into the room with Lillie and a tray of goodies right behind him. "Thanks for coming."

"Sure thing Dr. Dan," Gavin replied.

"Come on and sit down," Daniel motioned. "We have a great deal to discuss."

Gavin nodded and took the seat Angeline's father offered him. Lillie placed the tray on the coffee table in front of him and took the seat directly opposite, while Daniel chose to stand.

"I'm going to come right to the point, Son." Gavin nodded and waited for Daniel to continue. "Lillie tells me that you hope to marry our daughter."

Gavin swallowed hard. "I intended to talk to you first."

"I know you did," Daniel nodded, trying to put Gavin at ease. "Now before you go getting all worried, I want you to know I like the idea. Not only do I like it, I couldn't have chosen better for Angeline, if I'd been given that right."

Gavin physically let out a sigh of relief, causing Lillie to smile sympathetically. "Did you think we were going to roast you over hot coals?"

Gavin smiled. "I was ready for just about anything."

"Good," Daniel said before Lillie could reply, "because we have a problem."

"I suppose Angeline's in the middle of it," Gavin surmised.

"No," Daniel replied. "She is the whole problem."

Gavin grinned at his father's best friend. In all the world, Garrett Lucas had told his son, there was no better man than Daniel Monroe. "Go on," Gavin urged.

"Angeline has run away," Daniel began. "She got it in her mind to join the Women's Suffrage Movement and travel the country whistlestopping and stumping for equal rights and the vote."

Gavin shook his head. "Angel does enjoy her causes."

"That's not the half of it," Lillie joined in. "We forbade her to go. We tried to reason with her and thought we'd made her see our side of it, but last night, she sneaked out of the house and caught the train for Springer. From there she plans to travel south to Santa Fe with a suffragist named Willa Neal."

"What do you want me to do?" Gavin asked, coming to the edge of his seat. He hoped Daniel's and Lillie's words would affirm what he already had in mind.

"We'd like for you to go after her," Daniel said solemnly. "We'd of course pay your expenses."

"No need for that," Gavin said, getting to his feet. "I was serious about marrying Angel. I know she cares for me the same way I care for her. But, she's also young and stubborn. This time, though, she may well have gotten herself into more trouble than she can handle."

"Our thoughts exactly," Daniel concurred. "I don't care what it takes, I just want her back here safe and sound. From that point we'll just have to take it day by day."

Lillie reached out and poured a cup of coffee. "Why don't you have some," she said, extending the cup to Gavin.

"No thank you, Aunt Lillie," he said, knowing that one day he would call her by another name. That was, if he could find Angeline before she caused herself harm. Then, he'd have to somehow convince her to marry him, but that was all immaterial at this point.

"I'll need to go home first," he said, already heading for the door. "My folks will need to know what I'm up to."

Lillie and Daniel followed him. "Of course," they said in unison.

Gavin turned at the door. "Try not to worry. Angeline's stubborn, but she's got a good head on her shoulders."

"Thank you, Gavin," Lillie said, reaching out to hug the stern-faced young man.

"I'll get her back," he whispered for her ears only, and Lillie hugged him even tighter.

"I know you will."

~

Gavin found a captive audience when he returned to the ranch. Maggie and Garrett immediately sensed the urgency in their son and shooed his brothers from the room in order to privately speak with their eldest.

"Is something wrong?" Maggie asked, the worry clearly written in her eyes.

"Yeah," Gavin said with a nod, "it seems Angel has run off to join the Suffrage Movement." Maggie and Garrett both looked rather surprised before Gavin continued. "Lillie and Dan want me to go after her, and I told them I would."

Garrett grinned at his wife, who'd already told him that their son intended to marry their best friends' daughter. "Bet that was a hard decision to make."

Gavin couldn't help but flush a bit. "Who told you?"

Maggie laughed out loud at the look of surprise on her son's face. She reached out and rumpled his hair as she'd done when he was a small child. "Does it matter? Do you mind us knowing that you're in love with Angeline?"

Gavin shook his head, then rolled his eyes heavenward. "Please tell me they don't know," he moaned, motioning in the direction Maggie had sent his brothers.

Garrett fairly howled at his son's grim expression. "Gavin, my son, you are the oldest boy, and therefore the first to experience the ribbing and teasing that your brothers will good-naturedly dish out. But, just remind them," Garrett added with a wink, "their time will come and the shoe will be ever so neatly on the other foot."

Gavin smiled, just a bit. It really didn't help matters now. "I hope it's all right with you, my going after Angel, that is."

"Certainly," Garrett said, and Maggie nodded her assurance.

"She's in Santa Fe," Gavin offered. "I'm leaving this afternoon."

"I don't envy you going after a willful young woman," Garrett said with a sly glance cast at his wife. "Retrieving spiteful, head-strong girls, especially ones you fancy yourself in love with and plan to marry, is no easy task."

Gavin looked quizzically from his father's amused expression to his mother's reddening face. "You look as if you have a story to tell," Gavin said with a grin.

"You might say," Garrett began, "that I started a family tradition."

"You might say," Maggie interrupted, "that unless you want to sleep with that horse of yours, that you'll choose your words carefully."

Garrett grabbed her around the waist and pulled her close. "You know that your Grandfather Intissar, Maggie's pa, and I were good friends long before your mother came here to live."

Gavin nodded. "Mom lived in Kansas with her grandmother because Grandfather Intissar had some problems to work through."

"That's right, and when those problems were worked out, he sent for Maggie. Only problem was, she didn't want to come. That's when I came into the picture. Jason Intissar sent for me and knowing that I was half love-sick for his daughter, he put me on a train to Topeka and paid me to fetch his only child home."

"I guess I knew that," Gavin said as if suddenly remembering the story.

Maggie interrupted his thoughts. "What your father might be hesitant to say is that I nearly outfoxed him several times, in escaping to return to my grandmother."

Garrett laughed. "She thinks she nearly outfoxed me. First, I caught her coming down a trellis outside her second story bedroom window. Then she nearly got herself killed when she slipped off the train in the middle of the night and wandered around on the rain-drenched prairie for several days." His voice grew quite sober. "When you find her, Gavin," he stated quite seriously, "don't let her out of your sight. Women get peculiar notions when they feel caged in, and I wouldn't want Angeline to get hurt."

Maggie had thought to make a snide remark, but the truth was, Garrett's words were an accurate portrayal of why she'd run away from him. Now Gavin would perhaps face the same thing with Angeline. Maggie put a hand on her son's arm. "Unfortunately," she said softly, "your father is right. Angeline won't be easy to bring home, and it might risk the both of you before the matter is settled."

"Don't worry," Gavin said, patting his mother's hand, "God's my partner on this one, as with everything else. I prayed long and hard about Angeline and this time won't be any exception. You keep me in your prayers too. That way, when I'm having to concentrate on what she's doing and where I'll still be covered."

"You'll have our prayers, Son," Garrett replied proudly.

"And I know you'll have Lillie's and Dan's," Maggie added.

"Thanks," Gavin said and turned to leave. "I know it will make all the difference."

Chapter 7

Angeline had already been told more than ten times by Willa that tonight's rally was an important one. She had been instructed to send messages to all of her family's good friends and encourage them to attend. After that, Willa had suggested that Angeline rest up, and with special emphasis she added that Angeline should wear something pretty to the rally.

Pacing in her hotel room as twilight fell in a golden glow against the adobe churches and plaza structures, Angeline picked up one of Willa's books and read for several minutes. From outside her window came the sound of a baby crying and, for some reason, it caused Angeline to think of home.

Going to the window, Angeline gazed out on the ancient city of Santa Fe. "I wonder if they hate me?" she whispered. She couldn't help but envision her father and mother sitting down to the empty dining table and gazing at her vacated spot the way they had when John and James had gone into the army.

"I don't know what to do," she moaned and wished that God would open her eyes miraculously. She'd gone to church since she was a little girl, but none of that or the multiple sermons and Bible verses that had made their ways to her ears, seemed to help now.

Down in the center of the plaza, Angeline could see the makings of a crowd starting to gather. Willa had told her that many of the local politicians were shy about their cause, but with a little encouragement from solid citizens and people such as Angeline, they would turn out in mass number. If for no other reason, just to see what the fuss was all about. If they were lucky however, as Willa told Angeline they must be, these men would offer their support for the suffrage movement.

Angeline felt torn like never before. She really did want to help Willa. More than that, she wanted to do something worth while with her life. Something that people would remember her fondly for. Women's suffrage seemed to be a worthy enough cause, but Angeline knew her heart wasn't in it completely. How could it be when part of her heart was several hundred miles away in Bandelero?

The knock on her door startled Angeline, because she knew Willa would simply enter with her own key.

"Who is it?" she asked softly.

"Douglas."

Angeline opened the door. "Mr. Baker."

Douglas smiled revealing his perfect teeth, and Angeline immediately thought of a tooth powder advertisement she'd recently seen in one of her magazines.

"I hoped to escort you to the rally tonight. Willa will undoubtably have her hands full, and I wouldn't want you to arrive alone."

"That's very considerate of you, Mr. Baker."

"I thought we dispensed with that earlier today. Call me Douglas."

Angeline nodded and offered him a shy smile. "Very well, Douglas. I shall meet you in the lobby at seven o'clock."

"I will look forward to it." He gave her a slight bow and left without another word.

Angeline closed the door behind her and leaned against it heavily. Every time Douglas was near her, she couldn't help but think of Gavin. The troubling part was that she couldn't for the life of her figure out why.

～

Ten minutes 'til seven, Angeline put on the finishing touches by adding a pink ribbon to her carefully pinned up hair. She wanted to make Willa proud, and so she had chosen her very delicate white eyelet dress with the pink ribbon waist band and snug bodice. Checking herself in the mirror one final time, Angeline opened the door and made her way to the lobby.

Douglas was waiting for her at the bottom of the stairs. He cast an admiring glance at her, quickly running his gaze up and down the full length of her.

"You look ravishing, my dear." His tone was sincere enough, but something in his expression seemed almost leering.

"Thank you," Angeline murmured, uncertain why she suddenly felt so uncomfortable.

"Come along," Douglas commanded, taking hold of her arm. "They are about to begin, and Willa has instructed me to have you close to the stage."

"Why would Willa want me there?"

"I'm uncertain as to her exact reasons," Douglas stated, making his way with Angeline into the street, "but I believe she holds you in high esteem. You will offer her great support as you have all along."

Angeline said nothing but immediately began to pick up on the atmosphere surrounding the plaza grounds. Somewhere in the midst of the people, a band was playing popular ragtime tunes and most of the people seemed in high spirits. The crowd was growing by the minute, and though most of the participants were men, Angeline counted a great many women among the group as well. It should please Willa, Angeline thought.

Douglas manuevered them expertly through the mass and finally arrived at the place where Willa, in a stiff looking suit of blue serge and a banner proclaiming her cause, awaited the moment of her speech.

"Good, you're here," she said, noting Douglas's possessive control of Angeline's movements. "Sit here and I will start the rally."

Angeline allowed Douglas to lead her to the chair, while Willa had the small band stop playing their ragtime tunes and cued the percussionist to give her a drumroll.

"Ladies and gentlemen, we are happy to welcome you here tonight." The crowd seemed to still and move in closer to the stage. Willa began to speak in earnest, commanding everyone's attention and enrapturing Angeline as she had the very first night in Denver.

"For centuries women have played a vital and necessary role in the lives of their families. When God first created the universe and mankind, He showed the necessity for womanhood and, by special design, created her for life on this earth."

Angeline smiled. Willa said she always liked to start with something about God, because who could argue with the Bible? True to form, she was leading the crowd where she wanted them to go.

Willa continued, "The position women have maintained over the last several hundred years, however, has been less of a helpmate to her male counterparts and more of a servant. A servant whose mind has been closed to the reality of what she was created to do. Women all across this great nation, and even throughout the world, have offered important progress in the lives of all people. They must be rescued from obscurity and thrust forward in the limelight." Willa paused to see how the crowd was effected by her stern words before moving on.

"Madame Marie Curie in 1911 won the Nobel Prize for chemistry. Her contributions to the field of science have been magnificent and will continue to be so. And only a few years ago, an upstanding Southern woman named Juliette Low created an organization for our young women—the Girl Scouts. This association promises to help girls everywhere to formulate leadership qualities and push forward into the future. However," Willa paused, and everyone seemed to lean forward, "that future cannot be mastered, and those young women cannot be sufficiently utilized until they are able to exercise their choices for the leadership in this country. Women need the right to vote. Men need for women to have that right."

The crowd murmured unintelligible things, while Angeline seemed to momentarily forget Willa and concentrated instead on the people nearest her. She hated to eavesdrop but she wanted to know, no, she needed to know what they were thinking. Douglas seemed to immediately sense her contemplation and leaned down to whisper in her ear.

"Smart men will know she speaks the truth, and if their women are motivated to seek the vote, they will rally behind them."

Angeline looked up at Douglas for a moment and nodded, while Willa finished her speech and prepared to move from the stage to walk amidst her listeners and answer questions.

For some strange reason, Angeline suddenly felt very misplaced. She felt the people around her shifting to accommodate those in front of them and a fearfulness gripped her momentarily. With a quick glance at Douglas, Angeline assured herself that all was well.

Willa shook hands with people, while Douglas helped Angeline to her feet. "She's very good at this," Douglas said as if sensing Angeline's uneasiness. "Just watch her and you will learn a great deal."

Suddenly, a man approached Willa with an narrowing of his eyes that quickly told Angeline he wasn't a supporter of the "cause."

"Madam," the man began in a loud enough voice that everyone around immediately fell silent. "I have listened to you suffragettes from one end of this country to the other. You spout about rights that were never extended to you, because frankly, Madam, they were never necessary. Proper women, women who are biblical-minded as you so clearly like to associate your cause with, seek the protection and authority of men. Men, whom I might add, the good Lord made first and put in charge of everything else." At this, a roar of approval went up from the crowd.

"Sir, proper women are women who seek to do their best. They are women who, knowing God gave them many gifts, choose not to waste a single one. They seek not to usurp the authority of man, but to augment the benefits they might offer their fellow human beings."

The man made several notes on a tablet before questioning Willa again. This time the attack was far more personal, and an ugliness was born of the group that startled Angeline.

"Why is it, Madam, that all of you suffragettes are homely, spinster-type women, who obviously can't seem to attract the attention of a man any other way than to try to steal the pants from him?" The people surrounding them roared in laughter, and Angeline moved closer to Douglas, feeling fearful that things might get physical as Willa had warned her had happened on occasion.

Without any warning, Willa seemed to part the crowd with the wave of her hand and pulled Angeline forward. "This lovely young woman is my assistant. Perhaps you would like to tell her how homely and spinster-like she is."

The man stared at the stunned-faced Angeline and smiled. "No, Madam," he said to Willa, and a broad smile crossed his face. "I doubt anyone could accuse this beauty of being homely."

Angeline wanted to crawl into the nearest hole, but Willa's hand firmly gripped her arm and moving away was out of the question. The man quickly motioned to someone, and Angeline blinked her surprise when a man thrust a camera into her face and started snapping pictures. The flash blinded her momentarily, but Angeline stood fast.

"Tell me, Miss," the man began.

"Her name is Angeline Monroe. She is the very model of virtue and grace," Willa stated for the newspaperman.

"Tell me, Miss Monroe," he began again with pencil in hand, "do you honestly support the cause of suffrage and if so, why?"

Angeline felt Willa's hand tighten on her arm, but she wasn't schooled enough to know this was her mentor's signal to remain silent. Willa opened her mouth the speak but found Angeline's soft voice answering instead.

"I hold the highest regard for womanhood. I believe that God has given women a very special place on this earth, and that place is neither to usurp the man's place, nor to exceed it." The crowd grew completely silent as everyone strained to hear the delicate voice.

"My own mother is an intelligent woman who works at the side of my father, a physician. She is often consulted for her opinion, and my father, even with his college training, supports and honors my mother as a colleague. Other women I know are just as resourceful and just as important. And, Sir, I find it sad indeed that you seem to place a woman's value only in her appearance. One cannot always help the way one looks. Should we scorn the cripple because he," Angeline paused, "or she, cannot walk as we do with strong, sturdy legs? Do we not love the unlovable, just as Christ did when He walked this earth?"

The man stopped writing and stared at Angeline in earnest. Several women in the crowd dabbed at their eyes with handkerchiefs, while their men stared down at their feet and shifted uncomfortably.

"The Lord made us all," Angeline continued. "Who are we to condemn that which He created? You, Sir, report the news with the critical eye of one who has seen many things and perhaps has seen too much. You have lost in your sense of vision what it is to feel the heartfelt sorrow of the people around you. We are not seeking to thrust you from your place. We are merely asking to join you there. We are asking you to be proud of your women—your wives, mothers, sisters, and daughters. If we lack wisdom and education, then teach us. If we lack courage, then bolster us with your own, but don't turn us away as though you were ashamed. Not a single man here can boast of an entry into this world without the assistance of a woman. We are now asking for the return of that favor in assisting us into the world. We are asking for the right to vote."

For several minutes, no one said anything. There were sniffling sounds that were heard, then the sound of a solitary pair of hands clapping, then two, then a dozen, then a hundred. Willa smiled and gave her protégée a hearty pat on the back before nodding to Douglas. Angeline Monroe would be a bigger asset than even Willa Neal had imagined.

Chapter 8

It was as though that one small speech had somehow justified Angeline's existence in Willa Neal's eyes. She beheld the girl with a new respect and the fervent, driving knowledge that Angeline just might get them voting rights in New Mexico.

The papers that ran the following morning were plastered with front page photographs of Angeline Monroe. Her speech was recited, almost word for word, and the article citing it listed Angeline as a remarkable and clear-minded suffragette.

Willa was thrilled at the coverage. They often had to pay out precious money to get the kind of newspaper attention that Angeline's one, heartfelt outburst had surged. She pored over the stories and the multiple requests which had started arriving as early as six that morning, for interviews with Angeline Monroe.

Further evidence came in the form of flowers and cards from the political connections whom Angeline had invited to the speech. Willa read one card after another, noting the dates and times of invitations to dinners, small parties and teas. She intended to work the situation to her benefit no matter the consumption of Angeline's time and energies.

The one bit of attention that Willa would not tolerate came from the more conservative suffragists who sought to have Angeline join their cause instead of Willa's more militant one.

Willa refused to even admit these women into the hotel suite, and Angeline couldn't help but wonder what the real threat might be. Willa passed it off as unimportant, however, and insisted Angeline read a speech that had been given by Alice Paul several years earlier and not concern herself with the merits of the less passionate.

～

Angeline, herself, loved the attention. Used to the limelight, she was once again thrust front and center, and it was everything she'd hoped it would be. A surprising sideline came to her in the form of Douglas's ardent regard.

Angeline enjoyed Douglas's pampering, but her heart nagged at her and reminded her that Gavin was at home in Bandelero, waiting for her. *But I never committed myself to him,* Angeline thought. *In fact, I told him that I*

269

wasn't interested in marriage. She reminded herself of this at least twenty times a day, for all the good it did.

When Willa announced they were moving on to the next city, Angeline was a bit taken aback. She hadn't thought of how far she was drifting from home and the people she loved until Willa pointed out that they would be traveling for several weeks. Guilty at the thought of her parents' suffering because of her disappearance, Angeline suggested to Willa that she write or telegraph them, but Willa quickly dismissed the idea.

"They won't understand, and they'll only insist that you come home," Willa replied. Angeline nodded in acquiescence, but felt a terrible lump in her throat at the thought of her parents worrying over her.

~

Two days later, Angeline found herself sitting to the far side of the stage, where Willa, front and center, urged the people of the small town to see the merits of women's suffrage. This town was much smaller than Santa Fe and far less progressive in its thinking. Many of the men and women gathered there were natives to the area and cared little for the ideals behind voting when they were worried about water for their crops and animals.

Angeline was amazed at the crowd's seeming indifference, but even more amazing was the way that this indifference changed to anger at one simple statement made by Willa.

"I have seen the treatment of animals in this country and deemed it better than that of women," she announced in a heated fury.

"Animals are our life's blood," a man yelled from the murmuring crowd.

Willa shook her raised fist, and Angeline felt herself cower against the hard wooden chair. She didn't much care for this side of Willa. "Women gave you life, not those animals you pamper to market."

This created quite a stir in the gathering and, before Angeline realized what was happening, there were angry shouts and rocks being thrown at Willa.

Staring in dumbstruck silence, Angeline watched as several men approached the stage. They were shouting and cursing about Willa's inability to understand their plight. It wouldn't be learned until days later that several boxcars filled with sheep headed to market had derailed and consequently pushed more than one of the local families into financial ruin.

Angeline came to her feet at the sight of the first dissenter coming on stage. She backed up against the edge, not knowing what would happen next, fearful that she would be unable to protect herself from the rushing crowd.

Glancing around into the inky shadows of full night, Angeline began to pray as never before. "Please God," she whispered, "please help me."

Utter pandemonium broke out after that, and the stage was rushed with Willa being safely spirited off in the opposite direction of where Angeline stood. Without warning, Angeline felt herself being lifted and thrown heavily against the broad shoulders of a stranger. She fought for all she was worth, kicking, screaming, and beating at the man's back, but nothing could stop him.

The man pushed through the crowds, leaving the dissenters behind to tear up the stage and suffrage banners. He wormed his way through new arrivals who were clearly endowed with false courage from the assistance of the local saloon. When her captor started to run, Angeline felt the wind knock from her as her mid-section slammed against his shoulder again and again.

"Dear God," she breathed aloud, feeling herself grow faint.

Then as quickly as it had begun, it ended. The man stopped, glanced around, and opened the small wooden door that entered a tiny adobe building.

He had to stoop to get through the doorway, but once inside, he straightened back up and pulled Angeline down into his arms.

Angeline kept her eyes closed tightly. Partially because she was afraid to see her captor and partially because her head was spinning.

"Hi, Angel," the stern, but familiar voice called out, as Gavin Lucas cradled her to his chest.

Angeline's eyes flew open and a small gasp escaped her lips before she threw her arms around Gavin's neck and squealed his name.

"Gavin! I'm so happy to see you. I thought I was going to die back there!"

"You very well could have. Those people weren't a bit happy with your cause." He said the word in such a snide way that Angeline immediately took offense.

"They just don't understand," she began. "They don't see the necessity of women being allowed to choose their representation in government." She wound down a bit and looked around the room. "Where are we?"

"I haven't the slightest idea," Gavin replied. "I looked in the window and saw the place was empty and figured I needed to check you out and see if you were all right. Are you?" His expression was one of sober consideration, while his eyes traveled the length of Angeline's simple white shirtwaist and blue serge skirt.

Angeline noted that her suffrage ribbon had somehow been torn from her and was probably beneath the muddy boots of the town's male population. Otherwise, she felt fine now that she could breathe. "I'm perfectly well," she finally answered.

"Good." Gavin's voice still sounded rather indifferent. "We'd better get out of here and get back to the hotel."

"You're staying at the hotel?" Angeline questioned. "Why are you here,

Gavin?" she pressed without giving him a chance to answer her first question.

Gavin opened the door and peered down the alleyway in each direction. He motioned her to the door with his finger pressed to his lips to insure her silence.

Angeline was never good at keeping quiet, however. Especially when she wanted answers to important questions. She stared up at the handsome face of the man who claimed to love her and whispered, "Why?"

Gavin looked down at her as though she'd asked the stupidest question possible. "Why do you think?" he replied softly and pulled her into the shrouding darkness.

Angeline didn't like leaving the lighted room, but she liked the idea of awaiting the return of an angry owner even less. She allowed Gavin to pull her along until they approached the main street and saw that at least twenty or thirty angry men still surrounded the front doors to the hotel.

"Come on," Gavin growled in a barely audible voice. He pushed Angeline toward the end of the boardwalk and ended up pulling her into the livery at the edge of town before he'd allow her to rest.

"What in the world is wrong with you, Gavin Lucas?"

"Me? You think there's something wrong with me?" His voice was indignant.

"Yes," Angeline began, but Gavin wouldn't hear any more.

"I came here because your mother and father are sick with worry and grief about your well-being. I've followed you from Santa Fe and tried a hundred times to get close enough to talk to you, but you have more watchdogs than prime herd of beef on its way to market." Angeline started to respond to his reference but closed her mouth quickly at the look of warning Gavin gave her.

"I nearly get killed in that crowd just to save your scrawny, ungrateful neck, and you have the audacity to ask me why I came here?"

Angeline was quite taken back at this side of Gavin. She knew him to be quite serious and decidedly dedicated to his loved ones, but she'd never seen him this mad. "I'm. . .I'm. . ." she wanted the words to be just right, but they wouldn't come together.

"You're what?" Gavin asked her as if he thought her reply might actually be important.

"I'm sorry." Angeline finally managed to say. "I never meant to hurt my folks, but the cause is important."

"You and your causes!" Gavin exclaimed in disgust. "Your cause got a little out of hand tonight, don't you think?"

"I didn't expect it to result in a fight," Angeline admitted, taking a seat on a nearby bale of straw.

Just then the livery keeper entered from outside. "Oh!" he exclaimed. "I didn't know I had company. Sorry to keep you waiting, but it seems we had a bit of excitement at the hotel tonight."

"No problem," Gavin replied and nodded, toward Angeline. "I had a bit of excitement tonight, myself."

The man looked at Angeline, nodded, and gave Gavin a sly wink. "I'll be out back if you need me, but I suppose you won't." Then the man left as though it were perfectly normal to find two strangers arguing in his livery.

Angeline jerked herself upright and glared at Gavin. "I'll not have you besmirch my reputation by implying that you and I, that we, that we. . ." She blushed furiously and fell silent.

"That we what? That we raced through the streets, fighting to save our own necks?"

Angeline stomped her foot, unable to unleash enough words at once to tell Gavin Lucas just what she thought of him. "Go home, Gavin," she finally uttered and turned to walk toward the door.

Gavin spun her around and pulled her into his arms. "They're using you, Angel. I've heard the way they talk behind your back. I've been following them, remember? They just want to use you until you can't help them anymore."

Angeline pushed against Gavin and, to her surprise, he released her. "Mind your own business, Gavin."

"You are my business, Angel," he replied softly. "I intend to marry you or did you forget that?"

Angeline tried to sound self-confident when she laughed. "It's immaterial what you intend. The cause needs me, and I intend to fight for women's suffrage in any way I can. It's a cause worth fighting for."

"Is it a cause worth dying for?"

Gavin's words seemed to hit some deeply buried reality in Angeline, but she hated to yield that conquest to him. "I'm not sure any cause is worth dying for," she replied honestly. "At least, I'm not sure I've found a cause worth that to me."

Gavin stepped forward and reached out to her. When Angeline didn't refuse his touch, Gavin pulled her close. "What about God, Angel? Where does God fit into your cause?"

"Why do you ask that?" Angeline whispered, staring deep into Gavin's smoky blue eyes.

"You were sure calling on Him for help a little while ago. I was just wondering how He figures into your plans for the future. Or does He have a place in your plans?"

The spell was broken, and once again Angeline pushed away and headed for the door. "He has a much more secure position than you do, Mr. Lucas." The words were delivered with stilted exasperation. Lifting her chin defiantly, Angeline continued, "Now if you don't mind, I intend to return to my hotel room. I'm quite exhausted."

Chapter 9

Gavin left Angeline at the door to her hotel room and went downstairs to make plans for going back to Bandelero. He figured he had more than enough money to get them home, but he had no idea of how he was going to convince Angel to go, short of hog-tying her and throwing her over his shoulder. Laughing to himself, Gavin thought even that plan had its merits.

~

Inside her room, Angeline tiptoed to avoid disturbing Willa, but the woman had incredible hearing and quickly came to investigate.

"Angeline! Where have you been? I was worried that you'd been hurt in the unrest."

"Unrest? Is that what you call that riot of out-of-control rock slingers?" Angeline shook her head. "I've never seen people like that, Willa. There was no reasoning with them at all."

Willa's brown hair hung in a loose braid down her back, and when she smiled at Angeline's statement, she was almost attractive. Angeline couldn't help but think that with just a little makeup and the right clothes, Willa could actually be beautiful.

"You're smiling at me," Angeline sighed in exasperation. "You were nearly killed and you're smiling?"

"I'm smiling because this entire ordeal was mild compared to what we saw in Washington D.C. in years past. Angeline, you are young and innocent. It is hard for you to realize that things worth fighting for often come at a high price." Willa paused and looked around the room. "Did you read those speeches I gave you? The ones given by Alice Paul and Lucy Burns?" Angeline nodded with a shudder. Willa smiled patiently. "It wasn't a pretty picture that they painted about the treatment of suffragettes in England, was it?"

"No, it wasn't," Angeline recalled. "I found it deplorable that one human being could treat another in such a fashion."

Willa looked thoughtful for a moment. "Those women believed in the cause of suffrage so strongly that they starved themselves in massive hunger strikes. The public was enraged, shocked, surprised, and concerned. The feelings ran from the extremes of wanting to put these women in insane asylums

275

to the sympathetic desires of those who understood their plight."

"But they forced them to eat," Angeline said with disgust, then shook her head. "No, it couldn't be called eating. They ran tubes down their throats to their stomachs. I could never have imagined such actions possible."

"They are, and even worse things than these have been endured by our sister suffragettes."

Angeline put her hand to her head. The entire evening had been too much for her. "I need to go to bed."

Willa watched her carefully for a moment. "How did you escape the crowd? Did Douglas find you?"

"No, I never saw Douglas. A friend of the family, someone my parents sent to find me, did just that and rescued me as the stage was overrun."

Willa frowned at this news, glad that Angeline had already turned to walk towards her door. "A friend? Did he sympathize with the cause?"

Angeline laughed. "No, Gavin Lucas only sympathizes with his own causes. The main one of which seems to be his desire to marry me." Without another word to consider the situation, she left Willa.

～

Willa stared at the closed door of Angeline's room for several minutes before quickly going to her own room to dress. She had to get to Douglas and see what could be done to discourage this Gavin Lucas character. She couldn't lose Angeline now. Not when there was so much at stake.

Forty-five minutes later, Douglas Baker finished counting out several dollars to each of three scruffy looking characters. Men could be bought easily in the small town and getting what he needed had been no trouble at all.

"You understand," Douglas stated before turning to leave, "I don't want him killed. I just want him too busy with his own problems to stick his nose in ours." The men nodded and watched the well-dressed man disappear down the alleyway. Looking at each other and sensing that the time to earn their ill-gotten pay was at hand, the men took off in the opposite direction.

～

"But I don't understand," Angeline protested, taking her seat on the train. "Why are we running away and to Denver of all places?"

"We aren't running away, so much as tactically regrouping," Douglas said with an air of concern. "We have to consolidate our forces, much like an army. We need to approach these small towns with proof of the benefits that can be had through acceptance of suffrage." Douglas seemed unruffled by the entire episode, while Angeline had slept very little the night before. The dark circles under her eyes betrayed her exhaustion, and Douglas reached out his hand. "Come sit beside me," he spoke softly. "You may use my shoulder for a pillow."

Angeline was touched by his kind gesture but shook her head. "I'm afraid that would hardly be proper, Douglas."

"But we are friends and in clear view of everyone on board. Come, Angeline." His words lured her into obedience. "No one will think a thing of it."

"Maybe for just a short time," she whispered, feeling incapable of refusing.

While Angeline slept she dreamed of Gavin. It had been with a bit of sadness and relief that she had been unable to see him before leaving town with Willa and Douglas. Had her words and declaration of independence put him off so that he left without her? Perhaps he was too busy elsewhere to concern himself with Angeline's needs. Needs? Angeline wondered even in her sleep what those needs might be. Restless from her thoughts, she turned away from Douglas's rather soft shoulder and sought the hard, cool glass of the window beside her.

After two days on the train, Angeline was grateful to be in Denver. She loved Denver with it's big buildings and bustling streets. She liked the automobiles and smartly dressed people who always seemed to be hurrying to someplace important.

She was immediately whisked away to one of Denver's finer hotels and given a suite to herself, much to her surprise. Willa suggested she bathe and sleep, something that Angeline surmised Willa longed for herself.

Angeline looked the room over casually. It was very nice, in fact, it was the nicest hotel she had ever stayed in. There was a small sitting room with a door leading off to a private bath and another door leading to a bedroom. The sitting room was tastefully furnished with several velvet upholstered chairs and a round table of walnut that held a crystal vase of freshly cut flowers. The plush draperies had been pulled back to reveal a charming view of the city, with a small park across the street in which Angeline hoped to find time to walk.

"I can't say that I haven't been well cared for," Angeline murmured and went to prepare her bath. In the back of her mind, however, she once again let her thoughts travel back to Gavin.

"I wonder why he didn't come to tell me good-bye?" Then as soon as the words were out of her mouth, Angeline realized there was no way Gavin could have known of her plans. Angeline herself hadn't known they were leaving until Willa had her dressed and on the train.

Soaking in the tub of hot water, Angeline let down her long blond hair. She eased down into the tub, sighing at the soothing comfort it offered. *With very little trouble,* she thought, *I could fall asleep here.* But, knowing the bed would be more conducive to her needs, Angeline forced herself to finish the task at hand.

~

When the loud knock sounded on her hotel room door, Angeline forced herself to wake up. She glanced quickly around her, forgetting momentarily where she was. Another fierce knock, followed by the sound of a key being fitted in the door, caused Angeline to jerk up in the bed.

"Angeline!" It was Willa.

"In here," she called out and forced herself to leave the comfort of the bed.

Willa bounded in with all the energy of six women and smiled. "We've got a great deal of work to do. I've ordered supper to be sent here so get dressed and join me."

Angeline nodded and reached for her blue serge suit. It was one of only four outfits she had, and she was rapidly beginning to tire from her limited wardrobe. With a sigh, Angeline couldn't help but remember the closet filled with clothes at home in Bandelero.

By the time Angeline had dressed and repinned her hair, supper had arrived and with it a very pleasant aroma.

"Umm, that smells heavenly," Angeline voiced, coming to join Willa.

"This hotel offers the finest meals," Willa said, motioning Angeline to sit. "Of course you'll soon find that out for yourself."

Angeline looked down at the steaming food and realized it had been a long time since she'd eaten. Happily, she joined Willa, offered a small prayer of thanks, and sliced into the most tender veal cutlet ever created.

"Douglas and I both realize that this constant moving about is taxing to you, but you are young and can adapt easily." Willa took a bite of food and chewed thoughtfully as though carefully considering what she was about to say. "I need for you to understand, Angeline, that often you will have no say in what happens and you may have questions. I hope that you will have the wisdom to not question me in public, but when we are alone you may of course seek me out."

"What are we going to do next?" Angeline jumped right in.

"Well," Willa said, "we have a great deal of planning. We have the march on Washington coming up, and we must somehow rally our sisters there to aid the cause of winning New York. They will put the suffrage issue to a vote this November and we must take that state or it will notably hinder our cause."

"Why is that?" Angeline asked innocently.

"Because Washington can only be swayed by powerful people. It matters little what the common man wants, if the palms of those in control are being tied to the purse strings of the rich. New York is filled with persuasive people. Rich, famous people who can see the thing done," Willa stated almost feverishly. "We must win in New York, and to do so, we must make a good showing in Washington."

Angeline listened while Willa continued, but her heart was elsewhere and far from the cause of suffrage. Something caused her to remember the warm way Gavin's arms had held her, and from that moment on, Angeline heard nothing that Willa said.

"You aren't even listening to me."

"I'm sorry, Willa. My mind and heart are heavy."

"The young man in New Mexico?" Willa questioned without sympathy.

"Yes." Angeline sighed and hoped Willa could relate to her feelings. She could not.

"You cannot trust this person, Angeline!" Willa was quite adamant in her statement. "Men are corrupt. Why even Douglas is only trusted so far."

Angeline's head snapped up. "I don't believe you can just sum up an entire group of people like that, Willa. Isn't that what men are trying to do to us?"

"It's different." Willa seemed to have to think on the matter for a moment. "It's an entirely different matter."

"How?" Angeline questioned. "Men state that women shouldn't be allowed to vote because we are poorly educated and easily swayed. Now you're telling me that men as a whole are corrupt and incapable of receiving our trust. How is it different?"

Willa got to her feet as if deeply hurt. "I can see this conversation will get us nowhere. You are naïve and young, Angeline, and you need to trust my wisdom on the matter. I will leave you to yourself. See if you can't sort through your childishness." With that Willa left the room, slamming the door behind her.

Angeline stared in surprise for several moments before going to the door and locking it. "Whatever got into her?" Angeline wondered aloud. It never crossed her mind to recognize Willa's confusion in how to control Angeline.

"Well, what am I to do now?"

Crossing the room to look out on the darkness that had captured the city, Angeline spied a black-covered book on a small table by the window. A Bible. Angeline recognized it immediately. Almost against her will, she picked up the book and held it close. All of her life she had been taught to center herself around the teachings here. All of her life she'd been told to make her stand on this book alone.

Taking a seat, Angeline opened the Bible and flipped casually through the pages until she came to rest on 2 Timothy 3:13–15. "But evil men and seducers shall wax worse and worse, deceiving, and being deceived. But continue thou in the things which thou hast learned and hast been assured of, knowing of whom thou hast learned them; And that from a child thou hast known the holy scriptures, which are able to make thee wise unto salvation through faith which is in Christ Jesus."

The words were a powerful message to Angeline, and she read them over many times before leaning back in the chair to close the Bible. "I've known since I was a small child that the truth of God could be found in Scripture," she murmured. "I know the answers must be here, but I'm so confused. I care for Gavin and I know he cares for me, but the cause is also important and Willa is right about the corruption of men and powerful people."

With a sigh, Angeline shook her head and put the Bible aside. There didn't seem to be a clear understanding. At least not one that came easily.

Chapter 10

The next week and a half passed in a flurry of activities for Angeline. She met many of Willa's more militant suffrage supporters and found these women to be even more intolerant of opposition than Willa was. Angeline listened graciously as each woman recited her entry into the "cause" and tried to be sympathetic or enraged at exactly the precise moment for each, depending on the subject on which the woman spoke.

Angeline then found herself in a grown-up school of sorts. She was given printings of lectures, handwritten copies of letters, as well as lists of statistics regarding suffrage worldwide. Next, she was lectured morning, noon, and night until she no longer questioned why she was asked to respond in a certain way, she simply did it. Which, of course, was exactly as Willa Neal planned it.

After an intensive period of this oppressive training, Angeline found herself at a reception the governor was throwing. People from assorted causes gathered at this party with the hopes and planned intentions of gaining the ear of the powerful. And, while suffrage had already been achieved in Colorado, there was a great deal the suffragettes hoped to obtain from their political representatives.

Angeline passed through the beautifully decorated ballroom and spoke with a number of people. Some she knew vaguely and others quite well, and to whomever she spoke, she spoke of suffrage.

"Angeline Monroe?" the voice of an elderly gentleman sounded behind her.

Angeline whirled around, surprised that the man seemed to know her, while she hadn't the faintest clue as to who he was.

"You don't remember me and, in truth, had I not overheard someone speak of you a moment ago, I wouldn't have recognized you from the scrappy ten-year-old I met long ago."

"I'm afraid you have me at a disadvantage," Angeline replied with a smile.

"Jefferson Ashton," the man replied and extended his hand. "I'm a good friend of your father's. He was a great ally in the fight to win statehood in 1912."

Angeline remained confused, struggling to put his face with the newly given name. "My father has many friends, Mr. Ashton. Forgive me if I don't remember you."

The man chuckled. "There's naught to forgive, my dear. You were just a child. Your father first met me when I sought him on a medical emergency. One of my entourage became quite ill from bad oysters. Your father saved his life and, in the process, he and I discussed the volatile politics of the day. Now I find you here in Colorado and at a political gathering no less. Tell me, what is it that you are about these days?"

"I'm in support of suffrage," Angeline told the gray-haired man. She liked his kindly face and long droopy mustache. He had a glint in his eyes that bespoke of a brain that never stopped working. "I'm here with Willa Neal."

"Ahh," the man said as though the mere name of Willa Neal said it all. "Then you are in agreement with the more militant champions of suffrage."

Angeline smiled thoughtfully at Mr. Ashton. "I don't always believe they go about things in the proper manner. I'm not sure that I would go on hunger strikes and storm the president's house with threats of forming a separate country for women."

Ashton laughed at this. "I've heard of the extremists also. I say give them a country somewhere, as long as it's not here."

"I suppose that would get them out of your hair." Angeline enjoyed the older man's sense of humor.

"In truth, those women do far more to harm the cause than to help it. When Colorado first accepted suffrage many other states were interested and encouraged. Now many, many years later, we still haven't seen nationwide suffrage come to pass, and I believe it is because of the frightening antics of the more dramatic of your sisters."

Angeline's lavender eyes narrowed a bit as she considered his words. "I have often wondered if having the vote merited civil disobedience. It seemed to me that children do not often get their way with tantrums as much as with cooperative behavior. The same seemed to be a natural assumption for national causes."

"Right you are, my dear." Jefferson Ashton accepted a drink from a passing waiter. "You are very wise, Miss Monroe, and, I believe, cool-headed like your father."

Angeline smiled. "Yes, I rarely get angry. But, as my mother would say, when I do, watch out!"

"So what will you do now, Miss Monroe?"

"It is Miss Neal's desire that I accompany them to Washington and join in the rally there. We are to speak with the president and request more support for a nationwide push for suffrage."

"My advice to you, regarding Woodrow," Mr. Ashton remarked, noting his close friendship with the president, "is to be clear-minded and open to suggestion. He is a fair man, but he has a great deal on his mind these days. Things that far outweigh the necessity of suffrage."

"But suffrage is very important!" Angeline exclaimed. "Some of these women are dying for the cause."

"And some of our young men may be called upon to die for another." Jefferson Ashton's words hit Angeline hard.

"The war in Europe," she murmured.

"Yes. It isn't likely that we can remain neutral much longer."

"My brothers both joined the army," Angeline said with a fretful look on her face. "I pray you are wrong."

Mr. Ashton offered her a sympathetic look and gently touched her arm. "I pray also that I am." He tried to be consoling while giving her the honesty that she desired. "Wars are ugly things, Miss Monroe, and I have no desire for us to enter into this particular mess without the deepest of regard."

"We shouldn't have to go at all," Angeline said rather hostilely. "Neither side is right."

Jefferson Ashton smiled.

"My dear," he began in an almost indignant tone, "war in and of itself is never right. This issue goes beyond whether war is immoral or not, but whether one side is more right than the other. And in this case, there is evidence to clearly support the issue. Consider the *Lusitania*."

Angeline shook her head. "It may be true that the Germans sunk the *Lusitania* and violated the lives of Americans, but how very different is that from the way the British board our ships on the high seas? Ships, I might remind you, which are from a neutral country and headed for yet another neutral country."

"Ah, but how neutral are those countries?" Ashton questioned. "The export of food commodities to neutral countries surrounding Germany has greatly increased. Coincidence? I think not. The British confiscate our foods, label it contraband, and often haul our ships into port to avoid being attacked while sitting motionless on the ocean."

"Exactly my point," Angeline declared. "Where lies the difference between the British and the Germans?"

Jefferson Ashton smiled sadly. "The British injustices could be compensated to us later; for while the British seize ships, Germany is sinking them and taking the lives of innocent people with them. Do we, as responsible, God-fearing people, ignore the suffering and pain when we have it in our power to put an end to it?"

"But at what cost?" Angeline questioned. "Do I send my brothers to die for another woman's brothers?" Angeline was near to tears.

"My dear," he spoke softly, "it is not for us to decide. We must pray and allow God to work His course and pray for those who make the choices for us." Angeline nodded, but she felt a heaviness in her heart that ruined the evening for her.

∽

From a distance, Douglas Baker had watched the exchange between Angeline and Jefferson Ashton. When Willa passed by on her way from one group of congressmen to another, Douglas pulled her aside.

"Do you know who that is?" he questioned, motioning to Angeline and Ashton.

"Of course," Willa replied rather indignantly. "Everyone knows him."

"It would seem our little Angeline knows him quite well."

Willa watched for a moment as Angeline and Jefferson Ashton continued in deep conversation.

"Perhaps another family friend," Willa said with a smile. "I must say that this child has proven to be more beneficial than I'd originally believed."

"Yes," Douglas murmured, watching with envy at the casual way Ashton touched Angeline's arm.

Just then, Angeline pulled away from Ashton and seemed to be making her good-byes. She passed by Douglas with a hint of tears in her eyes.

"Angeline, are you all right?" Douglas questioned her, sounding far more concerned than he really needed to.

"I'm fine," Angeline replied. "I think, however, I'm going to go upstairs to my room. I'm feeling rather tired and a bit hungry."

"They're serving a wonderful buffet," Willa reminded Angeline. "Why not have something to eat here?"

"I need to get away from all of these people," Angeline stated.

"Why not come with me to dinner? The hotel has excellent fare, which you already have learned, of course. We could go to the dining room and order something there. It would be both quiet and private," Douglas offered.

Willa sensed his game and encouraged Angeline to accept. "Douglas is right. Go on with him and afterwards, if you are still feeling poorly, Douglas will escort you to your room."

Angeline looked into the warm glow of Douglas's green eyes.

She forgot for a moment about the threat of war and her brothers, but no matter how hard she tried, Angeline couldn't forget Gavin.

"I suppose I could. . . ," she began, but Douglas wouldn't allow her to finish.

"Come," he whispered in her ear.

~

The atmosphere of the dining room was warm and inviting. Candles graced each table, giving off a romantic glow to the room, and from the upstairs alcove, chamber music floated down upon the patrons like a soft satin coverlet.

Angeline tried to enjoy Douglas's praise for her work with the suffrage cause. She tried also to relish his admiration for her physical attributes, appreciative that he worked hard to keep from becoming too personal in his assessment of her.

Douglas spoke on, or droned on as Angeline heard it, while in her mind were images of that warm night when Gavin had rescued her from the angry crowd. She could feel Gavin's arms around her and smell his spicy cologne. Why hadn't he come to see her? Had he taken seriously her words of dismissal?

Unable to concentrate on Douglas, Angeline ate and tried to nod from time to time as though she were paying him the strictest attention.

"What will you do when suffrage is won?" Douglas questioned, and Angeline snapped her head up as though she'd just been accused of taking the silver.

"What?" her voice betrayed her surprise.

"What will you do when suffrage is won? Will you return home to New Mexico or will you go on to fight another cause?"

Angeline stared at Douglas for a moment and thought of Gavin's harsh words for her causes. Yet, without giving it much thought at all, Angeline answered Douglas in a way that surprised him almost more than she surprised herself. "I suppose I'll go home and marry."

"Is there someone waiting for you?" Douglas asked, trying to make the question sound as though it were unimportant.

"Yes," Angeline replied, realizing for the first time that there really was someone waiting for her and that she was glad he was. But was he? She'd told Gavin to leave her alone. She'd insisted to him that she wanted nothing to do with marriage.

Just then, Douglas spotted an old friend and excused himself to corner the powerful land baron. While Angeline watched, Douglas laughed and pounded the equally pleased man on the back. They seemed completely engrossed with each other. When Douglas took an offered seat at the man's table, Angeline felt rather put out and summoned the waiter.

"Please tell Mr. Baker, when he returns," she said, refraining from using the words "if he returns," "that I have acquired a headache and have retired to my room." The man promised to deliver the message and helped Angeline from the table.

She hated to lie. She didn't have a headache, but in truth, Angeline knew she soon would, if she had to listen to Douglas any longer. Making her way to her room, Angeline grew deeply troubled by her thoughts of Gavin. In a sense, she was planning to marry him, and the thought shocked her. She'd known Gavin all of her life. He was probably her best friend in all the world. Could she jeopardize that with marriage?

Angeline wearily entered her hotel room, thankful for the electric lights that snapped on at her touch. She closed the door behind her and turned to lock it.

"Evening, Angel. I wondered if you'd ever make it back."

Angeline turned around and gasped Gavin's name before she even saw him. "What are you. . ." Her words fell into silence at the sight of Gavin's battered face. "Oh Gavin!" she rushed to where he sat and lost her footing.

Gavin reached out and caught her, pulling her to his lap. The effort caused him much pain, which was quickly reflected in his expression.

"What happened to you!? How did you get hurt?" Angeline seemed unconcerned that she was sitting on his lap. She tenderly reached up to touch his face. "Who did this?"

Chapter 11

Gavin eyed Angeline suspiciously for a moment, then sighed. "I wondered if you knew about it," he muttered.

"Knew about what?" Angeline questioned, her eyes roaming his face, itemizing his injuries.

"About the men who attacked me." Gavin's voice was very grave, and Angeline suddenly realized that he thought she had a part in his injuries.

"Gavin Lucas!" she exclaimed and tried to get up from his lap. "How could you ever believe me capable of hurting you. I could never hurt you. I. . ." Her mouth snapped shut when she realized that she'd very nearly told Gavin that she loved him.

Seeming to sense what she nearly said, Gavin gave her a lopsided grin. "No, I never really thought you were in on it, Angel. But it's good to know how you feel."

"Let me up," Angel demanded, feeling herself blushing from head to toe.

"You sure?" Gavin asked, his smile broadening. "I kind of like it like this."

Angeline pushed away and got to her feet. "You would. Now tell me what happened to you. Who did this?"

Gavin winced as he shifted his weight. "I don't know the names, but I'd be able to pick out the faces, or what's left of them."

Angeline grimaced. "How many?"

"Three," Gavin said rather proudly. "But they were puny ones." His words sounded more like an accounting of a poor fishing day than an assault on his life.

Angeline ran a glance the full length of Gavin's body before she spoke again. "Are you hurt anywhere else?"

Gavin laughed weakly. "You could say that. I've got some pretty tender ribs and about fourteen stitches where the knife went through my shoulder."

"Knife!" Angeline exclaimed and not caring how it looked, she went to Gavin's side and fell on her knees. Taking his hand she said, "I'm so sorry, Gavin. Oh, if you hadn't followed me you would never have gotten hurt."

Gavin was rather taken aback by her reaction.

Gavin tightened his fingers around her hand. "It's okay, Angel."

"No, it's not. I knew the crowds could get violent. It is, after all, my cause. But you had no way of knowing that people could be so set against the suffrage movement. If you hadn't come to try and talk me into going home, you wouldn't have had to deal with those crazy people."

"Angel, those folks who nearly trampled you to death had nothing to do with this."

Angeline looked up at Gavin, her lavender eyes melting his heart in a single glance. "What do you mean?"

"I mean, the men who attacked me were paid to do so. They were given all the information they needed as to where they could find me, and they were well paid to see to it that I couldn't interfere with you."

"With me? But who would care whether you talked to me or not? Who even knew that you were there?" Angeline questioned, her voice raising slightly.

Gavin smiled. "Yes, who knew I was there besides you?"

Angeline thought back to that night. "I told Willa. She saw me after you brought me back to the hotel. She wondered how I'd managed to escape unharmed, and I told her about you." Angeline paused and shook her head. "Willa would never hire someone to harm you. She'd have no reason."

"Why not, Angel?"

"Like I said, she'd have no reason."

"What did you tell her about me? Think hard," Gavin said softly.

Angeline's brows knitted together as she tried to remember. "I told her you were a friend of the family. She asked me if you were in support of the cause."

"What did you tell her?" Gavin's eyes were intent.

"I told her. . ." Angeline paused, remembering her words with some embarrassment.

"Tell me."

"I told her that your cause was getting me to marry you."

"So she'd have no reason to feel threatened. No reason to suspect that I might take you away from her cause?"

Angeline jumped to her feet, mindless of the way she pulled at Gavin's arm and shoulder as she did. She released his hand indignantly. "I can't believe that Willa would hire hoodlums to come beat you."

"Calm down, Angel. As far as I could learn, your friend Douglas Baker is the one who did the hiring." Gavin got to his feet slowly, and Angeline took a step back.

"I don't believe you. You're just jealous, that's all."

"Jealous of Baker? Is there something there that merits my jealousy?" Gavin questioned seriously.

"Douglas is a wonderful man, and he isn't at all the type that needs to resort to illegal activities. He has powerful friends and plenty of money. I don't think you would threaten him in the least. As for whether he merits your jealousy, well that simply isn't for me to say." Angeline moved away, unable to look Gavin in the eye. She knew full well that Douglas was more than a little interested in her as a woman.

"Angel, I overheard one of the men say that Baker expected to get his money's worth. The others agreed, and that's when the man behind me stuck his knife into me."

Angeline turned, a look of shock on her face. Her hand went to her head. "I can't believe Douglas would be capable of such a thing. It's monstrous."

"If I can give you proof it was Baker, will you realize just how much danger you're in and come home with me?" Gavin questioned, moving forward to take hold of her shoulders. The effort caused him to grimace, and Angeline stood very still to keep from further irritating his wounds.

"What kind of proof can you give?" Angeline asked softly.

"What if he admits it himself?" Gavin's fingers played with the wisps of hair at her neck.

"Well of course, that would prove. . . But how in the world are you ever going to get him to just come out and say. . ." Angeline refused to finish. She shook her head. "He couldn't have been a part of it."

Gavin's finger traveled up Angeline's neck to her jaw. "Angel, you are such a good-hearted woman. So good-hearted, in fact, that it's difficult for you to believe anyone capable of the kind of evil that lurks in the world."

Angeline relished his warm touch against her skin. She felt her breathing quicken and wondered if Gavin knew how he affected her. How could he? She was only learning about it herself.

"Angel, I'll get the proof, but you didn't answer me. Will you come home with me when I do?"

Angeline was so confident of Douglas's innocence that she saw no reason to withhold her agreement. "If you can show me, beyond any doubt, that Douglas was responsible for your injuries, I'll go home with you." She was lost in his touch and the look in his eyes, but somehow she found the strength to add, "But, if you can't get your proof, will you agree to go home without me?"

Gavin grinned, his eyes twinkling as though he'd already won. "Of course. If I can't prove what I said is true, then I'll leave you to traipse all over the world, and I'll even explain to your parents why you didn't return."

"Deal," Angeline said softly.

"Deal."

The clock chimed the hour, breaking the spell. Angeline looked away from Gavin and, for the first time, realized how very alone they were. "You shouldn't even be here," she said and pulled back. "If anyone finds you here, you'll compromise my reputation."

"That would be a pity," Gavin chuckled. "I might have to marry you then."

Angeline wanted to slug him, but she was too painfully aware of his injuries. "Gavin Lucas, you would try the patience of Job himself."

"So my mother has told me."

"Mine says the same thing about me," Angeline couldn't help but add with a grin. "But even my mother wouldn't approve of you being here with me, like this."

Gavin nodded. "Sorry. I had to see you alone, and I didn't want to risk having Baker see me. Since you two were having such a pleasant dinner, I thought your room would be the safest place to wait."

"But what if he'd accompanied me back here?"

Gavin frown. "Then I would have had to accompany him back downstairs. He'd better never try anything with you, Angel. You belong to me."

Angeline felt both hemmed in and pleased at Gavin's declaration. "I only meant that being a gentleman, he would have seen to my safety and escorted me at least to this floor. Douglas has never tried to impose his will on me. I can't say the same thing for you." Gavin took a step towards her, but Angeline outmanuevered him.

"I make no apologies for my actions, Angel. Your folks like the idea of adding me to the family, and my folks adore you. Frankly, I'd appreciate it if you'd give all this up and come home now. I've got a great deal of work waiting for me at the ranch, and I've already endured more than I bargained for."

"So go home!" Angeline declared. "You're the only one stopping you. I have no intention of pretending that I want you to stay."

Gavin moved faster than Angeline expected. He swept her into his arms and planted a passionate kiss upon her lips. "Tell me again how you don't want me to stay."

"I don't want you to stay," Angeline said without conviction.

Gavin kissed her again, only longer.

"Tell me."

Angeline's lavender eyes met Gavin's smoky blue ones. "I, uh," she began and saw the amusement on his face at her confusion. "Go home, Gavin."

Gavin lowered his lips to hers once more and, this time, Angeline kissed him back. "All right!" she declared and forced herself to step away from him, breathless and flushed. "I don't want you to go, but I don't want you to cause trouble, either."

Gavin laughed, picked up his hat from a nearby chair, and cautiously opened the door. "Good seeing you, Angel. Be careful." He started to leave, then pulled back into the room and shut the door. Reaching into his pocket he pulled out a piece of paper. "This is my room number. I'm just one floor down, so if Willa or your precious Douglas try to move you out of town, I'd appreciate it if you'd get word to me."

Angeline took the paper and nodded. "Now, go. Please." She was more disturbed by his kisses than she cared to admit.

"You'll be in my prayers, Angel."

"Thank you," she whispered. "And you'll be in mine."

When Gavin had gone, Angeline sighed and leaned heavily against the door. Her mind raced with thoughts. Could Douglas really have paid to have Gavin beaten? She'd never known Gavin to lie, and he'd have no real knowledge of Douglas Baker, otherwise.

"Oh, Lord," she whispered the prayer, "what am I to do? Who can I trust?" Her mind quickly referenced a verse she'd memorized from childhood. Proverbs three, verse five. "Trust in the Lord with all thine heart," she recited, "and lean not unto thine own understanding."

"Everyone is running my life, Father," she said, going to stare out the window. "Gavin comes here with his plans and dreams. He insists I marry him and won't take no for an answer. Willa tells me what to do and say. She makes me read horrible things and tells me what I should feel. She plans my days out in complete detail without ever considering my needs." Angeline smiled to herself when she thought of Gavin's surprise arrival. "Of course, Willa didn't plan on Gavin." Then a thought crossed her mind. She mustn't say anything to give away Gavin's presence. If she told Willa, and Douglas had been responsible for Gavin's attack, she'd end up being the cause of him being hurt further.

With a heavy sigh, she let go of the drapes. "Oh, God, please keep him safe. Please don't let them hurt Gavin again."

Chapter 12

The dry, warm days of mountain summer caused Angeline to think of home. She remembered her father and mother with such fondness that she ached at the thought of the distance between them. Despite their differences, they had always shared a closeness that Angeline cherished. It was that obvious void in her life that began to make her rethink her devotion to the cause of suffrage.

Twice she'd made her way to the lobby telephone, but both times she'd stopped herself. If Gavin found the proof he was seeking, then she'd be headed home in a few days anyway. If he didn't find something substantial to prove Douglas's involvement in his attack, then Angeline would give her folks a call and let them know about her trip to Washington D.C.

But Gavin remained mysteriously absent. Angeline had assumed he would spend some time with her now that he was here in Denver. She'd even imagined romantic evenings at the theater or opera with Gavin on her arm. But he never called on her or even so much as sent a message. After nearly a week of this, Angeline began to wonder if he'd admitted defeat and gone home.

"Maybe he couldn't find his proof," she said aloud to herself one day. "At least he could have said good-bye."

The hotel room was more confining as the days passed and Angeline decided an outing was in order. Pulling on her well-worn blue serge skirt, she gave serious thought to her wardrobe. If she stayed on with Willa, she'd have to send for more of her things. Trying to look the part of a smart, young suffragette was most difficult when you had to alternate between three or four changes of clothes.

A knock came at her door, and Angeline found that her heart skipped a beat. Maybe Gavin had come to talk to her again. If so, she'd ask him to accompany her across the street to the lovely park she'd watched for days from her window.

"Who is it?" she called, unlocking the door.

"It's Willa, open up. I have a surprise for you."

Angeline opened the door and greeted her friend. "You certainly seem excited about something. Come on in and tell me all about it."

Willa entered the room with little flair or grace. Instead, she more or less took over a room as a general would claim a piece of ground. "We leave for Washington in two days. The march is already scheduled, and the president has agreed to receive us in the White House."

"Two days?" Angeline questioned, uncertain that she could manage on such short notice.

"Yes, is that a problem?"

"Well, I was just considering my clothes," Angeline replied. "You see, I never planned to be away from home more than a week or two. I only have four outfits at best and they are becoming a little worn."

"Umm," Willa said, surveying Angeline intently. "Yes, it would be appropriate to clothe you better."

"I have a vast wardrobe at home in Bandelero, but I would need to send for my things and there's no real way of knowing whether my folks would send them or not. I have some money, but it certainly isn't enough to refurbish my attire." Angeline's words were straight to the heart of the matter.

"You can't very well show up as one of our best speakers and look unkempt. I'll work on the matter immediately. In the meantime, I've brought you these." Willa pulled out a stack of papers from her valise-styled bag.

"What are these and what do you mean 'best speaker'?" Angeline questioned, taking the papers from Willa.

"You have a gift, Angeline. I've already made up your agenda. You will give three speeches while we are in Washington. You will speak first at a small reception where there will be several representatives from each of the forty-eight states. You will speak no longer than ten minutes." Willa motioned Angeline to the table at the far side of the room. "For that occasion, you will give this speech. I just finished writing it for you about an hour ago, so you will need to memorize it and make it characteristically your own."

"I have no intention of speaking, Willa. I'm too new to this," Angeline protested.

"Nonsense. You'll do as you're directed and you will do quite well at it. The next speech will be given at a luncheon for our suffrage association. This again, will last about ten minutes. Here is the speech for that occasion." Willa pointed out the paper and pushed it aside. "Lastly, during our rally at the Capitol, I want you to speak similarly to the way you did in Santa Fe. I tried to recapture the mood and the gist of what you told those people. They were moved to tears there, and you will no doubt capture the hearts and minds of many in Washington. You might even catch the national paper's eye and that would truly be a boon to our cause."

Angeline couldn't believe the way Willa had it all planned out. "Do I get any say in this?"

Willa stared at her in mute surprise. "Of course not. I am your mentor, I will teach. You will listen. The time is right for a young, beautiful woman to step forward and help open the eyes of the nation."

"But I'm not even old enough to vote, if we had the vote," Angeline declared.

"It is unimportant. Now you read these over and memorize each and every line. I will get to work on clothing you and will come back this afternoon to see what progress you've made. Don't bother going downstairs for lunch. I'll tell them to send something up." Willa got to her feet and moved to the door. "It is very important to the cause, Angeline, that each of us be prepared."

Angeline remembered Douglas's words about preparation. "I don't mind being prepared," Angeline muttered, "I'd just like a say in what's being prepared for me."

"Pshaw!" Willa denounced her concern. "You're just a child, Angeline. What would you do differently?" Angeline's blank expression gave Willa the fuel she needed to continue. "You know nothing about what is necessary to plan a march or a rally. I have the experience and you don't. It's that simple." With that, Willa was gone before Angeline could even open her mouth to reply.

Angeline did as she was told, although her heart was far from in it. She read the speeches over and over, wondering if she believed any of the words. Women's suffrage had seemed an important cause, but now Angeline just felt used. Used? Wasn't that what Gavin had said they were doing to her?

"Oh, Gavin," she whispered and sighed heavily. "Where are you?" She thought instantly of the hotel room number he'd given her. *Perhaps I should check on him,* Angeline thought to herself. *After all, he was injured. Maybe he's taken a turn for the worse.* She had just gotten to her feet, intent on finding out, when Willa barged in without bothering to knock.

"Well?" she questioned the surprised Angeline. "Have you memorized the speeches?"

"No," Angeline replied in a rather stilted manner.

Willa frowned. "Why not?"

"I haven't had the time for one thing. For another, I'm just not sure I can give these," Angeline said and held up the papers. "They aren't my words. They aren't the way I feel."

"No one needs to know how you feel, except that you demand equal rights for your sisters. Angeline, we've been all through this before."

Angeline plopped down unladylike into the nearest chair. "Willa, I don't even know if I'm going to Washington."

Willa was genuinely taken aback by the younger girl's response. "Of course you're going."

Angeline frowned. "Willa, I've tried to be patient about this but I feel like everyone is telling me what to do and no one cares about my feelings. I have parents who are no doubt worried about me and love me. I know they want me to return home, and I believe I can remain here and still help suffrage. After all, I have good connections in New Mexico and can write letters. . ."

"Write letters, bah!" Willa interjected. "You need someone like me to teach you. Angeline, you can't keep your head buried in the sand forever. The world is an ugly, cruel place out there, and this is war!"

"Yes, exactly," Angeline stated, quieting Willa. "I have two brothers who are in the army. The entire world is waiting to see how the United States will respond to the sinking of the *Lusitania* and the atrocities in Belgium. It is war and while it very well may be a European war at this point, it could easily become an American interest as well."

"It doesn't matter," Willa protested.

"It does to me! You and Douglas both seem to think you can lead me around on a chain and I will perform like some type of circus animal. Well, I have news for both of you." Even though Angeline spoke Douglas's name, she also thought of Gavin's pushiness. "I have a good mind of my own, and I will make my own decisions."

Willa eyed Angeline suspiciously, then gave her a tight-lipped smile. "You're just overtired. Douglas is a good man, and he is quite attracted to you. You could do far worse."

"What are you talking about?"

"I think you know very well what I'm talking about," Willa answered. "You are falling in love with Douglas and it frightens you. Douglas would make an excellent husband, so stop fretting."

Angeline's mouth dropped open and, for a moment, she couldn't say a word. Willa took that as confirmation of her statement. "Douglas Baker is a wealthy, powerful ally, and to have you aligned with him in marriage could be quite beneficial to all concerned."

"I have no intention of marrying Douglas Baker!" Angeline exclaimed. "Willa, you must stop this at once. You may look upon me as a child with no will of my own, but my own mother could very well set you straight on that."

Willa held her angry reply and crossed to the door. "Memorize the speeches, Angeline. I'll return in the morning and we will go over the material."

Anger raged up inside of Angeline, and as Willa closed the door, she couldn't help but hurl her shoe against it. Unable to think clearly, she took herself to her bedroom and threw herself across the empty bed in order to decide what she should do next.

Angeline never realized how very tired she was. When she awoke the next morning, still fully dressed from the day before, she began to calculate the toll that Willa and the cause were taking on her. She'd barely had time to wash her face and fix her hair when noises sounded from the sitting room, bringing Angeline to investigate.

Willa instructed several bellhops where she wanted them to put the boxes they carried and quietly ushered them from the room with a handful of change to share between them.

"I have your new clothes," she announced unceremoniously. "Try them on and make certain they fit." The order didn't set well with Angeline. Especially in light of the way she'd spent the night.

"Willa, would you please leave. I'm afraid I just woke up and need some time to bathe."

"Nonsense." Willa was already pulling open boxes. "Try this first," she said and tossed a burgundy gown to Angeline.

Angeline caught the heavy satin and held it up to inspect it. "The style is much too old for me," she muttered.

"Your manner of dress is too childish. I want to present a beautiful, sophisticated woman of the world. I want to mold you into an image that women will strive to emulate. Beauty and grace should be synonymous with the suffrage cause, and with your help, it will be."

Angeline felt hostile, and there was little charity in her words to follow. "You could benefit by your own advice, Willa. You aren't an ugly woman, yet you dress in a mannish style, and you wear your hair entirely too severely to look feminine."

Willa was unmoved. "I dress as I do because I have too little time to waste on frills and pampering. You, however, can draw a new generation. These younger women will look to you as a role model. Now go try on the dress."

Angeline did as she was told, quite unhappy that Willa was unwilling to listen to reason.

The gown rustled lightly as Angeline pulled it over her head. The graceful princess lines of the dress were accentuated with painfully narrow stays that would barely allow Angeline room to breath. The cut of the neckline draped alluringly across the bodice and left little question as to the femininity of Angeline's form.

"Come, let me see," Willa called from the sitting room, and obediently, Angeline did as she was told.

Willa nodded in approval. "You look most lovely. There are shoes to match in one of these boxes. You may wear this to the reception."

Angeline could take no more. "Willa, the dress is beautiful, but it isn't me. I would like to have a choice in my clothes and in my itinerary. I want a say in where I go and what I do, not to mention with whom."

"Angeline, we've discussed this before. Now, why don't you try on this white dress?" Willa tried to ignore the fire in Angeline's lavender eyes.

"No!" Angeline stared hard at Willa and put her hands to her hips. "I am not a child to be ordered about. If you want my cooperation in any matter, then you will discuss it with me as an adult. If you do not see fit to treat me in a respectful manner and include me in the planning of situations that involve me, I will return home and forever leave the cause of suffrage behind me."

Willa paled just a bit, but not enough to make Angeline believe she'd taken her seriously. "I mean it, Willa! Stop trying to run my life or I'm going to leave!"

With that Angeline fled from the room and stormed down the hotel hallway, uncertain as to where she would go or what she should do. Dressed as she was, Angeline drew appreciative stares from the men on the staircase and it wasn't until she'd made it all the way down to the lobby that she knew she had to return to her room and change.

Grudgingly, she turned and made her way back upstairs. What was she going to do, and how in the world could she convince Willa Neal that she was not an ignorant child?

"Lord," she whispered, "I know I've put You alongside as one of my many causes, but I'm starting to see a real need for a better walk with You. I need a deeper understanding of what You want for my life." Shaking her head and continuing the hushed prayer, Angeline wished most adamantly that she could speak with Gavin.

～

Gavin had heard the murmurs and hushed comments before he'd even glanced up to see what the commotion was all about. What he saw was rather shocking, but like everyone else in the lobby, he was mesmerized by the vision on the staircase.

"Angel!" he whispered, and she did seem very much like a heavenly illusion. Then, much to his amazement, she turned on the bottom step and rushed back upstairs as though she'd forgotten something important.

Gavin got to his feet as if to follow her but realized he needed to stay put. Douglas Baker was due to join his cronies for a drink, at least that's what a well paid bellhop had passed on to Gavin not fifteen minutes earlier. With the picture of Angeline in the burgundy gown still fresh in his mind, Gavin forced himself to sit back down and wait.

"One of these days, Angel," he breathed almost painfully. "One of these days."

Chapter 13

Willa left Angeline's room quickly after the younger girl had stormed from the premises. She had to find Douglas and talk to him about Angeline. Rather, she had to figure out how they could better control Angeline.

Painfully aware of the asset that was about to slip through her fingers, Willa cautiously made her way to the lobby via the back stairs. It would do her no good to have another confrontation with Angeline just yet. No, it would be better to discuss her thoughts with Douglas and see if together they couldn't get the spirited girl under their control.

The hotel lobby was busy as always. This seemed to be one of the many gathering places in downtown Denver where business deals were made and broken. Willa had chosen the hotel for just such a reason. It never hurt to find oneself rubbing elbows with the very powerful and very rich. It cost a small fortune to maintain the four suites they held here, and Willa knew that without Douglas's additional help in the matter she would never have enjoyed the luxury.

Spotting Douglas in his exquisitely tailored suit, Willa ignored the men who surrounded him and pleaded with him for a private moment of his time.

"I must say this is a surprise," Douglas said, following Willa to a small sofa in a far corner of the lobby.

There were people everywhere and Willa uncomfortably glanced around her at the nearest occupants to ascertain whether they could prove harmful. "I'm sorry for the disruption, Douglas," Willa began, deciding that the people around her were of no consequence. "Angeline is fast becoming a problem. She had a bit of a fit this morning when I brought her the clothes."

"A beautiful young woman and she got angry at new clothes?" Douglas questioned with a chuckle in his voice. "I find that hard to believe."

"Well, believe what you want, but it's true. She's even more angry about being told what to do. She wants to call her parents. It seems perhaps that friend of hers, you remember, the Lucas man? Well, I think perhaps he stirred up feelings in her that she can't quite deal with. She hasn't been the same since he came into the picture."

"I took care of him in New Mexico," Douglas stated flatly. "What more do you want me to do, kill her parents?"

Willa seemed aghast for a moment. It was impossible to tell if Douglas was just saying the words for effect or if he really meant to offer the solution as a viable possibility.

"Don't give me that shocked expression, Willa. Just cut to the heart of the matter and tell me what you want me to do."

"We need better control over Angeline. She's threatened to walk out. I need her connections and the money behind them or we'll never get the vote in New Mexico."

"And where do I fit into this?" Douglas questioned, remembering to keep his voice down.

"Perhaps you would woo the girl and get her to marry you. As your wife, Angeline would have to respond more respectfully to instruction." Willa's statement was offered so matter-of-factly that Douglas was now the one silently stunned.

Finally, a slow grin spread across his face. "I would very much enjoy the pleasure of husbanding Angeline Monroe. However, I doubt very seriously that you could convince her to agree."

"I'm not suggesting you ask her, but rather you tell her. Force her if necessary. Use the threat of her parents. It doesn't matter. If you have her under control, then we can get at her connections."

"Angeline doesn't strike me as the kind of girl who will be easily swayed by idle threats," Douglas replied.

"Then don't make idle threats!"

Willa's voice rose enough to cause Douglas to glance around at the nearby hotel guests. No one seemed interested in their rather lively conversation, however. In fact, the man directly across from them was thoroughly engrossed in a copy of the *Denver Post* and seemed not to even notice that other people occupied the same room.

"Look," Douglas whispered. "I'll do what I can. I also could use Angeline's connections as you well know. But I'm going to have to persuade her to marry me, and perhaps that will result in her spending less time involved in the suffrage cause and more time on my arm."

"I can't give her up to you," Willa declared firmly.

"What do you think you would be doing if she married me?" Douglas questioned. "Did you think I'd invite you on the honeymoon?" His face was twisted in a leering expression.

"Don't be vulgar with me!"

"Then don't be foolish in your dealing with me. I will get Angeline to marry me, but there is price to pay, my dear, dear Willa. You may control the child to a degree, but after we are married she's mine and everything she does must come through me first. That includes the suffrage cause and any political contacts you make through her."

Willa considered the words for a moment and nodded. "Very well. If we are to be adversaries for her attentions, at least let us be cooperative ones."

"Rather like the United States and Germany and this insane agreed upon neutrality?"

"Neutrality serves my purpose very well," Willa stated and got up to leave. "I'd rather we never enter war and take the focus away from the rights of women in this nation."

Douglas got to his feet. "You seem rather unconcerned with the rights of one particular woman," he said with a smirk. "I doubt you'd ever tolerate such a heavy hand upon your will."

"Just bring her under control, Douglas."

"So that she responds more respectfully to instruction?" Douglas used Willa's words against her.

Willa's eyes narrowed, and Douglas realized quickly that it wasn't best to have this powerful suffragette against him. At least not in this manner. "Just see to it, Douglas."

"Certainly, Madam," he said with a slight bow. "May I escort you somewhere?"

"No, I have a meeting nearby." With that Willa went one direction and Douglas the other, and neither saw Gavin lower his newspaper with an intent look of concern edging his features.

"If this weren't becoming just a little too dangerous for my taste," Gavin muttered, folding the newspaper under his arm,"I'd like to see Baker try to tame Angel. What a laugh!"

"Did you say something, Sir?" A hotel attendant was quickly at his side.

"Yes," Gavin replied and thrust the newspaper at the man. "Dispose of this for me, please." The man quickly took the paper, while Gavin made his way to the main staircase.

I'd better warn Angel, he thought. Taking the steps two at time, he glanced quickly over his shoulder to assure himself that Douglas Baker was still moving towards the men's club entryway. Noting that he was, Gavin slowed his step a bit and tried to figure out a plan.

Angel will be suspicious no matter what I say, so I'd best just come clean with the truth. Gavin reasoned that he'd have certain information to give Angeline that would prove he'd overheard Douglas and Willa in conversation. Perhaps that would be enough, he tried to convince himself.

Making his way to Angeline's room, Gavin began to pray in earnest. "Father, she's so innocent and she doesn't begin to understand what these people are trying to do to her," he whispered the words under his breath. "Please help me to convince her. Please show me a way to reveal the true nature of these people so that she won't be hurt by their scheming. Amen."

He finished the prayer just as he reached Angeline's door. Knocking for several minutes, with worried glances down the hall toward the stairs, Gavin finally gave up and tried to think where Angeline might have gone.

Heading down the backstairs, Gavin immediately thought of the park across the street. Angel would love it there! He raced down the remaining steps and made his way to the park. She just had to be there, he thought. "Please God, let me find her first."

~

Angeline had found the confines of her room unsettling and more than once had hoped for a stroll in the city park across from the hotel. Willa's absence from her room had allowed her to change out of the very grown-up burgundy satin and into her serviceable blue serge skirt and shirtwaist. Before she realized what she was doing, Angeline found herself strolling among the park's aspens and pines as though she'd been there a hundred times before.

It was summertime, soon to be heading into fall, and Angeline marveled at the colorful flower beds. Carefully cultivated rosebushes were in full bloom and the scent that lingered on the warm air was heavenly. Taking a seat on a nearby park bench, Angeline wondered what she was to do. On one hand, she wanted to be helpful to the cause of securing women the right to vote. But, on the other hand, she knew that Willa's ideals and forceful ways were not her style. Furthermore, Angeline knew they were not God's ways, either.

"I hoped I'd find you here," the familiar voice called out, and Angeline didn't know whether to be relieved or concerned.

"Hello, Gavin," she replied and looked up to find his gaze fixed on her. My, but he was a welcome sight!

"You look a little upset. Want to talk about it?"

"No," Angeline stated emphatically.

"Well, I do." Gavin took a seat beside her and put his arm around her.

Angeline stared at him hard for a moment, but when Gavin's grin only broadened, she stiffened her shoulders and sat on the edge of the bench.

"You can't get comfortable that way," Gavin teased.

"It wouldn't be appropriate for me to sit beside you like that." Angeline nodded backwards toward his arm.

"But we're engaged," he argued.

"It doesn't matter. It still isn't appropriate," Angeline answered and only after it was too late, realized that she'd affirmed Gavin's possession of her.

Gavin wasn't shy about grasping onto the words for security. "So maybe we should set the date."

Angeline glared at him and scooted away from him. "Have you found the proof you need?"

"Yes, as a matter of fact," Gavin said, causing Angeline to drop her stuffy look. "I see that surprises you."

"Well, I suppose it does. Well, maybe not surprise, oh, I don't know." Her hands went to her head as if she could sort everything into perspective with wave of her hand.

Gavin pulled her back against him and forced her to remain. "Don't go, Angel. We need to talk. You're in danger, and I have to warn you in order to keep you from making a very grave mistake."

"What do you mean, I'm in danger?" she questioned and stopped her struggles.

"Willa wasn't very happy that you didn't like the new clothes," Gavin stated, and Angeline gasped at the words. "I see that verifies for you that I have a reliable source. Matter of fact, this time it came straight from the horse's mouth." He grinned hard. "So to speak. Of course, I thought you looked real nice in that little red number."

"Burgundy," Angeline muttered without realizing until too late the compliment he was paying her.

"It was a little out of your routine style of dress, but I thought it looked great." His warm breath was against her ear, and his words were so soft and alluring that Angeline found herself nearly hypnotized. Nearly, but not quite.

"When did you see me in that dress?" she asked quietly, trying to steady the racing of her heart.

"When you came storming downstairs. My, oh my, but you did look fit to be tied." Gavin was laughing softly, and Angeline jabbed him quickly in the ribs.

"Why am I supposed to be in danger, and why should I believe anything you say?"

"I've been trying to get the proof you asked me for, remember? Well I was sitting in the lobby when Douglas Baker and your friend, Willa Neal, came sauntering over to where I was and began talking about the need to control you."

Startled at his words, Angeline jerked away and stared at Gavin. "You were sitting right there, and they didn't see you?"

"Nope, I had the paper in front of my face the whole time. Anyway," Gavin began again and paused. "Are you listening to this, Angel? I don't want to have to repeat myself."

"I'm listening. Just get on with it."

"Well, it seems Miss Neal is quite worried about you and your political associates slipping away. Seems you threatened the old woman that if she didn't stop interfering and planning your life you were going home."

Angeline nodded. "I did say that, so I guess I should believe that what you say is true."

Gavin looked hurt. "I've never lied to you, Angel."

"No, I suppose you wouldn't, even to get me back home," she responded, sorry that she'd hurt his feelings.

The seriousness of Gavin's expression only deepened. "Angel, Willa Neal wants you to marry Douglas Baker. He's going to try to court you and get you to marry him right away. Miss Neal even suggested force." He wasn't about to tell her that this included the death of her parents in that threat.

"Oh really, Gavin!" she exclaimed and got to her feet. "You must be over-exaggerating. Douglas has no interest in me outside of the political arena." She faced him with her hands on her hips and eyes fairly blazing. "I know you mean well, but this is too much."

One minute Gavin was seated on the bench with that all-knowing look that Angeline had come to know better than to argue with and, the next minute, he'd pulled her into his arms.

"Angel, you have to listen to reason." His voice was nearly hoarse with pent emotion. "I love you, and I know you love me too. You're just too pig-headed to admit to your feelings and leave this nonsense behind. They're using you, and I can't stand by and let that American kaiser dictate to you how you'll spend the rest of your life. Marry me, Angel. Come away with me and marry me now." Before she could speak, Gavin lowered his lips to hers and tenderly kissed her. It was a kiss like no other Angeline had ever known. And though her experience was quite limited, she found the urgency in his manner most confusing.

Slumping against his chest and letting him support her full weight, Angeline nearly broke into tears. What was she to do? Had Gavin spoken the truth? Of course he had, she chided herself. She'd never known him to lie, but if he hadn't lied then that meant Willa and Douglas cared nothing about her as a person. Feeling Gavin's arms tighten around her, Angeline knew the blunt, harsh reality of what he'd shared. Gavin's truth was no different than the conclusions she'd already come to.

"Let me take you away from here, Angel. You belong with me."

～

From the seclusion of his hiding place, Douglas Baker snapped a twig in half. The scowl on his face was enough to distinguish his mood had his actions not already made that clear. He found it hard to believe he was witnessing

Angeline in the arms of that Lucas man. Hadn't he paid well enough to have Lucas out of the picture, permanently?

"I won't be so gracious next time, Lucas," Douglas muttered and watched as Gavin kissed Angeline. Dropping his hand from where it divided the brush, Douglas turned back toward the pathway and made his plans. "I'll put an end to this entire charade, once and for all." His words were low enough to offer comfort to their speaker, but not loud enough to give away his plans.

"I'll teach Willa Neal the meaning of respectful response to instructions," Douglas announced, emerging from the park with a plan already formulating in his mind. "I'll teach them all."

Chapter 14

A ngeline was nearly back to her room when she spotted a red-clad bellhop knocking on her door.

"May I help you?" she asked.

"Are you Miss Angeline Monroe?"

"Yes, I am."

"Then this is for you." He handed her a folded piece of paper.

The note read: *Please meet me in the hotel restaurant in fifteen minutes.* It was signed, *Elaine Cody.*

"Who is Elaine Cody?" Angeline wondered and folded the note and handed the bellhop a nickel from her skirt pocket.

"Not sure, Ma'am," the young man replied, "but she said it was urgent."

"I see," Angeline said thoughtfully. "Please tell her I'll be there." The boy nodded and took off down the hall.

Angeline pulled her key out and entered her room. A quick glance revealed no sign of an intruding Willa or anyone else, and for that Angeline breathed a sigh of relief. It seemed of late that nearly everyone had a way in and out of her room.

Deciding to quickly freshen up, Angeline went to the wardrobe. A survey of the clothes hanging there revealed that Willa had once again meddled in Angeline's affairs. None of Angeline's original clothes remained, forcing her to either continue wearing the serge skirt and shirtwaist or give in and utilize the new attire.

Stomping her foot in a private protest, Angeline muttered to herself and fingered through the dresses. Willa had thoughtfully provided for her daytime needs as well as evening wear. Choosing a sedate forest green suit, Angeline didn't stop grumbling about the interference until she reached the bottom step of the grand staircase.

Angeline was led to the table where Elaine Cody waited. "Miss Monroe," the woman said, motioning her to take a seat.

Elaine Cody was a simple woman in her thirties. She wore her brown hair short and curled and a simple gown of lavender and cream. "Are you hungry?"

Angeline smiled. "I've had such a busy day that I hadn't even thought to eat." She took the chair across from Elaine. "I hope I don't sound rude, but I don't know why you've called me here, Miss Cody."

"Mrs. Cody," the woman said sweetly. "I know this is a surprise, but we've been trying for several weeks to talk to you, but Willa Neal always managed to put a stop to it."

"Why would Willa keep us from talking?"

"I represent a less radical approach to the suffrage movement," Elaine said softly. She paused long enough to allow Angeline to order something to eat when the waiter approached their table. When the man had graciously left the table, Elaine continued.

"Willa Neal and her comrades believe that change can only come through militant action. They've caused civil upheaval all across the nation, even the world. On the other hand, our organization believes that a direct but less radical approach is the best."

"I must say I do agree, Mrs. Cody."

"Please call me Elaine."

"And you must call me Angeline."

"Angeline, Willa Neal does more to harm the cause of suffrage than to aid it. She gives people the impression that all suffrage supporters are violent in nature and care nothing for legal processes. Suffrage is an important, no, a vital issue, but we can win this cause through rational, straightforward behavior and by educating people to the importance of women voting."

Elaine's words mirrored Angeline's thoughts exactly. "I have long felt," Angeline began, pausing only to accept the lobster salad that the waiter placed in front of her, "that Willa's approach is worrisome. I was with her in New Mexico when the crowd stormed the stage. It was terrifying. Willa seems to enjoy stirring people up, however, and she won't hear reason from me."

"Perhaps you would consider attending one of our functions," Elaine said with a smile.

Angeline shared her smile. "I think it would be a welcome change, but I'm leaving soon for Washington. Willa has a march on the Capitol planned and a meeting with the president."

"Yes, I know," Elaine replied. "Maybe you should reconsider your plans, however." Elaine grew thoughtful for a moment. "I don't know how to say this without sounding rather trite, but do you realize that Willa preys on people like you?"

Angeline put down her fork. "What do you mean?"

Elaine shifted uncomfortably. "You have friends or at least your family has friends who can offer Willa and her cause a great deal of support and money."

"And you believe that Willa's sole interest in my participation is that I join her with these friends?"

"I'm sorry, but I've seen her at work before. You have to remember Colorado has had suffrage for many years. Willa Neal actively pursued the vote for women and, even then, she wasn't opposed to breaking the law. She uses whomever she can and always she weighs the benefit of each participant before she pulls them into her circle."

Angeline's frown and sudden lack of appetite caused Elaine to reach her hand out to Angeline's arm. "I am sorry, but it is important that you know what you're up against. Willa is looking for power. Unfortunately, she doesn't care who she uses, nor what happens to them when she's accomplished what she's set out to do."

Just then the waiter came with a silver tray holding a piece of paper. "Excuse me, but I have a message for Miss Monroe."

"I'm Miss Monroe," Angeline said, reaching for the note.

Angeline scanned the note quickly. It was from Gavin, and he requested that she join him immediately in the lobby. How was it that he always seemed to know where she was?

"I'm afraid something has come up, Elaine. A friend of mine has asked me to join him and says that it can't wait. I hope you will excuse me."

"Of course," Elaine replied. "I hope we have a chance to speak again."

Angeline nodded. "I hope so too." She turned to the waiter. "Please put this luncheon on Miss Willa Neal's account." She winked at Elaine with a knowing smile.

Making her way through the dining hall, Angeline searched the lobby for Gavin. People seemed to occupy every corner of the busy lobby, but Gavin was nowhere in sight.

"Looking for me, Angel?" Gavin whispered from behind her.

"What's wrong?" she asked in a worried tone. She looked Gavin over in case he'd once again come into harm. Seeing that he was unhurt, Angeline relaxed a bit.

"Nice to know you can come quickly when you're called." He grinned mischievously at her and took her arm in his hand. "You look real nice, Angel. More new clothes?"

"Yes." She sounded irritated, and Gavin raised a brow in question. "Willa took all of my clothes and left me with these."

"You still have that red one?"

"Burgundy," Angeline corrected again, but this time she couldn't help but smile. "You kind of liked that one, eh?"

Gavin's grin broadened. "Kind of." He pulled her along with him to a closed, ornate wood door. "Do you know what's in here?"

"I have no idea," she replied dryly and added, "but I'm sure you're going to tell me."

"This is the men's private smoking lounge. Women are strictly forbidden entry."

"How nice," Angeline said, trying to sound offended.

Gavin pulled her closer. "Baker and his men are sequestered in there. I believe, if I may offer a guess, that they are planning how to force you into marriage. I think perhaps, if I can get you close enough, you will overhear the proof you want of Baker's guilt."

Angeline paled only a bit, but it was enough to make Gavin feel concern for the younger woman. "I promise I won't let him hurt you, Angel."

"How are you going to get me in there?" she asked softly, steadying herself on Gavin's arm. "I thought women weren't allowed."

"I have a plan," he said with uncustomary seriousness. "Come on."

Angeline let Gavin take her along a servant's corridor. A sense of antic-ipation and dread seemed to hang over her. Wasn't this her moment of truth? No, she thought, she'd already come to believe what Gavin had told her as true. She put her hand out to stop Gavin from opening the door.

"You don't have to do this," she whispered, her lavender eyes seeking his.

Gavin understood at once what she was saying. "Just this once," he said softly and touched his finger to her cheek. "Just this once I will give you absolute proof of what I told you to be true. Then, in the future, when I give you my word on a matter, you will remember this and not doubt me."

Angeline suddenly felt a cold chill. "No," she said again, as Gavin slowly turned the doorknob.

"Where's your spunk, Angel?"

The room was dimly lit, and the low rumbling of male voices rose up with the assaulting cigar smoke. Gavin held Angeline tightly to his side and moved slowly through the storage room where crates of whiskey were care-fully concealed in wooden boxes marked "Medical Supplies."

Angeline's eyes gradually adjusted to the light, and she took in her sur-roundings with a great deal of interest. The room was paneled in a dark wal-nut with brass fixtures and emerald green draperies. "So this is where men come to get away from women," she mused. "What do they talk about when they get here?"

Gavin chuckled low. "Women, of course." Angeline started to giggle, but Gavin quickly clamped his hand over her mouth. "Shhh." He lowered his hand and pointed to where a massive plant blocked a clear view of the occu-pants behind it. "Baker." Angeline's eyes widened as Gavin pulled her further behind the plant and held her close.

"You took your time getting here," Douglas was saying. Angeline couldn't see who he was talking to, but she was very much aware of Gavin's arm around her waist.

"We're here, ain't we? What'da you want?"

"Yeah," a second voice chimed in. "What'da ya want?"

"We have a particular matter that I want taken care of," Douglas began. "It's a problem I thought I'd rid myself of in New Mexico."

"One of those pain-in-the-neck women?"

"No," Douglas replied. "A man. His name is Lucas. Gavin Lucas. I hired some local thugs to put him out of my misery, but they failed to do the job right."

Angeline nearly gasped at the casual way Douglas spoke of trying to have Gavin incapacitated, but she caught herself in time and put her hand over her mouth.

"So you want us to finish the job?"

"That's right. I thought it could be dealt with, without having to be permanent, but I was wrong. He's staying here in the hotel. I have his room number and a pass key. Take care of it tonight."

"Sure Baker, but it'll cost you extra."

"You'll have your money when the job's done," Douglas replied. "After Lucas is out of the way, we're going to put an end to Miss Neal's planned Washington trip. The last thing we need is a bunch of addlebrained women marching on the Capitol."

"Thought you supported their votin' cause," one of the men said with a laugh.

"I'm the only cause I support. Giving women the right to vote is like giving them a purse full of money. They won't know how to handle it properly, and they'll only ask for more once that's gone."

Angeline forgot herself and pushed away from Gavin to confront Douglas. "How dare you! How dare you sit here plotting to end a man's life and ruin the efforts of an entire movement!"

Douglas's eyes registered his surprise, but his tone indicated nothing out of the ordinary had happened. "Angeline, you would have been wise to stay out of this." He sounded like a parent scolding a child. "And you, Mr. Lucas, you should have learned your lesson in New Mexico."

Angeline hadn't even realized that Gavin had joined her. "You leave Gavin out of this. He was only doing what my parents asked him to do. You had no right to interfere in my life that way, Douglas."

"I had every right. Now if you'll calm down, perhaps we could discuss this more privately. Say upstairs."

"I don't want to discuss this with anyone but the appropriate authorities," Angeline stated angrily. She felt strengthened by Gavin's presence, certain that no harm could possibly come to them here.

The seclusion of Douglas's table worked to his advantage. No one seemed close enough to be able to overhear the commotion, and even if they could, people here weren't given to interfering in one another's business. With a nod at his companions, rough looking characters who made Angeline take a step back, Douglas got to his feet.

"And what proof will you offer?" Douglas questioned, staring intently into Angeline's eyes.

"My word will be good enough for starts. I'll call on Jefferson Ashton, and he'll help me in whatever I need." She turned to ask Gavin to take her to her room, but Douglas stopped her with an iron-like grasp on her arm. Gavin reached out to free Angeline, but Douglas pushed something cold and hard into his ribs. "I have a gun trained on your young man, Angeline. Please tell him it would be wise to do things my way."

The two men with Douglas stood up and produced their own weapons. Angeline turned ashen and nodded her cooperation, while Gavin gritted his teeth and stared daggers into Baker.

"Good," Douglas said when he saw they were going to cooperate. "Now let's go upstairs and talk about this like rational adults."

Chapter 15

W here should we take them?" Douglas asked one of the ruffians.
"We still got that room up on three," the man replied.
"Good," Douglas said with a satisfied smile. "Let's go there."
He pushed Angeline in front of him, then took hold of her with one hand and steadied the gun between them. "Now, Mr. Lucas, I won't have any problem from you, will I?"

Douglas made certain Gavin could see the gun. "You won't have any trouble with me." Gavin's voice was deadly in its tone.

"Douglas, this is ridiculous," Angeline protested. "This isn't the old West. You can't simply walk up to people and pull guns on them. Why even back in Bandelero, as primitive as it can be, people don't walk around doing this."

"Dear, sweet child," Douglas said, tightening his grip on her arm, "keep your voice down, or my good friends are going to put an end to your good friend."

Angeline paled and felt her heart pound harder. She couldn't let Douglas hurt Gavin, no matter the cost. She steadied her nerves and lowered her voice to a whisper. "He's got nothing to do with this. If you don't like the suffrage movement, deal with Willa or even me, but leave Gavin out of it."

"Mr. Lucas has become, shall we say, a personal challenge," Douglas replied and turned a leering smile on Angeline. "But never fear, I do intend to deal with Willa, and my plans for you are more promising with every passing moment."

Gavin growled from behind them and moved at Douglas as if to separate him from Angeline. "I wouldn't do that, Mr. Lucas," Douglas said quite seriously. "If this gun accidently goes off, guess who's hands the police will find it in?"

"Don't push him, Gavin," Angeline said in a pleading voice. "Please don't risk it."

Gavin backed off, feeling the presence of the other two men at his side. Douglas led the way, pulling Angeline along as though they were sweethearts. Together, the strange-looking group made their way through the smoking room

311

and into the lobby. Crossing the room cautiously, Douglas motioned in the direction of one of the back staircases, and the men nodded and prodded Gavin to follow.

Angeline tried to think of something to do or say, but Douglas seemed comfortable and far too familiar with the gun that he occasionally nudged into her side.

Lord, she prayed, *there's no one but You to help us. Please Father, Gavin and I need your mercy.* Angeline climbed the last set of stairs, feeling a bit light-headed. The altitude had little to do with it. This dizzy feeling came from fear. Fear that if something in Angeline's and Gavin's favor didn't happen soon, someone was going to get hurt. If not killed.

I should have gone home with Gavin when he first found me, Angeline thought to herself. She glanced over her shoulder to catch Gavin's eyes. It rallied her heart a bit just to see that he was so near and very much alive.

One of Douglas's men unlocked the door and shoved Gavin in, while Douglas walked through casually. With Angeline still on his arm, Douglas pointed to a nearby chair. "Sit there, Lucas. Joe, tie him up."

Gavin stared at Baker for a moment. His steely blue eyes seemed to darken to black, and Angeline saw an anger in him that she'd never known him capable of. "You'd better not hurt her," Gavin growled.

"That, my dear Mr. Lucas, is entirely up to you. If you behave yourself and do as you're told, then Angeline will remain perfectly well." Douglas paused and ran his finger along Angeline's jaw, further tormenting Gavin.

Clenching his fists at his side, Gavin took a seat and allowed the men to tie him to the chair. His eyes never left Douglas Baker, however.

"Now, gag him," Baker said and pointed Angeline to an empty chair. "Sit there, my dear. We're going to discuss our wedding."

"Our what!?"

"You heard me. Sit."

Angeline stared in disbelief at Douglas, but it was Gavin's words that calmed her. "Easy, Angeline. Just remember God's the One Who's in control—not Baker and not Willa."

Angeline's head quickly went to the source and met Gavin's eyes for reassurance. The hope went out of her at the sight of Gavin's captivity. *Oh, this is all my fault!* She wanted to say the words but wouldn't give Douglas the satisfaction.

"I thought I told you to gag him," Douglas said and pushed Angeline to the chair. The men produced a strip of material and gagged Gavin's mouth, while Douglas addressed Angeline.

"Now, let's get to the heart of the matter. It seems you've placed me in an awkward position, but it isn't without its remedies."

"I'm going to see that you get what's coming to you!" Angeline said, angrily twisting away from Douglas.

"That's my plan," Douglas grinned and pulled a chair beside her. "You and I are going to get married, Angeline."

"Never! I'll never marry you!"

"Never is a frightfully long time, my dear. Now, the way I see it," he paused and motioned her to look at Gavin, "our friend over there is in need of your utmost cooperation. If you don't marry me and keep what you know to yourself, I will see to it that he dies."

The words left Angeline cold. She couldn't take her eyes from Gavin, and even though he shook his head at her, she knew there was no other choice.

"And if I marry you, what proof do I have that you won't kill him anyway?"

Douglas smiled. "We need each other, Angeline. You need me to keep my word and allow your Mr. Lucas to live. I need you to keep your mouth shut and to get me the support of your New Mexican politician friends. Now, once we're married, I will release Mr. Lucas. I will, of course, keep track of his whereabouts, just in case you decide to share any secrets with Willa. Should that unfortunate thing happen, I will send one of these gentlemen to even the score. You might try to ruin me, Angeline, but just remember," Douglas's voice lowered to barely a whisper, "you'll already be my wife. There won't be any way you can escape."

Gavin made noises from behind his gag, but Douglas only seemed to enjoy his agony. "That's right, Mr. Lucas, she will be my wife. That is, if your life means anything at all to her, and I can clearly see that it does."

Gavin grew quiet, his eyes narrowing in on Baker. It wasn't the first time Douglas's had seen death in the eyes of a man. A man who very much wanted that death to be his own. It unsettled Baker for only a moment.

"Do you plan to kill Willa, as well?"

Angeline's words brought Douglas's attention back to her. "Kill her? No. That would be a waste of time. The woman is only one step away from an asylum. I'll see her put away where she belongs. I'll also see an end to this infernal suffrage movement."

"I thought you supported the cause," Angeline said, hoping he'd forget about the marriage idea. "What changed your mind?"

"I've never supported women having the vote," Douglas said simply. "I saw a group of people I could benefit from, and I ran the risk of associating myself with their cause. Causes are stepping stones for me, Angeline. They mean very little," he paused, "except in relationship to how they can benefit me."

Angeline felt as though she'd been slapped. It was exactly the same way she'd perceived causes. Was it possible that others saw her as distasteful and dishonest as she now saw Douglas? With her brows knitted together thoughtfully, she looked at Gavin who seemed to understand her sudden revelation. It was like growing up ten years in one single moment.

Angeline looked away, unable to meet Gavin's eyes. *I've only sought to benefit myself,* she thought. *I've run from one cause to another, including Christianity, and now I've nothing.* Angeline was miserable. Then a still, small voice stirred inside her.

It isn't true. You have God. You have the foundations of the faith you were born to. Reach out to Him. Trust His guidance.

Angeline squared her shoulders. "I have a headache, Douglas. Would you please get on with this. What is it that you expect me to do now?"

Douglas seemed quite pleased with her seeming acquiescence. "We will announce it to Willa, of course. She'll be quite pleased, you know. She's the one who originally put me onto the idea of marrying you. I saw the potential and decided it was a wise suggestion."

"So we just go to her now and announce it?" Angeline was trying not to let anything Douglas said affect her one way or the other. *I have to keep my head,* she thought. *I have to remain calm or they will kill Gavin.*

"I don't see why not. I know she'll want to be a part of it."

"Very well, Douglas," Angeline said and got to her feet. She refused to look at Gavin for fear she'd break down. "Let's find her."

～

"My, but this is exciting," Willa said with a broad smile and a knowing glance at Douglas. Angeline saw the exchange but chose to ignore it and play dumb. *If they think I'm a simpleton,* Angeline thought to herself, *so much the better.*

Angeline tried to smile and appear excited. "Douglas is so spontaneous," she said as eagerly as she could. "He wants us to marry right away."

"But of course!" Willa declared and embraced Angeline, who stared menacingly at Douglas over the older woman's back. "This is big," Willa announced. "Really big. We must make it public."

"I don't understand," Angeline replied. "What is it that you have in mind?"

"A public wedding!" Willa's mind was already making preparations. "We'll put off the Washington trip. I received word today that President Wilson couldn't meet with us anyway."

This was the very thing Douglas wanted, and Angeline noted the pleasure in his eyes as he came to stand beside her. "Of course, money is no object," he said smugly. "My family will be happy to. . ."

"No, no, no," Willa interrupted him. "This is much bigger than that. I'll speak with Jefferson Ashton. He's a good friend of Angeline's family and can probably arrange something with the governor."

Douglas nodded, yielding to the older woman's wisdom, while Angeline remained silent. She was plotting in her mind how she could rescue Gavin and escape Douglas's plans.

"Are you all right, my dear?" Douglas's charming concern was almost too much for Angeline to stomach.

"It's my headache. I can't seem to be rid of it."

"Douglas, take this poor child to her room. You and I can plan the details of this event."

"Certainly, Willa," he said with a smile that revealed his perfect teeth. "I wouldn't want my bride-to-be to come down with something serious."

Angeline batted her eyes at Douglas as though he could hang the moon and the stars in the sky, making Willa laugh.

"I knew you two were made for each other," she said with an undercurrent of mastery in her voice.

"That you did, Willa," Douglas said knowingly. He took hold of Angeline's arm and led her to the door. "I'll be free in a few minutes. Perhaps you would take dinner with me downstairs?"

"That would be fine, Douglas. I'll meet you there," Willa replied.

Angeline remained silent until Douglas had walked her down the hall to her suite. "Why do you hate suffrage so? Willa has worked very hard for the cause, and whether she believes in it for all the right reasons or not, it is worthy of passage."

"You are dangerously naïve, Angeline," Douglas answered, taking her key and unlocking the door. Handing it back to her, he closed his hand over hers. "Soon, we'll share a room."

Angeline wanted to smash her foot down on his, but instead she lowered her eyes as though embarrassed. In truth, she was, but it wasn't something she'd ordinarily have allowed Douglas to see.

"Why is it not worthy of passage?" she asked again.

Douglas was unconcerned with the way she ignored his suggestive words.

"Suffrage is only the start, Angeline. I am a futurist. I see down the road and know the turn of events that will come to pass, by those that have already happened."

"No one can see the future. Only God has that power."

"God may well have made the future, but He isn't the only one who can see it coming."

"For example?" Angeline questioned.

"War," Douglas replied, and Angeline's spine tingled.

"War?" Her voice was shaky, her face clearly pale.

"Yes. We'll be involved in the European war soon. Probably before next year is out, although since it is an election year for Wilson and, overall, the people love the fact that he's kept us neutral, it might be 1917 before we actually get around to it."

"What else?" Angeline felt that she needed to know what Douglas could see. After all, maybe he was right.

"We'll win it, of course. But it will be bloody and senseless. Some will make a great deal of money on it and others will suffer for it. When it's all said and done, I predict a great deal of prosperity for this country, and I intend to be in on it from the start."

"What about suffrage?"

"Unfortunately," Douglas said with a faraway look in his eyes, "I believe that unless I can stop this thing now, it will get out of hand and passage will be accomplished."

"And would that be so bad?"

"It would be a nightmare. It's bad enough they gave slaves the right to voting. Look what that's brought us to."

"And what is that?"

"They want more rights, of course. If women were given the right to vote, what would they want next?"

"I'm sure I don't know," Angeline replied evenly. "Perhaps they would strive to marry for love and not because someone, some man, arranged to force it upon them.

"Perhaps," Douglas smiled. "But then again, women are like children. You need a good pat on the head when you behave properly," he said and did just that to Angeline. "And a firm hand otherwise when they step out of line."

"I see," Angeline said in a stilted voice.

"I'm glad you do," Douglas said and dropped his hand from where he'd rested it casually on her shoulder, "because Gavin Lucas's life depends on you."

Angeline entered her room and closed the door gently. Leaning hard against it, she began to cry. At first the tears just welled up in her eyes, but soon she was sobbing and there was no turning off the water.

"What do I do?" she cried and threw herself down into a chair. Her hand fell across the table and beneath it she felt the Bible and suddenly knew what she had to do.

Chapter 16

The Bible fell open to the fifteenth chapter of Luke, and Angeline immediately read the story of the prodigal son. She saw herself in the selfishness of the prodigal. She felt the heaviness of guilt weigh her down as she read of the childish demands the boy had placed on his father.

"I placed so many demands on my parents," she whispered and wiped at her tears with the back of her sleeve.

Continuing to read, Angeline watched the tale unfold much like her own. The boy had gone away to a far-off land in order to live as he wanted. Then one day the joy of it was gone and there was nothing left. That was exactly how Angeline felt.

She thought for a moment of Gavin facing death knowing that he couldn't help himself, and she shivered. "I have to help him, Lord." She looked up at the ceiling and wondered if God even bothered to listen to her anymore.

"The prodigal repented," Angeline whispered and moved her gaze back to the Bible. "I will arise and go to my father, and will say unto him, Father, I have sinned against heaven, and before thee," the eighteenth verse said. Nineteen continued, "And am no more worthy to be called thy son: make me as one of thy hired servants."

Angeline paused and tears anew streamed from her eyes. "I'm not worthy," she said with a moan. "I've followed God only because it suited my purpose to do so. It was my cause and I wore it proudly, but it means nothing. Oh, God," she whispered and threw herself to her knees. With hands clasped together she raised them heavenward. "Please forgive me! I know how wrong I've been. I see it all now. When I was young it was a game to play. I went to church because that was the place to be seen. I played at being good, because that's what people expected. I mocked You and Your service, however, and I don't deserve forgiveness, but I plead for it."

She sobbed into her hands, her heart nearly tearing in two from the admission of all that had gone along in the past. "I am a vain and prideful woman, Father. I also sought my will first and never considered what other people wanted. I certainly never considered what You might want. And now. . ." She couldn't say it. She couldn't bring herself to imagine that even now Gavin might already lie dead in some dark alleyway.

"I love him, Father. Oh, I really, really do. I couldn't see how much, until. . .until. . ." She looked at her hands and felt the helplessness and hopelessness threaten to swallow her. "Oh, God, help him. Take me, but don't let them kill Gavin." She thought of her words for a moment, then knew without a doubt that she meant them with all of her heart.

"Yes, Lord," she nodded, suddenly more sedate, "take my life, if a life must be given, but please spare Gavin. I can't bear it that I've put him in this position. He wouldn't be here if it weren't for his love for me. Now, Father, I realize my love for him and I want to exchange places with him. You sent Your Son Jesus to take my place on the cross, so I know You understand about exchanges. Forgive me, Father. Forgive me and let Jesus live in my heart as King. I want only to serve You now. I'm not worthy to be a son, but I will happily be a servant." Angeline's words brought immediate comfort. They didn't offer her an answer to her plight, but they did give her the peace that God was now in control. And for the first time in her life, Angeline knew she'd truly come home.

Getting to her feet, Angeline picked up the Bible and finished reading about the prodigal. He too pled his case to his father and his father, like her Heavenly Father, accepted him home with open arms. "For this my son was dead, and is alive again; he was lost, and is found. And they began to be merry," Luke 15:24 stated.

"I want to be merry, Lord," she whispered, "and I want Gavin. I want us together and I want to share his life. Please help me to free him from his captivity, and if I can't help him, then please, God, please don't let me harm him with my carelessness."

Angeline's first thought was that somehow, some way, she had to get to Gavin. But how? And even if she got there, how could she free him? No doubt Douglas would have left him guarded by his two friends. "What do I do?" she questioned aloud. Then as if her mother were standing beside her, Angeline remembered her saying, "God guides our every step, Angeline, but we still have to be the one to pick up our foot and move forward. When we do, we find out that He was there all along, just waiting for us to trust Him." Angeline smiled. She'd move forward and trust God to show her what to do.

Feeling revived, she stripped out of the jacket and skirt she wore and went to the wardrobe. She wanted to find something attractive, yet sedate. She needed to find Douglas and try to talk some sense into his head. She would plead for Gavin's life, and she would happily offer up her own if necessary. Flipping through the dresses, Angeline gave each one careful consideration. She didn't want to encourage Douglas to believe her truly happy with their arrangement, yet she wanted to keep his eye on her.

A black satin gown crossed her eye and Angeline pulled it from the wardrobe to consider it. It was absolutely stunning with its flared skirt and fitted sleeves. The bodice was cut low, then overlaid with a fine, black lace that came high and was secured to the neck with pearl encrusted, black velvet ribbon. Angeline immediately knew it was the gown she should wear. Digging through the dresser drawer, Angeline found that Willa had thought of everything. Beautiful black lace gloves were carefully resting beside white and rose colored ones, and beautiful things to wear underneath the dress were waiting just one drawer down.

Angeline quickly went to work. She knew Douglas and Willa were to have dinner together and what happened afterward would be anyone's guess. She washed and dressed, noting that the hour should still afford her enough time to catch them in the dining hall.

With rapid brush strokes, Angeline quickly twisted her hair into a stylish chignon and looked at her face in the mirror. She couldn't do much about her eyes. They were red but looked more like she'd missed many hours of sleep rather than spent many hours in tears.

"It'll have to do," she said aloud and made her way to the door.

Outside, she was surprised to nearly run into a man who was trying to unlock the door adjacent to hers.

"I'm so sorry," she said and tried to back up.

The older man steadied her and smiled. "Angeline Monroe. My, my, but you've grown up to be a beautiful young woman."

"Dr. Jacobs!" Angeline exclaimed. The man was a good friend of her father's. "How nice to run into you here. Are you taking some time away from your practice?"

"No, I'm afraid it's all business for me. I'm here to attend a lecture," he said with a smile. "What about you? You look like you're on your way to some place important."

"Oh, it's really nothing. I've been kept very busy helping with the suffrage cause, but I'm hoping to go home very soon."

"You look quite tired," he stated in a concerned tone. "Are you all right?"

Suddenly a thought came to Angeline. "I am tired," she admitted. "I haven't been able to get much rest." *It certainly wasn't a lie,* Angeline thought with relief. She wanted to rescue Gavin, but she didn't want to sin against God in order to do so.

"You mustn't let it take its toll on you, Angeline." The doctor's words led Angeline in exactly the direction she wanted to go.

"I know," she said with a sigh. "Perhaps you could give me something to help me sleep at night. Denver is such a noisy city, and this hotel has so very much going on. . ." She let her words trail off, hoping it was enough to elicit sympathy from the old family friend.

"Of course," Dr. Jacobs replied. "I have some excellent medication for just that purpose." He reached into his bag and pulled out a small vial. "A little of this in warm milk will put you to sleep in no time. Just don't mix it with alcohol or you'll sleep a whole lot longer than you planned."

"You mean it would kill me?" Angeline asked, trying hard to sound horrified.

"No, no," the man answered. "Not unless you used the whole bottle. It's just that the effects are magnified with alcohol, but I don't imagine that's a concern for you anyway."

"No, of course not," Angeline smiled. "Thank you so much, Dr. Jacobs. I will tell my father how very kind you were to me. I'm running a little short of cash, but if you would send him a bill for this medication, I will personally see to it that it's paid."

"Nonsense. It's my pleasure to help. Now you run along and tell whomever you are meeting that you have doctor's orders to be in early tonight."

"I will," Angeline said with a smile. She hurried down the hallway and felt for once that the answer to all of her prayers were held in her hand.

⁓

It took almost a half an hour, but by the time Angeline was finished, she was more than confident the plan would work. Standing outside the room where Douglas had taken her and Gavin earlier, Angeline could only pray that they hadn't moved him. She also prayed that Douglas would be nowhere in sight, otherwise she was certain her scheme would fail.

Knocking lightly on the door, Angeline was relieved to find the one Douglas had called Joe answering the door.

"What'da ya want?" He growled the question.

"I've brought you boys some refreshment," Angeline said and batted her lashes coyly. "Douglas thought you might enjoy some food."

The man leered a smile, giving Angeline the once over and allowed her into the room. "Look at this, Ralph. Baker must be softenin' a bit. He let his woman bring up some eats."

"Good thing too," Ralph replied and did a double take when he spotted Angeline. "Whew! I thought you were a looker," he said and sported a grin which revealed several missing teeth. No doubt acquired, Angeline presumed, from the fist which had left his nose permanently listing to the left side of his face.

"What'd ya bring?" Joe asked, taking the tray from Angeline.

Angeline refused to look at Gavin for fear she'd lose her nerve.

"I hope you like ham sandwiches." She rather purred the words. "I also brought coffee."

"Ugh! That all?" Ralph asked, taking a look at the tray's contents when Joe put it down.

"Well, you know how it is, boys. Douglas figured you might like something to help flavor that coffee." Angeline produced a quarter bottle of whiskey and poured a generous amount into each cup of coffee.

The men eagerly took the treat and without so much as thank you, slammed it down and asked for the remaining contents of the bottle. Angeline shrugged her shoulders and shared the whiskey between the two men. "Sorry there wasn't more, but you know how it is these days. It was hard enough just to get this much. I suppose you can get something else later."

"That is if Baker turns us loose. You and him patch things up, eh?" Ralph asked her, helping himself to a sandwich.

Angeline nodded, still refusing to look at Gavin. She was painfully aware that he was watching, but she knew she couldn't see his expression just yet. It would be her undoing for sure.

"Certainly. Douglas and I have an understanding, and I've promised to be most cooperative. I never knew what a helpful man he could be." Angeline hoped she sounded convincing.

"Helpful, eh?" Ralph seemed unconcerned and yawned with his mouth full of sandwich. "Hey," he called to Joe. "Kinda warm in here isn't it?"

Joe suppressed his own yawn and nodded. "I'll open the window," he said and put his empty mug on the table.

Angeline wondered silently how long it would take the sleeping medication, via the whiskey and coffee, to drug the men into sleep. They were already showing signs of fatigue. *Please God,* she prayed, *don't let it be much longer.*

Ralph sat down and yawned again. "I've been working too many hours."

Joe finished opening the window and stuck his head out into the crisp night air. "Me too," he grumbled and pulled back inside.

Angeline felt her nerves begin to fray. "We could play cards," she said as though the men had complained of boredom instead of exhaustion.

Joe shook his head and sank into the nearest chair. "I don't think so." His eyes were drooping, and his speech sounded slightly slurred.

Angeline couldn't risk a look at Ralph without having something to say. "How about another sandwich, Ralph?"

"Huh?" Ralph yawned and put his head down on the table. "Think I'll just rest for a minute."

Angeline held her breath and looked back at Joe. "I guess Douglas really is working you too hard. I'll have to speak to him about it." She waited for a response from Joe, but his thick eyelids were closed and a light snoring was already coming up in reply.

Ralph, too, began a kind of duet with Joe, snoring in loud exhales, while Joe inhaled. Angeline refused to move and refused to look at Gavin. She had to be certain Douglas's thugs were asleep.

Tiptoeing to Ralph, she shook him hard and only succeeded in breaking his rhythm of breathing for a moment. "Ralph, wake up," she said and shook him again. He was out cold.

Moving to Joe, whose head bobbed up and down on his thick chest, Angeline repeated the action. "Joe, wake up." Nothing! Not even a snort or a cough to indicate she'd even disturbed him.

All right, she thought. *That's done. They're both asleep. Now I get Gavin untied.* Straightening up, Angeline felt her head grow light. With a pale face, she turned to look at Gavin just as her knees gave out, and she sank to the floor.

Chapter 17

Angeline steadied herself against Joe's bulky leg. *I can't faint,* she thought and caught the look of concern in Gavin's eyes. Poor Gavin. She smiled weakly at him, but nevertheless, it was a smile.

"I suppose you're wondering why I came here today," she began as though about to offer a lecture. Sucking in her breath and using Joe for support, Angeline got to her feet and adjusted her skirts. Looking back at Gavin, she could see his raised eyebrows.

"You like it?" she questioned, moving toward him in small hesitant steps. "It's another of Willa's dresses," she mused, trying hard to keep her nerves steadied with the casual banter. Gavin nodded.

Angeline felt better after the first few steps and hurried toward Gavin. She worked at the knotted scarf they'd used to gag him with. "Oh, Gavin!" she exclaimed, pulling at the material. "I'm so sorry I got you in all of this. I promise to make it up to you, and I promise not to be any more trouble."

She pulled the material from his mouth and planted her lips firmly on his, much to Gavin's surprise. She pulled away, noting his stunned expression. "I'll go anywhere with you and do anything you tell me. I love you, Gavin!"

"You sure took your time coming to that conclusion, Angel," he finally said with a stern expression replacing the shocked one. "I hope you're quicker about getting me out of these ropes."

Angeline smiled and pulled up her skirt just enough to reveal a knife carefully tucked into her knee garter. "I came completely prepared to assist you, Mr. Lucas." She pulled the knife out and quickly sliced through the ropes.

Gavin came up off the chair like it was on fire and pulled Angeline into his arms, crushing her against him. For several moments he did nothing but hold her, and for Angeline it was enough. She clung to him, needing to feel strong again. It was all so right, and she wondered silently how she could have ever doubted that her place was with him.

"Did he hurt you, Angel?"

"No," she assured Gavin. "He didn't lay a hand on me. He did, however, tell Willa that we were to be married. They're planning a big, public wedding even now as we speak."

Gavin frowned and held her even tighter. "Over my dead body."

"It nearly was," Angeline replied flatly.

Voices sounding in the hallway disturbed their reunion and with the grace of a cat, Gavin flew across the room and locked the door. With a finger to his lips, he pointed to the open window.

Angeline paled and shook her head. She had an idea what Gavin had planned, and if her assumptions were correct, there was absolutely no way she was going to agree to the arrangement.

Gavin crossed the room and took her in hand, with Angeline frantically shaking her head in protest. He pulled her close and bent his lips to her ear. "I thought you said you'd follow me anywhere." He was grinning from ear to ear as he put his head out the window.

Angeline was terrified and shaking so hard she didn't think she'd be able to move. The voices in the hall grew louder, and one of them clearly became recognizable as Douglas. Without second thoughts, she was out the window and standing beside Gavin on the ledge.

Trembling with her back against the cold brick wall, Angeline thought she would die. She felt Gavin's warm hand on her arm and prayed God would rescue them from their perch. She heard Gavin lower the window and scoot closer to her.

"It's going to be all right, Angel. You'll see."

"Oh, Gavin," she said, and her voice was full of emotion. "What if I faint out here?"

"You won't," he said confidently. "Open your eyes and look at me, Angel." She did without considering the consequences. "God's with us. He's been with us from the start, but I think maybe you're just learning that. I love you, and I'm not about to let anything happen to you. Especially not now that you've agreed to be my wife. You will be my wife, won't you, Angel?"

Angeline looked deep into Gavin's eyes. There was barely enough light from the window to reflect the love he held for her there. "If we live through this," she whispered, "I'll most gratefully marry you."

Gavin chuckled and kissed her forehead. "Good, now don't look down and keep quiet. Someday you can tell our children how I proposed on a ledge three stories above Denver." Angeline swallowed hard and nodded.

The words were no sooner out of Gavin's mouth when a storm came up from the hotel room inside. Angeline could hear Douglas raging and knew that he'd found his men sleeping and Gavin gone. She began trembling anew and felt Gavin squeeze her arm.

Oh, God, please help me to be strong, Angeline prayed. She shifted her weight and felt the satin skirt wrap around her legs. She had to be careful or she'd cause them both to fall. Gently, she eased her body back into its original position and felt the dress free itself again. Relieved, Angeline decided that if she had to stop breathing in order to remain in one position, she would. She couldn't jeopardize Gavin's life again.

The voices from inside the room ceased, and when the door slammed, Gavin braved a look into the room. Douglas had apparently gone in search of Gavin or Angeline, he surmised.

Sliding the window up, Gavin pulled at Angel's arm. "Come on," he said softly. "Just take little side steps. I've got a good hold on the windowsill, you aren't going to fall."

Angeline forced her feet to move, but she felt like she was going nowhere. "I can't do this, Gavin," she moaned, certain that she'd be the death of them yet.

"Yes, you can, you're almost there," Gavin encouraged. "Now, I'm going to step back and let you in first. Can you pull up your skirt so that it doesn't bind your legs?"

"Sure," Angeline said and reached for her skirt with her free hand. "Are you sure this isn't just a ploy to get a look at my legs?" She tried very hard to sound teasing.

"Seen 'em already," Gavin answered in good humor, "when you pulled the knife and on the way out here."

"Oh," Angeline replied nervously, but nevertheless smiled. She lifted her leg to the windowsill. "I can't say I get bored with you, Mr. Lucas."

Gavin laughed and helped her through the window and into the hotel room. Quickly following her, he pulled Angeline into his arms and kissed her soundly. "I can't imagine life without you, Angel."

"Nor I without you," she admitted. "I'm afraid it's my stupid pride and stubborn determination that's nearly gotten you killed not once, but twice. Gavin, I would have died if I'd caused you to be hurt again."

"Shh, don't talk like that. God knew what He was doing. I've never been out of His care, and I know our mas have never stopped praying for us the whole time we've been gone."

"Yeah, and you know how they can nag," Angeline grinned. "Poor God must have had an earful by now."

"We should call and let them know we're coming home. Let's go to my room and get my stuff, then we'll go to your room and get yours." Gavin didn't wait for her reply, but quietly opened the door and looked down the hall. "It looks clear, come on."

Gavin led Angeline through the dimly lit hall. They passed without incident to Gavin's hotel room, where he unlocked the door and put his finger to his lip. Quietly pushing the door open, Gavin snapped on the light and surveyed the room. It was void of any uninvited guests, so he pulled Angeline into the room and slammed the door shut.

Angeline felt her heart in her throat. It was pounding at an insane rate that left her feeling breathless. "Are we safe here? Remember, Douglas knows your room number."

"He knows the room that Gavin Lucas is registered to. I wasn't stupid enough to underestimate him this time. This room is registered under my granddad's name."

"Oh?"

Gavin grinned. "Jason Intissar, at your service."

Angeline smiled and hesitantly noted the intimacy of the room. "We'd better get out of here. I'm afraid my reputation won't survive a visit to a man's hotel room."

"Now we have to get married, Angel," Gavin's lopsided grin only broadened.

"Guess so," she said, trying hard to sound disappointed. "You think you can tolerate life with a suffragette? I make a pretty good speech if I do say so myself."

"I know. I heard you in Santa Fe."

"I didn't know that!" Angeline exclaimed. Her eyes were shining with pleasure that he'd taken the time out to listen. "What did you think?"

"I think you could talk a guy into just about anything," he said softly, and his eyes warmed with a sparkle of mischief. He took a step toward her. "At least I know you could talk me into just about anything."

Angeline's eyes widened. "I knew coming to your hotel room was just a trick. Wait till I tell my father!"

"Ahh, I seem to remember that battle cry from your childhood. Good to see you got some of your spunk back," Gavin said and turned away to reach under the bed for his suitcase. "Let's go."

"Aren't you going to get your things?" she questioned.

"They're all in here." He shrugged his shoulders at her surprise. "I've learned to live on the run, what with following you all over the countryside."

Angeline shook her head. "It won't happen again, I can assure you."

"Ready to settle down, eh?"

"Very ready."

Gavin seemed more than a little pleased to hear the news. "Come on, let's go get your stuff."

Angeline stopped him, the look of grief marring her sweet face. "Please, let's just forget it. You know they'll be there. That's the first place they'll look. They won't have expected me to manage your rescue, so I'm sure Douglas came first thing to my room, thinking it would be the first place you'd go."

"It's all right, Angel. No one is going to stop us now."

"Please, Gavin, I can't bear it. I can't stand the thought of going there for a few of my baubles and trinkets and have it cause your death." She clung to him, her eyes wide with fear. "I'd gladly give my life for yours, Gavin. Stay here and I'll go, but don't come with me."

Gavin put down his case and encircled Angeline with both arms. He could feel her shaking as though she might never stop. "God is in control. You do believe that, don't you?" Angeline nodded ever so slightly. Her hold on Gavin tightened, however.

"You belong to Him, don't you?"

"Yes," she whispered weakly. "I might not have until earlier this evening, but I do now."

"God will protect us. Remember that verse in the Psalms, Angeline," he said, calling her by her full name. She looked up at him, shaking her head.

"Which one?"

"Ninety-one, verse eleven."

"I don't think I do," she said, struggling to remember.

" 'For he shall give his angels charge over thee, to keep thee in all thy ways.' " Gavin lifted her chin to look deep into her violet-colored eyes. "You're an angel God gave me," he whispered. "Just one of many. We're surrounded by them, and they have been given charge of us by God Almighty Himself. Can you doubt that anything but the very best can happen now?"

Angeline tried to let the words dispel her fear. "I want to believe that. I truly do, but it seems foolish to test God by going after material things that mean nothing to me."

"Do you trust Him, Angel?" Gavin questioned, then added, "Do you trust me?"

Angeline realized that never had she been so certain of anything in all her life. God had given her new life. He'd helped her rescue Gavin. How could she believe He'd let her down now? "I trust you both," she stated clearly. "I'll do whatever you want."

"Good girl," he said and kissed her forehead. "Let's go get your things and go home."

Angeline held him back for just a moment. "Could we pray first, together?"

Gavin smiled a gentle, sweet smile at her. It gave her all the strength in the world and left her with no doubt that she was doing the right thing. "You bet."

Chapter 18

Angeline jumped at every sound, most of which seemed to come from her. The black satin swished noisily, and despite the carpeted floors, Angeline felt as though she was clumping instead of tiptoeing. The further they went, the worse it was.

Angeline felt her chest constrict as she tried to keep from gasping for air. Her heart alone pounded so loud that she just knew it would give them away. She followed Gavin closely, afraid that at any given moment, Douglas would jump out with a gun and shoot them both dead. Twice, Gavin had to pull her along but did so with a look of reassurance that made Angeline feel better.

They hadn't gone all that far when Gavin spotted a bellhop and called to him. "Wait here, Angel," Gavin said and slipped away to speak in a hushed whisper to the boy.

Angeline had no idea what Gavin was up to and, furthermore, she didn't believe she really cared. *I've had about as much adventure as a body can stand,* she told herself. It was easy to think of going home, and even easier to think of doing it with Gavin at her side. Wringing her hands, Angeline was relieved when the boy nodded enthusiastically and accepted some coins from Gavin. Now if she could only talk Gavin into forgetting this nonsense about her things.

When Gavin rejoined her, Angeline slipped her arm around him coyly and batted her lashes. "We could just leave," she suggested with a nod at the stairs leading down. "It'd get us home just that much quicker."

Gavin laughed and shook his head. "No."

Angeline turned and put both arms around his neck. "I promise I won't ask for another thing."

"No, Angel." Gavin stopped laughing as she raised herself up on tiptoes and pressed her lips to his. "Angeline!"

"Oh, all right," she said and walked away in complete dejection. Grabbing handfuls of her skirt, she headed up the staircase. "I thought you said I could talk a man into anything."

Gavin followed her, chuckling at her mutterings. "Just wait until I get you home, Angel. Then you can talk to me all you want."

Angeline had to laugh in spite of herself, but she quickly grew quiet as they

329

reached the last step. Taking her hand in his free one, Gavin led her down the hallway to her room. There was no need for Angeline to retrieve her key; she could tell by the light under the door that someone was already inside.

Reaching out, Angeline pushed the door open and found Willa standing in the middle of the room.

"It's about time!" Willa exclaimed. "Douglas and I have been frantic."

"I'll bet," Angeline said softly.

"Where is Baker?" Gavin questioned, putting his case by the door.

"Why, he's out looking for her, of course," Willa stated and came to where Angeline stood already unfastening the buttons of the black gown. "Who are you?"

"I have to change," Angeline said, ignoring Willa's question and moving to the bedroom. "I'll pack my things, Gavin, and be right back."

"Pack your things?" Willa questioned after Angeline's retreating form. Getting no answer from her, Willa turned to Gavin. "What is she talking about? Who are you?"

"I'm Gavin Lucas, and I'm taking her home," he replied. "We're leaving tonight."

"You're going to find that kind of hard to do, Lucas." Douglas Baker stood in the open door, filling it ominously as though he offered himself as some kind of barrier.

"You gonna threaten to kill me again?" Gavin asked, turning to face Douglas.

"I don't have to threaten. It won't take all that much to accomplish the matter."

"Douglas, save it for later," Willa said irritably. "Angeline's in there, and she'll be hard enough to handle without you threatening him."

"She'll cooperate plenty if she thinks I'm going to hurt him. See, she's quite gone over him, and that offers me all of the control I need."

"Not quite, Douglas," Angeline said, coming through the door, suitcase in hand. She had dressed in the shirtwaist and blue serge skirt, the only things left which belonged to her.

Douglas sneered in contempt at Gavin. "You think he's going to stop me?"

Angeline shook her head. "It doesn't matter what you say or do, Douglas. I'm not going to marry you, and I'm not going to keep your secrets." She put down the case and turned to Willa. "He's using you Willa. He plans to destroy the suffrage movement through you. I heard him talking, and he believes giving women the vote is a big mistake. He thinks we're too stupid or uncontrollable or some other such nonsense. Either way, he plans to see you ruined and put away."

Willa turned to Douglas, her eyes narrowing suspiciously. "Is that true? Is that your plan, Douglas?"

Baker laughed and left the open doorway. He moved first toward Angeline but found Gavin a formidable wall between him and the girl. Instead of pushing his luck just then, Douglas shrugged and moved across the room to Willa.

"You're an idiot, Willa Neal. Suffrage is a nightmare that must never be allowed to continue. I will personally put forth every effort possible to see it squelched." He looked as though he wanted to put an end to Willa then and there, and for the first time ever, Angeline saw Willa back away.

"I must say you were a convincing actor," Willa said in a fearful, yet determined voice. "Did you tell Angeline about your plans? Did you tell her that you planned to marry her to get close to her political connections? Did you tell her that even murder wasn't beneath you in order to get what you wanted?"

"I didn't have to," Douglas said with smug satisfaction. "She overheard my plans, and I took her and Lucas captive. I threatened them with each other. It was really quite simple."

"It's true, Willa. That's when I learned about Douglas's plans for you. He threatened to kill Gavin if I refused to marry him and, even afterwards, he said he'd kill Gavin if I revealed to you his plan to put an end to the suffrage movement."

Willa was enraged. "How dare you!" She moved toward Douglas, no longer afraid, but sufficiently incensed. She tried to slap Douglas, but he easily warded off her blows.

"Don't sound so persecuted, Willa. You were using Angeline yourself." He smiled confidently at the way Willa's face turned ashen. "You wanted Angeline for nothing more than who she knew and whose support she could get you."

She could tell by the way Willa reacted that it was all true. It hurt Angeline deeply to finally accept what everyone had already told her to be true.

Her reaction was not missed by Douglas. "You know, Willa, you very well might have pulled it off," he said smugly, "except you weren't expecting to deal with someone of my caliber. I've been operating one step ahead of you, all the way. Learning your routines. Mapping out your routes. Now is the time for me to step out and put you in your place."

"Just what do you have in mind?" Gavin asked dryly from where he'd gone to lean casually against the open door.

Douglas seemed unconcerned that his back was to Gavin. He didn't even bother to look away from Willa's worried expression. "There's a nice asylum near Chicago. I have some good friends there who will ask no questions. I thought the change of scenery would do you good, old girl."

"You'll never get away with it!" Willa declared.

"And who will stop me?"

"I will," Willa declared. "I'll tell everyone what a fraud and reprobate you are. I'll expose every single thing you have planned." She was nearly yelling at this point. "You haven't seen anything yet, Douglas Baker. I'll see you ruined."

Douglas laughed sinisterly, causing Angeline to pick up her case and back away toward the door.

"No one is going to ruin me," Douglas said so softly it was nearly a whisper. "No one will believe you, Willa. You have no one but this addle-brained girl to back you up, and she'll be my wife, so I'll have no trouble out of her."

"I'll never marry you, Douglas!" Angeline exclaimed. "Never!"

"We'll see about that." Douglas's eyes raked over Angeline before turning back to Willa. "Like I said, no one is going to believe your story."

"I don't know about that," the voice came from a stranger outside the door to Angeline's room. The well-dressed man walked into the room, still writing notes on a pad. He looked up long enough to introduce himself. "I'm a reporter with the *Post*. I've stood out there long enough to take down just about every word, Mr. Baker. I think the public will find this story fascinating."

Willa laughed aloud, and Douglas glared at her hard. "This means nothing. I have friends at the *Post*."

"Had friends, Baker," the man said, still writing. "Had friends. No one is going to want to admit to being anything to you after my story runs."

Angeline glanced past the man to Gavin, who had obviously expected the man's entry. She loved him all the more for his insightfulness. Beaming a smile at him, Angeline knew he understood her unspoken praise.

"See there, Mr. Baker!" Willa declared, feeling quite vindicated.

"As for you, Miss Neal," the reporter continued, "I'm sure there will be more than enough interest in you to generate a thorough investigation into your activities."

"You just hate me because I'm a suffragist."

"No, Ma'am, I don't hate you or the suffrage movement. I just want to see manipulative people like you put in their place."

Douglas made a move for the door, but quickly backed away when two uniformed policemen revealed themselves from the hallway. Angeline took that opportunity to retrieve her suitcase, which Gavin quickly took from her. Then looping her arm through his and nodding with a smile of contentment on her lips, Angeline let Gavin lead her to the door.

"By the way," the reporter called after her. "You're Miss Angeline Monroe, are you not?"

Angeline paused and smiled. "That's right. At least for now."

The man jotted down the information and motioned. "Who's the guy with you?"

Angeline didn't even bat an eye. "He's just about to become my husband!" Her reply shocked Willa and infuriated Douglas, while the reporter just nodded with a grin and noted the broad smile of amusement on Gavin's face.

"I'd say the groom looks pretty happy about that prospect," the reporter said with a chuckle.

"You might say that," Gavin answered for her, then swept her into the hall. "Ready to go home, Angel?"

Angeline looked up at Gavin with eyes that declared their love for him. "Ready," she replied.

⁓

That night, Angeline fell asleep to the gentle rocking of the train. She felt free and so completely at peace that she no longer questioned what she'd do with herself once they were home, or what cause she'd seek out. Gone were her little girl selfish ambitions and the desire to conquer the world. Gone were the searches for causes of great magnificence to occupy her time and energies with. All she really ever wanted was the man she slept contently against and the stillness that God had put in her heart.

⁓

Sighing in her sleep, Angeline missed the look of contentment on her husband-to-be's face. Gavin relished the feel of his arm around her and the way her blond head seemed to fit naturally against his shoulder. Thoughts of the decision he'd made so very long ago came back in pleasant memories. In his mind he could see Angeline as a twelve year old pulling a wagon filled with half-dead kittens. She'd found them tied in a sack and left to drown in the creek.

"What are you going to do with those mangy things?" Gavin had asked her in his sixteen-year-old bravado.

"I'm going to love them," Angeline had replied, her lavender eyes wide with surprise that he should even question such a thing.

"Looks like they'll need a lot of it," Gavin had laughed.

Angeline was undaunted. "That's all right," she'd replied confidently. "I have a lot of love to give."

It was then that Gavin knew she had his heart. Without even concerning

333

himself that she was just a child, he knew that she was the woman he'd one day marry. Now, with Angeline having come to the same conclusion, Gavin Lucas was truly happy.

"You do have a lot of love to give, Angel," he whispered against her hair. "And I'm just glad to get a part of it."

Chapter 19

Angeline took herself into the garden, away from the well-wishers and the revelry of her wedding. The sweet rich scent of roses and honeysuckle wafted on the warm afternoon air, and the vivid colors were a startling contrast to the white-gowned woman.

Angeline had wanted to wear an older style wedding gown, but neither her mother nor Gavin's had married in a traditional manner, and so it was necessary to search for just the right gown. She had finally managed to locate the perfect creation hanging in a dressmaker's shop in Raton.

The dress was styled after gowns popular at the turn of the century. It was fashioned out of heavy slipper satin with intricate lace pinaforelike flounces at the shoulder and along the bodice. The basque waist was snug and showed off Angeline's tiny twenty-inch waist to perfection. After arguing with the dressmaker for over an hour, Angeline finally settled on a price and purchased the gown. Now, after having worn it, receiving scores of compliments, and the warm glow of appreciation in her husband's eyes, Angeline felt the ridiculously high amount she'd paid had been worth it.

Laughter and music rose up as the festival-like atmosphere engulfed Piñon Canyon Ranch. Angeline was glad that Gavin chose his home for their wedding ceremony. It had been a beautiful affair with all of their friends and family present. Even John and James had managed to finagle time away from the army, although when they showed up in uniform flying an army biplane, Angeline wondered just how legitimate their escape had been.

The aeroplane had caused more of a stir than the arrival of Joelle Dawson, but not much more. Angeline had to laugh, to herself of course, at the way her brothers and every other man on the ranch, fell all over themselves to see to Joelle's needs. She was a beautiful woman, Angeline had to admit, and for once she didn't feel at all threatened.

Joelle was Nicholas Dawson's little sister, making her Gavin's sister-in-law, and it was announced that she would be living for awhile with Daughtry and Nicholas, who were once again expecting a child. Gavin had good-naturedly teased Angeline at the announcement of the impending arrival that they would have to work hard to catch up. Angeline had flushed scarlet, but in her heart it was exactly the thing she wanted. A family, a husband, a home.

That was the only kind of cause Angeline perceived as lasting.

Looking across the garden beyond the ranch valley to the mountains in the distance, Angeline felt a sensation of contentment wash over her that she couldn't begin to describe. The ineffable feeling bubbled up inside until Angeline didn't know whether to laugh or cry.

"God, You have been so very good to me," she whispered. "Thank You for the bountiful blessings. Thank You for all that You've bestowed upon me. I know now how the prodigal must have felt when his father placed the fine robe upon his shoulders and killed the fatted calf. You've given me more than I deserve, and I promise to strive hard to be worthy of it all."

Gavin stood in the adobe archway and watched his wife with intense interest as she moved about the garden. She was the most beautiful woman he'd ever seen, and she was all his. He stood there silently, afraid to go to her, afraid to break the spell that seemed to have woven itself over her. She was radiant and everything about her countenance spoke of her happiness and joy.

"Thank You, God," he whispered softly.

He studied her for a moment, seeing her lips move as though she was speaking to someone. With a sudden realization, Gavin discerned she was probably praying. It blessed him in a way he couldn't explain. It was gratifying to be a part of her life and to know that he'd have a long, long time to love her.

Angeline fell silent and closed her eyes for a moment. Drinking in the peace and pleasure of the moment, she didn't hear her husband come up from behind her. She didn't even sense him there until he put his arms around her and pulled her back against him.

"I couldn't find you. I thought maybe you'd run off again."

"Never!" Angeline declared and hugged his arms closer.

"What are you doing out here?" Gavin questioned softly.

"Just thanking God for everything." She turned, giving Gavin a beautiful smile that lit up her lavender eyes. "I'm so very grateful."

"Me too," he said and kissed her lightly on the lips. "I still can't believe you're really mine. I mean, I prayed about it long enough. God knows that I nagged Him often enough, and now, it just seems unreal. Almost like a dream."

"Umm," Angeline said, snuggling against his chest, her head fitting perfectly under Gavin's chin. "Then I don't want to wake up."

"I love you, Angel. I think I have loved you forever."

Angeline giggled. "Since you first saw me as a tiny, squalling baby?"

"Well, maybe not quite forever," Gavin chuckled. "After all, I was barely in pants when you came along."

"I know," she whispered. "Your mother showed me the most precious picture of you holding me. She said, 'And now Angeline, he'll be holding you forever.' It made me cry, because I knew she was right. Somehow, from that one little picture, that one small, seemingly insignificant moment in my life, our love was born and grew to be this."

Gavin kissed her head. "Brides are supposed to cry on their wedding days, but not grooms. Too many more stories like that and you'll have me sniffling. Come on, let's take a little walk, I want to show you something."

Angeline released her hold and let Gavin direct her down the path that led away from the main house. "I've been talking to my dad," Gavin began, "and I know you said you didn't care where we lived, so I took it upon myself to plan our home."

"What?"

Angeline's surprised tone caused Gavin to frown. "Is that a problem?"

"Not at all, I just presumed from what you said that we'd live here with your folks."

"We will, for a time," Gavin said. He kept walking past the outbuildings and fruit trees which his mother had faithfully nurtured into maturity. "But eventually we'll have our own place. That is, if you want your own house."

Angeline laughed and tried to keep from tripping over her gown on the rocky path. "What woman doesn't?"

"Good, then you'll like my surprise," Gavin grinned down at her.

Angeline felt her heart skip a beat whenever he looked at her that way. She could only imagine the joy of waking up to see that smile every day.

Gavin slowed his steps to accommodate her more hesitant ones. "See, I figured that we'd live with my folks while we build our own place. We'll want to be close enough that it isn't a chore to come over, but far enough away for privacy."

Angeline grinned up at him. "So we can talk?"

Gavin laughed. "Something like that. Fight too," he added. "I don't figure the spunk has left you in place of that wedding gown. I know we'll have more than our share of misunderstandings and problems."

"I'm sure you're right," Angeline said with a serious nod. "You are after all a very stubborn man, and you can be rather serious."

"And you are a flighty thing, running from one cause to the next and always thinking you have to be the center of attention."

Gavin's words made Angeline stop and eye him cautiously for a moment. "Are we about to have our first fight?"

"What do you mean, first fight?" Gavin asked with a twinkle in his eyes. "I've been having fights with you since you were six."

"Yes, I do seem to recall a rather nasty incident where you tore my red sash and pushed me in the creek," Angeline said rather sternly.

"And I don't suppose that you remember what you did to me first," Gavin replied, hands on hips.

"I believe it had something to do with your lunch pail," she said with a mischievous look.

"Something like you took it and threw it in the creek," he answered. "With my lunch in it, I might add."

Angeline giggled. "Yes, then you said I could just go in after it and pushed me over the bank."

"Yes, but I had a change of heart and tried to be gallant and rescue you."

"I remember. You grabbed my sash to pull me up and it ripped off in your hands, and I went backside first into the water."

"But you got my lunch pail back," Gavin grinned.

"Yes, I did and a lecture when I got home and no dessert for a week," Angeline said with a pouting look on her face.

"That's nothing," Gavin said with a serious expression replacing the grin. "I couldn't sit for a week."

Angeline laughed and threw her arms around her husband's neck. "You really have loved me forever, haven't you?"

"Pretty much so. I guess I was just hoping you'd get around to putting me on your list of causes."

"I'm done with causes," she said firmly. "Now show me what you plan for us."

Gavin took her hand in his and they walked a little further down the path. "You see that valley over there?"

Angeline looked out across the open ground to where a small stand of trees grew beside a well fed spring. "There?" she pointed and looked at Gavin.

"Yes." He sensed her satisfaction with the place. "I thought we'd put a house just beyond the trees. We'll have seclusion and privacy, yet be close enough for a helping hand if we need it."

"And you can still work the ranch with your father and not have to be that far from home. I could even fix you lunch every day and make up for the lunch pail incident." Angeline spoke with a pride and contentment in her voice that warmed Gavin's heart.

"You made up for the lunch pail long ago, Angel. Just promise me that you won't go running off again and I'll be the happiest man alive." He took her in his arms gently as if he were afraid of breaking her.

Angeline looked up at him. For a moment she just watched him, and when clouds passed over the sun, shadowing the land, she shivered. "I want nothing more than to stay at your side." She looked away with an awful thought running through her mind.

"What is it, Angel?" Gavin reached out to draw her face back to his.

"There's so much that could separate us, Gavin. The war in Europe is getting worse. I heard John tell mother we'll probably go to war before much longer."

"That's a very real possibility, but we can't let it ruin our happiness."

"Oh, Gavin!" she exclaimed and embraced him tightly. "I don't want you to go away. I can't bear the idea of losing you. How could I go on without you?" The shadows from the clouds seemed to make her feel worse.

"Don't," he said simply. "Don't take away what we have now by worrying about what we might not have tomorrow. We don't know what God has planned for us, Angel. But we do know that He has it figured out, and He knows what's best. He's in control just like He was the night we were on the ledge together. Just think of the stories we'll tell our children."

"Men never understand," Angeline said, surprising Gavin with her dismal outlook. "Mother told me men face war with pride and patriotism." She pushed away, stepping on her wedding dress. She would have fallen if Gavin hadn't caught her. The move forced her to look at his puzzled expression. Reaching up her hand, she touched his cheek. "I don't want you to be heroic. I'd rather have you be safe and sound, right here with me."

"I'd like nothing better," he said, looking at her as if seeing her and the responsibilities of taking a wife for the first time. "I've thought a great deal about the possibilities of having to serve my country in war." He looked beyond her to the valley. "But in all honesty, that was when I was single."

"Being married makes everything different," Angeline replied softly.

"Yes, it certainly does." He seemed to struggle with something inside himself, more than with her. A look of frustration crossed his face, and he walked away from her, stopping after just a few paces.

Gavin's silence frightened Angeline, and for a moment she hadn't any idea what to do. Then without any real thought, Angeline felt the need to be with him. To somehow let him know that she could stand beside him, whatever came their way.

She reached out to him and Gavin turned, surprising her with a hint of moisture in his eyes. "All I've ever wanted was to build a home here, marry you, and raise a family. I don't want to play soldier, and I don't want to fight a war I know nothing about," he said honestly.

"You were right earlier," she whispered. "We needn't borrow trouble. God is in control just as you said. From now on, Gavin, my only cause will be to serve God faithfully as His child and to love you faithfully as your wife.

Whatever else comes, whatever the need, we'll face it together."

Gavin smiled. "No more causes, Angel?"

"Positive." Angeline was glad to see his mood lighten.

"You sure about that? You've been so caught up in causes most all of your life, I'm not sure you could function properly without your hand in some problem, somewhere."

Angeline laughed. "You and God will be cause enough."

Gavin took her into his arms and lifted her chin. "I love you to pieces, Angel, but I'll believe that one when I see it." He silenced her reply with a kiss. Then, testing her reserve, Gavin pulled away and added, "I heard tell there was a committee getting together to raise money to build a bigger school in Bandelero."

"Not interested," Angeline replied with a wide grin.

"Then there was that talk about knitting mittens and socks for the soldiers in the trenches."

"I never could knit," Angeline said even more confidently.

Gavin glanced upward. "And I guess you wouldn't be interested in knowing that Elaine Cody is coming to Santa Fe to work with the local politicians on suffrage."

Angeline's eyes widened. "Elaine? Coming to New Mexico?" Gavin glanced down at her with an "I told you so" smile, causing Angeline to bite her tongue. "That's very nice, Gavin. Perhaps she'll call on us, and we can show her the ranch."

"Uh huh," Gavin said with delight in his voice. "Maybe she'll tell you about the war orphans."

"What war orphans?" Angeline questioned almost sharply.

"The ones whose folks have died in the war. They're trying to raise money to. . . ."

"Gavin Lucas, you aren't being fair!"

"No, I'm not," he laughed and brought her back into his arms.

"I said no more causes and I meant it," Angeline restated, then a look of consideration passed over her expression. "Of course, I didn't know about the war orphans and Elaine was very nice to me in Denver. . . ."

Gavin kissed her before she could say another word. It looked as if Angel's causes were about to strike again. "Just so long as I'm in there somewhere," he whispered against her lips.

"Always," Angeline murmured with a smile. "Say, Gavin. . ."

"Huh?"

"What do you suppose those war orphans need most?"

Come Away, My Love

Chapter 1

There it goes again," the pilot yelled over the roar of the Jenny's engine. "Don't tell me you didn't hear it that time, Flipflop." The young man in grease-smeared khaki shrugged his shoulders.

Lieutenant John Monroe, the Jenny's pilot, switched off the engine and leaped to the ground as though he might take issue with the confused private. Flipflop, as he was affectionately called because of his nervous stomach at flight time, backed up defensively.

"I mean it, Preacher, I didn't hear it missing out!"

John stopped short and offered a grin. "Then you take her up."

The private smiled back. He knew John's words were said in jest only. There was not a pilot around who would let another man take up his lady, if he were able to fly her himself.

"I'll help you take the engine apart again," Flipflop offered.

"Naw," John said and tossed aside his leather cap and goggles. "Go get some grub. I'll stay here and see if I can't figure out which cylinder it is. Say, where's that worthless brother of mine?"

Flipflop shrugged. "Last time I saw J.D., I mean Sergeant Monroe, he was heading to the mess. You want me to send him out here?"

John shook his head. "No, go on. J.D.'s no doubt managed to finagle a pass into town. I won't have him feeling obligated to help me here." The private shrugged again and gratefully headed to the mess tent.

John gave the Curtiss Jenny a determined stare. "You are sure one cantankerous lady today," he muttered. At twenty-five, John had realized his dream of flying. It was a young dream, just like the art itself. But nevertheless, it was in his blood, and John could think of nothing that gave him more enjoyment and pleasure than soaring overhead, master of the Jenny.

He laughed at that thought. "Some master. I can't even figure out what's wrong with you. Why don't you talk to me, Honey?"

The biplane sat in smug silence. If she were a flesh-and-blood woman, the cold-shouldered indifference could not have been more simply stated. But she was not a woman, not in the sense of flesh and blood, and she certainly was not a lady.

Yet, John could not help but grin at her in the same affectionate manner that he would have his beloved Joelle. Ah, Joelle, he thought. He could see her dark eyes blazing with the same love and excitement he felt.

"Pity the woman who shares a man with his plane." Those famed words from John's good friend and commander, Major Bob Camstead, were followed up with a haunting prediction: "She'll always run a close second."

But John did not think so. He considered Joelle Dawson to rank right up there with his aggravating Jenny. The only problem was, would Joelle see it the same way?

John heard the unmistakable approach of another Jenny overhead and stared out wistfully to where she was. There was absolutely nothing like it, he thought. John watched on in silence as the pilot cut back the engine and bounced to a rough landing with the Jenny's tailskid absorbing most of the impact.

"Flying up there gives a man a great belief in the reality of God," Bob Camstead had once told him. "But landings were sure to get you religious in a quick way, if you weren't already set in your thoughts."

John smiled and went to work on the engine. He had no doubt about the existence of God, nor of the love and peace that could be found when an obedient heart sought His way. Landing Jennys on rocky desert strips had not given John religion, but it had kept him regular in his prayer life.

~

It was late that night when John finally managed to locate the problem with the engine. After a quick bite of food and a shower, John sat down to write to Joelle. While sweating over the engine, he had made up his mind that he was going to ask her to be his wife. Picking up his pencil, he wondered how he should go about it.

He started to write, then shook his head and discarded the piece of paper and picked up a clean sheet. Maybe she would think it was too soon. What if he had misunderstood her feelings? No, he reasoned, that was not possible. He put the pencil down and thought for a moment. It had to be just right.

The well-worn Bible that he had brought with him to army life sat on his bed. It had been his habit to make it the first thing he read when he woke up in the morning and the last thing he saw before going to sleep at night. Picking it up, John began to leaf through the pages.

~

Joelle Dawson fairly danced through the kitchen of Piñon Canyon Ranch. Her tiny frame seemed as light as air, and her face was radiant in its joy.

Joelle's sister-in-law, Daughtry, rolled her eyes and suppressed a giggle. "John must have written another letter," she mused to her mother, Maggie Lucas.

Maggie watched the dark-eyed Joelle float from the room into the hallway. "She's completely gone over him, isn't she?" Maggie laughed, then looked back to her daughter. "Of course, you are just as bad, oh daughter-of-mine."

"I beg your pardon?" Daughtry feigned indignation.

"Oh, don't play ingénue with me, Daughtry Dawson. You still get gaga every time Joelle's brother comes waltzing through the door. A body might think that Nicholas Dawson hung the stars and the moon in the sky."

"I'm no worse than you are about Daddy," Daughtry countered. "I've seen the way you run to the mirror and check to make sure you look your best when you hear him coming up the walk." The look on her mother's face caused Daughtry to laugh, and Maggie could not help but join her.

⁓

Joelle could hear the two women giggling like schoolgirls as she moved away from the main section of the ranch house and down the west wing. Here, the Lucases had kindly provided her a room to live in when their daughter, Daughtry, and son-in-law, Nick, had come to the ranch to anticipate the birth of their second child. Joelle was a kind of tag-along who had happily lived the last few months on Nick and Daughtry's ranch. The youngest of her family, Joelle had come to stay on with her brother in order to help care for Kent, their firstborn, and keep house for Daughtry.

At least that is what she had told her mother and father when she had pleaded to be allowed to do the deed. They had had little idea that she saw this as the best way to position herself close to the man she would come to love.

Joelle had met John Monroe at the Lucas's Christmas party just two years earlier. He was not the kind of guy who caught everyone's eye when he walked into the room, but when Joelle first caught sight of him, she had immediately felt her heart skip a beat. He was a half-foot taller than she, with sandy blond hair and the most stunning blue eyes she had ever seen in her life.

That evening had been the most perfect one she had ever known. Although there had been many other men trying to get Joelle's attention that night, she had enjoyed talking to John the most. Daughtry alone had five brothers and John had a younger brother who was not to be outdone by his sibling. There was also another young man, John's cousin, Sam, but no one else mattered much after she had met John. By the time the party was over, Joelle knew that John Monroe was the man she intended to marry.

Clutching the latest letter from her beloved John, Joelle dreamily closed the door behind her as she sought her privacy. Unable to contain her excitement any longer, she tore open the envelope and read the words of Song of Solomon 2:10-11.

"My beloved spake, and said unto me, Rise up, my love, my fair one, and come away. For, lo, the winter is past, the rain is over and gone."

Joelle loved John's romantic notions and the way he used Scripture to court her. Her own faith in God was still a tender mystery to her, but John's was robust and invigorating. She found strength in it. She continued to read.

My beloved Joelle,
    I would like to be at your side when you read these words, but the army doesn't care how or when a man proposes his love. They only care that when duty calls, I answer and that I do it in double-time.

Joelle felt her heart beat faster. This was the letter for which she had been waiting. After what had seemed an eternity of time, Joelle knew herself to be hopelessly in love with the handsome army lieutenant, and she could only hope he felt the same. She closed her eyes, savoring the letter, wanting to make the moment last as long as possible.

She pictured in her mind John's tousled, blond hair blowing across his forehead and falling haphazardly across his sky blue eyes. She had not seen him in person since his sister, Angeline, had married Daughtry's brother, Gavin Lucas. That was nearly three months ago, not that it mattered. She could still hear his voice, soft against her ear. . .still see him waving good-bye from the cockpit of his biplane.

"Oh, John," she whispered his name as praise and turned her eyes back to the paper in hand.

    Once, it was only a dream of mine that I might find a woman to love. A woman with whom I could plan a future. You, Joelle, are that woman. I can't imagine life without you, and every day that passes without knowing that you officially belong to me grieves me as surely as anything has ever grieved me. I know this lacks the flowers and candlelight that you deserve, but, Joelle, I am hopelessly in love with you and. . .

Joelle paused to take a deep breath before she continued reading.

ask, with humble, loving heart, that you would consent to be my wife.

Joelle let out a scream of delight without even being consciously aware of what she had done. The sound of hurried footsteps in the hallway soon brought Maggie through the doorway, followed by the slower moving Daughtry.

"What is it, Joelle?" Maggie questioned in worried overtones. "Are you hurt?"

Joelle clutched the letter to her breast. She shook her head and breathlessly replied, "He's asked me to marry him!"

Daughtry leaned against the door and smiled. "Is that all?"

The three women were soon embracing one another joyously. Joelle was the first to pull away. She could not stand still for very long, and Maggie laughed at the way the petite woman flitted from one corner of the room to the other.

"I'm so happy, I shall cry," Joelle said, the emotion heavy in her voice. "Oh, Daughtry, Maggie, this is exactly what I've hoped and prayed for."

"I can't imagine a finer wife for John," Maggie stated, meaning every word.

"Or a better husband for Joelle," Daughtry added. "I certainly wouldn't wish any of my brothers on her."

"Oh, hush," Maggie said, waggling a finger at her daughter. "You have excellent brothers, and what with Gavin married to John's little sister, I have only four others to marry off."

"Good luck," Daughtry continued her mock harangue. "You're going to have to send away for wives. The women around here know them too well to be taken in by that Lucas charm."

All three women laughed, but each knew the merriment was not credited to Daughtry's words. It was clearly Joelle's joyous expectation of marriage to John.

"We should go right away and tell Lillie," Maggie suggested, thinking of the woman who was her lifelong best friend and John's mother. "No doubt John will write to his folks when he gets a chance, but a mother likes to know these things right away, and Lillie won't be any exception."

Joelle sobered a bit. "Do you think she'll approve? She won't think it rushed, will she?"

"John's mother is as romantic as the next woman," Maggie said, reaching out to smooth back a strand of Joelle's dark hair from her face. "Besides, I think Lillie already has a good idea of what John's intending to do."

"Honestly?" Joelle's eyes were wide in anticipation of Maggie's response.

"She told me, not two days ago, that she thought John was quite sweet on you," Maggie replied. "In fact, she commented that knowing John's penchants for moving right ahead with things and his rather romantic outlook on life, that she expected to have a daughter-in-law by spring."

"Oh, Maggie!" Joelle gasped. "That's wonderful. Then you think she really won't mind? I mean, I know John will want to get married right away."

"I don't think she'll mind at all. Why don't you get a letter of acceptance off to him, and when you're finished we can ride into town together and post it, then go see Lillie."

Joelle threw herself into Maggie's arms. "I don't know how to thank you. You've all been so kind and good to me."

"No thanks are necessary," Maggie said, giving Joelle a hug. "You've been a blessing to Daughtry and that in turn has blessed me. What with the way Kent runs around here like a wild banshee—"

"Speaking of my son," Daughtry said with a sudden worried tone, "I'd better locate him and see what mischief he's gotten himself into."

"Don't worry about it," Joelle said, pulling away from Maggie. "When Jordy brought me this letter, I traded him Kent."

Daughtry grinned. "That ought to teach my baby brother to go fetching mail for moon-eyed young ladies."

"I am not moon-eyed," Joelle protested, but very weakly. "I'm in love! And, I'm getting married!"

About fifteen minutes later, Joelle appeared in the kitchen, her readied response in hand. Maggie was nowhere to be seen, but Daughtry was vigorously kneading down bread dough. Glancing up, Daughtry could not help but smile. Joelle had apparently not only written the letter but had also changed her clothes and rearranged her hair.

"Wanting to make a good impression on your future mother-in-law, I see?" Daughtry teased.

"Oh, Dotty," Joelle answered, staring down at her outfit, "do I look perfectly awful?"

"Not at all. I think you look very fit. Mother is having the buggy brought around. I don't know why Daddy won't just get a car and make it easier on all of us."

Joelle wriggled her noise. "They smell funny, anyway."

"So do horses," Daughtry laughed.

"I guess that's so. But truly, do you think I look all right? I was going to wear the blue serge but it looked too stuffy. Then I tried on my green skirt with the plum piping, but it just didn't seem right, either."

Daughtry left her bread, wiping her hands as she came to where Joelle stood. "Turn around and let me see." She motioned with her hand and Joelle pirouetted in slow motion. Joelle had finally settled on a lavender print dress. "Yes, you look just fine. That dress really sets off your figure."

"What about my hair?" Joelle questioned, her hand going up to readjust her hat. It was a wide-brimmed straw affair with a lavender scarf to tie it smartly to her head. "Does this hat seem a bit too much?"

"Don't all hats, these days?" Daughtry questioned lightly. "Nick says if they get any larger we can just turn them over and use them as laundry baskets."

Joelle looked at her sister-in-law in horror. "Does it look that bad?"

Daughtry laughed. "The hat is fine. You hair is perfect. Your face is free of smudges and dirt, although given the ride into Bandelero, it won't take long to rectify that. Joelle, relax. You know Lillie Monroe adores you. She'll want only the very best for her son and for you."

"I suppose you're right," Joelle replied, nervously biting at her lower lip. "It's just that I love him so much. I'm so afraid something will happen to spoil it all."

"Trust in the Lord, Joelle," Daughtry advised. "He's the One Who holds the future. If it's right for you and John to marry, God will see to it that nothing else interferes."

"But what if it isn't what God wants?" Joelle questioned, suddenly realizing for the first time that perhaps there was a larger stumbling block to her happiness than she had even allowed herself to imagine.

"If it's not right, Joelle, then you certainly don't want to defy God and marry John." Joelle's panic-stricken face caused Daughtry to hurry ahead. "But I know John, and I know he wouldn't have asked you to marry him without having first asked God. He must feel quite confident about it, or he wouldn't have come this far."

Joelle's smile was back in place. "Of course, you're right! John would never propose marriage without feeling sure that God was leading him in this. All right, Daughtry. I shan't worry another moment about Lillie. I know God will see to the entire matter. I just know it!"

～

John was up to his elbows in grease when Flipflop approached him with Joelle's letter. The Jenny was causing him problems again, though in all honesty it was not her fault. The army was experimenting with the loads she could carry. They continued to add and take away various items from the plane until John was not all that certain if the engine had been removed by direct order of his superiors.

"You got a letter, Preacher," Flipflop said with a grin. "I think it's the one you've been waiting for."

John quickly picked up a rag and wiped his hands. His face was smudged from the oil, and his hair, which was due for a trimming anyway, had taken on a darker appearance from his time spent over and inside the Jenny's V-8 engine.

"Give it here," John said, throwing the rag down.

"You wanna be alone, Preach?" Flipflop asked hesitantly. The tone in his voice left little doubt that he hoped to be a part of the missive.

"Naw," John said, trying to keep his voice even. "Might as well stay. You've earned it just having to work with me these last few days."

Flipflop smiled his gratitude and matched the way John sucked in his breath as the top of the envelope gave way. Unable to slow his fingers, John tore at the folds of the letter until it opened to his scrutiny.

> *"His mouth is most sweet: yea, he is altogether lovely. This is my beloved, and this is my friend. . . ." The words of Song of Solomon 5:16 reminded me of you, John, and I could scarcely contain my joy when I received your marriage proposal. I will most happily rise up and come away, my love. I am yours, now and forever, and joyfully I will become your wife at the first possible moment.*
>
> *Your beloved Joelle*

John gave out a whoop that was loud enough to be heard, not only across the airfield, but throughout all of El Paso, as well. "She said yes! She's gonna marry me, Flipflop!" John kissed the single-page letter and let out another yell. "She said yes!"

Chapter 2

January brought them mild and pleasant conditions. Joelle enjoyed a continuous flow of mail from John, as well as a new-found friendship in her soon-to-be mother-in-law, Lillie Monroe.

"I can't believe this weather!" Lillie exclaimed, coming into the house from outside. "I haven't worn a coat all week, and today I'm even tempted to roll up these long sleeves, but Dan would skin me alive if he caught me." Although Lillie teased as though her husband was a harsh man, Joelle had witnessed the deep love they held for each other.

Joelle glanced up from the receiving blanket she was embroidering for Daughtry's new baby. "I keep thinking how wonderful it would be if only John and I could get married now. Why, we could even have our wedding outside, like Angeline and Gavin did last fall.

Lillie nodded, a faint smile crossing her lips at the memory of her youngest child's wedding. She had seen very little of Angeline or Gavin since their marriage. Her smile broadened at the thought of the newlyweds.

"What?" Joelle questioned, catching Lillie's expression.

Lillie shook her head. "It's nothing really. I was just thinking how little I've seen of Angeline since she got married. Maggie says that Gavin is pretty scarce too, and except for working with his father, she doesn't believe he ever leaves Angeline's side."

"I feel the same way about John," Joelle confessed. "I hate the separation, and I'd give just about anything if he were here. I'd pray for God to find a way to muster John out of the army, but I know how much he loves flying." There was an unexpected heaviness in Joelle's voice. "I think it will be hard being an army wife. I can't imagine getting married, only to have to send him off for long separations."

Lillie sat down across from Joelle and picked up her own sewing. "I know. I wish neither one of the boys had run off and joined up the way they did. I'm so afraid we'll be drawn into the war in Europe. Every day we seem to get that much closer to choosing sides. Of course," Lillie paused, "there is really no contest in that. We can't possibly support the way Germany has acted. Dan tells me that there is a great deal of propaganda, some of it true, some of it exaggerated, but nonetheless, it doesn't come out in favor of Germany."

351

"I saw one of the posters at the post office," Joelle confessed.

"The one with the poor little children asleep in their beds with the outline of the Hun soldiers overshadowing them?" Lillie questioned.

"Yes," Joelle replied with a shudder. She took several tiny stitches and put the blanket down. "How can people be so cruel to children?"

"I haven't a clue. I wish I could extend the same cruelty to those who dish it out, but Dan says we must pray for even the cruelest of Germany's soldiers. God doesn't want our anger to turn into something just as ugly. Revenge belongs to God."

"I suppose he's right," Joelle said with a wistful look to the window beyond Lillie. "Still, it would seem justified. I mean, God can't possibly expect folks to allow such horrors to go unchecked."

Lillie nodded with a smile. "I feel exactly like you do, Joelle. We're going to get along just fine."

Joelle beamed, "Oh, by the way, I forgot to thank you for having me over today. I cherish our visits." She paused for a moment to take in her soon-to-be mother-in-law. Lillie Monroe was a very stylish woman. She wore her blond hair in a short, yet feminine bob. There was just a bit of silver amidst the honey gold that betrayed her middle age. The thing that fascinated Joelle most, however, was Lillie's seeming perfection. She was good at everything she touched and everyone in Bandelero loved her.

Joelle suddenly felt insecure again. " I was so afraid you wouldn't want me for a daughter-in-law," she confessed.

With a surprised look on her face, Lillie looked up from her work. Her eyes softened as she considered the young woman across the table. "I feel quite blessed to have such a lovely young woman join my family," Lillie said in reply. "I sincerely mean that, Joelle. I'm pleased with John's choice for a wife. He's a sound young man with a heart for God. If he's prayed about this and sought the Lord's guidance, which I'm sure he has, who am I to interfere?"

"Not all mother-in-laws would feel that way," Joelle said with a grin. "Maggie told me the other day that her son, Dolan, got a bit of a cold shoulder from Judy Miller's mother. It seems that even though Dolan's family has plenty of wealth, Dolan himself hasn't proved a thing regarding how he would support a wife. Poor Dolan," Joelle laughed, "he wasn't even that far along in thinking, but Mrs. Miller sure gave him an earful."

"I think it's well for a parent, a mother of a daughter in this case, to know what the prospective husband of her child plans to do with his life. After all, his life is no longer his own. He is suddenly a very important part of another human being. A human being on whom you, as a parent, have spent a great deal of time and energy to grow to adulthood."

"That does seem reasonable," Joelle agreed. "So how come you haven't asked me what I plan to do with my life?"

Lillie laughed. "Because I don't have to. You plan to love my son with all your heart. It couldn't be any clearer."

Joelle blushed. "I can't imagine not loving him, Lillie. He's so important to me."

"I know. I'm not so old that I can't remember what it felt like to fall in love."

Joelle looked rather surprised. "You mean you aren't still in love?"

Lillie paused for a moment to consider her answer. "In love, no." Joelle looked crestfallen. "But I deeply and completely love my husband. You see, to me, falling in love is like jumping into a cool pond on a hot day. It's shocking and exhilarating at first, then as you become accustomed to it, you find it more and more comfortable, even ordinary."

"My love for John could never be ordinary," Joelle protested.

"Good, I'm glad to hear it. You'll do well in marriage if you work toward that end. It's when things become routine and ordinary that you can get off track," Lillie replied, leaning back in her chair. "But just like swimming in a pond, Joelle, you dare not take it for granted. When you take the water for granted, you drown. The minute you take love for granted, you lose something very precious. And, it's extremely hard to get it back."

"I'll remember that," Joelle said, picking up her sewing again.

Lillie started to say something in reply when a knock at the door distracted her thoughts. "I wonder who's injured themselves now?"

Joelle found life at the Monroe house more than a little bit interesting. Daniel Monroe was one of only two doctors in the entire area surrounding Bandelero. And, given the fact that he had been the only doctor for over twenty years, people were still partial to his kind of doctoring. It was nothing for Lillie and Dan to see a steady stream of cut fingers, infected wounds, and hacking coughs, all in the same day. Of course, there were those times when the ailments were much more serious.

It took only a moment for Lillie to return, but when she did, her face was ashen and in her hand was the unmistakable cause.

"A telegram?" Joelle questioned, wondering at Lillie's worried expression. When their eyes met, Joelle felt her breath catch.

"It's from the army." The words lingered in the air for an eternity before Lillie added, "John's been in an accident."

"No!" Joelle abandoned her sewing and crossed the room to Lillie. "No, it can't be true. He's not. . .? He isn't. . .?" She could not ask the question.

"No, he isn't dead. At least not yet. Joelle, we have to send for Dan.

John's going to need him. We have to go to him right away." Joelle worried that Lillie might faint, and so she gently led her to the chair.

"I'll get him myself," Joelle said and pulled her shawl around her shoulders. "Where did he go this morning?"

Lillie tried in vain to remember. "I don't know. I think he had calls to make at Mrs. Brown's and maybe Joe Perkum's."

"I'll go to Mrs. Brown's house first," Joelle said. "Will you be all right here alone?"

"I'll be fine, Joelle. Just get Dan. Please, just bring Dan home."

Joelle raced down the sandy dirt street outside the Monroe house. She was grateful that she had spent so much time with Maggie and Daughtry in Bandelero. She was rapidly learning her way around and now was confident in her mission to locate Dr. Dan.

"Oh, God," Joelle breathed, completely unaware of the tears that streamed down her face. "Please, God." It was all that she could say, yet it made her feel better.

A quick visit to the Brown's red-brick residence revealed that Dan had been there earlier but had moved on to tend to another patient. Mrs. Brown had the presence of mind to pick up the telephone and ask the operator if she knew where Dr. Dan had taken himself.

"He's over at Morely Davis's place," the operator replied. "He just checked in with me not five minutes ago."

"Thank you, Sarah," Mrs. Brown said, then turned to Joelle. "He's with Morely Davis. Do you know where that is?"

"I don't think so," Joelle replied, her voice near to a sob.

The older woman nodded sympathetically, wondering at the young woman's dilemma, but uncharacteristically, she kept her questions to herself. "You go past the bank and turn down the alley. You'll come to Second Street, then turn left. Morely's is behind the Red Dog Saloon."

"Thank you, Mrs. Brown," Joelle barely had the presence of mind to mutter. She quickly took off running, hiking her long brown skirt higher to accommodate her leggy strides.

"Dan! Dr. Dan!" Joelle yelled, even before coming to Morely's door. Several passing residents of Bandelero paused to consider her cries, waiting and watching to see what the trouble might be. In a town the size of Bandelero, one family's troubles were quickly shared by all.

Just as Joelle reached out to pound against Morely's door, Dan himself opened the door and stepped outside. He was so like John in appearance, that seeing him caused Joelle's tears to start anew.

"Joelle! What is it, Honey? What's wrong?"

"Oh, Dan!" she exclaimed breathlessly. "You have to come home."

"Is Lillie hurt?" Dan's face drained of color.

"No," Joelle's voice broke. "It's John. He's been in an accident. Lillie says you have to come home. Please, Dan." She reached up as if she might have to drag him back to the house.

There was no need to beg. Dan quickly finished with Morely, retrieved his bag, and joined Joelle in the street. "Come on," he said, putting his arm around the trembling young woman. "We'll go home and find out what's to be done."

Joelle nodded, grateful for Dan's gesture. "I want to go with you." She stated the words so quietly that she wondered if Dan had even heard them.

"Of course," he replied with a tender smile. "I wouldn't dream of going to John without taking you with us."

∼

After several telephone calls, Dan was able to ascertain that John had crashed his Jenny while testing flight loads west of El Paso. The rest of the details were sketchy, at best. All they knew for sure was that he was in the hospital in Columbus, New Mexico, and it would take the better part of a day and night to get to him.

By evening, the Monroes, with Joelle in tow, were on the train headed to Santa Fe. From there they would catch a train on the Santa Fe main line and head south to Columbus.

For Joelle, it seemed that forever separated her from her beloved. She paced the train until the steward and, finally, the conductor himself, pleaded with Dan to keep her seated.

Around midnight, Joelle fell into a fitful sleep. She saw John in his biplane, circling overhead. She heard him trying to shout something above the roar of the Jenny's engine, but she could not make it out.

"What are you saying, John? I can't hear you!" she cried out in her dream.

John smiled down at her, and the engine fell silent. "Rise up my love, my fair one, and come away."

∼

Joelle stirred, crying in her sleep. Dan wished silently that he could comfort her. Staring down at his wife, equally as restless but nestled against his comforting arm, Dan wondered at what they would find when they reached Columbus. Had John died already?

Rubbing his weary eyes, Dan thought back to his conversation with the army doctor in Columbus. Afterwards, he had not shared the full details with Lillie, for fear that her own knowledge of medicine would leave her feeling hopeless.

John had sustained severe breaks in his leg and back. It was even possible that the spinal cord had been severed, but the doctor was unsure. Casts had been applied both to the leg and to the trunk of John's body. The doctor hesitated to say anything more. All he could tell Dan for certain was that John was conscious and had no feeling from the waist down. Perhaps, mercifully so, Dan reasoned and issued a prayer on behalf of his son.

The foreign scenery beyond the windows of the train held little interest to Joelle or the Monroes. There were vast stretches of desert land where the only thing to break the monotony was the cactus. At each and every small town Joelle perked up when the train began to slow. Time after time this was not the case, and the conductor had come to merely shake his head at Joelle before even announcing to the other passengers the town in which they were about to stop.

When the small border town of Columbus finally did come into view, Dan felt suddenly fearful. What if John had been too weak to survive? What if while they were traveling, he had died and the army had buried him?

"Everything will be all right," he murmured as if to convince himself.

Joelle nodded. "I want to believe that."

"Good," Dan said softly. Then looking from Joelle to Lillie and back again, he added, "then believe it. God has everything under His watchful eye. He controls our destinies, and He certainly controls John's." The women nodded but said nothing, and Dan was grateful for their silence.

～

"We've given him the best facilities available," the army doctor was saying. "We still know very little about his condition, but at least he is conscious. Coherent too. In fact, I must warn you he's easily agitated and can be difficult."

Lillie smiled her first smile in days. "I've lived with him long enough to know that side of him, Doctor. Have no fear, I've seen my son's temper on more than one occasion. I'm just grateful he's alive and capable of throwing his fits."

The doctor countered her smile. "Strange guy, your son, if you'll pardon my saying so. He never curses, although he's been in a great deal of pain."

"Pain?" Dan asked. "Has he regained feeling in his legs?"

Lillie and Joelle both looked up with a start.

The doctor shook his head. "No, but he has other injuries that are causing him discomfort. He rants and raves at all of us without regard to rank or duty. He's entitled, though. It is a miracle that he lived through that crash. There was little left of his plane."

Lillie cringed. "He's paralyzed?"

"I'm afraid so," the army doctor replied, hesitating only long enough to glance at Dan. "We don't know if it's permanent or not. Only time will tell."

"I see," Lillie murmured, throwing an accusing look at her husband. "And you knew this and didn't tell me?"

"Look, Lillie, I didn't want to worry you more than you already were. You know almost as much about medicine as I do, and I knew you'd understand the full implications."

"Which are what?" Joelle interrupted.

All three turned to take in the small woman who looked more like a frightened urchin than anything else.

"What does it mean? You have to tell me!" she insisted in a barely audible voice.

Dan reached out and touched her gently on the shoulder. "John may have severed his spinal cord in the accident. We don't know a great deal at this point, so speculating won't help anyone. It may just be that the tissue around the spine is swollen, if not. . .well. . ."

"What happens if the cord is severed?" Joelle insisted.

Dan looked helplessly to Lillie, then to his colleague. "It means that John would never walk again."

Chapter 3

J oelle took the news with surprising grace. "But John is alive, right?" She again looked to the three faces that stared back at her.

"Yes, he is," the doctor assured her. "And I haven't any reason to believe he won't pull through. He's already passed through some of the most critical checkpoints. He survived the casting, which is always a delicate matter. However, I can't begin to give you an accurate prognosis of his future condition."

Joelle squared her shoulders. "The future's in God's hands. What I want to know is how I can help the present."

The doctor nodded. "I understand. If you'll give me a moment with John, I want to make sure he's up to this visit."

He left quickly, and Dan smiled down at his son's fiancée. "That's the spirit, Joelle."

"I want to see him," Joelle said without returning Dan's smile. "But," she added with thoughtfulness, "I understand that you and Lillie should see him first. I'll wait until you call for me."

Dan shook his head. "No, you'll come with us. You're an important part of John's life. He wants to build his future with you, and I think you should be there."

Lillie reached out and squeezed Joelle's arm supportively. "That's right. We're in this together. If anything will see John through this accident it will be the three of us, working as a team. Agreed?"

Joelle now smiled. "Agreed."

"Agreed, with one exception," Dan replied. "God's going to head up the effort or it won't work at all."

"Of course," Lillie and Joelle said in unison.

The doctor returned and motioned them to follow. Joelle tried to brace herself for the worst, without having any idea what the worst might be. She tried to pray but found her lips unable to form words. Instead, she cried out with her heart and soul, feeling that her efforts were so very inadequate.

Dan and Lillie entered the room after the doctor, with Joelle following closely behind them. She could not see John yet but heard Lillie exclaim his name and rush to his bedside.

"How dare you crash your plane!" Lillie teased.

"I guess life just wasn't exciting enough," he replied. He was lying flat on the bed in his plaster-of-paris jacket and could not see anything past his mother and father. "You beat a path down here fast enough. You fly?"

"You won't get me up in one of those contraptions," Lillie stated flatly.

"Probably won't get me up in one again, either," John said with a bitter edge to his voice.

"You've certainly got your work cut out for you, Son," Dan said, his physician's eye sizing up the patient before him. He leaned over to better observe a particularly nasty cut on John's jaw. "Looks like they've put in about ten stitches here."

"Felt more like fifty," John declared. "I suppose maybe I should be grateful that I can't feel my legs. Doc said the one was pretty bad off. They spent a great deal of time putting me back together, or so I'm told. All I know is one minute I was in the cockpit and the next I was wearing this suit of armor."

Dan chuckled and straightened up. "I'm sure it gives you cause for frustration."

"You've got that right," John replied. "Eating is a real trick, and I won't even go into detail on the process for relieving myself."

"No need to," Dan said with a nod. "I'm very familiar with catheters and even more so with bladder infections. Cystitis wouldn't help you one bit, so just be grateful for what they can do. We're going to see to it that you get back on your feet so that you won't need any of this."

"That'll be a good trick," John said, seeming to take on a completely new personality. "In fact, I'd say it might very well be impossible." The bitterness was even more evident.

"Impossible?" Lillie questioned. "I can't believe that word even came from your lips, John Monroe."

John turned his face aside, unwilling to deal with the matter. "How did Joelle take the news?" he questioned instead.

"Why don't you ask her yourself?" Dan said and reached around to pull Joelle in front of him.

It was Joelle's first chance to see John, and although she wanted to cry out from the sight of her beloved with his blackened eyes still swollen and his face full of cuts, she smiled instead. "You look awful," she said as lightly as she could manage.

John stared at her for a moment as if seeing a ghost. "Get her out of here! How dare you bring her!" His voice was raised in anger, while his stony stare went past Joelle to his father. "Get her out!"

"Calm down, John," Dan said, putting supportive hands to Joelle's shoulders. "You asked this woman to be your wife. When you marry it's for sickness and health, the good with the bad. Don't you think she's strong enough to walk with you through this?"

"I know she's strong, but she didn't ask for this," John replied through clenched teeth.

"You didn't, either," Joelle said, breaking her silence.

"I controlled the situation," John answered. "I climbed into the plane, knowing that I was taking a risk. I had complete control, and I made my choice. A pilot knows these things are always a step behind him. My time came just as I always knew it might. You can't be expected to share this, Joelle. It's too much to ask of anyone."

"But I'm not just anyone," Joelle protested and took a step toward John. "I'm going to be your wife, and you are going to be my husband. My place is at your side and that is where I'm going to stay."

John shook his head. "No. You didn't know what you were doing. You didn't know this would happen. You have to go back home and forget about us, Joelle. I release you from your obligation." There were tears in his eyes, but he refused to look away.

Joelle put her hands on her hips to keep from burying her face in them. She stared in silence for a heartbeat, then turned to leave, surprising everyone in the room. Dan and Lillie stepped aside to let Joelle pass, but she stopped instead and turned back to John.

≈

"You are a coward, John Monroe, but I love you all the same and," she said with a smile that betrayed her determination, "I do not release you from your obligation to marry me, and until you're able to do something about it, I will continue to consider myself your bride-to-be."

She stalked from the room leaving John to stare after her in mute silence, while Lillie and Dan broke into laughter.

"I guess she told you," Dan finally said. "You've got your hands full with that one."

"I've got nothing of the kind. This isn't a game. Dad, you've got to put her right back on the train and send her home."

"I'd like to see you try that," Lillie replied. "You apparently think Joelle will just walk away now that you are less than the object of perfection you once considered yourself to be."

"I never considered myself to be perfect!" John exclaimed, surprised at his mother's words.

"Then what's the problem?" Lillie's voice softened, and she took a seat beside her son. "Would you leave Joelle if this had happened to her instead of you?"

"Of course not," John declared, "but it didn't happen to her. It happened to me. I can't marry a woman if I can't support her, and I certainly can't support her while I'm on my back."

"All the more reason to get up off your back," Dan said, coming to stand beside his wife.

"The doctor said he couldn't guarantee that that would ever happen."

"I don't recall life ever coming with guarantees," Dan answered. "Leastwise, not the kind of guarantees you're looking for. Son, before you give up on a matter, you've got to at least try."

"I can't," John said in complete dejection.

"Can't never did anything," Dan said in a firm tone.

"You've said that to me since I was five years old." John's voice was changing from one of self-pity to anger. "I hated it then, and I hate it now."

"It usually worked, though," Lillie remarked. "You'd storm off chanting, 'Can't never did anything! Can't never did anything! I sure wish "Can't" were here right now so I could punch him square in the nose!' " Lillie reached out to touch her son's cheek. "Remember?"

John's anger melted in view of his mother's smile. "I remember, and I'd still like to give him a good one."

"Looks like he snuck up and gave you one instead," Dan said simply.

"You got that right," John grimaced as a flash of pain streaked across his head. "I don't want to deal with it right now."

"I know," Lillie sat and patted his hand. "But I also know you're going to have to quit feeling sorry for yourself. The doctor says that despite the back injury, you're in pretty good shape. The bones in your leg and back will heal, and the swelling will go down. From there, we'll see what we can work with and," Lillie said with a new determination, "we'll make the best of what we have and trust God to provide the rest."

"That's asking a lot, Mom."

Lillie cocked her head to one side. "Why do you say that?"

"I don't think God much cares to provide me with anything," John answered. "I said some things that I shouldn't have when I found out about my back."

"God knows what kind of grief you were under, John. I'm sure He'll forgive you for what you said."

"He might," John replied, turning away from his mother's eyes, "if I were inclined to take them back."

~

In the meantime, Joelle found her way outside the hospital and paced a portion of the sandy street while waiting for Daniel and Lillie to finish their visit with John. She was angry, but more than this, she was hurt. Hurt that John would push her away when he needed her so much.

"He's doesn't even know what he's saying," Joelle muttered. "He's so mad at having his wings clipped that he doesn't even know what he's saying." Then her own words rang back in her ears. Joelle stopped and stared back at the hospital.

"He doesn't know," she whispered. "He truly doesn't know." The words made her feel instantly better. Everyone said things they did not mean when they were angry or shocked. John was certainly no exception.

The revelation made Joelle's heart feel lighter. She would just wait him out, she thought silently. It was not like he could get up from the bed and make her go home. She was a grown woman, entitled to make her own choices, and her choice was to stay put and help the man she loved.

When Dan and Lillie appeared on the street, their faces gave away grave concern. Joelle quickly joined them, wanting and needing to know what had transpired after her exit.

"He's angry, Joelle. You have to forgive him," Lillie said, pulling the younger woman to her supportively.

"I know. People say a great many things they don't mean when they're mad. I'm sure John will come around in time."

"That's a good attitude to have," Dan said, studying her face. "It's not going to be easy, however, and you must be ready for him to say a great many more things before it's all said and done."

"I kind of figured that," Joelle admitted. "But John has never seen me with my dander up. Papa used to say that had I been born first, the other three might never have arrived. I can deal with John's temper and his angry words, now that I know where they're coming from."

"And just where might that be?" Dan asked, wondering at Joelle's reasoning.

"His pain, of course." Her dark eyes turned upward to meet Dan's.

"His wounds will heal and the pain diminish. Even then, he still might say ugly things. Especially if he can't walk again," Dan said thoughtfully.

"His body might heal quickly, but the pain I'm speaking of is in his heart. His heart is broken because the life he loves has been taken from him. His love for flying isn't something he will give up easily or allow to just fade away. He's going to be angry for a very long time, and the sooner we all see that, the less hurt we'll find ourselves in the middle of."

Dan shook his head. "You are very wise for such a young woman."

"That and more," Lillie said, hugging Joelle. "You've a very precious love for my son, and I've a feeling it will do more to heal his pain than anything else we might do."

~

Later that night, settled into the hotel, Joelle tossed restlessly on her bed. The words she had spoken so confidently in the light of day seemed trivial and uncertain in the shadows of night.

What if he never walks? What if he loses his will to live? The questions raced through Joelle's mind. *What if he stops loving me?*

She pounded the pillow to make it more comfortable but found little comfort. "Oh, God," she whispered into the stillness of the night, "what am I to do?"

~

John lay in the silence of the hospital room, staring up at the ceiling as he had done for most of the last few days. He had realized that his parents would come, but it had shocked him beyond reason to see Joelle.

He looked down the sheet that covered his legs and tried to force some movement to prove to himself that he was not paralyzed. Nothing moved, however, and his frustration began to mount.

He could imagine Joelle waiting on him day after day, for the rest of their lives. She would never leave him, he knew that full well. She had too much respectability and compassion. No, she would see him as her mission, John reasoned and he could never let that happen. He did not want her pity and self-suffering. The life he had planned with Joelle had no part in those things.

"I have to make her see reason and leave," John whispered to the ceiling. "Even if I make her hate me, I have to convince her that what we had is over."

Waiting for sleep to come, John wondered how he might accomplish his task. He could be unreasonable and rude. Well, he laughed to himself, he had been that already. It would come quite naturally, and Joelle would never be ready for it. Little by little, she would see he was no prize, then she would go home. It pained him deeply to imagine the hurt on her face, the sorrow in her heart.

It's for the best, he reasoned to himself. *I have to make her stop loving me.*

Chapter 4

One week blended quietly into another, and the only significant method to mark time was John's steady progress of recovery. Joelle purposefully kept away from the hospital, and even after two weeks had passed, she still was not certain how she should handle the situation.

She had spent a great deal of time in thought and prayer. Everything had seemed so simple. Why had God allowed this to happen? Why should John suffer so when he was so devoted to God's will for his life?

There were few answers for her questions, and when Joelle was not sequestered away inside the two-story, concrete "Commercial Hotel," she was reviewing the town. And always, her mind was on John.

"He needs this time," she reasoned to Dan one morning, "to get used to the idea that I'm not going anywhere."

"He asks me every day if you're still here," Dan mused. "I think he's both relieved and unhappy that you haven't come to visit him."

"I'm sure."

Joelle's crisp, white shirtwaist made her face seem strangely pale. Dan wondered silently if she was eating properly. It was already apparent from the dark circles beneath her eyes that sleep was a stranger to her.

"Joelle," Dan said in fatherly overtones, "you have to take care of yourself or you'll be no good at all to John."

"I know," she said with a nod. Going to the hotel window, she stared down at the sandy, isolated town of Columbus.

Settled in the middle of nowhere, four miles north of the Mexican-American border, Columbus, New Mexico was all that Joelle would deem desolate. . .God-forsaken. It was like one of any number of nondescript towns she had seen while coming south on the train. It was nestled, if that could possibly be the correct word to use, on a vast wasteland of sandy, brown desert. There was nothing to break the monotony but miles of mesquite-dotted flatlands and more cactus than Joelle had ever hoped to see again.

She felt as though she knew every inch of the town by heart, she had paced it out often enough. There was Camp Furlong on the opposite side of the railroad tracks. Resident soldiers in khaki and leather seemed to take an immediate interest in her, even though Joelle gave them no encouragement.

She had had no less than five invitations to supper and two less respectable propositions. John would have been livid if he had known.

Joelle had tried not to take offense at their forward manner. Soldiers were soldiers, after all, and some were quite far from home. Also, they were unavoidable, and Joelle could not see punishing herself by remaining in the hotel.

While soldiers by far and away made up the largest portion of the town's population, there were other residents, as well. A whitewashed bank seemed to do an acceptable amount of business, as well as a handful of shops, several drinking and eating establishments, and, of course, the train depot.

It was quickly revealed that Columbus sported two major events in its daily life—the arrival of The Golden States Limited, eastbound and its reverse sibling, The Golden States Limited, westbound. The latter was often called the Drunkard Express, due to the fact it brought the furloughed soldiers back from El Paso, some sixty miles to the east. In a town where they enjoyed neither electricity nor telephones, people often turned out in droves to see who or what might arrive by rail.

Joelle, herself, had gone to the yellow train station, given the fact that it possessed the only means of communication with the rest of the world. She had sent two messages by telegram and received two in reply. One came from her brother, Nicholas, and the other from Maggie Lucas. Daughtry was still well and growing larger by the minute, and the Lucas family sent their prayers.

"You're at least a million miles away," the voice came from somewhere in her hotel room. Sleepily, Joelle turned from the window and caught her future father-in-law's worried eyes. "And I doubt you've heard a word I've said."

"Sorry," she whispered. "I don't want you to worry about me, Dan. I'm fine. Really, I am. I can't help but think of John and how much he's had to suffer. I know he must be in a great deal of pain, and it concerns me that he'll give up and stop trying to get better."

"Let's leave John out of this for a minute. I think you should eat better and get more rest." Dan took a step toward Joelle, then stopped. "We're going to move John to a small house on the edge of town. When we have him settled there, we'll move our things over as well. After that, we'll start preparing him for when those casts come off. You're going to need your strength then. That is, if you plan to help."

"Help? Of course, I'll help, but what can I do?" Joelle voiced the first real interest she had had in the conversation.

"It's going to be difficult to know exactly what will help the most," Dan said. "There are several things we can try. Exercises, hot compresses, salves, and rubs to keep the circulation going, things along those lines. I sent a telegram to a colleague of mine at Walter Reed Hospital in Washington. He's going to collect the latest information in spinal and back injuries and forward it to me."

Just then Lillie returned from the room she shared with Dan. Somehow along the way, Joelle's room had become their gathering place. "Are you ready for supper?" she asked with an expectant glance at Dan and Joelle.

"I believe we are," Dan replied. "I want to discuss John's recovery and supper would provide a good opportunity to do so."

Joelle smiled weakly, knowing Dan's purpose. He intended to see to it that she could not finagle her way out of eating. She quietly followed them downstairs and out into the street.

"I was told by one of the officer's wives," Lillie began, "that they are serving excellent meals at a small cafe just the other side of the newspaper office."

"I'm ready for a change," Dan replied, and Joelle nodded. "The hotel serves a substantial fare, but it isn't what I'd call excellent."

They arrived at the quaint establishment and were ushered inside with the greatest of enthusiasm. The robust owner, who introduced himself as Papa Santos, seated them at a small table that held nothing more than a red-and-white checkered cloth and lighted lamp. The soft glow from the table lamps gave the room a cozy feeling, and the delectable aroma of spicy Mexican food made even Joelle's mouth water in anticipation.

They ordered from Papa Santos's oral recitation of his menu, then sat back to await their meal. Joelle found that her mind was always on John and, remembering Dan's comments about the move, she questioned him.

"Why are you moving John?" she asked.

"I think the change would be good for him," Dan answered. "He hates the hospital and, frankly, I think they're beginning to hate having him there. I wanted to load him up on the train and move him to El Paso, but the army doctor feels that would be too harsh a trip for him to make. I guess I'm inclined to agree, although I'd like to get all of us out of Columbus."

"Why?" Joelle asked innocently. "Is there some kind of problem here?"

Dan looked at Lillie and the meaningful exchange was not lost on Joelle. She frowned at their silence, biting her lower lip.

Papa Santos seated several new patrons nearby and boisterously acclaimed the restaurant's merits. Dan waited until he had gone before leaning over and continuing. "The area isn't as safe as I'd like it to be," he began. "You know that Mexico is struggling against revolutionaries. They've had all manner of conflict and uprisings and, frankly, it doesn't look good."

Joelle was notably surprised. "Of course, I'd heard about the border raids. I read about them in the paper, but I had no idea we were in any real danger. This is still an American city. Why should we be afraid here?"

"We're only four miles from the International Boundary at the Palomas Gate, and we're the only town of substantial means for miles around. Pancho Villa, the revolutionary responsible for the trouble you read about, is wreaking havoc all along the border, and there's no way to tell what he might do next. He's already burned ranches and taken livestock, not to mention—" Dan halted abruptly and coughed. "Well, it probably should be left unmentioned."

Lillie's eyes betrayed her concern. She had already had this conversation with Dan and knew very well what his thoughts were.

"But the army is here to protect us," Joelle rationalized. "Surely this Villa person wouldn't be willing to face down the entire Thirteenth Cavalry."

"They faced worse at Agua Prieta," Dan replied and said nothing more until a plump, dark-skinned woman had settled plates of steaming food in front of each of them. "Shall we ask God's blessing?"

Lillie nodded and bowed her head. Joelle did the same, but not without exchanging another look at Dan's sober expression.

"Father, we thank You for the gifts You have given. We praise You for John's progress and for the bounty that lies before us. We give ourselves over to Your protection and guidance. In Jesus' name, amen."

"Amen," Lillie whispered.

Joelle's head lifted, and her dark eyes bore into Dan's. "What is Agua Prieta?"

"A town just across the border from Douglas, Arizona. Villa was enraged that President Wilson decided to back a man named Carranza as the official leader in Mexico. Villa attacked with ten thousand men and the *Federales* came from El Paso with equipment our government provided in order to defeat him. They say that after the battle, Villa was down to less than fifteen hundred men."

"So that's good, isn't it?" Joelle said, picking at the tempting food on her plate.

"It angered Villa even more. He feels the U.S. has betrayed him. At one time they had promised to back him and his people. Villa thought U.S. support would put him in the position of running Mexico. When we withdrew that support, he became just one more revolutionary. Now he has no more prestige in the eyes of our government than do the Red Flaggers."

"Who are they?" Joelle asked.

"Renegades of the worst kind. They're a trashy sort, not at all organized like Villa's men. They carry machetes and flag themselves with red. They are ruthless and even more aggressive than Villa, if that is possible."

"But why do you think they will come here?"

"Camp Furlong has a machine gun unit here. Villa would love to get his hands on those guns. The army knows it too, and they are looking out for him, but they can't do very much at this point. No one seems to want to authorize any counteraction." Dan put down his fork and struggled with an unpleasant thought. "I didn't want to add to the needless worry, so I haven't even told this to Lillie, but just a few days ago, Villa's men attacked a train and hauled off nineteen American mining engineers and killed them. That was at Santa Ysabel, Chihuahua, and it isn't that far from Columbus."

"Daniel Monroe!" Lillie said, a look of disbelief crossing her face. "How dare you try to keep things from me. I've been around you long enough to prove myself capable of keeping a cool head. If we're in danger like that, then I should be informed. Maybe moving John is worth the risk."

"Calm down, Lillie." Dan's voice became honey smooth. "You know how I feel about causing you needless pain. I've been leveling with you about most everything. Just hear me out."

Lillie seemed to take a moment to consider his words, then picked up her fork and began to eat. Dan took her lack of comment as acceptance and continued.

"I very much would like to move John out of Columbus, but the situation is such that we could end up permanently damaging his spine. . .maybe even killing him. That's not a risk I'm willing to take, and because there is so very little we can tell about his condition, I made the decision to wait things out right here. The army has assured me that they will patrol the area, even on the edges of town, to the utmost. They are increasing their patrols even now."

"Increasing their patrols?" Lillie questioned with a raised brow. "When did you learn about this?"

Dan tried to ignore the tone that told him he would have a great deal to explain when his wife got him alone. "Just a little while ago. So you see, I think the best we can offer John is a homelike atmosphere and an aggressive healing program."

"What can we do for him?" Joelle asked with pleading eyes.

"We can pray and wait with good attitudes and pleasant outlooks. I can't say much more than that. We need to give the broken bones time to heal and also to let John rebuild his strength. After that, we'll have to work the muscles in his legs, and hopefully the spinal swelling will go down and we will know the extent of his paralysis."

"I want to help," Joelle stated firmly. "He won't like it and it may seem completely improper, but I want to help. Anyway, it's not like I've never been around grown men. I do have brothers, you know."

Dan glanced at Lillie who wore an I-told-you-so grin on her face. "We knew you'd expect to help," he answered. "So we have decided to take you up on it. See, I have a theory. . .a plan, actually."

Joelle leaned forward. "What kind of plan?"

"You eat everything on your plate," Dan said with a grin, "and I'll tell you."

Joelle's eyes narrowed slightly as her head cocked to one side. "Now I see where John gets it," she said.

"Gets what?"

"His ability to manipulate people into doing what he wants."

Lillie laughed out loud at this, and although several people in the room glanced her way, no one seemed at all to mind. Embarrassed by her outburst, nonetheless, Lillie leaned forward and whispered, "John is so much like his father, that at times it's like seeing Dan when he was young."

"You calling me old?"

Lillie glanced from Joelle to Dan. "Never old, Mr. Monroe, just seasoned."

Dan's smile broadened. "That so, Mrs. Monroe," he stated more than questioned. "I guess we might call ourselves a bit spicy, at that."

Joelle had to laugh at their play. She hoped that she and John would one day find things to laugh about again. An aching in her heart made her want to leave the table and go to his side. But what would he say to her if she showed up in the hospital?

"So," Dan said, momentarily turning from his wife to face Joelle, "you gonna eat?"

Joelle jerked back to the present conversation and nodded. Putting a forkful of food up to her mouth, she spoke. "Start talking, Dr. Monroe."

Chapter 5

T he small adobe house that Dan secured was anything but spacious. It had a main living area with a kitchen and front room sharing the same space and two small bedrooms off the back. There was, of course, no indoor plumbing, but then Joelle had not seen the likes of that since living with her parents in Kansas City.

Joelle could not help but think of her mother and father as she watched Dan and Lillie work to ready the house for John. They had not wanted to let her come to New Mexico to live with Nicholas and Daughtry. It was only after a series of letters from Nicholas and the united efforts of Joelle and her older sister, Natalie, that Riley and Zandy Dawson had agreed to let their youngest leave home. They understood her need to be on her own, and this choice had kept her from sprouting wings and flying too far from their watchful eye. And, while Nicholas and Daughtry received a live-in nanny and housemaid, Joelle got to be nearer to John.

Seeing Dan stop to steal a quiet kiss from his wife, Joelle made a mental note to send her parents a telegram when time permitted. They would want to know about John's condition, Joelle reasoned, and it might help ease her homesickness for them.

The move from the hospital to the house came in February, and Joelle was on hand to see to it that John got properly tucked into the small but firm bed that Dan had personally made for him. Dan and Lillie had already agreed that Joelle should have the first chance at some private time with John once he was settled in. They started to leave the room, but John called out and stopped them.

"I thought I asked you to send Joelle home," John said with a glaring frown.

Joelle smiled warmly. "I told you I was staying put until you could make me leave. From the looks of you that ought to be a good long while."

John grimaced and muttered something inaudible under his breath. "You gonna let her torment me like this?" he asked, turning to his father and mother.

"I think she's earned the right to stay," Dan said. "In fact, I think it might do you two some good to have a few moments alone. Come on, Lillie."

"I don't want a few moments alone!" John yelled after his parents' retreating forms. "Do you hear me? Take her with you!"

Joelle closed the door behind Lillie and Dan, thinking as she did that she heard Dan laugh. Turning slowly and smoothing her muslin apron, she faced John.

"I gave you plenty of time to get used to my being here. You can't force me to leave you, John. You might as well stop fussing about it and accept the fact that I'm here and here I'm going to stay." Joelle kept her expression rigid and firm.

"I don't want you here!" His words were harsh and painful to Joelle's ears, but she swallowed her hurt and squared her shoulders.

"I'm staying, anyway," Joelle said with renewed determination.

"I told you to leave," he countered. The firm set of his jaw told Joelle he meant business, but there was something very boyish in his expression and this made Joelle smile. "You think I'm joking about this?" John asked, growing angrier by the minute.

"I think you're a little boy with his nose out of joint," Joelle replied. "Why don't you stop feeling sorry for yourself, John Monroe, and put that effort into getting better?"

"You don't seem to understand. I might not get better!" he proclaimed in a voice nearly loud enough to rattle the windowpanes.

"You don't understand," Joelle declared, coming to stand directly over him. "I. . .don't. . .care!" And with those words the shouting match was on.

"You're leaving!"

"I'm staying!"

"I mean it, Joelle!"

"So do I, John!"

"I'll make you miserable until you get back on that train and go home!"

"No doubt!" Joelle's tiny voice was no match for John's, but she put her heart and soul into the matter and found herself quite capable of holding her own. "Just go ahead and try!"

"If I could get out of this bed, I'd be tempted to throttle you!"

"If you could move out of that bed, we wouldn't be having this conversation!"

"Joelle, you're making me angry, and you aren't getting anywhere with this. I'm going to tell Dad to get you packed and on the next available train. Now, for the last time, I want you to go."

"For the last time?" Joelle questioned. "What a relief. I thought you might keep up this foolery for weeks to come." She leaned her face down, coming within inches of his face. Her voice softened and a loving smile touched her face. "You can tell me to go, but you can't make me leave. I love you, John, and your angry words and self-pity aren't going to change it one bit."

Without warning, Joelle pressed her lips against John's. She felt him resist, keeping himself aloof and refusing to return her kiss, but it did not cause her a moment's hesitation. Gently, she continued to kiss him until she felt his hands on her arms and the hardness of his mouth soften. Feeling him surrender his anger, Joelle broke away and stared at him for a moment.

"I'm staying," she whispered and pulled herself away from John's touch.

John closed his eyes, refusing to look at her. "Don't do it, Joelle. I'm only thinking of you. It's gonna be a long, hard haul, don't think I don't know it."

Joelle sighed. "I never thought it would be easy, but my love for you will get me through."

John's fury was back and his voice was a growl. "Your love will turn to pity. In fact, it probably already has. You just feel sorry for me. Isn't that true?" His accusation infuriated Joelle.

"Ha!" Joelle exclaimed and John's eyes snapped open. Seeing she had his full attention, Joelle nearly danced to the door. "The last thing in the world I feel for you is pity. You may have every other woman swooning over you with sad-faced sympathy, but not me. I know what you're capable of and I won't be charmed into letting you get out of it. When you're out of that cast, I'll expect a great deal of work out of you, John Monroe, and pity won't take you very far."

John was obviously surprised at her outburst, but he steadied his voice. "Go home, Joelle, and leave me alone."

"No," Joelle replied simply and waltzed out the door, closing it behind her.

"Joelle!" John yelled from the other side. Joelle leaned against the white-washed adobe wall and sighed. She was not aware of Dan and Lillie watching her until Lillie spoke.

"He's not going to make this easy on you, is he?"

Joelle shoved her hands deep into her apron pockets. "He thinks he has the upper hand, but I can already tell that you were right. If we can just channel his anger into determination to get out of that bed, he'll be on his feet in no time at all."

"It could get ugly," Dan reminded her.

Joelle sobered. "It could never be as ugly as him lying there, rotting away and feeling sorry for himself. I can endure his temper and his insults. He doesn't mean a single word of it, anyway. I'll stick it, out and when it's all over and he's back on his feet, John will owe me the nicest honeymoon trip to San Francisco that an army pilot's money can buy."

Lillie laughed. "Spoken like a true woman!"

Dan rolled his eyes. "That's for sure."

~

Within a matter of days, the four of them fell into a companionable routine. For Joelle, mornings were spent fixing breakfast while Dan and Lillie examined and bathed John. Each day, Dan charted John's progress and reported it to the army doctor, who in turn reported it back to John's superiors at Fort Bliss.

Dan devised a series of exercises for John that were designed to strengthen his arms. He reasoned with his son that once the swelling around the spine had sufficiently decreased, the time would come when John would need the extra muscle.

John was not the best patient and Joelle often told him so. She refused to give him a single bit of sympathy, and John's frustration with her presence seemed to take on new life.

"Did you enjoy your breakfast?" Joelle asked, coming into John's room.

"Did you make it?"

"Why yes, I did," Joelle replied sweetly.

"I figured as much," John said, looking away. The fact was, he had enjoyed the breakfast very much, but he was not about to let her know that. He had to force himself at times just to keep up the façade of being angry with her, in hopes that she would go home. Now was no exception, especially in light of the way she looked.

"Look at the mess you made," Joelle chided, coming to retrieve his breakfast tray. "I suppose next thing you know, I'll have to feed you as well as fix your meals."

"Nobody asked you to fix anything. In fact, nobody even asked you to be here," John stated in a low voice. His anger was evident, yet he still tried to tidy the messiness around his tray while stealing glances at Joelle.

She swept his hands away and took the task in hand, trying again to get some response regarding his food. "Did you enjoy your omelette? I got the recipe from a bona fide French chef." John said nothing, but seeing that he had eaten every bit of it, Joelle smiled. "I guess you did."

He watched her cross the room and thought that there had never been a more beautiful woman alive. He allowed himself to linger on her turned back, wishing he could touch the long, dark braid that bound her hair. *I can't do this to her,* he thought angrily. *I have to get her away from me.* With a heavy sigh he faced Joelle as she turned back to the bed. "Joelle, when are you going to get tired of playing nursemaid?"

"When are you going to get tired of playing invalid?" she shot back at him without so much as a blink of her eyes.

A noticeable tick in John's cheek warned Joelle that his wrath was not far behind. "I'm not playing at anything," he growled.

"Neither am I," she mimicked his tones.

"Joelle!"

"John!" she countered and paused to rid the bed of the remaining toast crumbs. Reaching out to brush the bits away, she found her wrist encircled with John's steel-like grip.

"I see you're gaining hand strength," she said, refusing to flinch under the increasing pressure. "Those exercises must be paying off."

"Go home, Joelle."

"I am home, John. Wherever you are, that's my home." Her words were soft and sure, and it was John who flinched and lost his nerve. Joelle's eyes were dark and her face was flushed from their confrontation.

"Don't look at me like that," he moaned, releasing her arm.

"Like what?" Joelle asked, straightening up.

"Never mind, just get out of here."

"I was going, but I'll be back after I wash the dishes. I'm going to help you with some new exercises," she said and went to retrieve the tray.

"Oh no, you're not," John declared. "Mom or Dad can do that."

"Your father has been asked by the army doctor to give him a hand at the hospital. Your mother is out shopping for some of the things we need. So you see, there is no one else and the exercises must be done." She stared back at him so matter-of-factly that John could think of no reply.

"Now, finish your coffee and I'll be back shortly." She handed him his cup and turned to retrieve the tray.

"It's not going to work, Joelle."

Joelle paused at the door. "What's not going to work, Beloved?" she asked innocently.

"This game you and my folks are playing. You think you can make me well by the sheer will of your desires, and it's not going to work. I may never walk again. You have to face facts."

∼

"I do believe you're afraid to walk again. What's the matter, John? Can't bear the thought of having to face your army buddies and explain the crash?" John's jaw dropped, and Joelle immediately wanted to take the words back. She did not like being contrary, especially when all she wanted to do was take him in her arms and hold him close. She wanted to convince him that if he stayed in a bed the rest of his life, she would still love him, but Dan had assured her there was nothing productive in that.

Steadying herself to keep the confrontational spirit alive, Joelle appeared almost smug at his continued silence. "I thought so. I've faced the fact that you might never walk again, John darling. But I think you haven't been able to face the fact that you very well may." With that she left the room, pulling the door closed. She had barely taken a step toward the kitchen when the reverberating crash of John's coffee mug hit the door behind her.

Setting the tray on the table, Joelle went back to John's room and opened the door enough to survey the shattered pieces of the cup. "Well, at least you drank the coffee. It makes less of a mess to clean up." Seeing John clench his fist, Joelle only smiled. "I'll tell your mom we'd better lay in a supply of cups."

Before approaching John's room again, Joelle finished the dishes and tidied the rest of the room. She was weary of their fighting, but she knew that a spark of life had come back into John, which Dr. Dan had said had been absent after the crash.

In the hospital, Dan had told her John had become quite complacent with his injuries. He was angry, yes, but totally uncooperative when it came to working through the healing process. He wanted no one to touch him, and he refused to allow the doctor to so much as to suggest the future possibilities of using a wheelchair or crutches. Now, Joelle knew full well that the exercises Dan had devised for John were intentionally designed to progress him toward one or the other of those very subjects. God help them all when John figured it out.

"Are you ready to get to work?" Joelle asked, coming into the room.

"I told you I wasn't going to work with you and I won't."

"The sooner you cooperate, the sooner I'll leave you alone."

"For good?" John asked her blatantly.

For the first time, John's words had cut her to the quick. Joelle was speechless for a moment. Was that the price of John's recovery? Did she dare to push him so hard that his resentment of her interference would forever sever their relationship? Was she killing their love?

Joelle studied him for a moment. The swelling had gone from his face and the healthy color had returned. For all intent and purpose, he looked the picture of health, except for the fact that he was in a cast and still unable to feel anything below the waist.

With tears in her eyes, Joelle made her decision. "If that's the price to see you walking again, then so be it." She turned away from him to retrieve some hand weights that Dan had fashioned, and she dabbed the tears from her eyes.

"I'm sorry, Joelle."

The words caught her off guard and her tears started anew. It was the first civil thing he had said to her since the accident. Refusing to acknowledge them, she froze.

"I didn't mean to hurt you. This isn't fair to either one of us, but then I suppose nothing in life guarantees us fairness." He paused for a moment. "I can't bear to think of you married to me like this. You're young and alive and healthy and whole, and you deserve to be with someone who is likewise. I can't give you the future you deserve. Can't you try to understand that?"

Joelle swallowed hard and turned to face him. The tears on her cheeks glistened when the sunlight from the window fell across her face. Her voice was but a whisper as she spoke. " 'Rise up, my love, my fair one, and come away. For, lo, the winter is past, the rain is over and gone.' "

Their eyes met. "Joelle," he groaned in a sad, childlike way, "please don't do this to me."

What all of John's anger could not accomplish, these simple words did. Broken completely, Joelle dropped the weights to the floor and fled the room with a sob.

Chapter 6

It was in the middle of the night when John woke the house with his anguished cries of pain. Lillie and Joelle both came running from the room they shared to find Dan bent over his son, rapidly massaging his right thigh.

"What is it!" Lillie exclaimed.

Both women were surprised when Dan turned to face them with a grin. "He's got a cramp in his leg and he feels it!"

Lillie and Joelle exchanged looks of astonishment. "He feels it!" Lillie said to Joelle. "Isn't that wonderful?"

"It doesn't feel so wonderful from this end of it, Mom."

Lillie moved to her son's bedside. "I hope it hurts enough to give you the desire to regain what you once had. I don't want you to live in pain, but I want you to feel everything that happens to that leg, for the rest of your life."

John looked up to meet his mother's eyes. "Me too, Mom." He winced painfully. "Me too."

Joelle stood back by the door and watched the scene. John caught sight of her in the amber glow of the room. She was wearing a long white gown with a soft blue shawl drawn around her. Her long dark hair, usually pinned neatly in a bun, fell in a swirl of curls to her hips, and John longed to touch the chestnut softness. She was the most beautiful sight he had ever beheld, and in that moment, he was glad that she had refused to leave him.

When their eyes met, it was like he was seeing her for the first time, and after the words they had exchanged earlier in the day, he could tell Joelle was still feeling cautious.

The cramp passed and everyone made their way back to bed. It was a long time before Joelle could drift back to sleep, however. She had seen the look in John's eyes and knew that he still loved her. The thing that troubled her most, however, was wondering if she was truly doing the right thing in staying. Maybe she was more torture to him, than help. How could she possibly know?

Within her heart, a voice seemed to whisper, *Trust Me, Joelle*. She knew instantly that the voice was not of her own doing. A peace began to filter through her body, and within minutes she was fast asleep.

The following morning brought a fierce wind that blew the sand about in such a vicious way that it nearly stripped the whitewash from the bank. It was nothing compared to the true sandstorms of the spring, folks assured Lillie and Joelle, but nevertheless, it was torturous and required that all of the windows be closed tight against the assault.

It was in the midst of this onslaught when a visitor arrived at the Monroe house. The weatherworn man quickly introduced himself as John's superior from Fort Bliss.

"Major Camstead, Ma'am," the man said upon entry. He removed his peaked campaign hat and tucked it under his arm. "I arrived this morning on business at Camp Furlong and they told me I might find Lieutenant Monroe here."

Lillie smiled at the man. "Yes, my son is here. He's still recovering from his accident, but I'm sure they told you this."

"Yes, Ma'am," he replied. "I would like to speak with him about the accident, if you think he's up to it."

Joelle moved to the bedroom door. "I'll check and see if he's awake."

Lillie nodded, while Joelle went in to announce the major's arrival to John. "I'm certain my son will be happy for the company, Major. Lately, he's seen little of anyone but family."

"Speaking of family," the major mumbled, reaching into his pocket, "Sergeant Monroe sends his regards." He handed an envelope to Lillie.

"It's from J.D.?" she questioned, then noted the handwriting. "How kind of you to bring it all this way. Thank you, Major."

The man blushed and feeling quite uncertain as to what he should do next, was greatly relieved when Joelle returned. "He's awake and said to join him at your convenience."

Major Camstead dismissed himself with a curt nod. "Ma'am," he said to Lillie, then again to Joelle as he passed to the bedroom. At the door he paused long enough to close it, much to the disappointment of both Lillie and Joelle.

Giving John a brief once over, Camstead grinned. "Well, Preacher, looks like you made a mess of yourself this time," he said, coming to pull a chair along John's bed.

"You're a long way from home, Bob," John replied, using his hands to push himself up on the pillows. The informality he took with the major had long ago been agreed upon between them.

"Had business with the Thirteenth and thought a visit to you was in order. How's it coming?"

"Slow," John replied. "Way too slow."

"Give it time. You can't expect everything your way. Say, that little brown-eyed beauty out there," Camstead said with a nod, "she doesn't belong to you, does she?"

John's grin broadened to a full-blown smile. "As a matter of fact, she does."

"Some guys have all the luck."

John nodded uncomfortably. "But you didn't come all this way to talk about my love life, now did you?"

"No, actually I wanted to know about the crash. Wanna tell me about it willingly or shall I order you around?" He smiled and John shook his head.

"I'm not sure I could take an order seriously. I can salute, but I sure can't get up and snap to."

"I'll take the story," the man replied. "You can salute me later."

John laughed, but thoughts of the accident sobered him rather quickly. "I was at about fifteen hundred feet when she started handling rough. The whole engine seemed like it was going to shake right out from the cowling. I shut her down to see what I could make of it, and when the prop was slowed to where it was just windmilling, I could see it had splintered apart. There was a good six inches missing off the end on one side."

"We're having a bad time of that down here. The air's so dry it's causing us to have to remove the props and put them in humidified rooms to keep them from coming unglued."

"Well, I wish you'd have figured that out before it happened to me."

"Me too, John. You don't know how sorry I was to hear about your crash."

John met his friend's eyes. They had known each other for little over a year now, but Major Robert Camstead had quickly become one of John's closest comrades-in-arms.

"I'm glad you came, Bob," John said, trying to move the conversation away from the maudlin. "I sure didn't know how I'd get to you."

"Is there anything you need that you aren't getting around here?"

"No, I have it all. Two beautiful women waiting on me hand and foot. My own personal physician and plenty of creature comforts. Who could ask for more?" John replied.

"Well, I promised J.D. I'd check you out in person," Bob said, referring to John's brother. "In fact, I just handed over a letter from him to your mother."

"Will you be here awhile?"

"No. Duty calls, and I have to get back in time to catch the eastbound."

"You mean to tell me you didn't fly over?" John questioned in disbelief.

"In case you haven't noticed, there's a sandstorm blowing around out there. It isn't a bad one, but I sure wouldn't attempt to fly through the thing. Besides, I came by train last night and that's the way they expect me to make it back."

"Yeah, well take the sand with you all the way back to Fort Bliss."

"For you, my boy, anything," Bob said and extended his hand. "John, you let us know if you need something. Anything at all, okay?"

"Sure. You know me. I never hesitate to speak my mind."

Bob paused, John's hand still firmly planted against his own. "It's a good thing God was watching over you when Jenny decided to dump you."

A frown crossed John's face. "He may have been watching, but to my way of thinking, He almost missed catching me."

"Those are strange words coming from you, Preacher."

"No stranger than the circumstance that gave them thought," John countered. "Tell J.D. I'm doing well and don't forget to ask my mother if she has any messages for him."

"I'll do that, John." Major Camstead released his hand, gave a brief salute, and left the room.

It was only moments before Joelle appeared. "You look tired, John. Why don't you try to get some rest?"

John glanced up at her for a moment. Things had changed between them since he had made her cry. He was more careful how he responded now. "I am tired, but no more so than you, I imagine. You don't look like you're getting much sleep."

Joelle defensively raised her hand to her face. "This is a harsh country, John. It isn't at all what I'm used to. The heat is starting to build and the dryness is hard on my complexion." Her words sounded formal and stiff.

"You're still the best looking woman I've ever laid eyes on," John replied, surprising them both. To cover up his embarrassment, he added, "Now get out of here and let me sleep."

Joelle did just that, smiling as she closed his door quietly behind her. He was more and more like the John she had fallen in love with. Soon, she thought to herself, soon she would have him back and he would walk again.

∽

March, 1916 roared in like a lion and continued to roar. The temperature rose, becoming quite uncomfortable in the afternoon. Used to the chillier mountain valley winters of Bandelero, Lillie and Joelle found their clothing heavy and cumbersome. Deeming that the heat would be much easier to bear in appropriate clothing, the women took Dan's suggestion and went shopping.

"Get something serviceable," Lillie suggested. "Something easy to wash out by hand and light enough to dry quickly."

"In this dry heat," Joelle said, mopping her damp brow, "everything dries quickly."

Lillie smiled. "It certainly isn't home. I miss the snow and our cold mornings. Dan calls it 'cuddle weather' and I think it's about my favorite time of year."

"You and Dr. Dan sure seem happy with each other," Joelle said with a sigh. "I just wish John could see that I love him and accept the fact that I want to be with him no matter what his physical condition is."

Lillie paused in her consideration of a ready-made skirt. "John knows you love him, Joelle. It's just hard for him to think of disappointing you. His love for you runs deep, and he takes everything very seriously. Marriage is no exception."

"I know," Joelle said and there were tears in her eyes. "It's just that I'm afraid he's going to put up a permanent barrier between us. I'm afraid. . ." Her voice cracked and Lillie put an arm around her.

"Don't be. God will help John to make it through this. Have patience and faith." Joelle wiped at her eyes and nodded. Lillie smiled. "Now, what do you think about this green skirt?"

⁓

Rumors of the war in Europe flooded the pages of the local newspaper and even in the local theater propaganda ran rampant. *The Beasts in Gray* was advertised for viewing at two bits a person, no children allowed. Women were discouraged from attending the picture with the ghastly posters outside the theater depicting the Huns in spiked helmets tearing at the puritanical white robes of Belgian women. Joelle shuddered at the thought of what those poor European women must be enduring, but she said nothing to anyone about it. Somehow, with it left unsaid, it seemed less real and more easily dealt with.

The saggy iron bed, with its groaning springs and lumpy mattress, became less and less appealing to Joelle, as night after night passed. Lillie, too, grew tired of the poor substitute. At home, she had a fine, down-filled mattress that was as soft and comfortable as any bed had ever been. This, combined with the growing heat, was beginning to wear thin on her nerves and caused Daniel to begin seeking a way, once again, to move John from Columbus.

By the eighth of March, the Monroes and Joelle had shared their cramped quarters for nearly one month. John had made remarkable improvements. He now had feeling in his legs and, although he was unable to walk, he endured hours of exercises devised by his father.

John and Joelle still had their occasional fight, but John admittedly came to realize just how much she had done for him. It was still hard for him to accept the fact that she had seen him at his worst, but even this humiliation was passing from John's concern. Now, uppermost in his mind, was to strengthen the tender threads that bound his heart to hers.

"I have tickets for us to leave on the twentieth," Dan shared that night after supper. "I even managed to secure a private car, thanks to Garrett Lucas."

Lillie smiled. "Had one sitting in the backyard, did he?"

Dan laughed. "Just about. You know how Garrett is. He's always managed to get his hands on just about whatever he needs. Anyway, he's making the arrangements to have the car put on and brought down for the trip home. This way, I can keep John in bed for most of the trip. I think he'll manage quite well with it."

"Well I for one, will not miss this heat and sand," Joelle said. "May I go tell John the news?"

"Sure," Dan said, sharing a smile with his wife. "Go on and tell him."

Joelle knocked lightly at the open door to John's room. No doubt he had already heard the exchange, but Joelle decided they needed to discuss the future.

"Hello," Joelle said, trying her best to gauge what kind of mood John was in.

"Hello." His voice was warm, almost mellow, and Joelle felt her heart skip a beat as John's eyes appraised her appearance.

"Did you hear your father's news? We're going home on the twentieth."

"Yes," John said softly, "I heard."

"I thought it might be good for us to discuss what happens when we return to Bandelero."

"What do you mean?" John questioned.

"Well," Joelle said slowly, "I thought it might be good for us to go ahead and get married." She held her breath for a moment, wondering if John would launch into a tirade. When he remained silent, she continued. "I mean, it just makes sense. I plan to be a part of your recovery. I certainly don't intend to go back to the ranch with my brother and Daughtry. I don't want to ever be that far away from you again." She felt as though she was rambling, but the fear of letting John speak something negative kept her talking.

"I'd be happy to live with your folks for however long it takes to get you up on your feet."

Here, John interrupted. "That might never happen. I told you once before, Joelle, I may never walk again."

Joelle nodded. "I know, but it doesn't matter to me. I still love you, John, in spite of everything we've gone through of late. I don't mind the fights we've had or the harsh words, but I don't want to be cast aside like old, worn-out boots."

John laughed out loud at this. "You're the best looking worn boots I've ever seen." Joelle blushed but cast John a shy smile. John sobered at the look. "You really are beautiful. Too beautiful to spend your life being a nursemaid to an invalid. I can't make you honor a promise you made when there was so much more hope to our future."

Joelle shook her head. "I have no future without you. Don't you understand? You're everything to me. Whether you walk or talk or run in circles. It doesn't matter."

"I can't expect you to understand, Joelle. You're a woman."

"And just what is that supposed to mean?"

"If I can't walk, I can't very well put bread on the table, now can I?" His voice held a bit of sarcasm and Joelle felt angry that he had taken such a tone with her.

"What's wrong with me getting a job? I could take in sewing or maybe open a shop. There are all kinds of possibilities. I know my father would advance me the money to start a business, if I asked him to."

John shook his head furiously. "No! I won't support a wife on the charity of others. My folks caring for me is bad enough. I certainly won't ask them to support a wife, as well."

"I didn't ask you to," Joelle snapped. "I've already told you that I'd be happy to support us. I just want there to be an 'us,' don't you understand?" she questioned, emphasizing the word "you."

"It wouldn't be right, Joelle. You and I both know what's expected of a husband and having you out doing my job wouldn't be right. Think of what people would say and how it would look."

"Since when have you ever cared what people had to say?"

"I care, Joelle. I care because I know it would hurt you. Besides, you've talked a million times of wanting to have a family. A large family, as I recall. You can't have that with me. At least not now, maybe never." John shook his head again. "I honestly believe it's best if you go home to your brother, then go on back to Kansas City. If I do recover and you're still available, then perhaps—"

"Perhaps nothing, John Monroe!" Joelle crossed the room to the door. "I don't want to hear any more of this. I refuse your solutions." She stormed out of the room and slammed the door behind her.

"Joelle!" John called. "Joelle be reasonable!"

Dan and Lillie exchanged a look as Joelle continued to the room she shared with Lillie, where she again slammed the door behind her.

～

That evening, as Joelle prepared for bed, she found herself thinking of John and what he had said. She did not want to admit that his words had any basis in truth, but in the quiet of her room, the evidence of that seemed blatantly obvious.

How much longer would it be before he could walk? His spine seemed to have fared better than anyone could possibly have hoped, and even Dan seemed confident that John's recovery was just a matter of time. But what if it wasn't? What if it was as John had said. . .that something might never happen?

Doffing her cotton day dress, Joelle slipped into her nightgown and slowly braided her hair. The heat, which was so unbearable during the day, was quickly replaced with the chill of the desert. Once the sun was down, Joelle was quite happy to light a fire in the stove and hover around it while fixing supper. A soldier friend of John's had even told her that the water often froze in their canteens overnight, but Joelle found it hard to imagine when the heat of day bore down on the small village.

Outside her still-open window, Joelle could hear the *clip-clop* of several horses and knew it was the cavalry patrol riding their nightly vigil. It made her feel safe to know they were so carefully watched over, and even though the house was situated on the edge of the town, the army clearly honored their duty to protect all of the citizens of Columbus.

Extinguishing her lamp, Joelle crawled into bed and drifted off to sleep. She was not aware when Lillie came to bed, but she did wake up when the army doctor sent an orderly to request Dan's help in surgery. Lillie got Dan's bag, while he finished dressing, and Joelle fell back to sleep without even hearing Dan leave.

In her dreams, Joelle heard the rush of water as though a flood were bearing down on their tiny hut. The sound rapidly changed to that of horses' hooves and, suppressing a scream, Joelle bolted upright in bed.

The thunderous noise had been no dream. Lillie shot out of the bed with a cry, and Joelle quickly followed her to the door. Without opening it, they huddled against it, listening for several moments.

"What's happening? Is it the army?" Joelle questioned breathlessly. She reached out to pull the curtain back from the window when shots rang out. "Is it Villa's men?" Joelle asked, cowering in fear.

At the sound of gunfire, Lillie grabbed Joelle's hand. "It doesn't sound like they're friendly, whoever they are."

Just then, John's voice rang out. "Mom! Joelle! Where are you?"

Lillie pulled Joelle with her to John's room. By now, the predawn silence was filled with gunfire and Spanish curses. Lillie shuddered when a voice rang out just outside their window.

"Death to gringo soldiers!" the voice yelled. It was soon joined by another. "Kill them all!"

Joelle turned to Lillie. "We have to hide John," she said urgently.

"I'm not going anywhere," John answered, coming to the edge of his bed.

"John, you can't fight anyone in your condition. Those men are seeking the blood of soldiers, and you are a soldier. Joelle is right," Lillie said firmly. "We have to hide you."

"Just give me a gun," John protested.

"We don't have a gun," Joelle replied. "The closet, Lillie, we can get him into the closet."

Lillie nodded. "I'll get his right arm, you get his left. John, you keep your feet under you and help us as much as you can."

John shook his head but found his mother very determined. "I'm not a coward. I can't let you face them alone. If they were to come in here—"

Gunshots sounded loudly and Joelle cringed. The army Hotchkiss machine guns fired off a rapid reply, but it did little to ease the worry of either woman.

Joelle and Lillie were already moving John toward the closet when the sound of someone trying to push in the front door caught their attention. There was another shout of curses and orders in Spanish that only John understood in full.

"They're going to knock the door in," he said flatly.

"Hurry, Lillie," Joelle whispered and nearly pulled John's arm out of its socket. "You get in there with John, and I'll go hold them off."

"Don't do this," John said, looking down at Joelle. "Stay here with me. You can't fight them, Joelle. You don't know what these animals are capable of."

"They're capable of killing you," Joelle said quite frankly. "Anything else, anything at all, is preferable to that."

She shoved John into the closet, feeling a twinge of guilt when he lost his balance and slipped to the floor. Lillie stepped over his legs and crouched down beside him.

"It's a tight fit, but it'll work," she whispered to Joelle.

"Good. Don't come out, no matter what you hear. You have to keep John here, Lillie. Please don't let him act heroic." Joelle's eyes pleaded with Lillie. Each woman understood the anguish of the other. Both were fighting to save the life of the man they loved more dearly than life itself.

"No, don't let her go out there," John was struggling against his mother and trying to ease past her in the darkness.

Joelle closed the closet door, sealing them inside. Silently, she prayed it would not become their tomb.

Chapter 7

Y ou have to stop her," John said, taking hold of his mother's shoulders. He could not see anything in the blackness of their hiding place, but he knew she was facing him.

"John, there's nothing we can do. If you expose yourself, they'll kill you. For Joelle's sake, if not mine, please be quiet. Maybe they'll leave when they see no one else is here."

The noise outside grew louder as shouts of American soldiers rallied hope in the night.

"Dear God, what have I done?" John moaned and slumped back against the closet wall. "If only I would have—"

"Hush, John," Lillie insisted with her hand to his lips. " 'If onlys' are behind us. We can't change what is. This is the time to give up the past. This is the time to maybe go to God about those things you said."

John realized how right she was. "I was so angry when the plane started to fall from the sky. I couldn't control her well enough. I should have been able to. I blamed God for letting me crash. I said—"

"John, it doesn't matter. Take it back to Him and seek His forgiveness," Lillie said softly. She put her arm around his shoulders and pulled him close. "He already knows how sorry you are. Let it go, John. Let Him forgive you."

John knew she was right. It was all he had wanted from the start. Why had he allowed his anger to eat away at him? Why had he allowed his self-pity and frustration to separate him from Joelle? There was so much he wanted to say to her, so much he needed to tell her. Only now, there might not ever be a chance to do so.

They could hear the pounding and gunfire outside the house. John sought God in prayer, and Lillie did the same. They heard the front door give way, followed by the yipping and howls of several men. Joelle was protesting loudly that she was alone and that the soldiers were already on their way to protect her.

The voices grew louder, with Joelle's shouted protests.

"I should go to her," Lillie whispered.

"No," John said. "It's bad enough she's out there, but if you join her, they'll probably kill you both. I can't bear it as it is. Please, Mom, stay here with me."

Lillie put her free hand over his. She opened her mouth to reply when Joelle's screams filled the house. John struggled to move to the door, but Lillie held him back, using her body as a block between him and his goal.

"No! No!" Lillie said as loudly as she dare. "John, stay here."

Joelle screamed again and several gunshots rang out. There were shouts and the sound of glass breaking, then after awhile the noise grew strangely silent. Lillie wondered if Joelle had run from the house to escape her attackers, while John prayed as he had never before prayed, for the safety of the only woman he would ever love.

Time passed in the pounding beats of their own hearts. Lillie had no idea how long they had been in the closet. She had no way of knowing if the sun had yet come up or if it was still dark outside. It felt like the world had come to a standstill, and a nightmarish eternity had somehow begun.

The gunfire continued, though much more sporadically than before, and the undeniable smell of smoke was heavy on the air.

"I'd better see what's going on," Lillie told John. "If they've set enough fires, we might be in danger of burning up."

"Let me."

Lillie pushed John back again. "You can't. You may have already injured yourself. Please, John, just stay here. I'll be right back."

Lillie opened the closet door the barest crack and found a faint glow of light giving view to the bedroom. No one seemed to be there and so Lillie eased the door open and crawled out.

Her muscles ached from the cramped quarters and awkward positioning. She was not a young girl anymore and it grieved her to feel the reminder. Favoring her right leg, which had fallen asleep beneath her, Lillie tried to tip-toe to the bedroom door.

Putting her ear to the wood, Lillie listened and heard nothing. *Do I open it or not?* she wondered silently. A sound behind her caused Lillie to start and step back. John appeared in the doorway of the closet.

"Listen!" he said in a voice just above a whisper. "They're leaving."

"How do you know?" Lillie questioned. She could speak very little Spanish even after all her years in New Mexico.

John crawled out into the room. "They're retreating. The army must have them on the run."

Lillie moved quickly to the window. "I can't tell what's happening," she moaned. "It's still too dark to tell. The sun's coming up, but I just can't make it all out."

"They're leaving, I'm sure of it. Find Joelle, Mom. Find her and make sure she's all right," John said, pulling himself to the side of his bed.

Lillie nodded. "John, you should stay in the closet until we're sure about what's happening."

"I'm all right," he said and motioned to the closed bedroom door. "Just find Joelle."

Lillie moved cautiously and turned the knob of the door as silently as she could. Peering out into the front room, Lillie could not make out a single thing except the faint glow of dawn against the front door opening.

"Joelle?" she whispered the name. A rush of mounted men raced past the front door, causing Lillie to momentarily pull back. Once they were gone, however, she pressed forward into the room.

Picking her way through the debris of overturned chairs and table, Lillie called again. "Joelle, are you here?"

Nothing. The silence was maddening, and Lillie knew she dared not light a lamp. Getting on her hands and knees, Lillie moved through the mess into the shadowy corners of the room. Her heart nearly stopped when her hand felt the warm touch of flesh.

"Joelle!" she exclaimed, but there was no reply.

Lillie ran her hand across the unmistakable feminine form. "Joelle, speak to me. Joelle," Lillie reached down and pulled the unconscious form to her breast. She felt revulsion as Joelle's nightgown fell away from her body in a tattered heap.

"Oh, God, no," Lillie moaned, rocking Joelle back and forth. "Oh, please, God, help us."

No longer caring whether anyone saw the light, Lillie raced to her untouched bedroom and got the lamp and one of her own nightgowns.

"Mother!" John yelled, sensing that all was not well. "What's going on out there?"

"Hush, John. Please be still, Joelle's hurt." Lillie knew that with her son's determination she might very well see him crawling through the doorway at any moment. Lighting the lamp and putting it to one side, Lillie dressed Joelle's battered body in the nightdress and eased her back to the floor.

Lillie assessed the situation gravely. Joelle had been hit repeatedly across the face. There were multiple bruises already forming, and her lips were bloody. She was mercifully unconscious, and Lillie could only pray that she had been that way throughout her attack.

"John, I have to find your father," Lillie said, coming to her son. "I'm going to get you into bed and go after him."

"Don't bother with me," John said sternly. "What about Joelle?"

"She's hurt."

"Is it bad?"

"Yes," Lillie replied gravely. "I'm afraid it's very bad, John."

"This is all my fault!" he yelled and pounded the bedframe with his fist. "All my fault!"

"John, it doesn't matter who you blame. It certainly won't change matters now. Joelle needs help, and I have to find your father. This isn't any more your fault than it is mine. The madmen who shot up the town are the ones we can blame for this fiasco. Now, stay here," Lillie instructed.

His mother's words rang over and over in his head. John was spent from crawling to the bed from the closet, but now he prayed for the strength to go to Joelle.

"I have to be there for her, Lord," he whispered. Making a slow, but steady progress to the door, John was consumed with guilt. He had brought her here. His accident had caused her to rush to his side.

"I told her to go home," he muttered, moving inch by painful inch. "I begged her to leave this place."

John concentrated on each movement. Pull with the right arm. Pull with the left. His legs, still weak and mostly useless to his efforts, dragged behind him like a seal crossing a beach.

He was through the bedroom door when he saw her. Even from several feet away, he knew she was badly hurt. John doubled his efforts, pulling himself alongside Joelle and nearly knocking over the lamp. Reaching down, he turned her face toward the light and cried out in anguish at the sight.

"Oh, Joelle! Why? Why did this happen to you?" His cries were like that of a wounded beast.

Gently, he lifted her against himself and cradled her in his arms. "Joelle, wake up, my beloved," he whispered against her ear. "Please, wake up. I love you, Joelle. Oh, how I love you."

He traced the swollen jaw and wiped at the dried blood around her lips. "God, please help her," John begged. "Please, God. Please!"

Lillie and Daniel returned to the house to find John, holding Joelle against himself.

"John, you should be in bed," Dan stated firmly. He took hold of Joelle and eased her back onto the floor. "Lillie, clear the way."

"I want to stay with her," John told his father.

Dan hoisted John to his feet and half carried, half dragged his son to the bedroom. "You can help her most by letting me work on her without interference. You aren't helping yourself or her by endangering the progress you've made. Now, do I have to sedate you to keep you here?" Daniel questioned, placing John in his bed.

"No," John answered. "I'll wait here. But, please, promise me you'll come back and tell me everything as soon as you can."

"I will," Dan promised.

By the time Dan had returned to the front room, Lillie had cleared away most of the clutter. Together they worked to treat Joelle's injured body and, much to Lillie's heartfelt sorrow, Dan confirmed her suspicions that Joelle had been raped.

The anger in Dan's voice was barely controlled. "What kind of animal does such a hideous and degrading thing?"

"Poor baby," Lillie said, brushing back dark brown ringlets from Joelle's face. "She's just a little girl, Dan."

"I know, Lillie. I know." He reached out and touched his wife's cheek. "We're going to see her through this," he told her.

"She saved John's life and mine," Lillie stated with a wavering voice. "Oh, Dan, we all might be dead but for Joelle's sacrifice."

"Let's put her to bed," Dan said softly. "You too," he added, pulling Lillie to her feet. "You've been through too much as it is."

"I couldn't possibly rest. You'll need me to help you now. No doubt they'll be coming for you to help at the hospital and I'll have to care for John and Joelle without you. So you must tell me what to do and how to care for them properly," Lillie said, and Dan knew that she was right.

"First, we put Joelle to bed. Then we'll wash her up and better treat the lacerations." Dan reached down and picked up Joelle as though she weighed no more than a sack of flour.

"You lead the way," he told Lillie, and she quickly complied.

Lillie smoothed out the covers as Dan placed Joelle's still body onto the bed. "Bring the lamp, Lillie, and a basin of water."

Lillie left her husband and hurried to do as he asked. John called out to her, begging to know about Joelle, but Lillie could tell him nothing for fear of breaking into tears.

"I'll send your father as soon as I can," she told her son and hurried to bring Dan the water. "John's asking about her," Lillie said as though Dan could have missed the exchange of conversation just outside the door.

"I know. I'll go talk to him."

"What will you tell him?" Lillie asked, meeting her husband's eyes.

"I don't know." Dan's voice was uncharacteristically hollow. "I suppose the truth is the best."

"It'll tear him apart," Lillie murmured.

"But he'll have to be told sooner or later," Dan reasoned. "Better now, while he's expecting to hear the worst."

Dan walked from the room leaving Lillie to care for Joelle and went to his son's bed. Sunlight was now beaming through the open window and John could tell by the gravity of his father's expression the news was not good.

"How bad is she hurt?" he questioned.

"I'm not sure," Dan replied. "She's still unconscious, but that's from a blow to the head. I don't know how bad a hit she sustained, but there doesn't seem to be a great deal of swelling. Her heart rate is strong and even, so I think she'll pull through."

John looked at his father suspiciously. "You aren't telling me everything."

"No," Dan said, bringing a chair beside the bed. Wearily, he sat down. "John, there's no easy way to tell you this and I desperately wish it weren't so."

"What is it?" John nearly yelled. "You said she was strong. Are you going to tell me now that she's not going to make it?"

"No, it's not that." Dan struggled for the right words. "Joelle wasn't just beaten."

John stared at his father for a moment. "What are you saying?" The truth of what he feared his father would reveal was starting to dawn on him. "Please, tell me you aren't saying. . ."

"John, these men were obviously animals. Joelle fought for all she was worth—"

"No!" he cried. "No! It isn't fair! She was saving my worthless life!" John pounded the mattress, while tears streamed down his face.

Dan reached out to still his son's fist. "Fair or not, what's happened has happened. Joelle is going to need you now more than ever. She's going to feel bad enough from the physical injuries she's sustained, but the emotional scars are going to run even deeper. She's not going to need someone who's going to spend his time pouting about its being his fault. She's going to need someone who can show her it doesn't matter. That she had no choice in the matter, and that she's still the beautiful and loving woman that you fell in love with."

John swallowed hard and nodded. "I can do that for her. God knows what she's done for me. I love her so much, Dad. Just make her well, and I'll do the rest."

"No, Son," Dan said, with a shake of his head. "You and I can't do it alone. God will heal Joelle just as He's worked to heal you."

Chapter 8

J oelle became conscious in waves of sensation. First she smelled smoke and feared that the house was on fire. Then she struggled to move but found her body racked with pain. Her lips refused to move as she tried to speak, and she tasted blood when she tried to wet them with her tongue.

What's wrong with me? Joelle's mind wandered through a shadowy maze. *Why can't I open my eyes?* She tried to force her eyelids to part, but they refused to do as she willed them. A deep moaning came from somewhere inside her, but even then Joelle could not rationalize the reaction.

"Don't try to move, Joelle," the soft voice of Lillie came from somewhere overhead. "You've been hurt. Just lie still."

"John," she moaned the name. "Where is John?"

"John is all right, Joelle. You saved his life. You saved me too."

Saved his life? What is Lillie talking about? Joelle's eyes opened a fraction and through the tiny slits she could barely make out Lillie's tear-streaked face.

"I hurt," Joelle murmured.

"I know. Dan left some medicine for you, and I'll see to it that the pain eases. Can you swallow some liquid?"

"I think so." The words barely croaked out from her raw throat. "What happened?"

"You don't remember?" Lillie questioned in surprise. She stared down at the battered face and ached to make the swelling go away.

"No," Joelle whispered and seemed to fall back to sleep.

"It's just as well," Lillie said softly. She retrieved the medication and poured out a measure for Joelle. Lifting the young woman's head just a bit caused Joelle to awaken again.

"Lillie?"

"Here, just drink this. It will make you feel better."

Joelle did as she was told and fell back to sleep. Somewhere in her mind she thought she heard gunfire and the raucous laughter of foul-smelling men, but then it faded and Joelle heard nothing.

∼

It was not until the next day that Joelle truly became conscious. She opened her eyes, again finding it a pain-filled effort, but this time a tiny seed of memory came to her. She remembered a gloved hand, slamming hard against her face.

"How do you feel?" Dan's voice was soft and full of concern.

Joelle turned her head and felt the dull ache inside grow to a throb. "I hurt."

"You will for a time. We can control it, though. I have medication for you. Are you hungry?"

"No." Joelle struggled to remember something, but she could not begin to think of what it was. "I'm thirsty."

Dan nodded and poured a glass of water from a pitcher at her bedside. "Here," he said and eased his arm behind her.

Joelle drank slowly, still trying to figure out exactly what had happened. She remembered there had been something wrong. The smell of smoke came back to her. "Was there a fire?" she whispered to Dan.

"Yes, there was," he said and laid her back against the pillow. "The Commercial Hotel was burned to the ground by the *Villistas*."

"Were we there?" Joelle questioned. Her mind struggled to clear the haze.

"No," Dan replied. "Good thing too. The *Villistas* killed several people there before setting it on fire. It's still smoldering."

"I smell it," Joelle replied.

Dan pulled out a stethoscope and leaned over Joelle. "I'm going to listen to your heart," he said softly. "Don't be afraid."

Joelle thought it strange that he would say such a thing, but when he reached for the front of her nightgown her hands instinctively shot out. "No!"

It was the one thing to trigger her memory. Someone else had reached out to her like that. Only that man had not been a doctor; his actions had been violent and ugly.

"It's all right, Joelle. It's me, Dr. Dan. I'm going to help you get better. I won't hurt you."

Joelle shook her head from side to side. The ugliness was coming back to her. She remembered the foul odor of whiskey on the breath of the men who had grabbed her. She tried to block the image of a leering grin and dark fiery eyes.

"No! No! No!" she screamed and threw herself to the far side of the bed. Crawling back away from Dan, Joelle began to cry. She was unable to stop the assault that relived itself in her mind, and all she could do was cower like a frightened child.

Lillie came running at the sound of Joelle's cries. She jumped up on the bed and pulled Joelle into her arms, cradling her as a mother would a small child.

"It's all right, Joelle. Don't cry. No one will hurt you anymore." Lillie's voice soothed Joelle's anguish.

"Make them go away," Joelle moaned, with her hands to her head. "Make them go away."

"They're gone, Joelle. They can't hurt you anymore." Lillie's calm insistence caused Joelle to still.

"Are you sure they're gone?"

"Yes," Lillie whispered, "I'm sure. Dan and John and I are the only ones here, and we won't let anything bad happen to you."

"I'm afraid," Joelle croaked in a barely audible voice. "I'm so afraid."

"God is your strength and salvation," Lillie whispered. "You need not fear anyone. He is with you, and He will keep you from harm."

Joelle rejected the words. "No, He doesn't care. He left me alone. He doesn't care."

Lillie looked at Daniel with deep sorrow in her eyes. "He cares, Joelle. He never stopped. Please don't harden your heart. God cares."

Dan reached out to hand Lillie a glass of medicine. "Drink this, Joelle," he said, being careful not to touch her.

Joelle opened her eyes and accepted the medication gratefully. She prayed it might cause her to sleep. She prayed it would take away the horrible images in her mind.

$\sim$

John heard the anguished cries and felt the helplessness of his situation. He could not go to her. He could not comfort her. What use was he to anyone?

"Stop feeling sorry for yourself, John Monroe." He could hear Joelle's words as if she were standing beside him. He had given much time over to self-pity.

"I have to stop this," he said aloud. "I won't be any good to anyone if I wallow here forever."

"Did you say something, Son?" Dan came into the room with a tired look.

"I heard Joelle. How is she?"

"She's starting to remember."

John closed his eyes and clenched his jaw. If only he could help her forget her pain and sorrow. "I want to see her," John said, opening his eyes to meet his father's.

"You can't, John. She's terrified. I think it would only make matters worse."

"But she loves me and I love her. I want her to know that none of this matters. It won't change my love for her."

"Now is not the time, John. She didn't want me there. She'll only allow Lillie to touch her. You have to understand, John. Every man, even you and me. . ." He hesitated. "She can't separate us from her attackers. She can't find comfort in you right now. Give her time. You must give her time."

John rubbed his legs and thought on his father's words. "All right. . .I'll wait."

~

Dan found himself on a constant run between the hospital and his house. When he was not trying to help with the severely wounded, it seemed there were other less serious doctoring skills needed. Always someone occupied his time, until in frustration and exhaustion, he slipped away and tended to the needs of his family.

Within a day, the train arrived to bring workers bearing Red Cross armbands and scores of white-clad nurses. Dan wondered where they had found so many people willing to volunteer for duty in the small, forsaken town. Gratefully, he relieved himself of the massive obligations and turned his affairs outside of home over to those who had come to help.

Joelle climbed out of bed on the fourth day and, although her body still ached, she said very little about her pain. In fact, she said very little of anything to anyone. Even Lillie found it difficult to draw out the tiniest detail and rarely did Joelle even seem to notice when Lillie spoke directly to her.

It was Joelle's way of dealing with her pain. She knew in full what had happened that night, and it was hard enough to come to terms with it, much less to talk about it.

John had pleaded to see her, but Joelle had refused. How could she face him now? She was soiled and used by others. She would never again be John's beloved, and she wanted nothing to do with anything that would remind her of her loss. That was the reason she began to plan how she would leave. Somehow and by some means, she had to leave Columbus and get as far from John and his parents as she possibly could. Only then, she reasoned, would the demons leave her mind. Only then, would she be free from the memories.

"Joelle?" Lillie questioned, coming cautiously into the room with a tray of food. "I've brought you lunch."

"I don't want it," Joelle replied flatly.

"You need to eat. It will help you heal."

Joelle shot her a look of disbelief, then quickly turned away. "Just leave it, then."

Lillie put the tray on the bedside table and went to sit beside Joelle. "You know I love you as a daughter, Joelle," she began. "I just want to help you through this. You've done so much for John and for Dan and me. Please let us help you."

"There's nothing you can do," Joelle stated simply, refusing to look at Lillie.

Lillie reached out and touched Joelle's hand. "When I was around your age, I lost my first husband and the child we were expecting in a tragic accident. I thought God the most cruel and inhumane Being. I railed against Him and felt that He, above all others, knew nothing of my pain. But I was wrong, Joelle. It was through my pain and that tragedy that I met Dan. He too had his own pains from the past. He had lost a wife in childbirth and was also very angry at God."

Joelle pulled back her hand. "I'm sorry for your losses, but it has nothing to do with me."

"It does in a way," Lillie replied softly. "You've lived through a hideous nightmare. You feel that God has shown you all manner of cruelty and punishment. But He hasn't, Joelle. He hasn't sought to harm you, and you mustn't turn away from Him now."

Joelle's eyes blazed. "I didn't turn away from Him, Lillie. He cast me aside. The night he allowed those men. . ." Her words fell into a void of silence. "He threw me away," Joelle finally said.

"No, He didn't." Lillie struggled for just the right words. "We often go through bad things, but not because of God. We are as wheat being sifted. . . being made pure. The bad with the good, you might say, and from both we grow and learn how to cope with the challenges of life. The evil in this world, those men, and their sinful natures caused this, not God."

Joelle got to her feet. "Please go, Lillie. I just want to be alone."

"John's asking to see you. He loves you so much."

"He won't love me when he knows the truth," Joelle stated with hollow eyes staring blankly at Lillie.

"He knows the truth, Joelle."

Lillie's words hit Joelle as though she had been slapped. "He knows?" Her voice was small and weak.

"Yes, and he loves you even more. He knows that what happened to you, happened because you were saving his life. Oh, Child, he knows what they did, and it breaks his heart. But not because he thinks you are less than what you were, but because you think you are less than what he could love."

Joelle's eyes rimmed with tears. "He'd come to hate me."

"Never!" Lillie declared. "He could never hate you."

"Please, just go. Tell him to forget me. Tell him I release him from the obligation of our engagement. It's what he wanted before the attack. Now I see the wisdom of it."

"No, Joelle. John doesn't want to lose you. He never wanted that."

"He just feels sorry for me like he feared I felt for him."

"Joelle," Lillie tried to speak.

Joelle just shook her head. "Please, just leave me alone."

When Lillie was gone, Joelle sat back down and stared at the food on the tray. Food, water, air to breathe. How simple it all seemed. The basic requirements to keep a human body alive. But what of the spirit? What of the heart and soul of a person? What could raise those from the dead, when murder had been committed against them?

"Joelle!"

Joelle's eyes tightened shut, and her hand went to her throat at the sound of John calling her name. He kept doing that. Kept calling to her. Kept declaring his love and begging her to come to him.

"Joelle, I love you! Please don't stop loving me!"

Joelle felt the hot tears slide down her cheeks. "I'll never stop loving you, John. But, I can't be your wife," she whispered. "You deserve someone pure, and that can never be me."

⁓

After Lillie left the house to take supper to Dan at the hospital, Joelle grabbed what few things she could handle and left the house. She had no idea where she would go or how she would make her way from Columbus. All she knew was that she could no longer bear to hear John's pleading voice.

She left a simple note explaining her undying gratitude and love, with emphasis for John that her heart would forever belong to him alone. She pleaded for understanding and hoped that in time, John's pain would pass and that he would love another.

Lillie found the note upon her return and with tears in her eyes, took it to her son. "She's gone," she stated simply and handed John the letter.

He scanned it quickly. "Go find Dad. Get him to send out a search for her. She can't be far. We have to bring her back."

Lillie nodded. "If you think it best, I will. But, John, what if Joelle only hates us for interfering?"

"She can get as angry and hateful as she likes," John declared. "I owe her that, given what I put her through. Just go quickly, Mom. We can't waste any time." Lillie nodded and hurriedly left the room to retrieve Dan.

John eased his weight to the side of the bed. *Useless things,* he thought, pounding his hands against his still-weak legs. *If only I could walk, I could go after her myself*, he thought. But no, he could not even get off the bed without help. Here he was in a land he did not know well, with the love of his life fleeing from him and no way to go to her.

"Oh, God," he whispered, "if only You would heal me and let me walk. If only You would give me the power to go after her."

Outside his open window, John heard the haunting strains of a Spanish melody. The guitar's rich strings poured out the accompaniment of the once-popular "*La Golondrina*"—"The Swallow."

The Spanish words drifted up to pierce John's heart. He easily translated them, and the realization of Joelle's flight was brought home in ineffable irony.

"Where will she go, swift and weary,
    The swallow that leaves from here?
But if in the country you strayed
    Seeking shelter and unable to find it!
Next to my bed I will place her nest,
    In which she can spend the season. . .
I, too, am in the lost land:
    Oh! *Cielo santo! Y sin poder volar*!"

Oh! Heaven! And unable to fly!

Chapter 9

Joelle had no means to escape Columbus and so, in desperation, she snuck aboard a freight car when the opportunity presented itself. The train moved out of Columbus leaving behind scores of national newspapermen and an ever-growing command of soldiers. Joelle had heard it rumored, while waiting for the train, that President Wilson was sending troops out after Pancho Villa and his men. She silently hoped the army would slaughter all of them.

It was easy to slip onto the train. No one paid her any attention and, without regard to her own safety, Joelle threw herself into the back of a halfway empty car and settled down for the ride. She fell asleep and in such complete exhaustion found the first peace she had known in days. She was still bruised and aching from her ordeal, but her real pain was emotional. The never-ending bombardment of nightmares usually allowed her little escape from her memories. Gratefully, she succumbed to the rocking motion of the train car, finally realizing that she no longer cared if she lived or died.

When she woke up, Joelle adjusted her eyes to the darkness. Somewhere along the way, someone had closed the freight car door, leaving it pitch black inside. At first it frightened her, then, feeling that nothing else could hurt her more than she had already been hurt, Joelle eased her body into a sitting position and waited for the train to reach its unknown destination.

She thought of John. She could not help it. Somehow she knew that no matter where she went, she would always think of John. She remembered with fondest memories his laughing eyes and quick wit. She even smiled at the memory of their arguments. John was so good and loving. She could only hope that the woman he one day married would be worthy of him.

"Let him marry and be happy, God," she whispered the prayer, then started at the thought of talking to God. Had she not concluded that God no longer listened to her?

I'm listening, Joelle.

It was not an audible voice, but Joelle heard it, nevertheless.

"But You left me alone!" Joelle declared.

Never, My child.

Joelle felt the train slowing, and whether it was due to a planned stop or merely the obligation of an upcoming town, Joelle prepared herself to exit the car.

The train groaned to a stop, and although Joelle had no idea where she had arrived, she thrust her full weight against the door and managed to open it enough to jump to the ground.

It was dark outside and cold. Colder than she had remembered in Columbus. But then, in Columbus she had never before ventured outside in the dead of night.

There was a small train depot and a smattering of people milling around the train engine. Joelle crept silently to the side of the depot and down the sandy roadway. She passed by several darkened adobe buildings. They seemed oblivious to her plight in their orange-brown silence.

The moonlight overhead did little to aid her journey, and finally Joelle sat down against the side of a small building and considered what she should do. The town seemed quite inhospitable at the lateness of the hour, and Joelle began to wonder if she should just seek out the nearest telegraph and wire her parents.

"No, I can't go home to them. I can't go home until I know," she whispered to herself. A frightening question had risen up to haunt Joelle, and she desperately desired to have it answered before she made any plans for her future.

"You'll freeze out here, Child," the voice was gentle, ancient, and kind.

Joelle would have jumped at the sound of the voice, but her weariness of spirit gave her no reason to care. She gazed up into the face of an elderly man, a priest it seemed from the look of his clothing.

"I'll be fine," she answered and clutched her bag for warmth.

"I dreamed of a lamb caught in a snare," the white-haired man replied as though Joelle had remained silent. "It was so real that I had to come check."

"Did you find one?" Joelle asked innocently.

The man's wrinkled face broke into a smile. "I believe I have."

Joelle felt immediately at ease. "I'm no lamb, but I suppose you could say I'm caught in a snare."

"Come along, little one. These old bones won't take the desert cold. I have a fire and a room that will serve you well. Rise up and come with me."

Joelle stared at him in mute surprise. His words were so like those of John's when he had quoted Song of Solomon. Struggling against the need for comfort and the desire to fade into oblivion, Joelle got to her feet and sighed.

"I suppose it would be nice to get warm."

The priest nodded and began to walk. "I am Father Cooper and I watch over the flock of this tiny parish."

"I'm Joelle Dawson." She offered nothing more, and the man seemed satisfied to leave it at that.

He motioned to the adobe dwelling that rested behind a small church. "It isn't a mansion, but it manages to meet my needs."

"It looks fine," Joelle said and followed him into the house.

A warm fire did indeed glow out from the domelike fireplace in the corner of the main room. Joelle gazed longingly at its cheery flames.

"Go ahead, Child. Warm yourself," the ancient priest invited.

Joelle hurried to the structure, dropped her bag, and held out her stiffened fingers. "It feels wonderful," she said softly.

"Are you hungry?"

Joelle could not ignore the rumbling of her stomach. She could not even remember when she had eaten a proper meal. "Yes," she replied, "I suppose I am."

"I have some beans and tortillas left over from supper. Would you care to partake of it?" He watched Joelle intently for her answer.

"I would be very grateful," Joelle replied.

"Then I will fetch it from the stove. You sit there by the fire, while I see to it."

Joelle watched Father Cooper go from the room. He seemed to be one of those antiquated characters from the previous century and Joelle instantly liked him. It was funny, she thought. It seemed very right and good to be under his care. Yet, here was a total stranger, a man whom for all she knew could very well be no different from those who had harmed her.

"You have traveled far, yes?" he questioned, returning with a plate of food. His voice held the slightest hint of an accent.

"I don't really know," Joelle replied. "I'm not sure where I am, but I caught the train in Columbus."

"Then you have come about forty miles north, northeast," Father Cooper replied. "I see you are injured," he motioned to her face. "Were you there during the attack on the city?"

Joelle's countenance darkened. "Yes."

"Your room is over here," he stated and picked up the bag she had left by the fire. "Please, light a candle for yourself. You will find them in the box by the door."

Joelle did as he instructed and followed him down a short hallway. Father Cooper opened the door to a tiny room. There was a single, old-fashioned bed in one corner and a cross on the wall. Joelle noted the furnishings with a heart of gladness. It was safe and warm and away from the painful memories of Columbus.

"It is small, yes, but it is yours."

"Thank you," Joelle murmured.

"God bless you, Child. Sleep well. We will talk in the morning," Father Cooper said, closing the door as he took his leave.

Joelle did not even undress. She put the candle on the sawed-off frame of the bed and sat down wearily. The bed sagged, betraying the roping that held the thinly stuffed mattress, but Joelle did not care. She blew out the candle, slipped off her shoes, and fell back against the scratchy woolen blanket.

The nightmares came, as they did most every time she slept. Joelle relived the anguish of her rape, over and over, with every dream. She could hear their laughter, feel their breath against her face. Always she would wake up in a cold sweat, unable to shake the feeling of being hit and mauled. Pulling her knees to her chest, Joelle clutched them tightly and squeezed her eyes shut. When would the images leave her? When would she ever be free?

❧

After a restless night, morning came, and with it, the delicious aroma of sausage frying. Joelle jumped from the bed, sought out her brush, and quickly rebraided her hair. She thought for a moment about changing her clothes, then decided against it. If she had to travel again today, she might as well wear the same old things.

"Good morning," she said shyly, entering Father Cooper's kitchen.

"Ah, so you are awake. I have begun the breakfast. Will you join me?"

Joelle smiled at the sight of the little man working his way along the stove and counter to prepare his fare. "I would be grateful."

Father Cooper motioned her to the cupboard. "There are dishes in there and cups. We will have hot tea with our sausage and eggs."

Joelle went to the cupboard and pulled down two plates and matching cups. They were an ancient pattern of a once-fashionable china set. She thought how like Father Cooper the dishes were. Castoffs from another time and place, yet still serviceable.

She set the table and clasped her hands together, wishing she knew something to say. Father Cooper brought the skillet and all to the table. Joelle peered inside to see the concoction of eggs and sausage all scrambled together.

"It looks delicious," she said, offering the slightest smile.

Father Cooper blessed the meal and offered Joelle a seat before taking one opposite her at the tiny table. "We are a poor people here, but the Lord does provide, *oui?*"

"You're French," Joelle said in surprise.

"But of course," the man replied as though she should not have been surprised. Joelle smiled but made no further comment.

"You are traveling to your home?" Father Cooper asked.

"No," Joelle said, shaking her head. She pushed around the food on her plate, spooning in several bites, trying to think of what to say next. "I guess I have no home," she finally managed.

"You are alone?"

"Yes," she replied. Then to the old man's delight, she added in French. "I'm without family or funds and seek refuge and work. Would you have knowledge of someone nearby who might need my assistance?"

"I have not heard my language spoken in a very long time," Father Cooper replied with a smile of sheer pleasure breaking the wrinkled paths around his mouth. "I believe I can help you. I could not pay you, but you could live here and share meals with me."

"What would I do?"

"You could gather wood for my fire and keep my house and garden," he offered.

"I can also cook. I know several wonderful French recipes," Joelle beamed at the man, with sudden interest in his suggestion.

"It would be to my delight, Joelle Dawson."

"Very well," she said, feeling great relief to have the matter resolved. "I will stay for a time with you, Father Cooper, and share your hospitality."

"You will share also your heartache, no?"

Joelle started at his words. She put down her fork and stared thoughtfully at her plate. She had no reason to fear this man or his condemnation. He was a man of God, and the loving kindness that he had already extended to her gave Joelle no reason to doubt his earnest concern.

"I will share what I can," Joelle replied softly. She looked up with wide, dark eyes to see the compassion in the aged face that looked back at her. "It is a great burden that I bear, and I'm uncertain that if shared it will be any lighter."

"All burdens shared make lighter the load. It is less work when two carry the water, instead of one."

Joelle nodded and looked back at her food. "Perhaps."

Chapter 10

B ut Joelle won't come back to Bandelero!" John protested. Once again
  he was under the roof of his parents, only this time things were much
  different. He was no longer the young naïve boy who had gone off to
join the army. Now he was a cripple, or nearly that, and hopelessly worried
about the whereabouts of the woman he wanted to marry.

"Well, she certainly wasn't coming back to Columbus," Lillie stated,
pushing John's wheelchair to one side. Squeezing past her son's intentional
roadblock, Lillie paused to give John's shoulder a pat. "Get well first, then
worry about finding her. Joelle will either come back here or go home to her
parents. She won't wander around forever."

"I don't like the idea of her wandering around out there at all. I want her
here, where I can take care of her."

"I beg your pardon?" Lillie said, looking down at her son. "You have a
great deal of healing to do yourself, John. How can you concentrate on caring for Joelle when you need to work on putting yourself back together?"

John shook his head and ran his fingers back through his hair. "I know
you're right. But. . ."

"But?"

"I need her. She makes me feel alive. Even when she was arguing with
me, I wanted to laugh with her, hold her, love her. She's got to understand that
what happened in Columbus isn't important to me, at least not in a way that
matters about my feelings for her. If anything, I just love her more. She said
that anything was preferable to letting me die. I feel anything is preferable to
going through life without her."

Lillie's face softened. "I know, John. Give it over to God. He knows where
she is, and He can lead her home."

John nodded and wheeled himself off to his bedroom. His father had
redone the bedroom to accommodate John's various needs and, closing the
door behind him, John prayed that wherever she was, someone would meet
Joelle's needs, as well.

He noticed the papers still lying on the dresser and moved the chair closer
to retrieve them. They were his discharge orders and, although he knew it had
to be that way, John felt as though a major part of his life was over.

He closed his eyes and could almost feel himself back in the cockpit of the Jenny. If desire and will could make it so, John would have already been flying again, flying and soaring high above the turmoil and unrest of the earth.

For several minutes he sat there motionless, seeing in his mind the graceful plane as she glided across the sky. It would never be his again, he thought silently.

"But at least it was mine for a time," he murmured. He needed to be glad for the time he had enjoyed as a pilot. Some folks never had a chance to enjoy what they really and truly loved.

A knock at his bedroom door ended John's dreams for the moment. "Come in."

Lillie appeared, and on her face was a strained look. "John, Joelle's parents are here. Would you mind talking with them?"

John shook his head. "I don't mind." He tossed the papers aside and wheeled his chair to the door. "Just lead the way."

Riley and Zandy Dawson were sitting stiffly, with grim expressions lining their faces. Riley got to his feet and extended his hand to John.

"It's been a long time, but I do believe we met at Christmas, after my son, Nicholas, married Daughtry Lucas."

"Yes, I remember that well," John replied. "How are you Mr. Dawson, Mrs. Dawson?"

"Please, just call me Riley," Joelle's dark-haired father requested. He reclaimed his seat beside his wife, and John became acutely aware of how much Joelle resembled him.

"And you must call me Zandy," the brown-haired woman at his side stated.

John noticed the soft touches of gray that peppered Riley's hair while, except for the lines of worry, Zandy Dawson seemed hardly older than her daughter. He smiled sadly. "I'm sorry we couldn't get together under better circumstances. I'd figured on us getting under one roof for a wedding this spring."

"We'd heard about that possibility," Riley said, as though he had not been entirely sure of the matter.

John folded his hands in his lap. "I love her very much."

Zandy leaned forward to cover John's hands with one of her own. She said nothing, but her eyes met his with an all-telling look.

"We're staying with Garrett and Maggie Lucas," Riley said, breaking the tense silence.

"I presumed you might be," Lillie said before John could reply. "Dan says that Daughtry's baby is due just about any day."

"We're quite excited," Zandy replied. "If only. . ." She grew quiet and eased back against the sofa.

" 'If onlys' don't get us very far," John whispered, remembering his mother's words. "I'm full of those, and they haven't served me well."

"Do you have any news at all?" Riley questioned.

"No," John answered. "Nothing. I put friends to work on it down in Columbus, but the army's kind of got their hands full with tracking down Villa. My brother, J.D., is searching for Joelle in El Paso—"

"Why there?" Zandy interrupted to ask.

"It was close and a pretty good size of a town. We figured she might have gone there just to lose herself in the crowds for awhile," Lillie replied.

"She couldn't have gotten far," John added. "She didn't have much cash with her."

"I see," Riley shifted uncomfortably and shot a quick glance at his wife. "I'm going to hire some men to look for her. We'll start in Columbus and work from there."

"As soon as I'm out of this thing, I plan to go after her myself," John said in a voice that betrayed his frustration.

"We know you will," Zandy said, hoping to give him comfort.

"We'll be at the ranch if you get any news," Riley continued. "I understand they still don't have a telephone, but I'll ride in here daily to check with you. If you don't mind, I'll give my men this number, as well."

"Of course," Lillie stated. "You're welcome to stay here, you know, but I'm sure you'll want to be near Daughtry and Nick."

Riley and Zandy nodded and got to their feet. "We'd better head back," Riley said and extended his hand to John. "We'll find her, keep the faith. God hasn't brought us all this far just to desert us."

John nodded and watched his mother walk them to the door. He felt even more useless, thinking of how he must have appeared to them. With renewed spirit, John was more determined than ever to get back on his feet. *If my life has to change, let it. But let me have some form of control over it*, he thought.

~

April brought the birth of Heidi Dawson. At seven and one-half pounds, she was healthy and strong, for which everyone sincerely thanked God. Daughtry and Nicholas, ever the proud parents, were joyful in their new arrival. Kent, Heidi's older brother who was not quite two, did not know what he thought of the squalling baby.

"Bebe," he said, pointing an accusing finger.

"That's right, my boy," Nicholas said, holding Kent close enough to touch his new sister. "That's your baby sister, Heidi."

"I. . .D." Kent tried his version of the name.

"That's right," Daughtry said from her bed. "Later we'll let you hold her."

"Did you give her a middle name?" Riley asked from where he stood with Zandy. They proudly shared the laurels of grandparents with Maggie and Garrett Lucas.

"Joelle," Daughtry stated softly. "Her name is Heidi Joelle."

Zandy's eyes filled with tears, and Riley pulled her close.

"That's beautiful, Daughtry. Thank you. I'm sure Joelle will be honored."

"We hope so," Daughtry said, glad for Nicholas's supportive hand, now resting on her shoulder. "Joelle was. . .is a great comfort to us."

Maggie came forward to take Kent from his father. "I think it's some-body's bedtime."

"No nap! No nap!" Kent chanted and could be heard all the way down the hall.

"I think I'll give your mother a hand," Daughtry's bearded father said. "If you'll excuse me."

When Daughtry's parents had gone, Nicholas noticed the worried look his parents exchanged. "Has there been any word?" he asked.

"No, nothing," Riley answered and pulled Zandy with him to Daughtry's bedside.

"Poor Joelle," Daughtry whispered. "She had to bear so much. I've prayed constantly for her."

"So have we," Zandy admitted to her daughter-in-law. The dejection was clear in her voice. "It's so hard to just stand by and wait. Sometimes I get so angry at her. She knows the torment she's putting us through. She couldn't possibly be unaware of the pain we're suffering."

"She's not aware," Daughtry said firmly. "I'm certain of that. She was always very concerned about you both when she was staying with Nicholas and me. I'm sure it's just that her own sorrows are so great she can't think beyond them."

"That's why she should come home," Riley retorted.

"That's why she should," Nicholas offered in reply, "but it's also why she won't."

～

Joelle sat quietly knitting, while Father Cooper strained against the poor light and his own thick spectacles to read a lengthy letter. Putting aside her work, Joelle went to where he sat.

"Would you like for me to read it?"

Father Cooper surrendered the papers to her youthful hands. "It would greatly please these weary eyes, if you would be so kind."

Joelle read him the letter, a missive from a brother in the service. The shaky handwriting was nearly as poor as that of Father Cooper's, and Joelle deemed them to be contemporaries in age. By the time she finished with the correspondence, Father Cooper sat dozing in his chair.

Joelle smiled and leaned back to close her own eyes. She had been Father Cooper's houseguest for nearly two and one-half months. It had been most difficult at first, but he had quickly disarmed her fears with his zany tales of France in his boyhood and how he had nearly gotten kicked out of the seminary for putting alum in the drinking water. He was quite a character, her Father Cooper, and Joelle was very grateful to have made his acquaintance.

She was also grateful for the friendship he had extended. He never pressured her for answers that she found impossible to give, and he always seemed to understand when her sorrows kept her silent and unresponsive.

Joelle ran her hand lightly across her abdomen and thought of the child who grew there. She now had the answer to that frightful question. She would give birth to a child in December. She grimaced and opened her eyes. What kind of child could possibly come from such a union? This baby was conceived in violence and rage. What possible good could come from that?

Joelle tried to shake the image that always flooded her thoughts. It was the picture of a monstrously deformed and hideous creature being placed in her arms. Her child, she thought. . .and she reasoned, her punishment.

Chapter 11

With the use of a cane, John limped across the floor. The broad grin on his face was directed at the two men who stood at the opposite side of the room. The first was his Uncle David, the second was his father.

"I'm almost as good as new," John said, sweat beading his forehead.

"I knew if anyone could do it, you could," Daniel told his son.

"You've got your father's determination," David said with a laugh. "And, it's done you well."

"I'd imagine those prayers you had your congregation saying for me didn't hurt, Uncle David."

David nodded. "You bet they didn't." After over twenty years of pastoring the largest church in Bandelero, David definitely believed in the power of prayer.

"So now what are you going to do?" Dan questioned. "As if I had to ask."

"You don't." John's face left little doubt to his plan. "I'm going after her."

"You can't overdo it, even now. You'll tire easier than before, and if you sit a horse very long, you'll spend the following days nursing your aches and pains."

"I'm going after her," John said firmly. "And when I find her, I'm going to marry her on the spot before she can get away from me again."

"Good for you!" David declared. "Is there anything we can do to help?"

"Keep those people praying," John replied with a grin.

"You've got it, and I know God is working through the details as we speak."

John limped to the door. "I'm going to get my things ready. I've got a train to catch."

"John," Dan said, coming beside his son. "Try not to expect too much at first. It has been over six months."

"You talking about my physical condition or my finding Joelle?"

"Both," Dan replied seriously.

"I'll be fine," John assured his father. "And, I will find Joelle."

◇

Joelle enjoyed the mild October weather. She had worked outdoors in the vineyards throughout the summer months, whenever she was not helping Father Cooper. Her time spent outside had darkened her skin to a golden brown and, thankfully, she blended in quite naturally with the Mexican and Indian residents of the small village.

Carrying a load of mesquite on her head just as the other women did, Joelle looked as though she very well might be the beautiful descendent of Spanish nobility. If they only knew, she laughed to herself.

Her condition had become quite obvious, and Father Cooper, sensing her need for privacy, had found Joelle a tiny adobe house near the church. Joelle repaid the owner by gathering extra firewood and taking in laundry. She would also bake bread in the *horno,* a domed-shaped, adobe oven that sat outdoors. She could not say that she was happy, but she had become complacent. She still thought of John and her parents, as well as Lillie and Dan, but the child she carried kept her from even letting them know that she was safe.

"What could I say to them?" she had said to Father Cooper one evening before supper. "John would feel obligated to make the child his own, or my parents would feel the need to shelter me and take over the task for themselves. I can't burden them like that, not even for my own comfort."

"What is it that you want, Joelle?" Father Cooper had quietly asked. They were strolling down the sandy roadway, enjoying the tapestry of colors in the autumn sunset.

Joelle had thought for a moment. "I can't tell you or you'd think me ungrateful."

"I would never think badly of you, my child."

They had walked on in silence, while Joelle struggled to come to terms with what she felt. She had stared past the ramshackle *jacales*, homes of little more than mud and wooden poles, and she had sighed. She had no words for the sorrow deep inside of her. The ineffable pain that came any time she tried to rationalize her choices caused her to distance herself from even her dear friend.

"I wish to die," she had stated simply. Snapping her head up to meet Father Cooper's eyes, she had frowned. "Does that shock you?"

"Shock me? No," Father Cooper had replied with a shake of his head. "You have borne your cross with grace, Joelle. You haven't complained or grumbled of the great injustice done you, although just that is true. However, God's Word is clear about life and death. It has never been ours to give or to take. So just as it is impossible for you to have created the life that grows inside your body, it is also quite unreasonable to imagine that you can take one day away from your life here on this earth."

"But I'm tired," Joelle had replied, allowing the weariness to creep into her voice. "I'm just getting through minute by minute, day by day. I have no will to see the future. . .no desire whatsoever to endure even another minute." She had paused for a moment. "You've been so good to me, but I need much more and there is no one who can give it. I'm alone and lonely, and to face the thought of delivering this child scares me to death."

"The place where we say our prayers may be different," Father Cooper had said in his gentle way, "even the way in which we pray, but we serve the same God. He requires only that we come unto Him. Matthew 11:28 says, 'Come unto me, all ye that labour and are heavy laden, and I will give you rest.' You are tired from your burden, but God will lighten it and give you rest and in rest comes strength, Joelle. Trust our Father to give you that need."

"But what of this life?" she had said with a hand upon her swollen middle.

"All life is sacred, Child. Just as I said, you could no more snap your fingers and create a life, than I could."

"But people create children all the time," Joelle had said rather indignantly. "I've known of many folks who've spoken of surprises they received in children they'd not expected."

"Man and woman do not create the life. They are but the receptacles of God's gift. God creates that life. He alone has the power to breathe spirit into flesh and blood. Joelle, be reasonable and forgive me for my bluntness, but people often join together in a marriage bed and no children come forth from that union."

Joelle had thought on Father Cooper's words for a moment. "I suppose that is true. I just never thought of it much. I guess I just imagined that husbands and wives would naturally have a child most every time they came together."

"But that is the glory of it, Joelle. It is never our decision or our predetermination. We cannot choose one time to create a life and another time to snap our fingers and choose against it. God is the One Who determines our paths. Just as He created your life, He also created the life you carry within."

"But this child was created out of sin. Out of violence and all that is unholy, this baby came into existence. How could that be something of God?" Joelle had questioned in earnest.

Father Cooper had placed his hands upon Joelle's shoulders. "My child, you may seek God in all things or you may seek the world. If you choose the world, you may find that you completely miss the blessings and wonderment of the Father's touch. And that, Joelle, is the true tragedy."

Joelle had stared back at the priest in silence. His words had pierced the hardness of her heart. Turning without a word, Joelle had begun to walk again. When they had reached her little house, Father Cooper had taken her hand and patted it ever so gently.

"God's blessings upon you, Joelle," he had said. "I am praying for you."

"Thank you," Joelle had whispered, then placed a kiss upon the weathered cheek of her friend.

～

America moved closer to the November presidential elections with one concerned eye on the Mexican border and another poised on the war in Europe. President Wilson's campaign promoted his reelection by saying, "He kept us out of war!" People could only ask themselves, "Yes, but can he continue to do so?"

Black Jack Pershing had been called in shortly after the Villa raid on Columbus to head up the "Punitive Expedition." This affair called for three brigades, two cavalry units and one infantry, supported by field artillery, engineers, wagon companies, ambulances, and the First Air Squadron out of San Antonio, Texas. Their objective was to go after Villa and his troops. But late into 1916, Villa was still leading Pershing on a merry chase, and Mexico was growing ever more angry at the U.S. invasion of their country.

Joelle heard very little of the news. She liked it that way, and she never really went out of her way to learn any more than what Father Cooper shared with her. To know more only caused her to worry about those she loved. Whenever she thought of war, she remembered John and J.D., as well as Daughtry's brothers and scores of old friends from home. She hated to imagine them marching off to war and hated even more to imagine them never coming home again.

As was her routine, Joelle went to Father Cooper's little church and prepared to clean it. It was a very unassuming building of adobe with a flat roof and dirt floor. The walls were four feet thick, and the windows were small but remarkably glassed with colored panes and artistry that captivated the imagination.

Inside, Joelle really had very little to do. The altar was simple, unpainted wood, and it was her duty to dust it for the services to come. Before her arrival, Father Cooper generally saw to the matter himself, but Joelle wanted to make herself useful, and so he conceded this task to her.

As was the custom, the church had no pews. The families of the area were mainly Mexican and, because of this, the men would stand and the women kneel throughout their mass. Joelle had watched the mass once and had found it most fascinating. The women while praying, crossed themselves frequently in the Spanish tradition and kissed their thumbs after each sign of the cross. She did not understand the reasons behind what the worshipers did, yet she found their sincerity and devotion admirable.

From her days spent with these women, Joelle knew she could never have asked for better neighbors or friends. She was never in want for anything, so long as someone knew she had need. Joelle had but to express a desire to Father Cooper, and inevitably, some dark-eyed woman would show up on her doorstep. With a smile and a string of explanations that Joelle was only coming to understand in bits and pieces, the desired item would be deposited into her hands. It made Joelle cautious in speaking her mind, but her love of these people deepened in the face of her own adversity.

Without realizing it, Joelle also came to see that the actions of men like Villa's did not necessarily constitute the support of an entire people. Of course, she knew these people lived in the United States, but their ties were strongly and quite obviously connected to old Mexico.

Stepping into the coolness of the building, Joelle was met with a deep sense of spirituality that she had not expected. The wooden cross that graced the front of the church drew her eyes, and Father Cooper's words came back to her in a rush of emotion.

The child inside her kicked hard as though compelling its mother to listen and heed the loving priest's words. "All life is sacred," Joelle remembered aloud. She ran her hand across her stomach as if noticing for the first time the way it bulged out in front of her.

"We cannot choose one time to create a life and another time to snap our fingers and choose against it. God is the One Who determines our paths. Just as He created your life, He also created the life you carry within," Father Cooper had told her.

"The child," Joelle said slowly, "this child. . .frightens me." She raised her eyes to the cross and paused to reflect on the symbol. "I don't know what to do. I don't know whether to go home or stay here and bear this shame alone. I don't know what to do."

Tears began to fall down her cheeks, and Joelle felt as though her legs could no longer support her weight. Going to the altar, she came to her knees and sobbed. "This is my fate, my destiny. But, God, what of Your will? What of Your protection and comfort and," Joelle paused to take a ragged breath, "and love? What of Your love? How can I find it in this?"

She gripped the altar and pleaded for direction. "Show me what to do. I have no one."

As if a warm blanket had been placed around her shoulders, Joelle felt the presence of God's love surround her. There was no immediate revelation. No simple answer to guide her in the complexities of life's mysteries. It was just a quietness of spirit that descended into her heart and gave her peace.

"I will do what You guide me to do," she whispered.

Getting to her feet, Joelle stared out across the room and startled when a flash of three gruesome faces came to haunt her memory.

Forgive them, a still, small voice told her heart.

"Never!" she said with a shake of her head. Looking back to the cross, she was still shaking her head. "You ask too much."

Chapter 12

John's arrival into Columbus, New Mexico was considerably calmer than the one he had made back in January. He was overwhelmed with the sights that greeted him and realized just how few memories he had made in the small community. Most of his time had been confined to bed and, outside of Joelle's lengthy descriptions of her day or his mother's prattling about her shopping ordeals, John had not seen much at all.

His first order of business was to go to the headquarters at Camp Furlong. He had friends there and knew, too, that it was here he would get his best information.

Leaving his bag at the train station, John limped slowly through the sandy street. His destination was less than a block from the depot, but the sand made his progress difficult. John knew better than to curse his condition. He was quite grateful for the progress he had made. Even though he could not walk with ease and might never again walk without a cane, he was happy just to be on his own two feet.

At the camp headquarters, John introduced himself and was soon directed to the officers' mess shack, where he was told he could find one of the commanding officers. A brief discussion with the officer in charge resulted in John's being given a place to bed down and the news that his friend, Flipflop, was quartered nearby.

"Private Campbell is working behind the stables," the officer instructed. "We have some problems back there, and I'm certain you'll find yourself quite interested."

"Thank you for your help, Sir," John said, raising his hand to salute. The habit died at midpoint, as John remembered he was no longer a part of this life and its requirements.

John limped silently from the tent. His leg was hurting him, and the aching in his back had grown from a tolerable dullness to a dedicated throbbing. Still, he moved on and prayed for the strength to continue.

Past the long row of stables, John could already make out the structured frames of biplanes. His breath caught and his chest tightened as he cleared the last obstacle and stood in full view of the airfield.

This had been his world and he had loved it more than most anything else

415

in his life. He loved the droning noise and the oily smell of the engines. He cherished the feel of exhilaration when, after a jolting run down the sandy runway, the Jenny would lift herself into the air and blow a kiss good-bye to the ground below. Then of course, there was the flight itself. The feeling of being above all the mundane and routine things of the world. The feeling that in flight, one came just a little bit closer to God.

John shuddered the images away. It was no longer his world. Never again would he work the rudders or feel the stick in his hand. It was someone else's world now.

"That you, Preacher?" the voice called out from somewhere to John's right.

Turning, John spied Flipflop and grinned. "So they promoted you to corporal? Who did you have to pay off to get that?"

Flipflop laughed and double-timed his steps to give John a bear hug. "It is you. I thought I'd never see you again. You back to join us?"

John shook his head and nearly moaned under the strength of Flipflop's embrace. He set the younger man away from him and eyed him carefully. "Those days are over for me." He held up the cane. "This is the only stick I get to handle now."

Flipflop sobered with a nod. "I heard they mustered you out. Heard, too, that you'd never walk again, but here you are."

John smiled. "Just as stubborn as I ever was." He looked beyond Flipflop and motioned to the Jennys. "So why are they on the ground?"

"We're in bad shape, Preacher. Those machines just can't tolerate what the army wants to put them through. We've messed around with the loads. We've given her more power and trimmed down her weight, but the air is too dry here, the sand too harsh. Why, there've been storms that ripped holes the size of baseballs in her fabric. I have to wonder if we'll ever get it right."

"Oh, they'll get it right. Flight is going to forever change the military, you just wait and see. Once someone figures out how to give us an air machine with enough power to go the distance and carry the loads, you'll see wars ending overnight. Why just look at what they're doing with them in France. Some good American pilots are over there flying in their corps."

"I know you're right, Preach," Flipflop replied, "but, down here, we just ain't havin' much luck. They try to put up a few planes to figure out where the *Villistas* are and inevitably they get knocked back down. We've lost quite a few to sandstorms and such, and at five thousand dollars a machine, I don't think the army's real eager to keep it up."

John stared thoughtfully across the field. He could see it all in the future. Row after row of airplanes, lined up, waiting for their duties. Flipflop could see only the frustrations of the early years at hand, but John knew there was a bigger picture that stretched beyond the problems of the present.

"Say," Flipflop said with a sudden revelation, "I had a letter from J.D. the day before yesterday. His unit has joined Pershing in pursuit of Villa. Did you know that?"

"No, I haven't heard from J.D. in some time. I suppose he'll write to Mom and Dad about it, but in case he doesn't, why don't you fill me in on it, and I'll send them the news."

John learned all that he could about his brother, then shared his search for Joelle with his friend. He left nearly a half-hour later, feeling somewhat better for the renewal of his friendship, yet no closer to knowing the whereabouts of Joelle.

For the next few days, John paced out every square foot of Columbus. He asked questions of everyone and showed Joelle's photograph to anyone who would stop long enough to look. No one had seen the dark-eyed young woman.

Stopping at the bank, John questioned the tellers and even requested to speak with the man in charge, before he felt satisfied that Joelle had not come there to receive money. He moved around to the businesses, always receiving the same shake of the head and negative response. In complete dejection, John decided to leave Columbus and work his way along with the rail lines.

He reasoned that perhaps Joelle had managed to keep aside enough money to take the train from Columbus. He questioned the ticket agent at the train station, but the man could scarcely be held to account for the purchase of tickets way back in March. He had not even held the job then and was of no help to John. Buying a ticket, John felt utter hopelessness engulf him. His father had told him not to expect too much; after all, Joelle's own father had hired professional men to search for her. The police were notified throughout the state of her disappearance, and her photograph had been hand carried to law enforcement people in all the surrounding large cities. If all of these people combined could not locate her, how could John expect to pull off the deed?

The train took him east, and when John realized that he had learned very little pursuing the matter in this manner, he got off at the first small town and went in search of a horse.

"This horse is a fine animal, *Señor*," the dark-skinned man told John. "He is very gentle," the man added, noting John's cane.

"I'll take him," John replied and began bartering for a saddle.

The man counted out his money, while John saddled his new acquisition.

He glanced up from his task to look around the small town.

"I'm looking for a young woman," he said to the man. "She's my fiancée, actually. We were separated after a tragedy, and I'm afraid she might be lost and not know how to get back home."

"Who is this woman?"

John left the horse and brought out his photograph of Joelle. "Ahh, she is *muy bonita*," the man said, noting Joelle's beauty. "But, I have not seen this woman."

"If she were here, would you know it?"

"*Sí*, we are a very small village here," the man replied. "There are no strangers."

"I understand," John said and tucked the photograph back into his pocket.

Within the hour, John was back on his way, and although he had to rest often and had found the ride most challenging, he strengthened his mind with the hope of finding Joelle.

After a week of searching and spending his nights out on the open desert plains, John was ready for a hot bath and a hotel bed. The desert was a harsh companion even in this late time of the year. He was constantly eating and wearing more sand than he had ever imagined existed, and he had run-ins with several rattlesnakes, making his horse a most unhappy companion. Wearily, John made his way to Las Cruces, the largest city in the area, and prayed he might find someone, anyone, who had seen his beloved, Joelle. If nothing else, however, he would rest here and regain his strength.

He was still some miles away from the town, when up ahead he spotted an automobile. A wizened old man stood staring down questioningly, when John came abreast of the vehicle.

John immediately recognized the man as a priest and slowed his mount. "Good afternoon."

"Good afternoon to you," the man said with a smile.

"Having trouble with your car?" John questioned, gingerly getting down from his horse. He pulled out his cane from where others might have carried a rifle and limped to where the old man stood.

"It seems I have managed to get off the road, and the sand has quite inconveniently trapped me here."

John sized up the situation. "I think between me and my horse, we can pull you out of this spot. By the way," John straightened and extended his hand. "I'm John. . .John Monroe."

"I am Father Cooper," the old man said. "I was on my way to Las Cruces. I must make the trip periodically," he added as an explanation. "I borrow this automobile, the only one in our village, for the journey, and up until this day, I have never had any problem with it. But now, alas, you see it is no longer so."

"Well, it won't cause you a problem for long," John said assuringly.

It took only a few minutes to free the vehicle, and Father Cooper was most delighted. "I thank God for sending you my way, Son," he said with a beaming face that John could not help but like. "Where are you bound now?"

"I'm going to Las Cruces," John replied. "I've been out here over a week and I'm stiff and sore. I was injured several months ago, and I'm still not able to get around like I used to. I find myself in need of a little recuperative time."

"Perhaps you would ride the rest of the way with me?" Father Cooper suggested. "The car is surely more comfortable than your mount, and I would be happy to have you share supper with me."

John nodded. "That sounds mighty good to me."

Father Cooper moved to open the car door. "If I might impose upon you to give the car a crank, we can be on our way."

"Just let me tie the horse to the back," John replied and went to the task.

"Is the switch on?" John called as he bent to crank life into the machine.

"Yes," Father Cooper called back.

John felt the ache in his back intensify but nonetheless saw to his duty. The engine sputtered to life with Father Cooper adjusting the throttle as John joined him. Easing into the padded seat, John sighed. Yes, this was much easier to tolerate than the rigid stiffness of the saddle. As soon as they began the bouncing ride into town, however, John was not all that sure the trade-off had been a positive one.

The twin towers of St. Genevieve's Church soon came into view with the rest of the rambling town of Las Cruces. The church was a massive, brick structure patterned after the Gothic-French revival style. It was an overpowering sight that commanded the attention of anyone who looked upon it. John felt hope in the sight of the crosses that graced the double peaks of the bell towers.

"Over there is the Loretto Academy," Father Cooper commented, steering the car around a massive hole in the road. "The Sisters run a school there and have an excellent music department. They assure me they are quite modern, whatever that means."

John smiled and resumed his survey of the city. There were more trees here, and the desert seemed less oppressive. Cottonwoods and numerous orchard trees dotted the banks of the Rio Grande, and in the background the silhouetted Organ Mountains, so named for their pipe organ appearance, rose in shadowy black against the pink and purple twilight.

"They have completed a dam at Elephant Butte," Father Cooper was saying. "It has helped to make the area water more predictable. They no longer worry so about the flood or drought, and the crops they grow are magnificent. Such alfalfa as you have never seen!"

John only nodded. They drove past the traditional adobe homes, with John noting a few houses built of brick or stone. He was grateful to see the word "hotel" labeling the tops of more than one building and sighed to himself in anticipation of his rest.

"Why don't you join me," Father Cooper said, pulling the car alongside an iron fence. "I am certain there is room for you to stay with me tonight."

"I couldn't impose," John answered.

"There will be no imposition. Come along, we will have supper and talk."

John felt there was little to do but follow the old man.

They settled in to a hearty meal of stewed meat and vegetables, with a young boy running back and forth to see to their needs. At one point he brought out huge loaves of fresh white bread that caused John's mouth to water instantly. Father Cooper was treated royally, and there was no question of John's ability to stay when the elderly man made the request.

"So you are traveling with a purpose, no?" the priest asked.

John grinned. "You might say that."

"And you will share that purpose with me?"

"Might as well. I share it with most everyone I meet," John replied in between bites of food. He shifted his weight in the chair and grimaced.

"Are your injuries causing you great difficulty?" Father Cooper asked softly.

"I'm pretty sore. It's just as well, though," John said and paused to straighten his aching back. "Months ago, I was bedfast, so I thank God for even the pain. Although," he added honestly, "I'd probably be even more grateful for a back without pain."

Father Cooper smiled. "There is good in everything. Even my inconvenience today brought me a new friend, yes?"

"I don't know that I see good in all things," John said, and there was a sadness in his voice. He thought of Joelle. "I don't see the original accident as being all that good."

"Tell me what happened."

John relayed some of the details of his crash, then added, "It was because of the crash that my family and fiancée were in Columbus when Pancho Villa and his men raided back in March. The woman I planned to marry was brutally attacked."

Father Cooper took on a new interest, eyeing John carefully. "Was she killed?"

"No," John said with a shake of his head. "She lived, but before I could recover from my own injuries, she ran away." John reached inside his pocket and pulled out Joelle's picture. "I'm searching for her, and even though it's been months since I last saw her, I'll never stop until I find her." He handed the photograph to Father Cooper and went back to the task of eating.

~

Father Cooper stared at the dark eyes that stared back at him from the picture. It was just as he had come to suspect. Glancing from the picture to John, he was glad that the young man had not watched his reaction. He was equally glad that John did not ask if he had seen the young woman, for Father Cooper would never have lied about it.

Stunned to realize that John was the man Joelle so often spoke of, Father Cooper could only hand back the photograph in silence. *There would be much praying to do,* he thought silently, *much praying, indeed.*

Chapter 13

Father Cooper was troubled and elated at the realization of who John really was. He knew that Joelle's future and happiness most probably lay in whether or not this young man's love for her was as strong as he seemed to believe it to be. After seeing John to a bed in the dormitory where he himself would sleep, Father Cooper began to pray about the matter and did not find his way into bed until late into the night.

John, relieved to feel even the marginal softness of the poorly stuffed mattress beneath him, had little difficulty falling asleep. It seemed one minute he was putting his head to the pillow and the next minute Father Cooper was standing over him, calling breakfast.

"I think I could probably sleep for a week straight," John sighed and kicked the covers away.

"Your body and mind are weary, and you carry a great weight. It is not easy to be laden as you are. Come. Dress for breakfast, and you can tell me more about your little friend. In case you are turned around, the water closet in which you bathed last night is at the end of the hall."

John dressed quickly, pulling on the same dusty jeans he had worn the day before. The pain in his back and legs was considerably lessened, and despite still feeling tired, he was greatly improved. Finishing, he took a halfway clean shirt out from his bag and tried to tidy his appearance by wearing it. Then after a quick shave, he joined Father Cooper in the dining room.

"Ah, you feel better, no?" Father Cooper smiled, pulling a chair out for John to use.

"I'm a new man," John smiled and limped to his chair.

John was surprised when two white clad Sisters appeared and placed food on the table before him. The aroma wafted up to greet him, and John's stomach growled a hearty greeting.

"It sure smells good," he said and waited for Father Cooper to bless the meal.

They ate in silence for several minutes. John nearly inhaled the food before him and found that the Sisters were happy to refill the plate again when he had finished. Rolling scrambled eggs up inside a tortilla, John happily continued the feast.

"Please tell me about your young woman," Father Cooper suddenly encouraged, and John's hand halted midway to his mouth.

With a sad smile, John spoke. "Her name is Joelle. We met in Bandelero. That's where I'm from." Father Cooper nodded, and John continued. "She came to visit her brother once and I met her at a Christmas party. She was young and sweet, very naïve and ever so popular with all the young men."

"But you won her heart, eh?" the priest grinned, causing the wrinkles on his face to shift.

John smiled. "Yes. It was almost love at first sight. At least, I was in love at first sight. I think Joelle was too. She didn't seem to have nearly as much to say to anyone else, and when I'd interrupt one of the other men's conversations, she always looked happy about it. One thing led to another, and we started writing letters. I joined the army so I could fly planes. There wasn't but a handful of people doing it, and I'm afraid I lied when I joined up and told them I was already a crack pilot."

"Your story did not catch up with you?"

"I was lucky," John replied. "No, I was destined to fly. I watched and listened, even read what little I could find on the matter. I finally managed to get taken under the wing of a good man, Bob Camstead. He saw through my story, but he also saw my drive. It wasn't long before we were working as a team. Later, when the army promoted him, we didn't get to fly together." John shrugged his shoulders. "But we stayed good friends."

"And what did the young woman think of your flying?"

"She loved it. I snuck her a ride once," John said, and a light came into his eyes at the memory. "I went off without permission and flew one of the army planes home just so I could see my sister, Angeline, get married to my best friend, Gavin Lucas. Before I left, Joelle was at my side insisting I take her up. I think that's when I knew for sure that I could never love another woman as I loved her."

"But what of your love now? She has fled with her sorrow, and you are here." Father Cooper seemed intent on an answer, and John could not help but wonder what he should say.

"I only wish I knew. My love for her is as strong as ever. But, I don't know how she feels. She ran away after she was. . ." He could not say the word.

"Raped?"

"Yes. Such an ugly word, and such a hideous thing," John muttered.

"She was unable to face you with her shame, is that so?"

"I guess," John replied softly. "I never saw it as her shame. She didn't do anything to deserve it. She was protecting my mother and me. I was still unable to walk when Villa attacked. They were killing soldiers, and Joelle was certain they would kill me if they found me. She was probably right, but it doesn't make her sacrifice any easier to stomach."

"Why do you say that?"

"Because I feel like I let her down. I failed her because I couldn't keep her safe from harm. How can any woman go on trusting a man after that?"

"This woman sounds capable of a great many things."

"Oh, that she is," John agreed. "I just pray she's been able to put the attack behind her. I want to find her and take care of her."

"It will be difficult to put such a thing aside," Father Cooper said, putting down his fork. "Your accident is not yet behind you, and you must deal with it constantly, no?" He did not wait for an answer but continued. "You did not choose to crash your airplane, but you did choose to fly. You knew the possibilities of crashing, and yet you still chose to pursue that vocation."

"Yes," John said with a nod. The words could have very well been his own. "I told my mother that a pilot always lives with the knowledge that something can go wrong." He stopped for a minute. "Joelle came to care for me in Columbus. I didn't want her there. I didn't want her to see me helpless and beaten down. I made the choice to fly, and the accident was my consequence to deal with, not hers. She never bargained for that kind of thing when she agreed to marry me."

"Ah, but neither then did you bargain to deal with this attack," Father Cooper declared.

"True, but Joelle didn't have a choice. I chose to fly. She didn't choose to be raped. She had no control, no say. She did what she did to unselfishly protect the people she loved."

Father Cooper toyed with a mug of now lukewarm coffee. He seemed to consider John's words quite profound. "It is well that you see this," he finally told John. "Your Joelle may struggle for a long time with the things that were done to her. As you said, her choices were taken from her. She was without the power to make that decision, beyond of course, the choice to protect you. However, an attack such as she must have endured is not a thing easily put aside. She may always suffer from it and never be capable of a physical closeness. Are you willing to give up such a thing?"

John felt startled by the priest's words. "I don't think I ever considered that. I mean, well, my father did mention the possibility."

"You may find your Joelle and also find that she is unable to return the love that you hold for her. Her scars may run so deep, that for a long, long time, she may be unwilling to love again."

John squared his shoulders and sat back in the chair. "Then I'll just wait her out."

Father Cooper smiled. "Your love can endure this wait?"

"If it has to." John knew that he spoke the truth. What was life without Joelle? Loving another woman was not even a consideration. "I'll wait as long as it takes. I know she's been hurt, but I believe my love for her will go far to heal her. She has to realize that the rape means nothing to me, at least as far as my love for her is concerned. I'll help her learn to put it in the past and forget about it. She won't need to carry it with her because I'll fill her heart and mind with the happiness and love that I know God has in store for us."

Father Cooper sobered again. "You forget there is the possibility that she may be unable to leave the attack in the past."

"I don't understand."

"There is always the chance that she suffered further consequences from the rape. She may be with child."

The words were like a slap in the face to John. His color paled considerably and he pushed back from the table with a startled expression. "I never thought of that." Getting up, he leaned against the chair and stared down at Father Cooper. "I never even considered that possibility."

"But it is one that you must consider. Especially before you go on and locate her. Should you find this situation is so, your rejection of her at that point could very well kill her." Father Cooper could picture Joelle's hurt expression in his mind. He would not risk her tenuous contentment by bringing to her a man who could never accept her fate.

John swallowed hard and looked away. *A child*, he thought. It was possible, just as Father Cooper said. He would always love Joelle but could he love a child who had been forced upon her? A child conceived out of her most hated nightmare?

"I have to think," he said, suddenly breaking the silence. "I have to be alone." He grabbed up his cane and limped quickly from the room.

Father Cooper lifted his eyes heavenward. *Such pain and suffering for children so young*, he thought. There was only one way to help them and that way was to pray.

~

John walked back to his room and sat there in the silence for several minutes. In all of his dreams of finding Joelle, he had never once considered the chance that she could be pregnant. Why hadn't his father mentioned it when talking to John? He had certainly mentioned the fact that Joelle would probably fear physical intimacy. Daniel had talked at length with his son regarding the complications that might arise from Joelle's experience, but never once had he thought to mention a child.

Picking up his Bible, John knew that God would hold the only answers.

Could he possibly look into the face of a baby born out of that rape and love it? The attack had cost him, as well as Joelle, although he knew her price to be much greater. Could she, herself, give birth to a child from that ordeal and nurture it at her breast. . .and call it her own?

"Oh, God," John whispered, "why must this happen? I don't even know if Joelle is with child, but if she is, how could it ever be a good thing?"

John's hand stopped roaming the pages of Scripture that he held, and his eyes fell to the writing of Matthew 1:18-20.

"Now the birth of Jesus Christ was on this wise: When as his mother Mary was espoused to Joseph, before they came together, she was found with child of the Holy Ghost. Then Joseph her husband, being a just man, and not willing to make her a public example, was minded to put her away privily. But while he thought on these things, behold, the angel of the Lord appeared unto him in a dream, saying, Joseph, thou son of David, fear not to take unto thee Mary thy wife: for that which is conceived in her is of the Holy Ghost."

John considered the words, lifted his eyes, and whispered, "But Mary's Child was Your Son, and His conception was a glorious act of love."

John thought for a moment of how Joseph must have felt when he received the news of Mary's pregnancy. Did Joseph feel the anguish that John was feeling at this moment. Were there doubts and hesitations as to whether he could love Mary's Child?

"There must have been," John whispered. "Joseph must have been as troubled as I am, or God would have had no need to send an angel to him."

The turmoil in John's heart began to lift. "I cannot compare the possible child who Joelle might be carrying to Jesus, Father," John prayed, "but I am just a man, like Joseph, and my fears are deep in this matter. If there is a baby, what should I do?"

John knew the story of Joseph and Mary by heart. Christmas was a festive celebration of the birth of his Lord and always had been so as he had grown up. Some of his fondest memories surrounded the telling of this story of love between Mary and Joseph. He instantly recalled to mind a time when his Uncle David had preached on Joseph's faith.

"Joseph was just a carpenter. A simple man who worked with his hands. He was probably considered a good man by his neighbors and friends. He no doubt kept the Commandments in the best way he knew how. He was certain to have appeared in the synagogue whenever it was appropriate to do so, and he was betrothed to marry a girl.

"No doubt Joseph had his moments just like the rest of us. He probably wondered if he was making enough money to support a wife and eventually a family. He probably felt concerned about the condition of his home and business. Maybe the roof leaked, and he wondered how he was going to get everything fixed up before Mary came to live there." The congregation had smiled at this and John could not help but smile now as he remembered it.

"But," Uncle David's words continued to come back to John, "Joseph was to receive a bigger concern. Joseph was given a shock that must have come pretty hard to deal with. He was going to be a father. A father of a child he knew nothing about. A father of a child that was not his flesh and blood and had not come out of his doing."

John looked back at the Bible. If Joelle were expecting a child, it would be the same for him. He was engaged to marry Joelle, and the child would not be of his doing.

"But Mary carried the Son of God," John said defensively. "Of course, Joseph could accept that. He wouldn't have to deal with wondering whose Child it was, and Mary certainly didn't have to face the retribution. . ." John's words fell silent. Maybe he was wrong.

It was entirely possible that Mary had suffered just as Joelle might be, if she were expecting a child without a husband. Surely there were those who did not believe Mary's explanation. Even Joseph had to be convinced by an angel of God before he found peace of heart in the matter.

"There must have been those who scoffed at them," John thought aloud sadly. He pictured the young couple who must have faced the doubtful faces of disbelievers. "But You would have protected them," John added thoughtfully. "You knew ahead of time how folks would react, and You gave Your Son, even knowing that eventually people would kill Him. If You didn't spare Your own Son, Jesus, from the persecution and ugliness of this world, how can I expect that You would keep it from me or Joelle?"

John's sudden revelation made him feel ashamed. "Forgive me, Father," he said with tears brimming his eyes. "Forgive me for the prideful selfishness of my thoughts. It would be no fault of the babe, should Joelle bring a child into this world. I love her, Father. I love my beloved Joelle, and I can love any child she bears."

A peace washed over John like a flood and, with it, he washed away the bitterness of his past. How could he hold onto the regret and pain and embrace the future with the hope that God had planted in his heart?

~

Father Cooper was on his knees in prayer when John came into the room. He started to back out the door, but the priest looked up at him with such expectation in his eyes that John froze in place. The unspoken question in Father Cooper's eyes prompted John to speak.

"I love her. It doesn't matter what's happened. I will always love her, and

I want her for my wife."

"And if there is a child?" Father Cooper questioned.

"It doesn't matter," John insisted.

"You can love this child and raise it for your own?"

"It will be my own," John said confidently. "Any child Joelle bears, will share my name and my love."

Father Cooper crossed himself and, with a smile, got slowly to his feet. "Then there is something we must talk about."

John looked quizzically at the priest and cocked his head to one side. "What is it?"

"Come." The old man put his arm around John's shoulder. "I must tell you news of our Joelle."

Chapter 14

Joelle moved slowly under the growing weight of her child. In another month, she would deliver the baby. By her best estimations, Joelle figured the child was due around Christmas.

She finished tidying the tiny church and took herself to Father Cooper's quarters. He was due back today, and Joelle was quite happy for this. She had missed the old man and his company. He had helped her through so many hardships, and yet Joelle knew she could not expect him to be responsible for her future needs.

Seeing the low supply of mesquite wood, Joelle went outside to bring in an armful. She had steadily added to the stack throughout the summer months, and even though November had been very warm during the day, nighttime cold required a fire.

She wiped sweat from her forehead and bent over to retrieve the gnarled sticks of mesquite. The baby kicked in protest, and Joelle rubbed her hand lightly across her stomach. She was growing used to the idea of motherhood, and although she still feared the outcome and their future, Joelle felt God had given her a love for the child.

She refused, however, to consider the matter further than the baby itself. She could not bring herself to wonder about its father or how she would provide for its care. She could not allow herself the memory of John's love and their planned marriage because it hurt too much to realize what she had lost.

Gathering the sticks, Joelle sighed deeply. So much would change when the baby arrived. She had to make plans, and all her considerations led her in the way of leaving Father Cooper's little community.

If I stay, she reasoned to herself, *he will only feel obligated to provide for us, and there is little enough for him. The people here are generous and would gladly help, but how fair is it for me to thrust my burdens upon them? No,* Joelle thought, *I must go. But where?*

She had given considerable thought to the matter. She knew the best choice was to contact her parents and go home. They would love her despite the child she carried, and knowing her mother as she did, Joelle knew that the child would also be loved. Still, it was hard to face the idea. Once she went home, John would no doubt learn of her whereabouts and come to her.

"Oh, John," she whispered, straightening under the load of wood. She wondered where he was and if he had ever recovered from his injuries. Nightly, she prayed for him, but never did she allow herself to linger on his memory. It was simply more than she could bear.

"If I go home, can I keep you from coming to me?" she wondered aloud.

The day's heat continued, and Joelle was exhausted from her tasks. She had replenished the wood supply, beaten the sand from all of the rugs, and seen to it that a pot of beans sat soaking on the stove. Should Father Cooper not return until tomorrow, Joelle reasoned that she would cook the beans for herself.

Taking off the scarf she had worn on her head, Joelle dabbed at the sweat on her neck and brow. The aching in her back was fierce, and she longed to rest. Perhaps a short nap was in line, she thought. Seeing that nothing else could be done for Father Cooper, Joelle took herself home and stretched out on her own bed.

Her furnishings were simple, even stark, especially in contrast to that which she had known growing up. She thought again of going home to her parents in Kansas City. Memories drifted through her mind of times spent in the huge house she had shared with her brothers and sister. She had had everything a child could want and, being the youngest, she had been spoiled beyond reason.

Clothes were her passion, she remembered with a smile. Her closets were overflowing with the latest fashions in an array of colors and materials. Now, she wore simple, peasant clothes and, running her hand down over the oversized blouse, Joelle laughed out loud. Her friends would never recognize the woman she had become.

The thought of her friends brought to mind other things. She recalled dances and parties and games of lawn tennis. There was always something going on. She had enjoyed wealth and affluence, yet her parents had seen to it that her values were not placed in money and things. She had matured with the notion that money was only good so long as it was being used to benefit and not harm. Things could not buy peace of mind, Joelle knew. Just as money and things could not help her now.

She faded off to sleep thinking on these things, but the simple peace was again taken from her when images of the attack rose up to haunt her.

Joelle could smell the smoke and the foul stench of her attackers. It always started that way, and it seemed as though it always would. She struggled to refuse the memories, but her mind was not willing to let the scene pass. Tossing and turning, fighting the attack in her sleep, Joelle opened her mouth to scream and felt strong arms encircle her.

Joelle slapped at the hands that sought her. She battled with their hold and tried to move away. She suddenly realized in sheer terror, that the hands that held her were not merely conjured in sleep, but were very real.

Her eyes snapped open in horror. The image before her was one of her attackers, and she reached out with her hands to push away the man before her.

"Joelle, wake up. Joelle, it's me." John called to her over and over, knowing that she was lost in her nightmare.

Joelle heard the words, but it was the voice that caused her to still. She knew that voice. Squeezing her eyes closed, Joelle concentrated on the sound.

"Joelle, my beloved." The voice sounded again.

"John," she whispered and opened her eyes to the vision of his face.

"Yes, it's me, Joelle," he said with a softness that melted away her fears.

Joelle allowed him to hold her for a moment as her mind struggled to comprehend his appearance.

John thought his heart would break at the look of fear in her eyes. Father Cooper had so kindly brought him to her, but when he had first laid eyes on her sleeping face, John knew the anguish of her attack was still a very real presence in her life.

He had watched her wrestle with her fears, and when it seemed that the nightmare might best her, he could not resist pulling her into his arms. How could he have known that she would feel only more frightened by the action? He was still pondering this and wondering what he should do, when Joelle suddenly pushed him away.

"Get out of here, John. I don't know how you found me, but I want you to leave." The realization that he was here and that he knew her condition was more than Joelle could deal with.

John stared at her in confusion for a moment. "Joelle, don't be afraid. I've come to take you home. I've come to make you my wife."

Joelle shook her head and pushed at him with all of her strength. "Go away!" Her voice sounded strange to her. "Get out! I don't want you here! I don't want you to see me like this!"

"It's all right, Joelle. I love you."

She sobered for a moment. "I said the same to you once, after the accident. You told me to go away then and I'm telling you to leave now. You remember the pain. Don't be so cruel as to stay."

John reached out slowly to take her hand. "I remember."

Joelle felt his touch and tried to recoil. When he would not allow her to move from his grip, Joelle looked down at his hand as it lay against her swollen abdomen.

"We have to talk, Joelle. I've missed you so much, and I've searched for you so very long. Don't try to make me go without even letting me tell you my heart."

Joelle felt her body begin to tremble. She was acutely aware of John's surprise when the baby kicked against their hands. Her eyes looked up to catch his expression of wonder.

"No," she said in a wavering voice. "You have to go."

"Joelle," the gentle voice of Father Cooper sounded from the doorway.

Looking up at the old man, Joelle was torn between a feeling of happiness at his return and betrayal for the man he had obviously brought with him. Her questioning gaze caused him to step forward.

"You should at least hear out what your young man has to say, no? He has journeyed far and suffered much for his love of you."

Joelle moved her glance from Father Cooper to John and back again. "He should have never come."

"But he did," the priest reminded. "The very least you can do is listen to him. He isn't here to harm you, Joelle. You know that as well as I do."

Joelle swallowed hard and tried to still her fears. "Very well. I will listen to him."

Father Cooper nodded. "I will be seeing to my flock."

He left the room as quietly as he had entered, and Joelle returned her eyes to John. "You should have never come."

John grinned. "Just like you should have never come to Columbus when I crashed the Jenny."

"That was different."

John shook his head. "I didn't want you to be there, just as you don't want me here. Yet," he smiled even broader, "we both know I was just being stubborn and that I was really glad to see you. What of you, Joelle? Aren't you really glad to see me?"

"It doesn't matter," Joelle stated in a quiet, reserved manner.

"I believe it does."

"Well, I don't!" her voice sounded harsh. "If I'd wanted to see you, John, I would have come back to Bandelero."

John was undaunted. He had fully expected her anger. He let go of her hand and touched her stomach lightly. With a look of love in his eyes, he spoke. "I worked so hard to walk again," he began, "and all because I had to find you. When you disappeared, I thought I would die. I prayed and cried out to God to bring you back. I had J.D. looking all over El Paso for you. There isn't a law enforcement officer in this state, or Texas for that matter, who doesn't have a copy of your photograph."

Joelle's eyes widened in surprise, yet she said nothing. She was mesmerized by the gentleness of his voice. "I had to find you, Joelle. I love you so much. We are destined to spend our lives together, forever."

Joelle shook her head. "No, the raid changed all of that."

"Did the raid change your love for me?" His eyes pierced her façade of anger. She refused to answer him and looked away. Gently, John's hand took hold of her chin and drew her face back to his. "Did it? Did the attack you endured cause you to stop loving me?"

Joelle felt a tear slide down her cheek. There were no words for what she felt. How could she tell him that she still loved him? He would only feel more obligated.

John seemed to know what she was thinking. "Tell me that you no longer love me and I'll go. Tell me the raid caused your love for me to die, and I'll never force you to lay eyes on me again."

"No," Joelle sobbed and struggled to regain control. "My love didn't die."

"And neither did mine."

"But I can't hold you to that," Joelle protested. "I released you from our engagement. I'd hoped you would find happiness elsewhere with someone worthy of your love."

"Ah, Joelle," he murmured her name, and it sounded like a song. "You are more than worthy. I'm the one who acted badly. I tried to push you away when you knew I needed you most and now," he paused and slowly smiled, "you're trying to do the same. It won't work, you know."

"I can't hold onto the past," Joelle stated flatly. "You have no obligation here. I broke our engagement when I left Columbus."

"Well, I didn't accept the break," John countered. "I don't release you, Joelle."

"Go home, John. Just put me from your mind and go home." Her voice was weary. "I can't bear the sorrow of seeing you here."

"You are a coward, Joelle Dawson, but I love you, all the same." He used her own words from long ago, against her. Joelle kept shaking her head as he continued. "I don't release you from your obligation to marry me, and until you're able to do something about it, I consider myself your husband-to-be." John grinned. "You're stuck with me, just as I was stuck with you then."

Joelle pushed him away. "You can't be expected to stay with me now."

"And why not? My love was never conditional."

"You didn't ask for this," she shouted with a wave of her hand over her protruding stomach.

"And neither did you." John said firmly. "Funny, but this conversation sounds mighty familiar."

"It's not the same, John, so don't try to make it that way!"

John got to his feet. "It is the same, and you really are a coward."

"How dare you!" Joelle moved from the bed as gracefully as her size would allow. "How dare you!"

"I dare because it's true. You're afraid, and it's gotten the best of you. Surely it's much easier to live behind the wall of fear you've built for yourself, but I wonder," John said with a knowing look, "how long before the wall comes tumbling down and you have to face the truth of what's real?"

Chapter 15

J oelle picked up the first object she could reach and hurled it across the room. John ducked with a grin, narrowly missing the empty glass as it shattered against the wall.

"At least you drank whatever was in it first," he commented, reminding Joelle of the scene she had exchanged with him. "Suppose we ought to lay in a supply of drinking glasses?"

Joelle's eyes blazed. "You can mock me all you want, John Monroe, and it isn't going to change a thing! I want you out of here! Go home and stop feeling sorry for me."

John crossed his arms against his chest and blocked the door with his body. "I'm not going anywhere and neither are you. At least not until we get this talked out."

"I'm in no mood to talk to you about anything." Joelle mimicked John's action by crossing her arms. For a moment they faced off without words.

"Joelle," John whispered her name. "Marry me."

Joelle's anger surged again. "No! I won't ever marry anyone. I'm not worthy of anyone. Don't you understand? The attack changed all of that!"

"It changed nothing."

Joelle stormed at him with her hands raised. "It changed everything! Are you blind? I'm carrying another man's child. I don't even know which man's child. There were three of them, you know!"

John reached out to still her flailing arms. "No, I didn't know that. I didn't know because you shut me out and ran away. I'm sorry, Joelle, but it still doesn't change my love for you."

"It can't be the same!" she screamed, fighting against his hold.

"Of course not," John reasoned softly. "No one said it would be. I don't even want it to be the same. I was so selfish and lost in myself back then. I surely wouldn't want you to have to live with that man." John pulled her tighter to him, and the baby clearly took issue with the action.

"This baby will always be between us," Joelle protested, and tears began to fall.

"No," John whispered, "this baby will always be a part of us."

Joelle began to sob in earnest. She stopped fighting John's hold and buried her face against his shoulder. "I don't know who the father is."

"I'm the father," John declared. "I'm the only father this child will ever have. . .the only one he'll ever need."

She had no idea how long she let him hold her. She only knew that the comfort he offered was exactly what she had longed for. It dispelled her fears that John's touch would be just like that of her attackers. She had worried she might never again be able to feel the embrace of a man without being reminded of the rape. But this embrace reminded her only of the love she had known with John. This embrace gave her hope.

Silently, John led her back to the bed and pulled her down to sit on the side of it with him. Joelle raised her head and caught sight of the broken glass on the floor. It seemed to stun her momentarily.

"I don't know why I did that," she said, surprising them both.

John smoothed back her hair. "You did it because you were angry and helpless."

"Yes," Joelle nodded, "I am angry."

John put a finger under her chin and lifted her face to his.

"Anger is normal, Joelle. After all you've been through, you are quite entitled to your anger. It's what you do with that anger that makes a difference. The Bible even says we can get angry, but we aren't to sin out of that anger."

"I don't understand," Joelle said wearily.

"But God does, Joelle." John's eyes were soft and warm. "We can get through this with His help. It's time to move ahead."

"I don't know if I can."

"You have to," John said with a smile. "You have no choice. You're going to have baby. A baby who's going to need you and need your love."

"John," she whispered his name, "I'm not the girl you fell in love with. I'll never be whole again. There will always be a part of me that's damaged and crippled."

John dropped his hold and got to his feet. "Then we'll be a perfect match."

"I don't understand. You aren't making any sense," Joelle said with a look of confusion.

John crossed the room to retrieve the cane he had left by the door. For the first time, Joelle noticed his limp. He turned back to her with a shrug of his shoulders. "Dad says I may never walk normal again. I might always need this cane. Do you love me less because of it?" He was completely serious, and his expression betrayed a pain that mirrored Joelle's own.

"Of course not," she stated firmly. "But that's different."

"Why?" John asked her, coming back to the bed. "Why is it different?"

Joelle could not answer and so he continued. "I struggle to forgive myself for letting you face those men alone. I wanted only to protect you and keep you safe from harm, and it was because of me that you had to face the attack. It eats me up inside, and I know it's something I'll always live with."

"I made my choice, John. I told you. . ." Her words fell silent as she remembered what she had said.

"You told me what?" John encouraged her to answer.

Joelle swallowed hard, dropping her gaze to the floor. "I told you anything was preferable to your death."

"And now you want to take that back, eh?"

"No!" she exclaimed, her head snapping up. "Never! You were unable to walk. They would have killed you. What happened wasn't your fault, so there's no reason to blame yourself."

"It wasn't your fault, either, Joelle. The entire matter was taken out of your hands. I guess we both need to forgive ourselves." John picked up her hand and kissed her fingertips. "We have to forgive and let go of the past. We have to forgive ourselves and," he paused to take a tighter hold on her hand, "we have to forgive those men, as well."

"They don't deserve to be forgiven," she said flatly.

"Neither do we, but God extended us that privilege."

"But they deserve it even less. We aren't like them. Our sins aren't like theirs," Joelle protested.

"Isn't that up to God to judge?"

"I don't know."

"Yes, you do," John softly insisted. "You know as well as I do that no matter how undeserving those men are, forgiving them is the only way we can go on and build a future. It's the only way we can leave them behind and concentrate on us.

"God offered us His Son, Jesus, as a means to receive forgiveness and salvation. We've both known the truth of that since we were children. And, if I remember correctly, we both made decisions to take Him up on that offer. Seems to me, just when trials came to us both, we questioned whether or not God was really and truly Who He said He was. That's human weakness and a lack of faith, but even that, God understands. We made a commitment to God. We accepted His free gift of salvation through Jesus. We repented of our sins and pledged to forgive others. Now, here we are, presented with that very situation, and you want to throw it all away?"

"No!" Joelle declared. "I don't want to do anything of the sort. I know God wants me to forgive." Joelle stopped. It was true. God had made it quite clear to her that forgiveness was the only way she could set herself free. Just like His forgiveness had set her free from eternal death.

"Your anger is a poor companion, Joelle. You have to break away from your old nature and let Jesus fill you with the new nature that only He can provide. I had to do it. I had to seek out God and His forgiveness. I had to admit that I was wrong, and even though He'd been faithful to me a million times before, when I came face to face with a monumental problem, I was still too human to trust. Our adversities can weaken us greatly, but He can make us strong despite their effects." John paused, seeing the conflict Joelle felt mirrored in her eyes. "Forgive them, Joelle. Forgive them for their cruelty and let go of the anger that holds you captive."

Joelle felt a rush of emotion at the suggestion. She had lived so long with the nightmares that her anger seemed the only way to deal with her fear.

"I need to be alone. Please," she said with a pleading in her voice, "just let me think for awhile."

John released her hand and got to his feet. "I guess that's reasonable enough. I'll be with Father Cooper if you need me." He went to the door without protesting, surprising himself as well as Joelle.

He turned back to look at her. She seemed so frail and small. It was his utmost desire to protect her and keep her safe from the pain and suffering she had known.

" 'Rise up, my love, my fair one, and come away. For, lo, the winter is past, the rain is over and gone.' " His eyes betrayed tears. His voice was a husky whisper as he added, "Come away, my love."

He spoke the words, then was gone, leaving Joelle to stare at the empty space where he had stood.

⁓

Walking away was the hardest thing John had ever done. Now that he had found Joelle, all he wanted to do was cling to her. He certainly did not want to let her from his sight.

"Dear God," he prayed, "please give her the strength to get through this. Give her the strength to let go of her anger and fear. I love her so much."

He sat down on a chair, mindful of the pain in his back. He would carry that pain for a long time, just as Joelle would carry hers. Even in forgiveness, John realized, only time and healing would ease the pain.

Father Cooper's slight form passed by the window, and John got to his feet and went outside to join him.

"All is well?" the priest asked, unable to read John's expression.

"I'm not sure," John replied. He leaned heavily against the cane.

"You must trust God, my son. He knows full well the sorrows you share with Joelle. He has brought you here for a purpose. The answers you've searched for are soon to be given. Trust Him to give you the strength to bear them."

"I just want her to be healed. I just want her to recover from the pain."

"Even if you cannot be a part of that recovery?" Father Cooper's words hit John hard.

A life without Joelle? How could he even imagine the possibility? "I don't want to live without her. I can't even bear the thought of it," John admitted.

"But, if that is required of you, are you willing to put aside your own desires for the betterment of Joelle?"

John realized he would do whatever it took to help Joelle. Even if he had to walk away from her forever, he knew he would do whatever was best for her. "If God shows me no other way," John said softly, "I'll leave."

"Your love for her is good, John," Father Cooper said, putting a supportive arm around his shoulders. "Come, let's give God time to speak to her heart."

～

Joelle sat, silently staring at the four walls of her bedroom. She had called this place home for quite awhile, and yet it held no fond memories or happiness for her. It was a prison. . .a tomb, she thought. She had come here to live out her sentence and, in some ways, to die.

John's sweet face came to mind. Why had he come? How did he find her? The questions raced through her head, and yet Joelle knew the answers were unimportant. She thought back to the day she had first seen him after the accident. He was angry at God and everyone else, but mostly he was angry with himself.

"Just as I'm angry with myself," Joelle murmured. She smiled as she recalled the determination with which she had faced John during the early period of his confinement. "He won't back down," she realized aloud. "He's just like me when it comes to being stubborn."

Exhausted from her physical exertion, Joelle fell back against the pillows. She stared up at the ceiling and in that instant it triggered the memory of her rape. She remembered staring at the ceiling, fixing her eyes on a single spot, in order to keep from seeing the faces of the men who were hurting her.

Her breathing quickened. She could nearly feel their hands upon her. *Dear God*, she thought, *must I forever live with this?*

Forgive them and leave them behind. Wasn't that what John had spoken of not moments ago? *Forgive them?*

"They don't deserve to be forgiven," Joelle said with clenched fists and hot tears. "I want them to suffer just as I have. I want them to know the same misery I've known."

Give them to Me, Joelle. The silent voice stirred her soul.

"No," she argued, "I can't. They took so much from me. They took everything."

Give them to Me, and I will give you rest.

Joelle let go a sob. She was so tired, so very weary. The burden had been so great and the exhaustion from carrying it so complete.

"I want rest," she whispered. "I do want rest."

Chapter 16

It was dark when Joelle awoke. She had slept peacefully in spite of her surprise at seeing John. A tapping sounded at her door and, sitting up with a yawn, Joelle called out.

"Come in." The soft glow of lamplight flooded the room. She expected to see John, but was taken aback when, instead, Father Cooper poked his head inside the doorway.

"Are you feeling up to a talk?" he asked.

"Of course," she replied and awkwardly pushed up into a sitting position.

Father Cooper came in and placed the lamp beside her bed. "I hope you don't mind the imposition but I felt there are things between us that needed to be said."

"Things between us?" Joelle questioned with a puzzled expression.

Father Cooper drew up a chair and folded his hands. "I brought John with me from Las Cruces."

"So that's how he found me."

"Yes. It was actually God's doing, though." He paused and smiled in his way. "I had trouble with the touring car. It became stuck in the sand. John came riding up and freed me. We shared supper together, and he told me of his mission to find you."

"I see," Joelle replied softly. "That must have come as quite a shock to both of you."

"John didn't know at first. I decided not to share my good news with him until I was certain of his commitment to you. You see, Joelle," he paused, "I would never have allowed him to hurt you. I waited until I was assured of his sincere love for you before I shared your location with him."

Joelle shook her head. "But how could you be certain of his love? John's the type of person who upon hearing of my plight would instantly feel obligated to care for me."

"But I did not tell him of your circumstances, Child. I did not reveal to him any knowledge of you whatsoever. I let John tell me about his search and about his love." Joelle started to speak but Father Cooper held up his hand. "Please, hear me out." Joelle nodded and waited for him to continue.

"I could see the anguish and misery in this young man. He was so filled

441

with the longing to find you. He had already searched far, and the very fact that he was on his feet was, in part, due to his determination to see you again."

"I can imagine that's true," Joelle stated, forgetting herself.

Father Cooper smiled. "I talked to John without letting him know I knew of you. I told him it was possible that the woman he loved would be forever scarred by what had happened in Columbus. You had said as much, yes?"

"Yes."

"I asked him if he could live with those scars and he assured me that what had happened to you had no bearing on his love for you. I believed him then, Joelle. I still believe him."

"But, Father Cooper, he couldn't possibly have known about the baby. Not unless you told him. Even so, he wouldn't have told you then that he couldn't marry me. John's not that type of person. He takes his obligations quite seriously."

"I did not tell him you were with child. At least not until after he assured me that such a thing would still be unimportant in respect to your future and his love."

"How did he convince you of this?"

"I merely suggested that a fear of physical intimacy was not the only possible residual effect of the rape. I asked him what he would do if he found you, then learned that you were with child."

Joelle paled a bit. "And what did he say?"

"It was something he'd not thought about. He left me for a time and came back with his answer, which was that he would love you and any child you bore. It changed nothing, Joelle. He still desired to find you and to make you his wife."

Joelle's eyes filled with tears. "He is a good man."

"Yes, that is definitely so."

"You once told me that even though we prayed in different ways and in different places, we still served the same God," Joelle said as she reached out her hand to the wizened priest. "I also believe that is so. You have taught me much about God and His love. You've shown me a side to God that I might never have seen. I can't say I am thankful for the attack or that I ask blessings for my attackers. However, I do believe I am ready to forgive and desperately ready to forget."

"It is well with your soul, eh?" Father Cooper questioned with a smile lighting up his eyes. "Our God is big enough for even these things that seem overwhelming."

"He seemed to have planned everything out in detail," Joelle replied. "Look at the way He put you and John together. Better yet, the way He put you and me together. He saw to my needs when I didn't even know what they were."

"He is like that, our God."

"Yes, He is."

"I am glad for you, Joelle. My heart sings within me, and I know that God will bless you forever. If I can ever do anything more, please remember your old friend."

Joelle reached out and embraced the priest in a fierce hug. "I do love you, Father Cooper. You have given me so much."

"And you, also, have blessed me."

Joelle pulled back and wiped at her tears. "Would you consider one more favor?"

"What is it?"

"Would you marry John and me?"

The old man's face broke into a beaming smile. "I would love nothing more." He paused for a moment with a seriousness overtaking his joy. "But, you know you are not of my church and. . ."

"John and I will remarry in our church at home. His uncle is our pastor. I'd just like the memory of standing before you and God."

"Then we will treat it that way," Father Cooper said with a nod. "But, should you not find your young man and let him know your heart? He was quite worried when last we spoke."

Joelle nodded. "Where is he?"

"He was walking down by the river."

Joelle got to her feet and, reaching to the end of her bed, she took up the warm, handwoven blanket that lay there. "I will be walking by the river, Father Cooper," she said, pulling the blanket around her shoulders.

～

John lingered by the water's edge long after the sun had set. He was so unsure of how Joelle would respond to his coming. He had prayed and sought peace and knew in his heart that if he had to leave her, he would. But he would never again be whole. . .not without her love.

Sitting there on the river bank, John silently thought of his life in Bandelero. What would he do when he returned? He had spent so much time just trying to heal. If Joelle did agree to come home and be his wife, how would he ever support them?

"Are you brooding or dreaming?" Joelle's soft voice called out from behind him.

Getting slowly to his feet, John limped to where she stood. "Both," he confessed. In the moonlight he could see her smile.

She glanced down at the hand in which John held his cane. She put her own hand atop his and looked up into his eyes. "We should talk."

"Yes."

"Would you like to sit again?" Joelle asked, mindful of his condition.

"Would you?"

"Yes, I believe so," she replied, patting her stomach. "It becomes increasingly more difficult to get around. You'll have to help me."

John reached out and took her by the elbow. "I've got the perfect place for us." He led her to the river bank and helped her to sit. Joining her there, he found himself nearly holding his breath. "You wanted to talk?"

"Yes," Joelle said and took a deep breath. "You were right to come. I'm glad you came." She paused for a moment to look out into the darkness. "It's impossible to know what's out there," she said absently.

John thought it profound. "Yes, but what we have here is easy to see."

Joelle turned and smiled. "We won't have it easy elsewhere."

"Probably not."

"We will start life at a great disadvantage," she murmured.

"We'll have each other."

"And a child," Joelle reminded.

"Yes. A beautiful child, born of a lovely and beautiful woman," John whispered, running a finger along Joelle's cheek.

Joelle's breath caught at the pleasure his actions caused. She stared longingly into his eyes for several moments, waiting and hoping that he might kiss her. *Kiss me*, she thought. *I have to know it's all that it once was*. When John refused to initiate the action, Joelle leaned forward and put her hand up to his face.

"Please, kiss me," she whispered in the silence of the night.

John's eyes took on a fire that she had once known long ago. He leaned closer to meet her lips and put his hand gently behind her head. The kiss was sweet and heartfelt and everything that Joelle had hoped it would be. She found herself clinging to John with such joy flooding her heart that she could scarcely believe it was real.

He pulled away first, leaving Joelle with a smile on her lips. Her eyes were still closed as she relished the moment.

"I remember the first time you kissed me," Joelle whispered and slowly opened her eyes. "Do you?"

"How could I forget? It was under the mistletoe at Maggie and Garrett Lucas's Christmas party. It was the moment I decided to marry you."

She grinned. "You'd just met me. How could you have decided a thing like that?"

"It was easy. I knew what I was looking for."

Joelle frowned ever so slightly. "A lot has happened since then, John. Are you sure I'm still what you're looking for?"

"More than ever," he replied, his voice hoarse with emotion. "I love you, Joelle. Now and for all time."

"No matter the past?"

"No matter the past, the present, or the future." John pulled her close. "My love for you will only grow stronger. You are my beloved."

" 'I am my beloved's, and my beloved is mine,' " she quoted from the sixth chapter of the Song of Solomon. A warmth spread throughout her body. "I am yours, John, if you still want me."

"Can there be any doubt?" he said and lifted her face to meet his kiss. Joelle melted against him and was sorry when he pulled away.

"Well," she said with a sigh, "if there were any doubts, I believe you've dispelled them all. You are one stubborn man, John Monroe."

He laughed heartily. "No more so than you, Joelle Dawson."

"We'll probably fight," she said quite seriously.

"Yes, very probably."

"Will you throw mugs?" she asked with a grin.

"Only if you throw drinking glasses."

"You were right about me being a coward," she said thoughtfully.

"Umm," John sounded with a glance upward, "I hate to admit it, but you were right about me being a coward, as well."

"You? Never!" she exclaimed.

"It's true," John replied. "I was afraid in Columbus. I was afraid I would be bedfast forever and never know what it was like to walk beside you again. I was afraid in Columbus when you left me and ran away. I was afraid when I couldn't find you and my search seemed in vain." He stopped and looked deep into her velvety eyes. "And then when I did find you, I was afraid that you'd stopped loving me."

Joelle put her finger to his lips. "That, I could never do, so put it from your mind and don't be afraid any longer."

"What of you, Joelle? Are you still afraid?"

She dropped her hand and looked away. "I'm terrified."

"Of me?"

"No," she whispered and drew his hand to her stomach. "This."

John placed his arm around her shoulder. "Don't be. I'll be with you every step of the way. Babies are wondrous things, and I hope we have a dozen."

Joelle's head came up in surprise. "A dozen? I thought four sounded like a nice number."

John smiled. "Whatever you say."

"You realize, of course," she said with a sudden thought, "this particular child is due next month."

"That soon, huh? I guess we'd better think about getting home then so Dad can deliver it."

Joelle nodded. "That would probably be wise."

"We probably ought to think about something else, as well," John said without reserve. "Don't you suppose we ought to get married?"

"I'm way ahead of you on that one, Mr. Monroe. Father Cooper is waiting, even now, to perform a lovely ceremony for us. I thought it might be nice for him to be a part of our marriage, since he's partially responsible for bringing us together again. After we get home, your Uncle David could marry us, if that meets with your approval."

"I see you have this all under control," John grinned.

"Do you mind?"

"Not in the least. I think it sounds wonderful. Come on," he said, getting to his feet. "I want to get married."

Chapter 17

"John!" Joelle screamed out his name in the agonizing final stages of labor.

"What!" John yelled from outside the room where his wife was giving birth.

"I've changed my mind!"

Dan and Lillie exchanged a look of amusement with Joelle's mother. John and Joelle had been yelling back and forth at each other for hours now and neither one seemed to think the exchange unusual.

"It's a little late for that, Darling!" John called back.

Joelle grimaced as another contraction gripped her. She waited for it to pass before explaining her thoughts. "Not about having this baby," she yelled. "I've changed it about having four of them!"

Zandy and Lillie laughed out loud, while Daniel tried to concentrate on the task at hand. There was an amused smile on his lips, however.

"Whatever you say, Dear!" John yelled back and grinned at his father-in-law. "I love that woman."

Riley shook his head and laughed. "She's not your run-of-the-mill society girl, is she?"

"Thank God for that," John mused with a laugh. He grew sober, however, when Joelle's scream filled the air. "How much longer do you suppose this will go on?"

Riley shrugged. "It always seems like forever." John nodded and resumed his pacing.

Inside their bedroom, Joelle bore down with all her might to expel the child from her body. "Mother!" she gasped and gripped Zandy's hand tightly. "I want this to be over with."

"It will, Darling, just a little longer. You'll see." Zandy wiped her daughter's brow with a cool cloth and prayed for the delivery to be an easy one.

Joelle rolled her head from side to side. She was suddenly overcome with fear. "Mother, what if the baby is hideous? What if it looks like one of them?" Joelle had tried to force such thoughts from her mind these last few weeks, but the old fears caught up with her.

Zandy soothed her daughter with words of encouragement. "Joelle, no baby is hideous. Your child will be beautiful and precious. You'll see." She prayed silently for her daughter, knowing that only God could give her peace in the matter.

"That's right, Joelle," Lillie assured her. "Once you see the baby, all your fears will disappear.

"And from the looks of it, that's going to be in just another minute or two," Dan said confidently.

Joelle felt the contractions begin again. They were coming one after the other now. The urge to bear down and push was stronger than ever. "I. . . don't. . .want," she gasped against the pain.

"Don't want what, Sweetheart?" her mother asked softly.

"Let. . .John. . .see. . .first!"

"See what, Joelle?" Zandy questioned.

"The baby!" Joelle said and screamed out in pain. "Let. . .him. . .see the baby. . .first."

"Push, Joelle," Dan commanded. "Push hard."

Joelle bore down with all her might. She was exhausted from the entire ordeal. "John!" she screamed and was answered with the sound of a baby's cry.

"It's a girl, Joelle!" Lillie announced, as Dan passed the squalling child over. "We have a granddaughter, Dr. Monroe."

Joelle fell back against the pillow and threw her arm across her face. "Mother, pray with me. Please."

Zandy leaned her lips down to Joelle's ear. The baby continued to cry while Lillie cleaned her up.

"Please, God," Zandy whispered in prayer, "please strengthen Joelle and help her through this frightening time in her life. Give her peace of mind and a love for her daughter that will surpass her fear, amen."

Joelle pulled her arm away to look into her mother's face. There were tears in her eyes. "Where's John? Please let John come in."

Zandy looked at Dan, who nodded his approval. She went quickly to the door and motioned for her son-in-law to join them. In a hushed voice she told him of Joelle's request.

"She's afraid to see the baby. She wants you to see her first."

John nodded a look that held no condemnation. He knew of Joelle's fears, and he could not fault her for them. Stepping to where Lillie was now wrapping the baby in a warm blanket, he could only stare in wonder.

"You have a daughter," Lillie said, handing to her firstborn child, his own firstborn. "Now this is what I call some Christmas present."

John looked down at the tiny bundle. The baby calmed in his arms and stared back at him with dark, wet eyes. She was beautiful! The most beautiful thing he had ever seen in his life, with the possible exception of Joelle. He smiled broadly at his mother and Zandy.

"She's perfect," he said with assurance.

"She looks like Joelle did," Zandy said, and there was no stopping the flow of tears from her eyes. "I have to go tell Riley," she said and took herself from the room.

Dan finished his tasks and patted Joelle on the hand. "You did a great job, Mommy. I think this is the best Christmas present I've ever had. Not everybody gets a granddaughter in their stocking." Joelle tried to smile, but her teeth began to chatter. "Lillie, do we have another blanket?" Dan asked.

Lillie nodded and left John to fuss over his daughter. She pulled a huge quilt from the drawer beneath the bed and unfolded it to cover Joelle. "I always got the shivers after delivery," she grinned down. "This ought to warm you right up."

"Thanks," Joelle whispered, relishing the feel of the added weight.

"Come on, Grandma," Dan said with a laugh. "Let's call up the town and announce our new granddaughter!" Lillie nodded and linked her arm with Dan's. They exited the room to join the laughter and conversation of Riley and Zandy, thoughtfully closing the door behind them.

John looked up from the baby to catch Joelle's worried look. "She's precious, Joelle. She has your coloring and your eyes. She has your cute little mouth, and she can yell almost as loud."

Joelle could not help but smile. "Does she have any hair?"

"A ton of it, and it's all dark brown like her mom's."

Joelle bit at her lower lip as the baby started to fuss. "Bring her to me," she finally said, and John quickly complied before she could change her mind.

He lowered the baby into Joelle's arms, while Joelle kept her eyes on John's face. Joelle felt the warm softness of the infant and the natural way she seemed to fit against her. The baby calmed.

John kissed Joelle on the forehead. "She's perfect. Just look at her."

For only a moment, Joelle thought back to Columbus. Then pushing the image aside, she lowered her face to the bundle in her arms.

Two dark eyes stared up at her with a sweet, tiny mouth opened wide in a yawn. Joelle felt a surge of relief and tears came to her eyes. "Oh, John," she whispered. She reached up her finger to touch the velvety softness of the baby's cheek.

"I told you she was perfect," he said with a smile.

"Oh, she truly is," Joelle murmured. "How could I have feared this?"

"No doubt she'll give our poor hearts plenty to fear in the future. The first time she climbs a tree or runs away from home."

"She'd better never!" Joelle declared.

"Well, if she's anything like you, she no doubt will," John insisted.

"Well, if she takes after you, she'll probably be hanging out of the cockpit of a biplane and soaring overhead."

John smiled at Joelle's reference. "No daughter of mine will hang out of the cockpit of a biplane," he retorted indignantly.

"Oh, really?" Joelle laughed. "And who will stop her?"

"I will. If she can't sit in it properly and fly the thing professionally, then she won't be allowed to do it at all."

Joelle nodded. "With her daddy to teach her, she'll be a crackerjack pilot."

The baby yawned again and closed her eyes. John reached up and smoothed back Joelle's hair. "You've done a good thing here, Mrs. Monroe."

"Yes," Joelle said smugly and glanced up into his eyes. "I have, haven't I?" John raised a quizzical brow, and Joelle laughed. "Of course," she added, "you and God had something to do with it too. I couldn't have done it without your support and love, nor His."

"God has done something quite wondrous, hasn't He?"

"Indeed," Joelle agreed. "She's everything a mother could hope for. She's absolutely complete and perfect."

"Except for one thing," John said. "What shall we call her?"

"Oh, I was so busy worrying about the outcome, I never thought to plan a name for her."

"Well, let's see. It is Christmas. We could call her Christina."

"No," Joelle said shaking her head. "I like Holly."

"Hey, how about Mistletoe?" John teased. "After all, that's where we first kissed."

"I like Holly," Joelle repeated firmly.

"You sure?"

"Yes." Joelle nodded and ran her hand lightly over her daughter's tiny head. "Holly Noelle."

"Hey, it rhymes with Joelle. Sounds good to me." He planted a kiss on Joelle's forehead, then leaned over to do the same for the baby.

"Holly Noelle Monroe," Joelle breathed the name.

"I still think Mistletoe would have worked. We could've called her Missy," John said with a prankish smile.

Joelle rolled her eyes. "Her name is Holly."

"Well, maybe next time."

"Next time? I told you I'd changed my mind."

John nodded. "I thought you meant about having four. I just naturally presumed that meant we were going to try for twelve."

Joelle gave his ribs a hard nudge of her elbow, disturbing the baby's slumber as she did. Holly protested with a whimper but quickly settled back to sleep.

"All right," John conceded. "You don't have to have any more, if you really don't want to."

Joelle was already forgetting about the pain of delivery. "Well, I'd hate for her to grow up an only child. I guess we'll see."

Outside, it had begun to snow, and Joelle could see the light, downy flakes from where she lay. "Look," she whispered to John, "it's so lovely."

"No more so than you, Beloved," John answered with a proud look of love in his eyes.

Joelle felt secure and happy in that look. "It truly will be all right, won't it, John? We're a family now, and God can help us to rise above the hurt we've known. We'll make a good home for Holly."

"The best," John promised. "The very best God has to offer."

Epilogue

Pancho Villa's raid on Columbus, New Mexico, was a failure in that few Americans were killed and most of the money and valuables that were stolen were lost in the frantic retreat of the *Villistas*.

The most poignant effect of the raid was psychological. It caused panic throughout the border region of the U.S. and proved to the U.S. government that the *Carrancista* government could do nothing or was unwilling to control Villa. It also made Americans aware that even in their neutral attitudes regarding the war in Europe, they were far from safe in the isolated cocoon they had woven for themselves.

Across America, many were opposed to the U.S. government's recognition and support of the *Carrancistas*, feeling that they were as bad, if not worse than the *Villistas*.

General Pershing's troops never managed to capture the elusive Pancho Villa. As the United States Army invaded deeper and deeper into Mexico, hostilities grew between the two countries and Villa became somewhat of a hero to his people. President Wilson found himself up against Carranza's rejection of U.S. interference in Mexican affairs, and even though Villa had attacked U.S. soil, Carranza wanted Pershing's troops immediately recalled.

Large amounts of money, along with the sweat and toil of the U.S. Army, were spent on the effort without success, and the "Punitive Expedition" was rapidly deemed a failure.

By 1917, America headed into another four years with Wilson at the helm and Pershing still struggling to overtake Villa. The underlying hope of Germany at this point was to keep the Americans so completely engrossed in the border conflicts that they would be forced to stay on the opposite side of the Atlantic and leave them to their war conquests in Europe.

This might well have worked had it not been for the Zimmermann Telegram, in which Germany offered Mexico a military alliance in return for their declaration of war against the United States. The interception of this coded message made it clear to Wilson that our entry into what was to be called World War I was imminent. Our passive neutrality was broken, and America went to war.

A Letter to Our Readers

Dear Readers:

In order that we might better contribute to your reading enjoyment, we would appreciate you taking a few minutes to respond to the following questions. When completed, please return to the following: Fiction Editor, Barbour Publishing, Inc., P.O. Box 719, Uhrichsville, OH 44683.

1. Did you enjoy reading *New Mexico Sunset?*
   ❑ Very much. I would like to see more books like this.
   ❑ Moderately—I would have enjoyed it more if _____
   _____
   _____

2. What influenced your decision to purchase this book?
   (Check those that apply.)
   ❑ Cover   ❑ Back cover copy   ❑ Title   ❑ Price
   ❑ Friends   ❑ Publicity   ❑ Other

3. Which story was your favorite?
   ❑ *The Heart's Calling*   ❑ *Angel's Cause*
   ❑ *Forever Yours*   ❑ *Come Away, My Love*

4. Please check your age range:
   ❑ Under 18   ❑ 18–24   ❑ 25–34
   ❑ 35–45   ❑ 46–55   ❑ Over 55

5. How many hours per week do you read? _____

Name _____

Occupation _____

Address _____

City _____ State _____ ZIP _____

E-mail _____

If you enjoyed

NEW MEXICO
Sunset

then read:

NEW MEXICO
Sunrise

FAITH AND LOVE HOLD GENERATIONS TOGETHER
IN FOUR COMPLETE NOVELS
BY TRACIE PETERSON

A Place to Belong
Perfect Love
Tender Journeys
The Willing Heart

If you enjoyed
NEW MEXICO
Sunset

then read:

Montana

A Legacy of Faith and Love
in Four Complete Novels by Ann Bell

Autumn Love
Contagious Love
Inspired Love
Distant Love

If you enjoyed

NEW MEXICO
Sunset

then read:

Heirloom Brides

Four Romantic Novellas
Linked by Family and Love

Button String Bride by Cathy Marie Hake
Wedding Quilt Bride by Colleen Coble
Bayside Bride by Kristin Billerbeck
The Persistent Bride by Gina Fields

Grace Livingston Hill Collections

Readers of quality Christian fiction will
love these new novel collections from
Grace Livingston Hill, the leading
lady of inspirational romance. Each
collection features three titles from
Grace Livingston Hill and a bonus
novel from Isabella Alden, Grace
Livingston Hill's aunt and a widely
respected author herself.

Collection #7 includes the com-
plete Grace Livingston Hill books *Lo, Michael,*
The Patch of Blue, and *The Unknown God,* plus *Stephen Mitchell's*
Journey by Isabella Alden.

paperback, 464 pages, 5 ³⁄₁₆" x 8"

Grace Livingston Hill Collections

Readers of quality Christian fiction will love these new novel collections from Grace Livingston Hill, the leading lady of inspirational romance. Each collection features three titles from Grace Livingston Hill and a bonus novel from Isabella Alden, Grace Livingston Hill's aunt and a widely respected author herself.

Collection #8 includes the complete Grace Livingston Hill books *The Chance of a Lifetime, Under the Window* and *A Voice in the Wilderness,* plus *The Randolphs* by Isabella Alden.

paperback, 464 pages, 5 ³⁄₁₆" x 8"

❤ ❤ ❤ ❤ ❤ ❤ ❤ ❤ ❤ ❤ ❤ ❤ ❤ ❤ ❤ ❤ ❤

Please send me _____ copies of *Grace Livingston Hill #8.* I am enclosing $4.97 for each. (Please add $1.00 to cover postage and handling per order. OH add 6% tax.) Send check or money order, no cash or C.O.D.s, please.

Name_____

Address _____

City, State, Zip _____

To place a credit card order, call 1-800-847-8270.
Send to:
Heartsong Presents Reader Service
PO Box 721
Uhrichsville, OH 44683

❤ ❤ ❤ ❤ ❤ ❤ ❤ ❤ ❤ ❤ ❤ ❤ ❤ ❤ ❤ ❤ ❤